D0592569

In Memory of

Herr Memorial Library
Mifflinburg, Pa.

Presented by

IN THE
EVENT OF
MY *DEATH*

ST. MARTIN'S PAPERBACKS TITLES BY
CARLENE THOMPSON

The Way You Look Tonight
Tonight You're Mine
In the Event of My Death

IN THE
EVENT OF
MY *DEATH*

HERR MEMORIAL LIBRARY

CARLENE
THOMPSON

St. Martin's

Copyright © 1999 by Carlene Thompson.

All rights reserved. No part of this book may be used or reproduced in any manner whatsoever without written permission except in the case of brief quotations embodied in critical articles or reviews. For information address St. Martin's Press, 175 Fifth Avenue, New York, N.Y. 10010.

ISBN: 0-7394-0661-2

Printed in the United States of America

To my niece Kelsey

Thanks to Pamela Ahearn, Jennifer Weis, and the staff of Four Seasons Floral

Prologue

Angela Ricci wished again she had a dog. She'd always wanted one, but her fastidious ex-husband said they were dirty. Stuart Burgess. How could she have ever found such a creep attractive? What a pain he'd been to live with, constantly washing his hands, throwing a fit if he found a spot on his tie, developing a migraine when he came home to find the place looking like anything other than a museum.

But she'd been divorced from Stuart for a year. The settlement had been generous. Very generous. And why not? Stuart wasn't as fastidious about his personal liaisons as he was about the externals of his life. He would die if anyone found out about his taste for prostitutes. Young male prostitutes. She'd never threatened to tell. She *wouldn't* have told, both because she didn't want the negative publicity and because Stuart had a dangerous streak that frightened her. Fortunately, paranoid Stuart had perceived a threat from her and decided money would keep her silent.

He'd retreated to their large upstate home and given her the brownstone in Manhattan. Ever practical, she'd rented the second and third floors—much to Stuart's snobbish dismay—and redecorated the first floor for herself. Now the place no longer looked like a museum. She had a warm and inviting home with a lovely courtyard in back, the perfect place for a dog—a big, protective dog. But she'd never gotten around to buying one, and now she regretted it because lately she'd begun to feel uneasy here. She couldn't remember exactly when the uneasiness began. A week ago? No, longer. The feeling was worse when she returned from the theater at night. Even though she was exhausted from singing and dancing all evening, as the star of one of the most popular musicals on Broadway, she came back to the brownstone feeling lonely and scared. A dog would definitely make her feel less alone and much safer.

She was more tired than usual tonight. Maybe it was the cold. Or maybe it was because her new fiancé, Judson Green, had been out of town for a week. She missed him terribly. In three more days he would be home. Three endless days.

Angela stripped and stood under a hot shower for ten minutes until some of the tension began to leave her neck. She was toweling off when she thought she heard something in the house. She couldn't identify the sound. It wasn't like something falling over. It was much softer, much . . . *stealthier.*

Angela paused, startled by the word that had popped into her mind. Abruptly she dropped the towel and reached for her heavy terry cloth robe, sliding it on as if she were donning a suit of armor. Her heart thudding, she pushed her long black hair away from her face and stepped slowly into the bedroom. Everything looked neat, undisturbed. Quickly she dashed to the dresser, opened the top drawer, and withdrew the .38 automatic she'd bought after the divorce. Stuart would never have allowed her to have a gun.

Holding the weapon with trembling hands, she passed through the dining room and into the living room, flipping on lights. In the living room she punched on the security system, furious with herself for having forgotten to do so as soon as she came in tonight. Her carelessness about safety had always driven Stuart crazy.

She paced through the brownstone once more, turning on the lights in every room. Fifteen minutes later, the place blazing with electric illumination, Angela fixed a glass of brandy and sat down, the gun in her lap.

She had never been the fearful type, not even as a child. True, there was that awful period thirteen years ago when she'd been troubled by nightmares, but who wouldn't have

been after what happened? But time had eventually done
its work. Although she could never forget that awful night,
at least her nightmares had abated.

That awful night. A shiver passed through her. She'd
been only seventeen, an exuberant, cocky seventeen. She
was pretty, talented, and nothing truly bad had happened to
her in her whole life. Not until that night. It had all started
so innocently and ended so tragically.

Maybe that's why she'd felt so unsettled lately, she
thought. It had been this time of year when it happened.
She scanned her mind for the date. My God, it had been
December 13—thirteen years ago this very week. Unlucky
thirteen.

But Angela didn't believe in luck. When people told her
how lucky she was to have landed this plum role on Broadway, she wanted to laugh in their faces. It hadn't been
because of good luck—it had been because of years of hard
work, perseverance, and tolerating crushing rejections. And
the terrible event thirteen years ago that she would remember to her dying day wasn't caused by bad luck. It was
caused by a girl's deliberate, devastating act.

Angela shivered again and wished she could call Judson,
but it was past midnight. She knew he had early morning
meetings and it would be selfish of her to awaken him. No,
she would just ride out her bout of nerves, and as soon as
Judson returned and they began serious plans for their
spring wedding, all of this uneasiness would seem silly.

An hour later she lay in bed still wide-eyed, watching
television. This was ridiculous. She couldn't sit up all night.
She'd be exhausted and look like hell tomorrow. She had
an interview for *New York* magazine at one in the afternoon, complete with a photo shoot, and a performance tomorrow night. No, this sleeplessness wouldn't do at all.

Angela knew too many actresses who'd become depend-
ent on pills. She would never let that happen to her, but
there were times when a little chemical help was necessary.
Reluctantly she went into the bathroom, poured a glass of
water, and searched the medicine cabinet for her Seconal.

It had been prescribed a year ago during her divorce, and since then she'd only taken ten of the powerful little red pills. She swallowed one now.

Later, while voices still poured from the television, Angela's head slipped sideways on the pillow. Within minutes she was breathing deeply. Not even the creaking of a closet door in the guest room disturbed her.

A figure wafted quietly down the hall. It stopped briefly on the threshold of her room. *Angela,* the figure thought. The name was apt. She looked like an angel sleeping deeply, peacefully, her dark hair a halo on the white satin pillowcase, her lashes long and dark against ivory skin.

Such perfect skin. The figure drifted closer to the bed, casting a shadow over Angela's calm face. She didn't deserve such beauty. She didn't deserve serenity. She didn't deserve wealth, fame, adoration, her blessed life. After what she'd done, she deserved nothing.

The figure raised a tire iron, letting it hover a moment. As long as it was in the air, Angela Ricci lived. But if it came down . . .

Angela's entire body jerked beneath the powerful first blow. Her skull cracked. Blood splattered and her eyes snapped open. But the movement, the awareness, were short-lived. Again and again the iron bar slammed down on her, splitting skin, breaking bones, crushing vital organs.

Two minutes later Angela Ricci lay shapeless and twisted, a horrifying crimson mass on her lovely, shining white sheets. Breathing heavily, arms trembling from the effort, the killer looked at the body and smiled. Such a good job, so carefully planned, and over so quickly. Too quickly. The killer glanced at the clock. Two-thirteen.

Unlucky thirteen.

One

A circle of girls dancing in the near darkness. Chanting.
Light—leaping, growing light. Flames. A scream. A chorus
of screams climbing the scale to shattering shrieks. Pain.
Then darkness.

Laurel Damron felt herself kicking wildly before her eyes
snapped open. She gasped, balling her hands into fists to
stop their wild clawing. Her breath came in long, ragged
gasps.

Suddenly weight descended on her and she looked down
at her prone body to see a long-haired black and white dog,
its eyes only inches from her own. "Oh, April," Laurel
breathed, unclenching a fist to stroke the dog who always
climbed atop her whenever she was having the dream. She
never knew whether April's intent was to soothe or to protect. "That was a bad one. Same scene, only worse. The
fire . . ."

She broke off, her mind wandering back to the terrible
flames until she became aware of panting beside her. Alex,
April's brother, sat by the bed, stretching his neck toward
her. "Did I scare you, too?" She rubbed him under the chin.
"It's okay, boy. I frightened you guys for nothing. I know
you're sick of my dream. So am I."

Laurel ran a hand over her damp forehead and looked at
the bedside clock although she knew because of the darkness in her bedroom that the sun had not yet risen. Six
forty-five. Fifteen minutes before the alarm would go off.
"An early start on the day," she muttered. *Again.* She
gave April a final stroke, then shifted beneath her fifty-

pound body. "Time to get up, you two. There's coffee to be drunk and dog food to be eaten."

April reluctantly rose and leaped off the bed. Laurel stretched, closed her eyes briefly, then threw off the comforter.

A minute later she stood in front of the bathroom mirror. A thirty-year-old woman shouldn't look this tired after a night's sleep, she thought. Dark circles hovered beneath her light brown eyes and her skin was unusually pale. Her shoulder-length brown hair curled wildly out from her head. She ran her hand through it despairingly. Time for another bout of straightener, she thought. Not that Kurt Rider, the man she'd been seeing for seven months, would care. She often wondered why she even bothered dressing up for their dates. He didn't seem to notice whether she was in jeans and barefaced, or sporting a new dress and a careful makeup job.

Not like her parents. She grimaced, remembering when she and her sister were in high school. Laurel was fifteen, Claudia seventeen. It was school-picture day and they'd both taken pains with their appearance. When they entered the kitchen, their father put down his coffee cup, beaming at Claudia. "Honey, you are a *vision,*" he'd crowed as she pirouetted, bouncing her blond waves. Then his smile flagged slightly. "Laurel, can't you do something with your hair?" When Laurel, hurt, muttered, "I think it looks okay," her mother had glanced up from the eggs she was scrambling. "Leave her alone, Hal," she'd said. "They can't all be beauties. Laurel will make a fine wife and mother someday."

Well, I failed at that, too, Laurel thought ruefully. At thirty she was still single and childless while Claudia had married ten years ago and now awaited her third child.

Ever sensitive to her moods, April pawed at her leg, jerking her back to the moment. Laurel smiled. "Enough of this self-pity. Time to leave the past behind and get on with the day. Who wants Alpo?"

Both dogs knew the word and bolted from the bedroom.

Laurel shook her head. They would not respond to "Come," "Heel," "Stay," or "Sit." Any word dealing with food, however, elicited immediate action.

She walked into the kitchen, which always cheered her up with its shining oak cabinets, stretches of pristine white Formica, and carefully placed, lush plant arrangements that gave color and life to what could have been a large, cold room. She put on coffee and while it brewed fixed food and water for April and Alex. As usual they ate as if they'd had nothing for days, April standing graceful and silky on her long legs, Alex small and compact with his short hair and stubby legs. Obviously they'd had different fathers, but exactly what their parentage was, she'd never know. She'd found them one rainy October afternoon, four weeks old, trembling and dirty, deposited under an evergreen tree beside her driveway. Someone had dumped them, and she'd happily taken them in. They'd given her more companionship the last two years than she'd known for a long time.

When the coffee finished brewing, she carried a cup over to the glass-enclosed breakfast nook. The view beyond was chilling. Acres of snow-covered ground and bare tree limbs stretching against a gunmetal gray sky. The radio she'd turned on in the kitchen announced it was thirty degrees. "Looks like we're going to have a white Christmas, folks. Remember, only ten more shopping days to go!" the announcer warned.

So far, Laurel hadn't bought a thing. Usually she had her shopping done by now, but this year had been hectic at the store. At least that's what she told herself. Actually, she just hadn't caught the holiday spirit. A vague restlessness, almost apprehension, had enveloped her for over a week, and she couldn't seem to shake it long enough to enjoy any of her normal activities.

The phone rang and she jumped, then closed her eyes. Mom and Dad, of course. Four years ago they'd bought a small house in Florida near Claudia's. Since her father's heart attack two years ago, they'd moved there permanently, turning over the store and the family home to Laurel. They checked up on her frequently, though.

A moment later her mother was jabbering happily and repeating everything Laurel said to her father. "Hal, she says they have snow. It's thirty degrees there." Back to Laurel. "How will the weather be next week? You *will* be able to fly down for Christmas, won't you?"

I hope not, Laurel said silently. Christmas Day with her father and Claudia's husband shouting deafeningly at football games on television and Claudia's two ill-behaved children incessantly squabbling was not Laurel's idea of a good time. To top it off, Claudia, expecting her baby in a month, was swollen, nauseated, and cranky as the devil. "I'm sure I'll make it," Laurel said, trying to force some excitement into her voice. "But if the weather does turn nasty, you'll have a good time without me this year."

"Don't be silly," her mother replied quickly. "Your niece and nephew would be crushed." Oh, sure, Laurel thought. The children barely took notice of her except to grab for their gifts. "We'd all miss you. Of course, if you have a good reason to *want* to stay home . . ." Her mother's voice had turned coy, and Laurel inwardly groaned, knowing what was coming next. "How are things with you and Kurt going? Expecting an engagement ring this Christmas?"

"No, Mother, I'm not," Laurel said more sharply than she'd intended. "I mean, we're really not serious."

"You've been seeing each other exclusively for seven months. In my day that meant serious."

"Well, it doesn't necessarily mean serious these days. Look, Mom, I'd planned to go into the store a little early this morning. Tell Dad business is fantastic this year."

"Hal, she says business is good."

Laurel heard her father's voice rumbling in the background, but her mother drowned him out. "Honey, you are still *seeing* Kurt, aren't you? You two haven't broken up?"

"Everything is fine with us. But I really have to go. Love to you and Dad. I'll be seeing you in a few days."

"Good-bye, sweetie. Take good care of yourself. And

don't give up hope. I think there's a ring coming for you this Christmas. I just feel it in my bones."

I hope your bones are wrong, Laurel thought as she hung up. She liked Kurt tremendously, but marriage was another matter. If he actually did present her with a ring, she would have to refuse it, which would cause her mother far more grief than it probably would Kurt.

Laurel let April and Alex out for a short romp in the snow. As she watched them play, she nibbled toast, wondering how she could get out of going to Florida next week, wondering exactly what she would say if Kurt actually started talking about marriage. Finally, she tossed down the toast in annoyance. "Laurel, it's *Christmas,*" she told herself sternly. "You used to love Christmas. This year you're too depressing for words. Snap *out* of it!"

Half an hour later, showered, dressed in brown wool slacks and a matching angora sweater, a gold and russet scarf tied around her neck, her hair smoothed from a careful blow-drying over a big brush, eyeshadow, blusher, and lipstick in place, she felt and looked better. Relieved, she knew she could face what promised to be a long day. Customers expected to see her bright and cheerful, and her father had taught her to always try to please the customer.

The snow was two days old so roads were clear. Laurel made it from her house to the store in fifteen minutes. As always when she saw it, pride flooded through her. Located in the historic district of Wheeling, West Virginia, Damron Floral inhabited a three-story Victorian structure painted robin's egg blue with ornate white shutters. She was the third generation of Damrons to manage the store. When her grandfather started it shortly after World War II, he and his wife and son lived on the third floor. During the fifties when business flourished and his family expanded to four children, he built the sprawling log home north of Wheeling, near the beautiful Oglebay State Park, where Laurel now lived.

She always entered by the back door and went into the

tiny kitchen off the workroom to start coffee before her
assistant Mary Howard arrived. She liked the store to seem
inviting, even to employees. Especially to Mary. She was
the best designer Laurel had ever hired. She was also the
younger sister of Laurel's friend Faith. Faith, so beautiful,
so insouciant, so bold. Faith, dead now for thirteen years.

Laurel felt a chill and pushed the image of Faith from
her mind. Good Lord, was she sinking into some kind of
holiday depression? For some reason, she wasn't allowing
herself to be happy. She seemed determined to dwell on
dark thoughts, the memory of Faith's death being the
darkest.

She went through the store turning on lights. She'd recently replaced the bland tan carpet that had covered the
floor of Damron Floral for as long as she could remember.
Every five to ten years when new carpet was needed, her
father chose the same nondescript shade. Now floors of
deep smoky blue stretched before her and soft pearl gray
walls replaced the former shade of bisque. Her parents
planned a trip home in the spring. She hoped her father
would approve of her decorating innovations, but she
doubted it. Hal Damron didn't like change.

A quick glance out the front window assured her the
street was nearly deserted. Good. She wouldn't put up the
open sign for twenty minutes, giving her time to go over
the day's orders. Aside from the usual holiday trade, three
funerals were being held tomorrow. They were swamped
with work.

Laurel took a quick inventory of the store's interior. The
glass shelves were loaded with lush poinsettias and holiday
planters decorated with various colored ribbons and silk
flowers. Grape vine wreaths hung on the walls along with
the more traditional pine wreaths. Laurel breathed in the
scent of pine mixed with potpourri coming from little sachet bags scattered throughout the store. The place definitely smelled of Christmas.

She heard the back door close and in a moment Mary
Howard called out, "Good morning, Laurel."

Laurel went to the back. Mary shrugged out of her long, heavy brown coat and smiled at her. She was a tall young woman of twenty-six with pale, frizzy red hair pulled back in a ponytail, light blue eyes, and a smattering of freckles over her high-bridged nose. She was attractive in a strong, rawboned way but certainly not the beauty her sister Faith had been. She didn't come close to Faith's vivid, sensual, almost Rita Hayworth look. Laurel had always thought of Faith as red satin, Mary as blue gingham.

"Hi," Laurel said. "You're early."

"Busy day ahead." Mary held up a bulging white paper bag. "Doughnuts."

"Bless you! I only ate half a piece of toast this morning and I know I'll be starving in a couple of hours."

"Have one now with a fresh cup of coffee. In a couple of hours you won't have time."

Laurel hesitated, then smiled. "Okay. You twisted my arm. Any chocolate-covered ones in that bag?"

"Are you joking? I know they're your favorite."

Mary was right. Two hours later the phone rang every few minutes and three customers browsed. Mary worked on arrangements in the back with Laurel's other designers, Penny and Norma, while Laurel manned the front. She'd just sold a set of artificial holly and pine candle rings when the phone rang for what seemed like the twentieth time. Sighing, she reached for her order pad. "Damron Floral."

A moment of silence spun out before a husky female voice asked, "Laurel, is that you?"

"Yes." The voice was familiar, but Laurel couldn't place it. Some customers were offended when she didn't immediately recognize their voices so she asked carefully, "How are you?"

"I'm fine. Well, actually I'm not fine this morning."

"Oh?"

"You don't know who this is, do you?"

God, I hate it when people make me guess their identity, Laurel thought in irritation. It's so rude and I'm so busy . . . Suddenly a face with clear green eyes flashed before her. "Monica! It's Monica Boyd."

"Right. Pretty quick after not having seen me for twelve years."

"We were close. Besides, you're a hard person to forget." A woman was holding up two pots of poinsettias, tilting them until dirt began sprinkling to the carpet. Laurel stiffened, wanting to snap, "Watch what you're doing!" Instead she asked pleasantly, "Are you still in New York, Monica?"

"Yes. I'm on my way to making partner at Maxwell, Tate, and Goldstein."

"Wonderful." More dirt fell. Laurel was ready to tell Monica to hold for a moment when Mary came to ask a question, immediately saw the problem, and rushed to the woman's side with a gracious smile and large, firm hands that relieved her of the poinsettias. "Big plans for the holidays?" Laurel asked.

"A change in plans. I'm coming back to Wheeling."

"After all these years?"

"Yes. I think it's important that I talk with you."

"Me?" Laurel was genuinely puzzled.

"Yes. You, Denise, and Crystal."

They'd all been friends growing up. Friends forever, they thought. When they were twelve, they'd formed a club called the Six of Hearts—Monica, Laurel, Crystal, Denise, Angela, and poor dead Faith. Anxiety abruptly gripped Laurel. "Monica, what's wrong?"

"You know Angie's been living here in Manhattan, too?"

"Of course. She's always kept in touch. I just got a card from her. She's the lead in a Broadway play."

"Not anymore." Laurel could hear Monica take a deep breath. "Laurel, Angie was murdered night before last. She wasn't found until yesterday, when she didn't show up for an interview and the theater couldn't reach her. It was . . . brutal. She was bludgeoned to death in her own bed."

"Oh, my God," Laurel gasped, her stomach clenching as

she pictured Angie's lovely face, remembered her beautiful voice. "How horrible!"

"Yes. But there's more, Laurel. I don't know how to tell you this, but Angela's death had something to do with the Six of Hearts."

TWO

1

Laurel's face slackened in shock. She saw the quick look Mary threw her way before she managed to speak again. "Monica, have they caught her killer?"

"No."

Laurel spoke softly. "Then what makes you think this had something to do with the Six of Hearts?"

"On the mirror in her bedroom the murderer drew a six and a heart. In Angie's blood."

"Oh," Laurel said weakly. "How do you know all this?"

"I'm good friends with a detective on the case. He knows I knew Angie. He gave me the details. They aren't known to the general public, but he thought I might have some idea of what they meant. I said I didn't."

"Why didn't you tell him the truth?"

"Because we never told *anyone* the truth about the Six of Hearts. Besides, I don't want to get involved in this. I doubt if any of us do."

Laurel realized she was clutching the receiver and forced herself to relax her grip. "Monica, the stuff on the mirror has to be some sort of coincidence."

"Coincidence?" Monica's husky voice rarely rose and Laurel heard the tension in it. "It's a coincidence that the killer just happened to put a six and a heart on her mirror when Angie used to be a member of the Six of Hearts? And something else. There was a tarot card lying beside her body—the judgment card."

"Judgment?"

"Yes. It seems to me the killer might want revenge for an old deed committed by the Six of Hearts."

"Judgment? Revenge? Monica, this is crazy. We were a secret club. No one knew about us."

"Laurel, we weren't CIA operatives. We were a bunch of young girls playing around with the idea of having a *secret* club because we were bored. It made us feel important even though most of what we did was just harmless, stupid stuff. Who says one of us didn't talk about the club at some point? It wasn't as if someone was going to get a bullet in the brain for revealing the Six of Hearts."

"I didn't tell anyone."

"I didn't, either, but that leaves four others."

"Not Faith. Faith is—" She broke off as she saw Mary standing in front of her, a frown creasing her pale forehead. "Monica, I'm afraid I have to go now. We're very busy today."

"Laurel, this is serious. You can't brush me off."

"I'm not trying to. It's just that—"

"I'm coming to Wheeling," Monica said firmly. "I'll be there tomorrow. Tell Denise and Crystal."

She hung up. Laurel stood mutely holding the phone.

"Was that bad news?" Mary asked. "It's not your sister, is it?"

"What?" Laurel blinked at her, then slowly put down the phone. "No, Claudia is fine. It was just someone telling me that an old friend of mine was murdered."

"Murdered! Who?"

"Angela Ricci. You wouldn't know her."

"She was a friend of my sister," Mary said promptly. "Is that why you mentioned Faith?"

Laurel nodded and Mary went on. "I remember Angela. Very pretty. Very talented. My goodness, what a shame!" Laurel nodded again. "Are you all right?"

"Yes."

"Are you sure? You don't look well."

"I'm fine, Mary, really."

But she wasn't fine. She was more horrified and frightened than she had been for thirteen years.

2

Laurel spent the rest of the day in a fog. She saw Mary, Penny, and Norma watching her closely and even some of the customers threw her curious glances when she didn't help them with her usual efficiency. She closed the store at five, forced herself to stay until six-thirty helping Mary with some last-minute arrangements, then gratefully headed for home.

April and Alex met her with one of their customary exuberant greetings. She petted both absently, rewarded each with a dog biscuit, threw her camel hair coat on a chair, and dropped onto the couch.

All week she'd felt odd. Had she somehow sensed something was going to happen to Angie? Impossible. Although Angie sent her Christmas cards and had even called when her mother told her about Laurel's father's heart attack, they weren't close. In fact, if not for Angie's efforts, they would have drifted completely apart, just like she and Monica had. After all, what did she have in common with a talented Broadway star?

Nothing. Not a thing except a shared youth in Wheeling and membership in a silly club formed by the precocious Monica when they were only twelve years old.

The Six of Hearts. Monica had come up with the name. She said symbolically the heart was the center of power and intelligence. When Crystal argued that she thought intelligence had something to do with the brain, Monica had snapped, "I said *symbolically*. Don't you even know what symbols are? Besides, do you want to be called the Six of Brains?" Sufficiently quelled, Crystal had ceased arguing. Never sure of her own intelligence, Monica had completely overwhelmed gentle Crystal. Lord, she overwhelmed all of us, Laurel thought. Monica was always a force. Apparently she still was, announcing that she was coming back here to talk to her and Crystal and Denise about Angie's murder, a murder she was certain had something to do with the Six of Hearts.

The club had started out so innocently. There had been a "secret" initiation, which consisted of eating foods blindfolded after being told olives were eyeballs and raw cow's liver was a human liver. Then they'd played harmless practical jokes on students they'd unanimously decided they didn't like. Sometimes they made anonymous phone calls to older boys, throwing their voices deep and sexy, then hanging up before they collapsed in giggles. When they were fifteen, everyone except Denise celebrated Bastille Day by sneaking out in the night armed with wire cutters, breaking out a window, crawling inside, and liberating nearly fifty dogs and cats from the local pound. That prank made the newspaper, but no one ever suspected them. It was all such fun. But as they got older, the games became darker.

The doorbell rang. Laurel frowned, wondering who it might be, then sat up slowly. Of all the evenings when she didn't want to be disturbed, unexpected company had arrived.

But it wasn't unexpected. "Hi," Kurt Rider said. "Hungry? I sure am."

Laurel closed her eyes briefly. "Oh, Kurt, I completely forgot we were supposed to have dinner."

"Oh, well, no harm done," he said easily, stepping inside, his six-foot-two frame towering over her. "Ready to go?"

"No, Kurt, I'm afraid I'm not feeling up to it tonight."

Disappointment flashed over his long, good-looking face and shone in his brown eyes. "Not up to it? Are you sick?"

"Not really." Laurel waved a hand at the big living room. "Come in."

He strode forward, then turned to look at her. "Why is it so dark in here?"

"Because I haven't turned on any lights?"

He grinned. "You're hilarious."

"You're the one who's supposed to make all the brilliant deductions."

"Hey, I'm just a simple deputy sheriff, not one of your flashy television detectives. And here I am, exhausted after a hard day of fighting crime, and my girl forgets we have a date."

"I'm really sorry, Kurt."

He flipped on a lamp and sat down on the long leather couch. "Stop apologizing and tell me what's wrong. You're pale. Getting the flu?"

"No. I got bad news." She sat down beside him. "Do you remember Angela Ricci?"

"Angie? Sure. She was just a year younger than me. She was in your class. Her mother's been telling everyone in town she made it big in some play in New York."

"Angie's dead, Kurt. Murdered."

Kurt stared at her blankly for a moment. "Murdered? What happened?"

"Angie was beaten to death in her own bed." And it seems to have something to do with a club we were in when we were kids, Laurel thought, although she said nothing. She didn't want to talk about the Six of Hearts with Kurt. Besides, Monica only had a theory.

"Laurel?"

"Huh?"

"I asked if you were still friends with her. I don't remember you mentioning her since we've been dating."

"I heard from her occasionally."

"How did you find out about her murder?"

"Monica Boyd. She lives in New York, too."

"Monica. I remember her. Tall. Bossy. Isn't she a lawyer now?"

"Yes. She's coming to Wheeling tomorrow."

"Why?"

Laurel paused. "The funeral," she said abruptly. Monica hadn't mentioned the funeral, but the Ricci family had been summoned to New York and had called back to tell a few people about their daughter's death and the funeral arrangements. Angie would be buried in Wheeling. Orders for funeral baskets and wreaths had begun trickling in a couple of hours before she closed the store.

Kurt frowned. "Well, it's a real shame Angie's dead, but you seem awfully upset about someone you hardly knew anymore."

"But I used to know her so well. We were friends for ten years. And the *way* she died . . . Kurt, it's awful."

"I know. But then murder is always awful." He put his arm around her. "Honey, I'm sorry."

"Thanks."

"I know there's nothing I can say to make you feel better, but you've got to eat."

"I'm not hungry."

"Your stomach is growling."

"It is?"

"Yes. Loudly."

Laurel smiled. "I didn't notice, but come to think of it, I haven't eaten anything except a piece of toast and a doughnut."

"No wonder you feel lousy. My mother is a firm believer in eating, no matter what."

"Your mother weighs two hundred pounds," Laurel said absently, then flushed in embarrassment. "Kurt, I'm sorry," she said quickly. "What an awful thing to say! I didn't mean . . . I don't know where that came from," she blundered. "Your mother is a lovely person."

But Kurt laughed good-naturedly. "She *is* a lovely person who weighs two hundred pounds. It's okay, Laurel. Facts are facts. And the fact is that you're too thin to be skipping meals. If you don't feel like going out, how about if I order a pizza for us?"

Laurel hesitated. "A pizza does sound pretty good."

"Great. Got any beer?"

"A couple of six-packs."

"I won't need that much. You go feed those hungry hounds of yours that are giving me such dirty looks from the doorway, and I'll call in the order. I guarantee that in an hour you'll feel like a new woman."

Kurt insisted on building a fire in the large flagstone fireplace. After feeding the dogs, Laurel sat on the hearth, clutching a pillow and warming herself. She hadn't realized until then that ever since Monica's call, she'd been freezing. When the pizza arrived, she ate ravenously. "Thought you weren't hungry," Kurt teased. "Glad I ordered the super size."

Laurel laid down a half-eaten piece. "You're right. I'm eating like a pig."

"No you're not. It's kind of nice to see you eat like this. You usually pick at your food."

"I don't have my sister's looks, but I can still stay slim."

Kurt smiled at her. "No offense to Claudia, but I never considered her the blond bombshell everyone else did."

"That's because she wouldn't go out with you."

"That did show a real lack of taste on her part, but I don't hold grudges. Besides, I only asked her out because it was considered a feat of success to go out with Claudia Damron. I always found your style more appealing than hers, though."

"I wasn't aware I had any style."

"You do. You've just never known it."

At nine o'clock, her appetite satiated, her body finally warm from the fire, Laurel asked Kurt if he'd mind leaving early. "I had a really busy day and tomorrow promises to be even worse," she told him.

"All right," he sighed. "First forget about our date, then kick me out in the cold."

"Kurt, I'm sorry—"

"I'm joking." He kissed her on the forehead. "Get a good night's sleep. Saturday evening we'll go out for a nice dinner. We might even stay up past eleven since you don't have to go to work the next day."

"That sounds wonderful, Kurt. Thanks for being so understanding."

She watched as he went down the long walk to his car.

He really is a great guy, she thought. Calm, steady, sweet. No wonder Mom wants me to marry him. I just wish I were in love with him.

As soon as his headlights disappeared at the end of the driveway, she shut the door and hurried to the phone. She hadn't lied to Kurt—she *was* exhausted—but she had a couple of calls to make.

First she dialed Crystal's number and was surprised when no one answered. Since Crystal's husband, Chuck Landis, had left her six months earlier, she'd become a near recluse. Maybe there being no answer was a good sign. Perhaps Crystal was resuming her life.

Next she called Denise Price. Although Denise had been one of Laurel's good friends growing up, after they graduated from high school Denise had cut off all contact. Laurel had been hurt at first, then she slowly accepted that none of the Six of Hearts had really wanted to remain close anymore. None with the exception of Angie. It was only through the local grapevine Laurel learned that after graduating from college with a nursing degree, Denise married a doctor, had a daughter named Audra, and was living in Chicago. Laurel was shocked when a little over a year ago Denise and her husband, Wayne, moved back to Wheeling. Shortly afterward Denise asked Damron Floral to decorate her lovely home for a Christmas party. It was then she and Laurel became casually reacquainted and Denise explained it was Wayne's idea to move to Wheeling where he felt their daughter would be safer than in a big city.

Wayne answered. "Why, hello, Laurel." His voice was deep and melodic. "Calling about decorations for our annual Christmas bash? You and Kurt *are* coming, aren't you?"

"We wouldn't miss it." Actually she'd forgotten all about it. So much for Kurt's plans for dinner out on Saturday evening. That was the night of the party. "I do need to speak to Denise about decorations and a couple of other things."

"All right. I'll see if I can find her."

It was nearly three minutes before Denise came on the line. When she did, she sounded abrupt and peevish. "Yes, Laurel, what's the problem?"

"No problem about the decorations." Laurel was a bit taken aback by her tone. She and Denise had not and never would regain the kinship they'd once felt, but they were friendly. "Are you free to talk right now?"

"It's a little hectic around here. Audra isn't feeling well and I have a headache."

"I'm sorry. I hope you and Audra aren't getting the flu that's going around."

"Me, too. We both feel awful."

"I'll be brief, then. Have you heard about Angela Ricci?"

Denise's voice lowered. "I heard she was murdered."

"Yes. Monica called me about it today. Denise, she knows a homicide detective working the case. He says a six and a heart were drawn on Angie's mirror in her blood."

"What?" Denise choked.

"A six and a heart. There was also a tarot card beside her body. It was the judgment card. Monica is certain Angie's death has something to do with the Six of Hearts."

Denise was quiet for a moment before she muttered, "That's absurd."

"I thought so, too, until I really considered how unlikely it would be that the six and the heart on her mirror are just a coincidence. Monica is coming to Wheeling tomorrow. She wants to talk to you, Crystal, and me."

"I don't want to talk to her," Denise said emphatically. "I don't ever want to think about the Six of Hearts again."

"Neither do I, Denise, but we have to."

"No we don't. *I* don't."

Laurel's reaction had been much the same this morning, but a day of thought had put her on Monica's side. "Denise, we *do* need to think about this. After all, if Angie's death had something to do with the Six of Hearts, the rest of us could be in danger. Monica's smart and she knows a lot about the case."

"Monica formed the Six of Hearts," Denise said bitterly. "She got us into the mess that resulted."

Laurel felt a wave of impatience. "Monica didn't force us to form a club or do any of the things we did. We're all responsible for 'the mess that resulted,' as you put it." Denise was silent. "Anyway, I just wanted to let you know exactly what happened to Angie and that Monica is coming. Whether or not you choose to talk to her is your decision."

"Yes, it is." Denise was quiet for a moment. "I'm sorry, but I'm very busy tonight. I'll talk with you later. Good-bye."

The phone clicked in Laurel's ear.

3

Laurel tried to be angry with Denise for her curtness, but she couldn't. Denise had a husband, a child, a safe and very comfortable life. The last thing she would want to be reminded of was the Six of Hearts. Then there was Angela's murder and Monica's theory that her connection with the Six of Hearts had something to do with it. She'd probably sounded as abrupt with Monica this morning as Denise had with her this evening.

She fixed a cup of cinnamon tea, went to the bookshelf and withdrew an old album whose vinyl cover was cracked. I should have taken better care of this, she thought as she sat down on the couch again. With Kurt gone, April and Alex jumped up to join her, cuddling on either side. Slowly sipping her drink, she flipped the pages of the album. Several albums on the shelf were devoted to Claudia, always posing and preening, in love with the camera. Only this one was hers. Laurel flipped past the pages showing her as a baby and toddler, stopping at the ones with photos of her with her first and best friend, Faith Howard.

She smiled. There they stood, arm in arm, in front of the dazzling flower bed in her backyard. Both had long hair, Faith's thick with natural curl and glowing like copper in the sun. Each wore a crown of daisies Laurel remembered weaving, thinking they made them look like Queen Guinevere. "Guinevere with two missing front teeth," she giggled, gazing at herself.

Laurel wore red shorts and a white top that looked as if she'd spilled chocolate on it. Faith flaunted a flowered sundress, one strap dangling rakishly off her seven-year-old shoulder while she pointed a dirty, bare foot like a ballerina. Quite the *femme fatales,* Laurel thought. It was a wonder Kurt Rider and Chuck Landis had ever become friends with them.

They hadn't wanted to, at first. They both lived nearby and Faith seemed to have a nose for finding them, determined to befriend the two good-looking, rowdy little boys, but the guys shunned them at first. "You're just skinny old *girls,*" Chuck had told them scathingly one day as she and Faith stood on the ground, watching the boys sitting up in their elaborate tree house behind Kurt's house eating Ritz crackers and peanut butter. "This is Tarzan's tree house and girls aren't allowed."

"Yes they are," Faith maintained staunchly. "What about Jane?"

The boys had stared at each other, puzzled about how to argue their way out of that one. Then Kurt looked triumphant. "Jane could swing on a *vine.* Only girls who can swing on vines get to come up."

They chortled as Laurel and Faith wandered away, Faith feigning tearful rejection. Fifteen minutes later both boys shrieked when Faith swooped through the air clutching an ivy vine and landed with a thud on the edge of the tree house. She broke her arm, but she'd won the admiration and acceptance of Kurt and Chuck. They'd agreed to be her friends, and she'd insisted they be friends with Laurel, too. The four of them had been close that summer. Naturally as they got older they grew apart, Kurt and Chuck spending their time with other boys, Laurel and Faith forming intense friendships with girls their own age, but the basic warmth of the relationship the four had developed that summer did not fade. Not until thirteen years ago, that is.

Laurel laid the album aside and stared into the flames in the fireplace, her mind spinning back over the years to a night not unlike this one.

She remembered the cold. She was supposed to be spending the night with Angie. They all were, although none of the parents knew the Riccis were away for the weekend and thought Angie was staying with Laurel. Five of them would have been content to remain in the Ricci home, eating popcorn, calling boys, watching videos, and drinking the wine Monica had brought along. None of them were drinkers and the presence of wine turned the overnight stay into a heady experience for everyone except Monica. She wasn't content to stay home. She wanted the Six of Hearts to make one of their visits to the Pritchard farm.

Monica had always been fascinated with the place, particularly the old barn. Everyone in the area knew about the Pritchards' slave, Esmé Dubois. In 1703, the Pritchards' eldest son was thrown from a horse and killed. Weeks later scarlet fever carried away four of the remaining five children and only days afterward Mrs. Pritchard was found drowned in the farm pond.

The Pritchards prided themselves on their devotion to God. They knew they didn't deserve such hardship and decided the devil must be at work in their midst. Esmé was from the heathenish islands where voodoo abounded. They quickly deduced that she had been practicing her black arts. She was found guilty of witchcraft in a court where the judge and members of the jury were all in some way beholden to the wealthy Pritchards. When she was only nineteen, Esmé was hanged in the Pritchard barn, the same barn that had weathered almost three centuries to become the sometime meeting place of the Six of Hearts.

On that cold December night Monica decided it was time for one of their trips to the barn. Everyone else groaned. "Monica, it's *freezing* outside. It's beginning to sleet," Crystal wailed.

"We have coats," Monica stated.

Laurel sided with Crystal. "Why can't we wait until it's warmer?"

Monica glared at her. "Because it won't be warmer for months. Besides, we stand less chance of being caught when no one else is out. I thought we could do something a little different tonight, something a little spooky."

"Oh, no," Denise moaned. "Not another one of those witchy things, those rituals. I don't think we should be messing around with witchcraft. It scares me."

Suddenly Faith, who'd been unusually quiet, came to life. "Yeah, it's a perfect night," she said spiritedly. "It's Friday the thirteenth. What better night for a ritual?"

Crystal looked at her in bewilderment. "Your dad's a minister. Seems like you'd be the last one of us to mess with witchcraft."

Faith rolled her azure eyes. "My father is the unordained minister of some crazy religion he made up. I think he and all of his followers are nuts. Witchcraft makes a lot more sense." She stood. "Let's go to the barn."

"Yeah, it'll be fun," Angie suddenly chimed in. She always enjoyed the theatrics involved in Monica's Satanic rituals. "It's a perfect night and we don't get chances like this very often."

Still grumbling, Laurel, Denise, and Crystal acquiesced. Monica, Faith, and Angie were by far the strongest personalities in the group. Looking back, Laurel realized the Six of Hearts was ruled by Monica, but Angie and Faith were her seconds-in-command. She, like Crystal and Denise, had always been a follower.

Laurel took another sip of her tea and shifted uncomfortably as she remembered the drive. Although the place had not been owned by a Pritchard for nearly a century, it was still known to locals as the Pritchard farm. In the days of Esmé, the farm encompassed over a hundred acres. Now it was reduced to twenty. The massive old barn, no longer used by the present owner of the farm, sat nearly a hundred yards from the house. They parked a quarter of a mile away and ran quietly through the night. Monica carried a duffel bag. She must have packed it before they left the house.

They opened the door of the barn only wide enough for each girl to slip through although the lights in the house looked far away. A dog barked somewhere and Laurel remembered being afraid it might come charging toward them, but nothing happened. Either it was tied up or behind a fence. She also remembered someone, probably Angie, giggling.

Once inside, Monica quickly found a kerosene lantern she kept stashed behind some ancient equipment for these occasions. She held a match to it and in a moment light bloomed, throwing shifting shadows around the barn's old, rotting interior.

Taller than any of them, Monica held up the lantern. Light danced on her long mahogany hair and turned her eyes to emerald above her high cheekbones. "Tonight we're going to bring back the spirit of Esmé Dubois."

"What?" Crystal squeaked. She looked fragile and child-like with her long golden hair, wide blue eyes, and small frame. At seventeen, she was only five feet two inches tall. "Bring back a spirit?"

"Yes," Monica said calmly in her husky, commanding voice. She withdrew a fresh bottle of wine from the duffel bag. "Red wine. Wine as red as blood." She pulled the already loosened cork from the bottle. "We'll each take a drink."

"I don't want any more," Crystal said. "I don't like it."

Laurel didn't like it, either. Only later did she learn she had an intolerance for alcohol. The smallest amount had an exaggerated, nauseating effect on her. But that night she'd drunk because she didn't want the others to laugh at her. They all drank. When the bottle was empty, Monica, seemingly unaffected, resumed speaking in her authoritative tone. "Tonight we will summon the spirit of Esmé Dubois." She withdrew a rope from her duffel bag. "We'll reenact the hanging."

Laurel was aghast. "You're going to *hang* someone?"

Monica looked at her disdainfully. "Of course not. We'll

only take things to a certain point. Then the spirit of Esmé
will return."

"I don't like this," Crystal ventured.

Monica ignored her and looked at Denise. "You'll be
Esmé."

Denise's gray eyes widened. "Why me?"

"Because I've decided you'd be best," Monica returned.
"Your hair is black and really curly like Esmé's. You look
the most like her. Angie, help me get this rope over that
beam. Then we'll make a noose. Denise will put her head
in it."

"Oh, no I won't!" Denise snapped.

"Yes, you *will*."

Denise gave Monica a steely look. "Esmé may have been
a slave but *I'm* not. I don't have to take orders from you,
Monica Boyd, and I will *not* put my head in a noose."

Monica stared at her for a moment, then laughed. "Denise, you're always so damned *serious*. This is just a game."

"I'll put my head in the noose!" Faith announced in a
slightly slurred voice. They all looked at her. Her long red
hair gleamed in the light and her eyes had a wild, abandoned expression. She'd been acting odd all evening, alternately withdrawn and aggressive. Maybe it was the wine.
She'd drunk more than any of them. "It'll be fun."

"Don't do it," Laurel told her. "This is crazy."

Faith giggled. "I like doing crazy things. Loosen up, Laurel."

"Faith—"

"I'm *doing* it!" Faith shot out. "C'mon, Monica, I'll help
with the rope."

By this time Laurel was beginning to feel sick. She sat
down on the straw-laden dirt floor while Monica and Faith
worked. Soon Monica was dragging a rotting bale of straw
beneath the noose. Faith climbed up on the bale. Monica
moved the kerosene lamp closer. Shadows flickered over
Faith's beautiful, sensual face. She seemed taller than she
really was and the whole scene took on a surreal quality.

"Faith, put your head in the noose," Monica ordered.

"Everyone else form a circle around her and join hands."

Laurel tried to stand but couldn't. Monica looked at her in annoyance. "You're drunk."

"I'm sorry," Laurel murmured. "Never had wine before."

"Just sit there, then. You look green. I don't want you throwing up on us. Everyone else get in the circle."

"I don't feel so good, either," Denise said.

"You're fine," Monica told her firmly. "Get in the circle."

Faith had climbed onto the stool and slipped the noose around her neck. "I'm standing up here with my head in a rope," she shouted. "Hurry up!"

"Be quiet," Monica hissed. "They'll hear you at the house."

"She's drunk," Denise said. "She's swaying. This is dangerous. Faith, take off that noose."

Faith stamped her foot. "No. Do the chant."

"Yeah, let's get it over with," Crystal said. "I'm freezing."

They joined hands and began circling Faith. Laurel watched a moment before their movement make her feel even sicker. The whole room was beginning to spin.

Monica began to chant, throwing her husky voice down a pitch, saying the words slowly, hypnotically. She went through the ritual prayer once with everyone staring at her. Then Angie began to repeat it, then Crystal, and finally Denise. "Hail, the Lords of Darkness. In the name of the rulers of the earth, the kings of the underworld, rise to this place. Open the gate, and bring forth your faithful servant Esmé Dubois, who died for doing your work among the God-worshipers." They circled faster. "Azazel, Azazel, scapegoat released on the Day of Atonement, its destination hell." Around and around they went, their voices ringing out in unison. "Appear before us, Esmé and Azazel. Appear before the Six of Hearts, your modern-day servants. Let us bask in your glorious presence."

Light flickered from the kerosene lamp they'd set near the stool. Laurel closed her eyes again, desperately fighting off nausea. She wanted to get away from this cold, musty place to somewhere warm where she could lie down and wait for the sickening effects of the wine to wear off. Clasping her arms around her waist, she opened her eyes again.

Although her memory until this point was so clear, the next few moments had always remained a blur. All she recalled precisely was the girls chanting, "Bring forth your faithful servant—" A scream. Then flames leaping from the overturned lamp, devouring the bale of straw, licking up the legs of Faith's jeans. Faith.

More screams erupted and suddenly Laurel realized Faith's feet no longer rested on the bale. They dangled limply as she swung slowly back and forth, her head twisted to the right, her dazzling eyes wide.

The girls scattered as the fire spread, jumping higher up Faith's legs. Horrified, Laurel scrambled forward. She heard someone shrieking "Laurel!" as she reached into the fire, grabbing at Faith, trying to get her feet back on the bale. But Faith's legs were on fire and Laurel couldn't touch them. "Faith," she wailed. *"Faith!"*

Someone pulled her away. "Stop it, Laurel. She's dead!"

"No!" Laurel sobbed.

"Yes. It's too late. My God, look at your arms!" More milling, more screaming. "We've got to get out of here!"

"We can't leave her!" Laurel cried.

"She's *dead!*" Monica shouted. "Denise, grab Laurel. We have to go !"

The next few minutes were a kaleidoscope of images. The cold. Sleet pouring down, hissing as it hit the fire. Being half dragged back to the car. Monica starting the engine and shooting down the rutted country lane. Looking back to see part of the barn engulfed in flames that leaped angrily against the starless winter night.

Laurel jerked back to the present, realizing she was hyperventilating. She set down her cup of cold tea and forced herself to take long, slow breaths. Although she dreamed about that night frequently, she rarely allowed herself to think about it when she was awake. It would seem that after thirteen years, the memory should have dimmed, but it hadn't. She still vividly recalled standing dazed in Angie's bathroom while she applied antiseptic to Laurel's burned hands and arms, then wrapped them in gauze and made her swallow a pill. "What is it?" Laurel had mumbled. "Antibiotic. I got a bunch of capsules out of Dad's office." "But your father's a *veterinarian*," Denise cried. "Sometimes animals take the same medicine as humans," Angie answered. "These are safe. Laurel, you have to take one every eight hours until you run out of capsules. Laurel, are you listening to me?"

So she'd taken the pills, told her parents she'd spilled boiling water on her hands, carefully kept her arms covered, and stayed to herself for the next few days. She'd also kept her silence. They all had, even when the talk of the town was Faith Howard's death. People were baffled at first. Although owners of the Pritchard farm had left on lights, they had not been home that night and hadn't heard the screams of the girls. Everyone assumed Faith had been in the barn alone, which seemed inexplicable. Then the medical examiner announced that Faith was ten weeks pregnant. That's when townspeople believed they understood what had happened. Faith, daughter of the fanatically religious Zeke Howard, was terrified of telling her father she was pregnant, and no doubt her boyfriend, Neil Kamrath, whom everyone considered a coldly intellectual oddball anyway, had refused to marry her. Faith, they thought, had intended to commit suicide by hanging herself. In her death throes, she'd kicked over the lantern and set the fire.

Laurel suffered agonies of guilt during all the gossip and speculation. She and the other Six of Hearts knew Faith hadn't intended to kill herself. They should tell the truth, Laurel and Denise argued. But Monica argued more forcefully. "Look, do you realize what people in town would think of us if they knew what we were doing? God, we'd be dirt in their eyes. Worse than dirt. And we *didn't* kill her. It was an accident. She was drunk. She slipped off that bale and when the rope jerked her neck, she kicked over the lantern, just like they're saying."

"But we should let people know she didn't commit suicide," Laurel maintained.

Monica had turned on her angrily. "If we tell the truth, we have to admit we ran off and left her."

Denise looked stricken. "But she was already dead. You said so."

"Exactly. *I* say so and I'm right. You saw the angle of her head, those blank eyes. She was on fire and she didn't make a sound. But what if no one believes us? What if they think we *murdered* her?"

"Why would they think that?" Denise asked in an appalled voice.

"Why? Maybe because we were drunk."

"They don't know that."

"They will if they do blood work on Faith's body. They won't think she was drunk and we weren't. And how do we explain that noose around her neck?"

Denise's fervor was flagging. "We say it was just a game. That's all it was—a harmless game."

"Brilliant, Denise. Is everyone going to think a harmless game involved sticking a girl's head in a noose? No, we are *not* talking. We *can't*. What happened wasn't our fault but people won't believe us. We could be charged with manslaughter or negiligent homicide. We could go to *prison!*" Everyone quailed. "Our lives will be ruined and for what? An *accident!* We're *innocent!*"

Throughout the whole thing Crystal had not spoken. She'd only cried, silently, wrenchingly. And in the end they'd kept quiet as Monica told them to, even though poor Neil Kamrath suffered the derision of Wheeling residents. He'd gotten Faith pregnant, deserted her, and she'd killed herself, they thought. He was a pig, they said. Laurel had worried about him, but Monica said that was silly. He had an alibi for the night of Faith's death. The police couldn't prove he'd killed her, and in the autumn he would be going off to Harvard on scholarship. Until then he'd live through the gossip. It wasn't like he'd ever tried to be popular. He didn't seem to care what anyone thought of him. Meanwhile, the Six of Hearts disbanded and the remaining five had gone their own ways the next year, none retaining the innocence of youth, each bearing black memories of their friend's terrible death.

Laurel pushed back her sweater sleeves. There were burn scars on her arms and hands, but they were so faint people rarely noticed them. It seemed to her that she'd tried valiantly to reach Faith through the fire, but if she had, wouldn't the scars be worse? They were barely visible. Maybe her memory of her actions was blurred by the alcohol. Maybe she hadn't tried hard to save her dearest friend at all.

The fire was burning low and Laurel pushed her sleeves down, realizing how chilly the living room had become. April and Alex were deeply asleep on the couch, Alex snoring lightly. Laurel wished she were sleepy, but she wasn't.

She got up slowly so as not to disturb the dogs and wandered around the room. Woven rugs lay over the polished hardwood floors and the paneled walls bore oil paintings of local scenes done by her grandmother. Laurel knew the paintings could garner an impressive sum today, but no one in her family would have considered selling them. Usually she found the room warm and charming with its casual, rustic style. Tonight it seemed too big and full of dark corners. She wished she had something to divert her mind for a while. She had thought of Faith and the Six of Hearts far too much today.

Suddenly she remembered she hadn't picked up the mail on her way in this evening. Looking for some diversion, she put on her coat, turned on the carriage lamp beside the front door, picked up a flashlight, and went outside.

The night was cold and clear. She turned on the flashlight and slowly made her way to the end of the gravel lane where her mailbox sat on a pole facing the county road. There was little traffic at this hour. The night was completely dark except for an icy crescent slice of moon. Laurel shivered and pulled her coat tighter around her. There was nothing frightening out here—no strange noises, no feeling of being followed—but she still felt uneasy. She reached in the mailbox, pulled out several pieces of mail, and half walked, half ran back to the house.

Once inside she slammed the door and locked it. When both dogs leaped up, barking in alarm, she felt silly. "It's all right," she said soothingly to calm the pair. "There aren't any intruders for you to attack."

Whether April and Alex would actually attack anyone was questionable. Both tended to be gentle, almost fearful dogs. She'd always wondered if their nature had something to do with their being taken away from their mother too soon.

Feeling a bit calmer now that she was inside with the door securely locked, Laurel took off her coat and sat down with the mail. Her hands still trembled slightly. This is ridiculous, she told herself. Angie's death was awful and Monica's theory chilling, but Monica had no proof. Maybe the six and the heart on Angela's mirror had been a coincidence. Maybe it hadn't even been a heart at all, but some arcane, smeared symbol the police had mistaken for a heart.

While her thoughts whirled, Laurel sorted the mail absently. She'd opened three Christmas cards and a credit card bill when she came across a thick envelope with no return address. It was postmarked New York.

With a feeling of dread, she opened the envelope and withdrew a sheaf of paper with a six and a heart drawn in red ink. Her heart picking up speed, she unfolded the paper. Two photographs fell out.

The first was old, a small black and white photo of a smiling Faith Howard wearing a black sweater and a simple string of pearls. Faith's school picture, Laurel thought, her eyes welling with tears. Then her gaze shifted to the second photo.

It was a color Polaroid shot of a body lying on white satin sheets, the features grotesquely crushed and bloody beneath a mass of long, black hair.

Three

1

Although Laurel crept into bed about an hour after opening the mail, she spent most of the night staring blindly at the television, unable to concentrate on any of the movies shown on cable.

Now she knew that Monica was not imagining someone was after the Six of Hearts. The Polaroid shot had been of Angie's mutilated body. Certainly it wasn't a police photograph. The killer must have taken it right after the murder.

Laurel shivered and drew the down comforter higher. The only bodies most people ever saw were embalmed, dressed nicely, made up in a semblance of life, lying in quiet repose in satin-lined caskets. She, on the other hand, had watched a girl swinging from a rope with fire climbing up her body. Now she'd seen a photo of a brutally beaten corpse. What made it worse was that both bodies had belonged to friends.

Faith's death had been an accident—a horrifying accident. But Angela's wasn't. What kind of person could bludgeon someone, stand over them and strike again and again until nothing remained but a bloody mass, then calmly take a photograph to send to her?

A person who knew about the Six of Hearts. A person seeking revenge for their part in Faith's death. Who was to be the next victim? Herself? Is that what receiving the photos meant?

Laurel finally drifted off to sleep around four in the morning. At seven she nearly leaped from the bed when the alarm went off. The previous three hours had been filled with bad dreams. She was relieved daylight had come at last.

Two hours later she saw Mary do a double take when she came into the store. "Laurel, are you sure you're feeling all right? You didn't look well yesterday and you look even worse today."

"Thank you."

Mary flushed in embarrassment. "Oh, Laurel, I didn't mean to hurt your feelings."

Laurel forced a smile. "You didn't. I haven't been feeling great the last couple of days."

"You look exhausted."

"I sat up and watched about twenty movies last night. At least it seemed like that many. I'm going to get another cup of coffee. I think I'll need regular infusions of caffeine to keep me going today."

Mary followed her to the kitchen. "If you need to go home, I'm sure we can manage."

"No you can't. We have too much work to do. I'll be fine."

Shortly afterward she called the wholesalers and ordered the flowers they would need for that day. News of Angela's murder had been in the evening paper and no doubt calls would begin flooding in for arrangements, although times for the viewing and funeral were not set because the New York police had not yet released the body.

She was taking an order on the phone when Crystal Landis rushed in, setting the bell on the front door clanging. "Laurel, I've got to talk to you," she said breathlessly.

Laurel held up a finger indicating Crystal should wait a minute. Can't she see I'm on the phone? Laurel thought. But Crystal was clearly overwrought. She wore an ugly plaid coat that looked as if it had been made from a horse blanket. Laurel knew it hid a body that had recently gained about ten pounds. The hair she'd once kept golden with artificial color had been allowed to return to its natural dishwater blond and was cut in an unflattering short style. The pretty little-girl face had aged before its time, three lines slicing deeply across her forehead, nasal labial folds beginning to appear, blue eyes looking perpetually worried and disillusioned.

Early in life, Crystal had seemed blessed. Her family had money and lived in one of the largest houses in town. Crystal was pretty and popular, an only child whose parents doted on her and denied her nothing. But things changed before she reached twenty. She married Chuck Landis, the old friend of Laurel, Kurt, and Faith. She'd been in love with him since her early teens, and Laurel understood why. He was the golden boy—handsome, charming, the school's star quarterback. Unfortunately, adulthood dulled his luster. In spite of the academic allowances made for athletes, during his second year he flunked out of the college that had recruited him for his football skills. Only months later, Crystal's parents were killed in a plane crash and, to everyone's surprise, they left barely anything. Her father's reckless investments had landed the family on the verge of bankruptcy. Everything had to be sold to pay estate taxes. Suddenly penniless and humiliated, Crystal had dropped out of college and she and Chuck returned to Wheeling where they moved into a tiny, dilapidated house owned by Chuck's grandmother. Afterward Chuck bounced from job to job while Crystal suffered three miscarriages. Finally, six months ago, after the stillbirth of their daughter, Chuck left Crystal for an attractive older divorcée named Joyce Overton. Crystal was devastated and looked five years older than she had before his desertion.

Laurel hung up and looked at Crystal. "Sorry, but I had to get that order."

"You know about Angie getting murdered," Crystal said bluntly.

"Yes. I tried to call you last night but you weren't home."

"I went to a movie." Crystal leaned across the counter. "Can you leave for a little while? I've got to talk to you."

"Crystal, we're awfully busy—" She broke off. Crystal

looked almost frantic. "Why don't we go down the street for coffee and pastry?"

"I don't care. Anywhere."

Laurel told Mary she was leaving for half an hour, grabbed her coat, and hurried out with Crystal. Minutes later, as they sat over French vanilla coffee and croissants in a secluded corner of a nearby café, Crystal blurted, "What do you know about Angie's death?"

"Monica called me yesterday morning. She knows a detective working on Angie's case. He told her the police found a six and a heart drawn on Angie's mirror in her blood. She thinks the murder has something to do with the Six of Hearts."

Crystal blanched. "Did she tell the police?"

"No." Laurel looked at Crystal closely. "What's the matter? You're not this upset over Angie's death."

"No. I mean, her getting murdered is terrible but . . ." She trailed off and lifted her coffee cup to her lips with trembling hands. "Laurel, I got something in the mail about an hour ago. It was postmarked New York." Laurel felt the breath go out of her as Crystal fumbled in her purse and withdrew an envelope. She handed it to Laurel. "Look inside."

Laurel really didn't need to look, but she couldn't stop herself from pulling out a sheet of paper. A six and a heart were drawn in red, probably with a felt tip pen. Inside the paper was the school picture of Faith and the color Polaroid. Crystal pointed a shaking finger at the Polaroid shot. "Is that what I think it is?"

"Yes, I believe it's Angie." Crystal made a small choking noise. "I got a package just like this yesterday," Laurel said.

Crystal's pale lips opened. "What? You, *too*?" Laurel nodded. "Where did this awful picture of Angie come from?"

"I'd say from the murderer."

"Oh, Laurel, that can't be!" Crystal burst out.

"Shhhh!" Laurel glanced around, then spoke softly. "Do you have any other suggestions about where it came from?

I'm sure the New York police didn't send it."

"But why is Faith's picture with it?"

"Monica told me the police found a tarot card lying beside Angie's body. It was the judgment card. Considering the six and the heart on the mirror and the picture of Faith we received, I'd say someone is saying judgment is being wreaked on us because of Faith's death."

Crystal reached out and took Laurel's wrist. "No one knew about our club or that we were there when Faith . . . died."

"I believe someone *does* know." Laurel didn't think it was possible for Crystal to lose any more color in her face, but she did. "Crystal, Monica is as worried as we are. She's coming to Wheeling today to talk with you, Denise, and me."

Crystal looked alarmed. "I don't want to talk to Monica!"

"Why not?"

"Because. . . ." Her gaze dropped. "Because she always scared me."

"Oh, Crystal, don't be silly. I know she dominated us a long time ago but we're adults now."

"I still don't want to talk to her," Crystal said stubbornly.

Laurel sighed. "Neither does Denise, but I think it's important. As I told Denise, Monica knows a lot about Angie's case, probably more than she told me on the phone. She believes we're all in danger and she wants to help us."

"But the pictures were sent from New York. The killer can't be in Wheeling."

"Crystal, New York isn't on another planet. Whoever murdered Angie could easily come here."

"Do you think so?" Laurel looked at her in amazement. "Of course he could. I sound like an idiot. This is a nightmare."

"It certainly is. *I* think we should go to the police."

"No!" Crystal said emphatically. "I won't do it. Do you know what people in town would say about us?"

"Is that really important now? It's been thirteen years and someone has been murdered . . ."

Crystal looked up and her eyes widened. "Oh, no."

Laurel followed her gaze. Entering the pastry shop were Joyce Overton and Crystal's soon-to-be ex-husband Chuck Landis. They placed orders at the counter. Chuck turned and spotted Crystal immediately. Laurel saw discomfort cross his face. He bent and murmured to Joyce, who shook her head. In a moment they were carrying their order to the only available table, forcing them to pass Crystal and Laurel. Joyce beamed at them as if they were old friends and this was the most natural situation in the world. "Hello, Crystal," she said brightly.

Joyce was slender and dark-eyed, with shoulder-length gleaming ash blond hair, and a year-round tan that spoke of hours in tanning beds. She was at least fifteen years older than Chuck and the age difference showed in her face but not in her trim body always sporting youthful, expensive clothes. Laurel had met her several times and thought Joyce was one of the brashest people she'd ever encountered. She was also quite affluent and Laurel heard she was setting up Chuck with a car dealership.

Crystal managed a slight nod in Joyce's direction, then looked at her husband. "Hello, Chuck."

"Crystal," he said stiffly. He still resembled the school football hero he'd once been with his strapping body and blond good looks. In fact, he appeared only a few years older than when he graduated from high school. Laurel could understand Joyce's physical attraction to him—he might be a loser and he'd certainly treated Crystal without an ounce of respect or affection, but he was strikingly handsome. Now, however, his cheeks burned crimson with embarrassment. "Cold enough for you?" he asked lamely.

That was Chuck—always quick with the small talk, Laurel thought. What an awful situation. Crystal was still so in love with him. Laurel had known him for over twenty years. Everything had once been so simple and easy. Now she had to choose between being friendly to Chuck and supporting Crystal.

"It *is* cold," Crystal said woodenly.

Joyce turned hard dark eyes on Laurel, who wondered if she were actually wearing false eyelashes. "I suppose business is really great this time of year."

"Yes, it is."

Joyce had her arm firmly through Chuck's and she pulled him a bit closer. "We're having a little get-together at my house this weekend. I thought perhaps you could do some decorating for me . . ."

The woman certainly had gall, Laurel thought as she saw Chuck blink rapidly, clearly appalled. "I'm afraid I can't, Mrs. Overton," she answered coolly. "I'm far too busy to take on any other jobs."

Chuck's face grew even redder ~~and~~ but Joyce didn't bat a false eyelash. "Well, there's always the Flower Basket. I usually use them anyway. Most people say they're the best." She looked at Chuck. "Come on, honey. Our cappuccino is getting cold."

Chuck followed meekly behind her. Even his neck was red. Laurel glanced at Crystal's trembling lips. "Oh, Crystal, don't cry," she murmured. "You'll ruin everything. Joyce was trying so hard to upset you and instead she just humiliated herself. *And* Chuck. He's not going to appreciate that. What do you want to wager they have an argument before they even get out of here?"

Crystal managed a weak smile. "You're right. Chuck can take a lot, but not embarrassment. Still, thank you for turning her down."

Laurel looked at her in mild astonishment. "Good heavens, Crystal, do you really think I'd do business with her considering the situation?"

"But business *is* business and we haven't exactly been bosom buddies the last few years."

"We used to be, and I never stopped caring about you, even though it was painful for all of us to see each other after Faith's death."

"I guess we can't avoid seeing each other now." Crystal bit her lower lip. "You're right. We're in danger. We have no choice but to get together with Monica and figure out what we should do before another one of us is murdered."

2

Monica called the store shortly before closing time. "I'm in Wheeling, Laurel. Have you talked to Denise and Crystal?"

"Yes. Crystal is willing to get together with us. Denise isn't."

"I'll call her. What's her number?"

"I don't have it memorized, but it's under her husband's name, Wayne Price. But Monica, I don't know if calling will do any good—"

"It will," Monica said with her usual assurance. "I'm staying at the Wilson Lodge in Oglebay Park, room 709. They were very stubborn about not giving me the Burton Suite."

Laurel couldn't suppress a smile. Monica always expected the best even at the last minute. "I'm sure all the rooms there are very nice."

"It's all right. Can you be here at seven?"

"Yes."

"Good. Call Crystal. I'll take care of Denise."

She hung up without saying good-bye. "Good luck with Denise," Laurel muttered.

She arrived home at six, making sure she picked up the mail. Before driving up to the house, she sorted through it quickly. More Christmas cards and a sales flier from a local discount store. Nothing frightening, thank God. She didn't know how she'd handle another grisly missive like the one she'd received yesterday.

Laurel pulled up to the house and let herself inside. The dogs greeted her noisily. "What have you two been into today?" she asked, bending to pet them. "Watching television? Making long distance calls?"

They gamboled after her into the kitchen, starving as usual. She opened a can of food for each and poured fresh

water. When they finished and dashed through the dog door
into the backyard, she fixed herself a cheese sandwich. She
could have used something more substantial, but she didn't
have time.

Twenty minutes later she was headed north toward Oglebay Park. Laurel had always loved the fifteen-hundred-acre
resort, particularly around Christmas when it became the
showplace for America's largest light show. Ever since
the Winter Festival of Lights began in 1985, she'd made
the tour. In the beginning the show was somewhat humble,
with only a couple of thousand lights. Now there were over
nine hundred thousand lights covering three hundred acres
of land. Claudia laughed at Laurel's continued childish
delight with the lights, but Laurel ignored her. Christmas
had always been her favorite time of year. At least until
this year.

Earlier she'd called Crystal from the store and she had
agreed to meet with Monica. As Laurel drove up the last
hill and circled the lodge, she looked for Crystal's red
Volkswagen but didn't see it. Maybe she was simply late.
Laurel hoped she hadn't changed her mind about coming.

She parked, taking a moment to look at the hills sur-
rounding the lodge. They formed a dark silhouette against
the lighter darkness of the night. Below her was Schenk
Lake and in the distance the glow of lights from some of
the giant Christmas displays. How nice it would be if she
were here merely for her yearly tour, not to see Monica
about Angie's murder.

She found Monica's room quickly and tapped on the
door. In a moment Monica answered. "Hello, Laurel," she
said pleasantly. "You're the first to arrive. Come in."

Laurel was amazed at how little Monica had changed
since she'd seen her over twelve years ago. Her hair was
still shining mahogany, worn halfway down her back and
nearly straight except for a slight curve at the ends. The
luminous skin was free of lines, her eyes a brilliant, clear
green. She was around five feet ten with wide shoulders
and perfect posture and she looked even slimmer than she

had as a teenager, tight black slacks and a cashmere turtle-neck sweater revealing a body that obviously underwent regular workouts.

"You're looking well, Laurel," she said, closing the door. "You've cut your hair."

"Years ago. It's easier to take care of."

"It suits you."

"Thanks. You look remarkably the same."

Monica cocked an arched eyebrow. "Is that good or bad?"

Laurel smiled. "Good and you know it. I thought a high-pressure job like yours would take more of a toll on your appearance."

"I've learned to manage stress."

"Like we're under now?"

Monica merely nodded and took Laurel's coat, laying it across one of the beds. She had a comfortable double room with blue-green carpet, white bedspreads with an ivy pattern, and a big window overlooking snowy rooftops and the hills beyond. A door led to a narrow balcony.

Laurel sat down on a bed. "We could have met at my place."

"I heard you moved back into your parents' house. We need to be alone."

"I didn't give up my apartment until my parents moved to Florida. I live alone in the house."

"I know, but someone might stop by. You *are* dating a cop, aren't you? That's what Angie told me. It wouldn't do for him to find us all together."

"Yes, I'm seeing Kurt Rider. Do you remember him?"

"Vaguely. One of those big jock types."

Laurel decided to overlook the faint derision in her voice. "Well, he's a deputy with the county sheriff's office now, but I already told him you were coming to town."

Monica's face tightened. "Why did you do that? Now he'll be suspicious."

Laurel felt herself stiffening, anxious to make excuses to appease Monica. She had to remind herself she was a thirty-year-old woman who should no longer be daunted by Monica, no matter how self-possessed and authoritative she was. "Monica, Kurt was not suspicious," she said firmly. "I explained you were coming for Angie's funeral. He remembers we were all friends. He wouldn't think it was odd if we got together for an evening."

"Did you tell him about the evidence at Angie's apartment pointing to the Six of Hearts?"

"Of course not. He doesn't know about the Six of Hearts. He doesn't know anything except that Angie was murdered."

Someone tapped on the door. Monica opened it and Laurel heard Denise's voice. "Well, I'm here. Satisfied?"

"I see time has done nothing to dull that sharp tongue of yours."

Over the years a tension had developed between Denise and Monica. They were the only two of the Six of Hearts who had started to squabble by the time they were sixteen.

Denise strode into the room. She was scowling, her gray eyes angry behind attractive metal-rimmed glasses. She'd let her curly black hair grow to almost shoulder length but it was carelessly pushed back on either side with tortoise-shell combs. She looked careworn and slightly flushed.

"Hello, Denise."

Denise's expression softened. "Hi, Laurel. Sorry if I was short with you on the phone last night. It hadn't been a good day."

"That's all right. Is Audra feeling better?"

"She stayed home from school, but I don't think she has the flu."

"How old is your daughter?" Monica asked.

"Eight, and a real handful. Where's Crystal?"

"Just late, I hope," Laurel said. "I talked with her this afternoon and she said she was coming."

Denise sat down but didn't remove her pale gray wool coat. "I really don't know what you expect to accomplish, Monica. Are you going to organize another club? A group of amateur detectives who can catch Angie's murderer?"

Monica's eyes narrowed and Laurel braced for a scorching retort when another knock sounded at the door. Crystal rushed in looking flustered. "I'm sorry I'm late. My car is so undependable. I didn't think it was going to start. You probably thought I wasn't coming. I should have called. Hello, Denise. Monica."

"Glad you could make it," Monica said, seemingly oblivious to Crystal's agitation. "Shall we get down to business?"

Same old Monica, Laurel thought. Always taking charge. As she glanced around the room to see Denise looking truculent, Crystal scared, and Monica commanding, she wondered how they'd all become friends. Maybe it could only have been possible a long time ago when they were softer, more malleable, before the dominant traits of their personalities took control. Or maybe they had all changed after Faith's death.

"I assume Laurel has told you about the evidence at the scene of Angie's murder that points to it having something to do with the Six of Hearts."

Denise said yes. Crystal nodded, watching Monica with wide, worried eyes.

"I know some of you feel this is flimsy evidence—"

"Excuse me, Monica, but there's something you don't know." Laurel withdrew the envelope from her purse. "I received this yesterday. Crystal got an identical piece of mail today. They're both postmarked New York."

Monica reached for it with a long slender hand with perfectly manicured nails. She glanced expressionlessly at the paper with its red six and heart, next at the photos, then said flatly, "I got the same thing yesterday. Aside from the symbols in Angie's apartment, it's what made me determined to come here."

Monica held the items out to Denise. She took them, cringing when she saw the picture of Angie's body. "I didn't get anything like this."

"Why would the killer send this awful stuff to Laurel, Monica, and me and not to you?" Crystal asked Denise.

"I have no idea."

Laurel's voice sounded to her as if it were coming from someone else. "Because the rest of us live alone. The killer didn't want Denise's family to see the photos."

After a moment, Monica said, "You could be right."

"How considerate of him," Denise returned dryly.

"You should be glad," Crystal said sharply. "What if Audra had seen that picture of Angie?"

Denise shut her eyes. "It would have been dreadful." She looked at the rest of them. "But I can't be sure he *won't* send me this stuff later. I have to watch the mail closely every day. If Wayne saw this . . ."

"Denise, did you tell him about the Six of Hearts and Faith?" Laurel asked.

Denise shook her head emphatically. "*No.* I've never told *anyone.*"

Monica looked at Crystal. "Did you ever tell?"

"N-no."

Monica pinned her with an icy green gaze. "You don't sound too sure."

Crystal twisted her hands nervously in her lap. "It's just that after my baby was stillborn I was sedated. Chuck said I kept muttering things about 'fire' and 'Faith,' but he thought I was just rambling about her death."

"Are you sure you didn't say anything about the club or our being there when Faith died?" Monica demanded.

"I don't think so."

Monica rolled her eyes. "You don't *think* so. Great."

"I'm sure if I had, Chuck would have mentioned it. He would have asked what I was talking about."

"All right. Stop looking so terrified." Monica sighed. "*I've* never told anyone and Laurel says she hasn't. We don't know about Angie."

"Or Faith."

"If Faith told someone about the Six of Hearts and that person figured out we had something to do with her death, they sure waited a long time to get revenge," Denise said. "Besides, who would she have told? Certainly not her father. Zeke Howard is a religious fanatic. He would have beaten her senseless. How about her sister?"

"Mary works for me," Laurel said. "She has for over a year. If she bears any animosity toward me, I've never seen a trace of it."

"How about Neil Kamrath?" Crystal asked. "He was her boyfriend and the father of her baby."

"He got married," Laurel said. "He's a successful writer. If he knew, why would he suddenly decide to start striking back after all this time?"

"His wife and son were killed in a car wreck less than a year ago," Denise told them. "As a matter of fact, he's in Wheeling because his father is dying of cancer."

"He's *here*?" Monica exclaimed.

"Yes. For a couple of weeks now. Wayne is his father's doctor. He says Neil is pretty shaky. First his wife and son, then his father all within one year."

"Pretty shaky?" Monica repeated. "Angie's fiancé, Judson Green, told me that a couple of weeks before she was killed, he was away on a business trip and she told him she had a visitor. An old friend from Wheeling was all she'd tell him. He was certain it was a man. I *know* it wasn't any of us. It could have been Neil. She was fairly friendly with him in high school and he could have been in New York to see an editor or agent or something." Monica pinned Denise with a glance. "Do you think after Neil's wife's and son's deaths he's emotional enough to suddenly fixate on Faith?"

Denise frowned. "How should I know? I haven't talked to him, and even if I had, I'm not a mind reader. Wayne did invite him to our Christmas party Saturday night. I doubt if he'll show up, but if you want to come and see . . ."

Monica looked interested. "It might be worth it."

"*I* don't want to see Neil Kamrath," Crystal said. "He was so weird in high school, the big brain who always stayed to himself. I never understood why Faith dated him. She said he was interesting, but how on earth anyone could find *him* interesting I'll never know."

"You found Chuck Landis more interesting?" Monica drawled.

Crystal flushed. "As a matter of fact, I did. At least he's normal. Have you read any of those awful books Neil writes?"

"They're horror novels and I think they're great," Laurel said.

Crystal frowned. "They're gruesome and you'd have to be nuts to come up with some of that stuff he does."

"You don't have to be nuts," Denise said. "You just need a good imagination."

Crystal shook her head. "No. Ghosts, vampires, monsters. I think you'd have to be crazy to think about stuff like that all the time and actually write *stories* about it."

Monica looked impatient. "Can we save this highly literary discussion until later? We have a much more urgent issue to solve. We have to figure out who murdered Angie and who's trying to terrorize at least three of us."

"Isn't that up to the police?" Denise asked. "Don't the New York police have any suspects?"

"Only one—Angie's ex-husband Stuart Burgess," Monica said. "He is *not* a nice guy, but for some reason he gave Angie a small fortune in the divorce settlement. The police wonder if she was holding some damaging information over his head. Nasty rumors about him have circulated for years, but no one has ever known anything definite. Maybe Angie did. Anyway, she never got around to changing her will so now that she's dead, all that he gave her, plus all that she made on Broadway, belongs to him. He's been arrested."

"Well, there you go!" Crystal said hopefully. "He probably did it."

"Maybe, *if* he knew about the Six of Hearts and Faith. If he didn't, why would he have put a six and a heart on her mirror? Why would he be sending *us* mail with Angie's and Faith's photos?"

"To throw the police off the track?"

"The police don't know about the Six of Hearts, Crystal."

Monica shook her head. "I agree Burgess had an excellent motive, but I don't think he did it. And the problem is that Angie was killed between midnight and three Tuesday morning. It's now almost eight o'clock Thursday night. After twenty-four hours the trail gets cold."

"That's still not such a long time," Crystal insisted. "I can't believe they solve all murders in twenty-four hours."

"Certainly they don't. I'm just saying the more time that passes, the harder things get for the police. In the meantime, three of the four of us have received what I interpret as warnings that our turn is coming." Monica gave each of them a hard stare. "I, for one, don't intend to sit idly by and let it happen."

"Go to the police," Laurel said promptly.

"No!" chorused three voices. "Absolutely no way," Denise stated.

"What do you suggest we do?" Laurel asked.

Monica took over. "For one, be extra careful. Be sure to keep your doors and windows locked. Carry Mace. Keep a gun by your bed."

"I'm sure Wayne will wonder why I have a gun by the bed," Denise said.

"Stick it in a drawer you can reach easily."

Crystal frowned. "I'm afraid of guns."

Monica looked at her in exasperation. "Aren't you more afraid of being murdered? Take another look at that picture of Angie and tell me you'd rather end up like that than keep a gun around." Crystal glanced away. "All right, the second thing we're going to do is look at *everyone* who might have knowledge of the Six of Hearts. Mary and Zeke Howard. Neil Kamrath."

"I knew it!" Denise crowed. "Amateur detectives."

"Would you rather tell Wayne the truth and then go to the police?" Monica snapped.

Denise looked at Monica for a moment, then uttered a reluctant "No."

"Well, we have two alternatives. Telling the police about our part in Faith's death, or trying to smoke out this killer ourselves, because if Stuart Burgess didn't do it—"

"Then it might be someone from around here," Laurel said slowly. "Someone who has a perfect chance to get at any of us."

3

Crystal and Denise left almost immediately. Monica asked Laurel to stay for a few minutes. Laurel could tell the others were curious, but Denise was anxious to return to Audra and Crystal looked as if she couldn't wait to get away.

When they were gone, Monica said, "There's a coffee maker in the room. Would you care for a cup?"

"Yes. I can't seem to shake this chill I've had ever since you told me about Angie."

Monica fixed coffee and came back to sit opposite Laurel. "You know, I feel you're the only one who's taking this seriously."

"You do? Crystal is scared to death."

"Crystal is always scared. Denise acts like the whole thing is just a nuisance."

"I think Denise is in denial. She's so protective of her family, of the life she's made for herself, she just can't face this kind of threat."

"She *has* to face it. We all do."

Laurel leaned forward. "Monica, do you really believe Stuart Burgess had nothing to do with Angie's death? She could have told him about Faith and the Six of Hearts, and the photos we received were mailed in New York. They could have come from him."

"But none of that would matter unless one of us tells the police about the club and Faith, and Stuart couldn't count on that happening."

"He could tell the police himself."

"That wouldn't be as effective, especially if we opted to deny it. There was no suspicion of us thirteen years ago. The only person whose alibi was even checked was Neil Kamrath. We all alibied each other. The only people we

HERR MEMORIAL LIBRARY

were in trouble with was our families for lying about Angie's parents being home when they weren't. Stuart Burgess, on the other hand, has no alibi for the night of Angie's
murder. He's too smart not to have provided himself with
something ironclad if he had killed Angie. No, Laurel, I'm
sure he didn't do it."

Laurel looked out the window. The lights were on in the
room so her face and Monica's were reflected. She looked
troubled. Monica looked determined. Monica rose and
came back with a cup of hot coffee. Laurel took it. "I still
think—"

"Don't even mention the police."

"But—"

"Laurel, *no!*" Laurel drew back and Monica softened.
"At least not right now. Please."

"All right," Laurel said reluctantly. "I'll give in for now.
But only for *now*. Tomorrow I'll find out what I can from
Mary."

"Be subtle."

"You don't need to tell me that, Monica. I'm not an
idiot."

Monica's lips twitched. "No, but you're a lot more con-
fident than you used to be. What happened?"

"I got older."

"So did Crystal but the years didn't do much for her."

"She hasn't had many confidence-building experiences.
The final blow was Chuck walking out on her."

"That dolt. He used to be handsome but he didn't have
much else going for him."

"He's still handsome and he still doesn't have much else
going for him except a wealthy new girlfriend. But I remember a time when you weren't so derisive about Chuck."

"What are you talking about?"

"You had a crush on him in high school."

"I did not!"

"Oh, Monica, you did, too. I used to see the way you
looked at him. It's not something to be embarrassed about.
He was great-looking and he was our star athlete, the most

popular guy in the school. Lots of girls had crushes on him."

"Do I seem like the kind of woman who would have a thing for Chuck Landis?"

"Not *now* but we're talking about when you were a teenager. I even suspected you went out with him a couple of times."

"Now that *is* crazy. He was Crystal's."

"Or so she thought. I never believed he was as smitten with her as she was with him."

"He married her."

"And he left her. She's crushed."

"How tragic."

Laurel looked at her angrily. "You never fought with her like you did Denise, but you were always jealous of Crystal."

She expected hot denial, but Monica looked away and sighed. "Yes. She had everything. She was such a damned princess."

"Well, she's not a princess now, especially after the miscarriages and the stillbirth. You know how she used to talk constantly about wanting to be a mother, and she's loved Chuck since she was about fourteen. Now he's gone and she can't have children, so don't be so damned hard on her."

"I'll try, but those perpetually fearful eyes and that mournful voice annoy the hell out of me." Monica shrugged. "What can I say? I'm not an easy person. That's probably why there's no one in my life. No one available, that is." Laurel looked at her questioningly. "John Tate. He's married."

"Your law firm—Maxwell, Tate, and Goldstein. That Tate?"

"Yes, but don't get the idea I'm close to making partner in the firm because of him," Monica said hotly. "I've worked damned hard. Next month I'm going to represent Kelly Kingford."

"The wife of that multimillionaire who's suing her for

divorce and trying to get custody of the children?"

"Yes. You don't know the publicity this trial will bring me." Monica looked at Laurel intensely. "That's why I *cannot* have anything about the Six of Hearts and Faith come out. It would hurt all of us, but it would ruin me."

So that's why Monica was so concerned, Laurel thought. She wasn't just worried about the safety of her, Denise, and Crystal. She was afraid they might have received the photos of Angie and Faith that she did and would go to the police, drawing Monica into a scandal.

Laurel remembered when she met Monica. Her mother had died three years earlier after a long, debilitating illness. Shortly after her death, Monica's father met another woman who didn't want her, so her father blithely dispatched Monica to Wheeling to live with a starchy great-aunt who never let her forget she was only taking in Monica out of a sense of duty. Monica had been a miserable nine-year-old, stiff and withdrawn, when Laurel went out of her way to befriend her. It hadn't been easy at first. Monica was hurt and defensive, humiliated and devastated by the rejection by the father she'd adored, but Laurel persisted. She'd pulled Monica into her circle of friends. She wasn't sure when Monica's quiet gratitude to the group had turned into equally quiet domination. Perhaps it was some time after the formation of the Six of Hearts when they were twelve. Looking back, Laurel could see that during Monica's teens, the seeds of her current almost total self-absorption had begun to sprout.

"Monica, none of us is going to the police now."

"Do you promise?" Monica asked. "Do you promise not to tell Kurt?"

"Yes, I promise not to tell him. We're not sure of anything and too many people could be hurt. But if this gets more serious—"

"Then we'll decide what to do. In the meantime, I plan to go to Denise's party. I know she doesn't really want me, but Neil Kamrath might show up."

"I'll be at the party, too. If he doesn't come there, he

might come to Angie's funeral. As for Faith's father, I don't know how I'll get to him."

"You can join that crazy church of his."

Laurel pulled a face. "There has to be an easier way. I'll figure out something." She stood. "I really should be getting home."

Monica touched her arm. For just a moment she looked like the girl Laurel had first seen, a vulnerable nine-year-old who'd stood self-consciously in front of thirty students, being introduced to the fourth-grade class by the teacher. "Laurel, you're the only one I can really count on. You always reached out to me, always helped me. I appreciated it then and I appreciate it now."

Laurel wasn't sure if Monica's words were genuine or an attempt at manipulation. It didn't matter. "This is very serious business, Monica. I'll do anything I can to help *all* of us."

When she went back out to her car, the night had become considerably colder. Atop the hill on which the lodge sat, a brisk wind whipped her coat around her and blew her hair mercilessly. She started the car, turned on the radio, and pulled out of the parking lot listening to "Up on the Roof." Tour buses and dozens of cars moved slowly along the narrow road, making their way around the light display route. If she weren't so cold and distracted, she might have taken the tour herself, but now she only wanted the safety and comfort of her home.

She had pulled onto Route 88 and started down the hill when she became aware of a pair of headlights bearing down on her. Dammit, she thought. Why did some people ride your bumper? The driver didn't need to come this close even to pass, not that this was a good place to pass anyway. The road was narrow, two lanes, and a steady stream of traffic came in the opposite direction heading for the park. Laurel pressed the accelerator, raising her speed by five miles an hour. There, a little breathing room, she thought.

She glanced in the rearview mirror to see the headlights bearing down on her again. Her hands tightened on the steering wheel as her anger grew. She squinted into the rearview mirror trying to see the driver, but she was blinded by the lights that were on high beam. All she could tell was that the car was larger than her own mid-sized Chevrolet Cavalier.

Tempted to go even faster, Laurel glanced at the speedometer. She was already over the speed limit. Besides, if she speeded up, so would the other driver. She would just have to grit her teeth and suffer through the next three miles until she reached home.

She was passing the Wheeling Country Club when the other car hit her rear bumper. The impact threw her forward. What the hell is he *doing*? she cried to herself. The car dropped back slightly as she regained her breath. Then it shot forward again, hitting her harder than before.

Oh, God, Laurel thought. Was this just a drunk having some fun or did this have something to do with Angie's murder and the photos she'd received? She'd thought they were a threat. Instead of being bludgeoned to death like Angie, was she to die in a car wreck?

No, she *wouldn't*. She was a good driver and it would take more than a couple of taps on her bumper to unnerve her to the point of running off the road. She focused on the highway, refusing to be distracted by continually looking in the rearview mirror.

Two miles from home. Another, harder bump. Her breath quickened. Concentrate on the road, she commanded herself. She couldn't let fear take over, although she knew that blow had been strong enough to damage her car. She'd heard metal crunching.

Finally the car actually rammed her. She swerved, nearly running off the pavement as she desperately fought the wheel, managing to regain control of the car. But she couldn't control the fear that gripped her. In spite of the cold she felt perspiration popping out along her hairline. One mile from home. What should she do? Make a couple of turns and reach her long, deserted driveway with this maniac right behind her? No way.

As they reached the place where she should have made the first turn, she couldn't help a quick glance into the rearview mirror. The other driver slowed slightly. He was *expecting* her to turn, she thought, appalled. That meant he wasn't some drunk playing games with a random car. The driver knew exactly who she was and where she lived.

Laurel sped past the turnoff, heading toward town. The other car picked up speed again and nosed close enough for another nudge. But that's all it was—a nudge. Maybe she'd thrown him by not heading for home as he expected.

Five minutes later she reached downtown Wheeling. The other car had dropped back. When she ran a yellow light, the car stopped. She made two unnecessary turns in case the driver was watching, then pulled up in front of Kurt Rider's apartment building.

Laurel jumped out of the car and ran up the walk and through the main door. Kurt's apartment was on the second floor. The heels on her boots slammed against each step as she hurtled upward. No doubt Kurt's cantankerous next-door neighbor, Mrs. Henshaw, would be complaining, but she didn't care.

She pounded on Kurt's door, looking fearfully behind her. The stairs were empty but for how long? She pounded again. Dammit, where *was* he? She knew he didn't go out much at night unless he was with her. He was too devoted to the weekly television lineup to hang out in bars and miss his shows. She pounded one more time before the door beside his was flung open.

"Do you know what time it is? What's all this racket about? You'll wake up the whole buildin'!"

Mrs. Henshaw—plump, red-faced, and sporting a head full of pink foam rollers—glared at her from small, mud-colored eyes.

"I'm sorry, Mrs. Henshaw," Laurel said, although it was only nine o'clock, not midnight. "I'm looking for Kurt."

"I figured that out for myself." The woman wore a bulky quilted robe in a patchwork pattern and huge fuzzy slippers with bunny faces, whiskers, and large pointed ears. She looked ridiculous. "You two have a fight or somethin'?"

"It's none of your business," Laurel started to snap, then caught herself. Kurt had enough problems with this harridan without her adding to them. "No, Mrs. Henshaw, we didn't have a fight. I had a bad scare—someone following me—so I came here."

"Someone followin' you?" she repeated. "Old boyfriend or somethin'?"

"No, I'm certain it wasn't. Just some crazy person, but I was frightened. Do you know where Kurt is?"

"What do I look like? His social secretary or somethin'?" Laurel had never known anyone who could end almost every sentence with "or somethin'." "Alls I know is he went out a couple a hours ago."

"Oh. Well, maybe I'll wait a few minutes."

"Suit yourself," Mrs. Henshaw said and slammed her door.

Thank you so much for inviting me in, Laurel thought sourly. Kurt always said she was the most disagreeable person he'd ever met and that her wimpy little husband had probably died at forty-five just to get away from her.

Laurel sat down on the stairs, her eyes fastened on the door leading outside. What would she do if the driver of the other car came in after her? God, she didn't even know what the other driver looked like. But if anyone who seemed threatening entered the building, she'd . . . she'd what? Bang on Mrs. Henshaw's door and hope the woman would take pity and let her in? What if she wouldn't? Monica said they should carry Mace. She had none. She had *nothing* with which to defend herself.

She looked at her watch. Twenty minutes had gone by and still no Kurt. And here she sat, backed into a corner, totally defenseless. She waited another five minutes, then decided she couldn't take it any longer.

She crept down the stairs, opened the main door, and peered out. Cars were parked along the street but she didn't see anyone in any of them. No one strolled along the sidewalk—it was a cold night. Clutching her keys, Laurel ran for her car. When she opened the door she checked the back to make sure no one was hiding on the floor. Then she jumped in.

As she drove toward home, she glanced in the rearview mirror every few seconds. Nothing but ordinary traffic. After what seemed like an hour she turned into her long driveway. Trees lined the drive so it would be difficult to hide a car along the way, but a person could easily conceal himself.

She pulled up to the garage, planning to open the door, pull in, then dash inside the house door leading to the garage. She pressed the automatic opener. The garage door didn't respond. She pressed again. The door remained down.

Oh, hell! Laurel thought furiously. The last few days the door had been sluggish, meaning that the battery in the opener was weak. Now it was dead. Why couldn't I have taken five minutes to buy a new battery? she berated herself. Just five minutes.

But thinking of what she should have done was no help at all. Reluctantly she separated her front door key from the car keys, took another look around, drew a deep breath, and ran to the front of the house. She was stabbing the key at the lock when her eyes lifted and she froze.

The cheerful Christmas wreath she'd hung on the door two weeks ago was missing. In its place hung a wreath with white silk lilies and a large black satin bow.

A funeral wreath.

Four

Laurel nearly fell in the door, slammed and locked it. Both dogs rushed to her, alternately barking and whining, Alex bouncing on his hind legs the way he did when he was excited. They were upset. They led solitary lives with Laurel gone six days a week and rarely entertaining anyone except Kurt. The dogs' agitation meant they had seen or heard something unusual. Laurel looked at the couch. Its back, usually covered with a bright russet, green, and gold afghan, faced the big front window. The afghan lay in a heap on the seat of the couch. Both dogs had stood on it, bracing their front legs on the couch's back. They'd seen whoever had come to her house and put the wreath on the door. Maybe the person had even tried to break in.

Although her legs were still trembling, Laurel knelt and pulled the dogs to her. "Did someone scare you?" she asked. "Did someone look in the window at you or try to open the door?"

April nuzzled as close to her as possible but Alex continued to bounce, making little talky noises as if he were trying to explain.

"This isn't the first time I've wished we could really communicate," Laurel said. "If only you could tell me what you saw."

Suddenly she thought of the dog door leading from the kitchen into the big backyard. Usually she never bothered with the lock panel—only a small person could wriggle through the opening and she'd never been bothered with prowlers—but now she quickly slid the lock panel into place. The dogs eeled around her feet, her fear adding to their own.

"I think all three of us could use a tranquilizer," she told them. "Instead you'll have to settle for treats and I'll have chamomile tea."

She filled the tea kettle and put it on the stove, then found their sausage treats. Luckily, they loved the treats so much they temporarily overcame their nervousness long enough to gobble them all in record time.

When Laurel finally sat down in the living room with her tea, she realized she hadn't even looked at her car to see how much damage it had suffered. It seemed insignificant compared to what happened, what *could* have happened. She'd almost lost control of the car when the other driver actually rammed her. And the presence of the wreath on the door erased the last of her doubts that the driver was merely trying to frighten a woman alone in a car. He'd been after her.

Someone rapped on the door and Laurel jumped so violently she sloshed tea onto her lap. She sat rigid on the couch while the dogs barked and the rapping continued, growing louder. Finally a man shouted, "Laurel, it's Kurt. Open the door!"

Was it really Kurt? she wondered for a terrified instant. Then he called to her again. She recognized his voice.

She opened the door. Kurt looked at her for a moment, his eyes worried, then enfolded her in his arms. "What's going on, Laurel? When I got in, the Henshaw woman came tearing over to tell me you'd been there pounding on the door and saying you were scared because someone was following you."

Laurel clung to him for a moment, then pulled him inside. "I was coming back from Wilson Lodge—"

"What were you doing there?"

"Monica is staying there. She called and asked to see me."

"Why didn't she come here?"

"The light show," Laurel said quickly. "You know I always go. I took the tour and stopped to see her." Not quite the truth but almost, she thought. "As I was coming home, someone began riding my bumper. They hit me lightly twice, then they rammed me."

"I know. I saw the back of your car."

"I started to turn in here, then changed my mind. I went to your place, but the ever-charming Mrs. Henshaw said you'd left a couple of hours ago."

"I had a few beers with Chuck. He needed to talk."

"I hope you convinced him to go back to Crystal."

"Not much chance of that happening from what I heard tonight." Kurt gazed at her earnestly. "Laurel, why did you go to my place? Why didn't you go to police headquarters?"

Laurel shook her head. "I don't know. I wasn't thinking. I was so scared."

"It's not like you to lose your head like that." Kurt's voice was rising. "Don't you realize how dangerous it was to come to my place and sit around in an empty hall when I wasn't home?"

Laurel stepped away from him. "Don't get mad. Yes, now that I'm calmer I know it was stupid, but I told you I was scared silly and not thinking clearly. Besides, the car wasn't still following me."

"As far as you know."

"Okay, as far as I know." Laurel felt tears rising. "Look, Kurt, after all that's happened tonight, the last thing I need is for you to come over here and yell at me."

Kurt took a deep breath. "You're right. I'm sorry, honey. I'm just worried."

He hugged her again. She clung to him with more than her usual fervor. "We haven't even shut the door yet and it's freezing outside."

Kurt stepped back, took hold of the knob, and started to swing the door shut. Then he stopped, staring. Finally he asked, "Why the hell is there a funeral wreath on your door? It's not for Angie, is it?"

"No. It wasn't there when I left to see Monica. I think whoever rammed my car put it there."

Kurt gave her a hard look. "You've been acting strange ever since Angela Ricci was murdered. Now someone's following you and hanging a funeral wreath on your door." He paused. "I'm not leaving here until you tell me what's going on."

2

As she drove to work the next morning, Laurel tried to convince herself she shouldn't feel guilty about not being open with Kurt. She'd told him the truth about having no idea who the driver of the car was. She'd also told him the truth when she said she didn't know who'd hung the wreath. "You just didn't tell him you received pictures of Faith and of Angie's mutilated body, and you didn't say you're afraid the person who was after you last night is the same person who murdered Angie," she said aloud. "No, you didn't leave out anything at all important."

But she'd promised Monica she wouldn't talk to the police, she told herself. She didn't tell Kurt because she didn't want to break her promise, that's all. And that is a very convenient excuse, the voice of her conscience said. You didn't tell him because *you* don't want anyone to know, either.

Not coming forward to tell the truth thirteen years ago was a shameful, craven act she could never forgive herself for and wouldn't expect anyone else to forgive. Isn't that why she'd broken her engagement to Bill Haynes five years ago? She'd tried a dozen times but couldn't bring herself to tell him. Obviously Denise had been able to marry without baring her secret, but Laurel would not pledge herself to a man who didn't know the truth, whom she felt could not *know* the truth and still love her.

Last night Kurt had stayed for an hour asking questions. He seemed frustrated she couldn't tell him more about the car except that it was large and dark. He badgered her for a description of the front grillwork, the placement of the headlights, whether or not there had been a hood ornament, until she was nearly in tears. "Kurt, I was being chased down the hill, rammed for God's sake. I was trying to keep my own car on the road, not studying the grillwork of the other car."

At last he relented, apologizing for his persistence. He asked if she wanted him to stay the night and she said no so definitely that he looked slightly hurt, but in spite of her fear she needed to be alone to think about her meeting with Monica, Denise, and Crystal, and especially what had followed. Before he reluctantly left, Kurt insisted on checking every door and window, told her he would buy Mace for her and take the car to several garages for estimates on the cost of fixing the damage because "mechanics think they can get away with highway robbery when they're dealing with a woman. Besides, the other car must have sustained a little damage. I can ask if any cars with dented grillwork have been brought in."

"Thank you, Kurt," Laurel said. "That's great of you."

"Checking garages about the other car is just part of my job," he assured her. Then he looked at April and Alex, who for some reason never came near him. They stood together near the fireplace, looking at him warily. "I wish you had a real watch dog instead of those two cowards."

"I like these two just fine," Laurel said tartly. "And they are *not* cowards!"

Kurt smiled. "I've never known anyone so touchy about a dog. I didn't mean to insult you, but you should think about getting a Doberman, one that's trained to attack."

"I don't want an attack dog," Laurel said stubbornly. "April and Alex can protect me just fine."

"Yeah, sure. They look like it."

Laurel glared at him and he let the matter drop. Finally, on his way out, Kurt retrieved her pretty Christmas wreath from the shrubbery and rehung it. "I'll throw this one away," he said, holding up the funeral wreath.

"You're not going to check it for hair and fibers?"

"Laurel, this is not a crime scene and we don't live in New York City or Los Angeles. We don't have a forensics lab downtown."

"I'm kidding, Kurt. I'll keep it for a closer look. Maybe I can get an idea of where it was made."

He shrugged. "You know more about this kind of thing than I do. See you tomorrow, honey. If anything happens, let me know immediately."

After he left, she'd studied the wreath. The wreath form was exactly like the ones they used at Damron Floral, but that didn't mean anything. Probably every floral shop in the area ordered wreath forms from the same wholesaler. There was also nothing distinctive about the flowers, although Laurel rarely bought white silk lilies. She carried many silk flower arrangements for household decoration. Sometimes people ordered artificial flower arrangements for funerals, and often she used silk flowers, sometimes lilies, to brighten up planters, and of course at Easter many churches ordered live lilies in vases to place on the altar in honor of those who had died during the past year. At this time of year, though, lilies of any color weren't too popular.

The flowers and the black leaves were wired onto the form with ordinary .22 gauge floral wire. There was nothing unusual about the wreath except that funeral wreaths seemed to be a thing of the past. Laurel had never had an order for one. Nevertheless, she decided to take the wreath to the store with her and see if it elicited any reaction from Mary.

3

The night had been long and dream-torn, images of fire and of plunging off a hillside in her car constantly awakening her. Now, driving into town to the store, she felt more tired than when she'd gone to bed.

Laurel stopped at a bakery for pastries and tried to stifle huge yawns while she waited for her order to be filled. Ten minutes later she pulled her battered car into its usual parking place, carried the wreath inside, tucked it in a cabinet, and started the coffee. She hadn't eaten at home and was halfway finished with a Danish and a fresh cup of coffee when Penny and Norma arrived. "Where's Mary?" Norma asked. They were mother and daughter, but Norma looked only slightly older than her twenty-two-year-old daughter. They had dark, shiny hair in identical pixie cuts, dark brown eyes, and small, compact bodies. They wore jeans and sweatshirts in the winter, jeans and T-shirts in the summer. "Mary's always here before we are."

"Help yourself to some pastry," Laurel said. "Mary hasn't called in, so I assume she's coming. She's only ten minutes later than usual."

Another fifteen minutes passed before Mary appeared, pale and flustered. "Laurel, I'm so sorry to be late," she said in a rush, shrugging out of her coat. "This wasn't a good morning for Papa."

Mary still lived with her father, Zeke Howard, whose wife, Genevra, had deserted the family when they lived in Pittsburgh and Mary was two, Faith six. Shortly afterward they'd moved to Wheeling. "What's wrong?" Laurel asked. "Is he sick?"

Mary hesitated. "Not physically. It's just that . . . well, his mind seems to be going." She gave Laurel a half smile. "I know most people in town think he's never been in full possession of his faculties, but he was. He just has a different way of looking at religion. Now he's getting strange. He gets confused easily and he forgets things."

"Everyone forgets things, especially when they're older."

"He's not a *little* forgetful." Mary closed her eyes. "This morning I found him wandering outside looking for Faith. He was terribly upset. I had quite a time getting him back inside and convincing him that Faith is dead."

"Oh?" was all Laurel could manage.

"Yes. Then he started sobbing that Faith didn't kill herself. She knew suicide was a sin and she wouldn't commit a sin." Laurel looked at her in silence as Mary poured a cup of coffee. "I guess he's forgotten that she was unmarried and pregnant. She wasn't the saint he remembers." She sighed. "But I still miss her so much. I adored her. I don't think I'll ever get over her death."

Laurel wanted to run from the room, but she forced herself to ask casually, "Did your father always believe Faith didn't commit suicide?"

Mary frowned. "I honestly don't know. He refused to talk about her death until lately. But the last couple of months I keep coming home to find him in the attic going through her things."

"You kept her things?"

"Oh yes, everything." Mary stirred milk into her coffee and reached for a doughnut. "After her death I carried it all to the attic. *Everything.*" She looked at Laurel. "Is something wrong?"

Laurel's mouth was dry. "No. It was just so sad. Faith's death, I mean." Her chest felt tight as she fought for composure. Was it her imagination or was Mary taunting her? "Is your father all right now?"

"Yes. The doctor prescribed Valium about a month ago. I gave him one."

"If you feel you should go home—"

"No. He was settling down by the time I left. He'll be fine. Once again, I'm sorry I'm late. I'd better get to work."

Laurel stood in the kitchen after Mary left. She pretended to be wiping off the counter in order to hide her turmoil. What had bothered her so much about the exchange with Mary? Was it the almost challenging way Mary had looked at Laurel after she announced she'd saved everything of Faith's? What comprised *everything*? Clothes. Photos. Faith's school photos, no doubt. And what about papers? Letters or a diary, *anything* in which Faith wrote about the Six of Hearts? Perhaps Mary had known about the club all along or maybe she had learned of it when Zeke began rummaging through all of Faith's papers and Mary had taken a second, closer look. Did she and Zeke now know about the Six of Hearts?

Stop it! Laurel told herself sternly. Mary didn't say anything about papers and even if Faith had kept a diary, she hadn't necessarily mentioned the club in it. In fact, Laurel seriously doubted if Faith *did* keep a diary. She probably would have been too afraid of her father finding it and discovering her secrets.

But what about the way Mary was looking at her? Had it really been an odd look, or was her own guilt causing her to misinterpret everything? She had to admit it was guilt that had caused her to hire Mary. She'd seemed almost desperate when she came into the store and told Laurel she'd lost her job as a waitress in a local restaurant and couldn't find anything else. She had no experience with the floral business, but Laurel had hired her on the spot, thinking that in some small way she was making things up to Faith by helping her little sister. It was only later Laurel discovered Mary's great talent for floral design.

Laurel tried to shake off her uneasiness. Mary had probably meant nothing by her comments. Still, it would be interesting to catch her reaction when Laurel showed her the funeral wreath later in the day.

She left the kitchen and went out to wait on a woman torn between a multicolored silk flower arrangement and one done entirely in shades of pink. She compared, studied, and dithered until Laurel thought she would scream. At last she wandered out the door, saying she'd have to give it more thought. "I love decisive people," Laurel muttered as the door shut behind the woman. Twenty minutes wasted.

Half an hour later she was on the phone with the funeral home to which Angie would be taken. The New York police had released the body. It would arrive at the undertaker's Saturday, the visitation would be Sunday evening, and the funeral Monday morning. Details would be appearing in the newspapers later in the day, and Laurel was already swamped with orders, both from local people and through the wire services. She needed to make sure the funeral home would be open Sunday afternoon so last-minute deliveries could be made before the visitation at seven o'clock.

Just before she hung up the phone, a man walked into the store. She barely took notice of him as he sauntered around, looking as if he weren't sure what he wanted. Laurel's father had taught her not to pounce on customers as soon as they entered. "Give them a little time to look, honey. Even if they came to place an order, they might see something else they like."

As he studied the flower arrangements and wreaths, Laurel stole quick peeks at him. He was tall and had thick, sandy hair with a bit of wave. His features were clean cut with high cheekbones. She got the impression of an introverted, intense personality, maybe because he looked at every item as if he were memorizing it, but he'd not smiled or even glanced at her. She was just about to ask if she could help him with something when he finally approached the counter.

She smiled. He didn't. His eyes were a smoky blue and had a look of weariness about them, as if he'd carried a deep sadness for a long time. He wore a well-cut gray cashmere coat and kept his hands in his pockets. "I'd like to order an arrangement for the Ricci funeral," he said, his voice deep but soft.

"I've just learned that visitation will be Sunday night from seven until nine," Laurel said. "The information hasn't been in the newspaper yet." He didn't say, "Is that right?" or "Thanks for letting me know." He just gazed at her patiently. "What size arrangement do you want?" Laurel asked, realizing he looked familiar but she couldn't place him.

"I'd like two dozen white roses."

Laurel nodded, writing on her order pad. People usually mentioned a dollar amount they wanted to spend on a mixed basket of flowers. They rarely asked for specific flowers, especially when the arrangement would cost as much as two dozen roses. "And what name shall I put on the card?" she asked.

"Neil Kamrath."

Laurel looked up. Of course! She hadn't recognized him

immediately because he was taller, his hair longer, and his
face much more angular than it had been in high school.
She'd even seen him on a talk show a couple of years ago,
but he still looked different. Older and slightly haggard.

"Neil! You probably don't remember me from high
school. I'm—"

"Laurel Damron." He finally smiled, although the smile
didn't touch his eyes. "How could I forget? You were a
good friend of Faith's. So was Angie."

"Yes." She felt color creep into her cheeks at the mention
of Faith's name. "Denise Price told me you were in town.
Her husband is your father's doctor. I'm sorry he's so ill."

"He hasn't been well for a long time. I think he's relieved
his suffering is finally ending."

Laurel knew most people would say something along the
line of "The Lord is watching over him," but she couldn't.
She had a sense the words would sound as hollow to Neil
as they would to her.

Neil was watching her intently with those penetrating
blue eyes, obviously not feeling the need to make small
talk. She totaled his bill, he handed her a credit card, then
signed. "Will you be coming to Denise and Wayne's party
tomorrow night?" she asked.

"No." He paused. "Well, I'm not sure. I might stop by
for a few minutes. Dr. Price has been especially good to
Dad and friendly to me. I wouldn't want to insult him."

"I'm sure he wouldn't be insulted if you didn't come,
but he'd be happy if you did."

At that moment Mary came out of the workroom. She
stopped in her tracks, gave Neil a searing look, then turned
on her heel and headed for the kitchen.

"What was that about?" Neil asked.

"Uh, I don't know. Probably nothing," Laurel floundered. He fixed her with those eyes that seemed to draw
out the truth. "That's Mary Howard, Faith's little sister."

"Oh," he said simply. "I haven't seen her since she was
a kid."

Laurel handed him his receipt, feeling embarrassed by

Mary's behavior and unnerved by his unflappable manner. "I certainly hope we see you at the party," she said a trifle shrilly.

"Well, maybe." The bell on the door jingled and Kurt strode in, tall and formidable in his uniform. Neil didn't look at him. "Are you going to the party?" he asked her.

"Yes."

"Then I might see you there." He finally glanced at Kurt, who stared at him balefully. Why did you have to come in right now? Laurel thought impatiently. I might have been able to talk to him a bit longer, get some feel for his personality. Neil looked back at Laurel, unsmiling. "Good-bye, Laurel. It was nice seeing you again."

Kurt's gaze never left Neil's back as he left the store. As soon as the door closed behind him, Laurel snapped, "Why were you looking at him that way? It was rude."

"That was Kamrath, wasn't it?"

"Yes, it was Neil Kamrath."

"What's *he* doing here?"

"Asking me to elope with him."

Kurt's head swiveled toward her. "*What—*"

"He was ordering flowers, for heaven's sake. Why do you think he was here?"

"Flowers for who?"

"For whom." Kurt raised an eyebrow. "It's 'for whom.' And the flowers were for Angie's funeral. Why are you asking me all these questions?"

"I don't like that guy. Never did."

"I wasn't aware you really knew him."

"I knew all I cared to. He was always strange. I don't know how you can be nice to him. He seduced poor little Faith then deserted her. Now he writes those sick books. He's a creep."

Neil had nothing to do with Faith's death, Laurel wanted to shout. But of course she couldn't. No, not without tarnishing your own precious image, the savage voice of her conscience reminded her. "Kurt, we don't know that he refused to marry Faith," she said, forcing herself to sound

calm. "I was her closest friend and even I didn't know she
was pregnant. Besides, look how Chuck has treated Crystal
and you're still friends with him."

"That's different. Chuck's always been my best friend
just like Faith was yours and he's not crazy like Kamrath."

"Kurt, just because Neil writes horror novels doesn't
mean he's crazy. Do you think Stephen King is crazy?"

"Probably."

Laurel rolled her eyes. "You and Crystal ought to discuss
books sometime."

"What do you mean?"

"Never mind," Laurel sighed. "Why did you come by?"

"To bring you this." He held out a canister of Mace.
"Don't go anywhere without it."

Laurel relaxed a bit. "Thank you, Kurt. This was very
thoughtful of you."

"Any more trouble last night?"

"None, except that I was nervous and didn't get much
sleep."

"I offered to stay."

"Yes, but I didn't want to impose."

"Honey, spending the night with you is hardly an im-
position," Kurt said in his booming voice.

Laurel heard stifled giggles from the workroom. Penny
and Norma. "Kurt, lower your voice!" she hissed.

"Sorry." He didn't look sorry at all. "I've got to go."

"Before you do, I didn't remind you that Denise and
Wayne's party is tomorrow night. We're expected."

Kurt made a face. "I'm not exactly the party type. I was
looking forward to a quiet dinner with you."

"We wouldn't have to stay long if you don't want to,
but Denise is a good friend . . ."

"Okay. I'll work on my party manners and get out the
tuxedo."

Laurel grinned. "You don't own a tuxedo and it's not a
formal party. Slacks and a sport coat will do fine."

"You got it." The phone rang. "I'll let you get back to

work." He winked. "Don't lose your cool and blind any customers with that Mace."

"Not unless someone annoys me."

After she hung up the phone, she picked up the canister of Mace. The directions said to make sure the nozzle was pointed away from you before you sprayed the Mace *directly* in the eyes of the assailant. "Directly in the eyes," Laurel murmured. "I only hope I never get that close."

4

Laurel had lost so much sleep lately the afternoon seemed interminable. In spite of three cups of strong coffee, she couldn't stop yawning.

Around three-thirty Penny and Mary were outside loading floral arrangments into the delivery van. The two elderly, blue-haired Lewis sisters who lived together diligently toured the store, arguing over which wreath they wanted for their front door—white pine or cedar. You'd think they were investing in a car, Laurel thought, amused. A young woman wandered around with a little boy of three who pointed to every item on display and announced, "I want that!"

Suddenly the front door flew open with such force it slammed against the outside wall. Everyone jumped and Laurel looked up to see an old man, thin and terribly wrinkled, stalk into the store. He wore an ancient suit sprinkled with food stains and no coat. His hair, thick and white, stood on end and his blue eyes blazed.

"Hark!" he shouted. "Listen to me for I speak for the Lord our God!"

Oh, Lord, no, Laurel thought in horror. Zeke Howard.

Laurel rushed from behind the counter. "Mr. Howard—"

"*Reverend* Howard!"

"Reverend Howard, are you here to see Mary?" she asked, touching his arm.

He slapped away her hand. "Don't *touch* me!"

"I'm sorry." Her hand stung. What should she do? "Mary

is outside right now but if you'll come and have a seat in the back, I'll get her."

"I don't want Mary! You. *You* are the one I came to see."

The three women customers stood frozen, gaping at him. The little boy had taken refuge behind his mother.

Laurel tried to sound calm and pleasant. "What do you want to see me about, Reverend Howard?"

Zeke pulled himself up straight and glared around the room. Then he drew a deep breath and began quoting in a thunderous voice:

" 'But it shall come to pass, if you do not obey the voice of the Lord your God, to observe carefully all His commandments and His statutes which I command you today, that all these curses will come upon you and overtake you . . . Your carcasses shall be food for all the birds of the air and beasts of the earth and no one shall frighten *them* away . . .' "

If Laurel could get him to move, the customers could escape. He seemed to know this, though, and stood like a boulder, blocking the door as he rambled on:

" 'But the day of the Lord will come as a thief in the night, in which the heavens will pass away with a great noise, and the elements will melt with fervent heat; both the earth and the works that are in it will be burned up . . .' "

By now the child was crying. The Lewis sisters clutched each other, trembling. Laurel didn't dare leave Zeke alone to fetch Mary. Who knew what he might do. Helplessly she stared at him as he drew another long breath and started again, this time aiming his words at her:

"And you, Laurel Damron!" His eyes narrowed and he pointed an incredibly long, large-jointed finger at her. " 'Your life shall hang in doubt before you; you shall fear day and night, and have no assurance of life . . .' "

"Papa!" Mary rushed into the showroom, her expression appalled. "Why are you here? How did you *get* here?"

He looked at her disdainfully. In spite of the web of

wrinkles and sprinkling of dark age spots on his face, his
eyes were as clear and azure blue as Faith's had been. The
difference was the febrile, insane glow behind them. Laurel
had never seen such frightening eyes in her life. "I'm here
to spread the word of God. And I *drove*."

Mary went to him. "Papa, you aren't supposed to drive.
I have to get you home."

"I am not going home!" he shouted. "Oh, I know *you*.
You give me drugs to keep me from doing God's work.
You're not like Faith. You with your sneaking around at
night and your lies, just like your whoring mother, Genevra.
Faith was taken too soon, against God's will, but she is
with me every day. She tells me what is true and she gives
me directions. She keeps me safe from you and all the
others who meant her and me harm!"

Mary clutched at his arm. "Papa, please, you're not well.
Let me take you home."

Zeke slowly placed his strong, sinewy hands on Mary's
shoulders and shoved her into a set of glass shelves. They
crashed deafeningly against the wall. Mary sank to the floor
and the broken shelves fell on top of her motionless body.

The Lewis sisters shrieked. The child wailed, clinging to
his mother's coat. Laurel took a step backward, not daring
to go near Zeke in order to help Mary.

He fastened his wild eyes on her. "Laurel Damron, you
purveyor of sin, 'In the morning you shall say, "Oh, that it
were evening!" And at evening you shall say, "Oh, that it
were morning!" because of the fear that terrifies your heart,
and because of the sight which your eyes see—' "

The front door burst open again and Kurt along with
another deputy surged into the store. Kurt glanced at Mary,
then grabbed Zeke. The old man fought wildly, roaring
threats of what the Lord would do to Kurt. Even at six two,
nearly two hundred pounds, Kurt was having trouble restraining him. Finally he wrestled him into position and the
other deputy cuffed him.

Kurt looked at Laurel. "You okay?"

"Yes, but Mary . . ."

"Call an ambulance." Zeke Howard continued thrashing, although Laurel could see his energy was flagging. "Now, Laurel!"

She suddenly came alive again as she watched Kurt drag Zeke out the door toward the patrol car. She was barely aware of the customers flying from the store as soon as the car pulled away from the curb.

Before she could reach the phone, Norma ran from the workroom. "I've already called for an ambulance. I phoned the police as soon as he came in here ranting. Maybe I should have called the city police, but I immediately thought of Kurt . . ."

"Norma, you did exactly the right thing," Laurel assured her. "I don't know what might have happened if you hadn't called Kurt."

She, Penny, and Norma gathered around Mary. Penny wanted to lay Mary flat on the floor, but Laurel said she should not be moved. Blood poured from the back of Mary's head and oozed from a dozen small cuts on her face and arms. She was alive, but Laurel had no idea how badly she was hurt. Mary's head rested at an angle that made Laurel fear she had a broken neck.

Ten minutes later he paramedics arrived and did a quick examination. Mary's blood pressure and heart rate were low. She was cold, in shock, her pupils dilated. Laurel couldn't concentrate on what they were saying about vital signs. All she saw were Mary's deadly white face and her limp body. The paramedics stabilized Mary's neck, placed her on a stretcher, and rolled her out to the ambulance.

Her heart racing, Laurel told Norma and Penny to close the store for her and ran to her car, following the ambulance to the hospital.

Five

1

All the way to the hospital Laurel kept replaying the scene at the store, wondering what she could have done differently to prevent Zeke from injuring Mary. She couldn't think of anything. Even Kurt had trouble physically subduing the old man, who'd come there in a fury, determined to tell her of God's wrath that awaited her. No one, not even Mary, could calm him.

But what had so enraged him? She'd only seen Zeke Howard a handful of times in her life, and then mostly around town. Faith had never wanted any of her friends to come to her house. Laurel had been there only once. Faith's father embarrassed her and Laurel knew how desperately she'd longed to be free of his tyrannical control. Perhaps that's why she'd been wild, why she'd jumped at the opportunity of doing every imprudent thing Monica came up with for the Six of Hearts, including experimenting with witchcraft.

Witchcraft. The Six of Hearts. Mary said her father had been going through Faith's things and Laurel worried that Faith might have left a diary detailing the members of the Six of Hearts and their activities. Is that what had triggered Zeke's visit and his prediction of doom for Laurel? Was he the one who had hung the funeral wreath? But he couldn't have sent the pictures of Angela. Her murderer had done that, and Zeke couldn't have made the trip to New York, found Angie, and wangled his way into her house. He wasn't stable enough to manage the planning and stealth Angie's murder required. Or was he?

Laurel parked and was heading toward the front door of the hospital when she passed a man. Distracted, she paid no attention until he asked, "Laurel?"

She looked at him. "Neil!"

"Twice in one day after thirteen years."

"Yes." Laurel went blank for a moment, then spoke in a rush. "We had an accident at the store. Well, not an accident. Zeke Howard came in ranting and raving. Mary tried to quiet him and he shoved her into some glass shelves. The police took Zeke away and an ambulance came for Mary. She was unconscious." Until now she'd thought she was in control, but suddenly to her surprise she burst into tears. "Neil, I'm afraid Mary's neck is broken."

"Good God," he breathed. He took her arm. "I'll go back in with you."

"You don't have to." She fumbled in her purse for a packet of tissues.

"If I were a real gentleman I'd offer you my handkerchief, but I don't carry one."

"That's all right," she sniffled, locating the tissues. "Really, you don't have to stay with me. You've probably been here all afternoon with your father."

"I have, but I'd just be going home to his dark, empty house. Besides, I don't want to leave until I hear how Mary is."

When they reached the waiting room in the emergency area, Neil steered her to a section of empty chairs, then went to the desk, telling the nurse they were waiting for news about Mary Howard's condition. Of course it was far too early for the doctors to know anything. Neil glanced back in at her. To her embarrassment, Laurel couldn't stop crying. He disappeared, then came back with two cups of coffee.

"I've had gallons of this stuff in the last week," he said. "It's so awful it's guaranteed to distract you from crying."

"Thank you." It was black and she used milk, but she

said nothing. "I don't know what's wrong with me. I'm usually not the weepy type."

He sat down beside her. "You had a bad shock and you're terrified that Mary is severely injured. I'd say that's reason enough to cry."

That's not all I'm crying about, Laurel thought. I'm crying for Faith and Angie and myself. I feel guilty and scared and lost. She took a sip of coffee and grimaced. "You weren't kidding about this stuff."

"As my father used to say, 'It'll put hair on your chest.' "

"Great. That's all I need."

Neil grinned. "At least you still have your sense of humor."

"Barely."

After a moment Neil asked, "Why did Zeke Howard come to the store?"

"I don't know. He burst in quoting a lot of Bible verses."

"Well, that's par for the course. I don't think the man's ever been able to hold a real conversation. All he ever did was quote." Neil shook his head. "My parents were part of his congregation, you know. Well, my father was the devoted one. My mother just went along to keep down trouble. But their membership is the only reason Zeke let Faith date me. He thought I was safe because I was one of his flock."

But you *weren't* safe, Laurel thought. You got Faith pregnant.

Laurel could feel color creeping into her cheeks at the thought and asked quickly, "Where are you living now?"

"Carmel, California. I did live in Virginia, just outside of D.C., but I moved after my wife and son . . . died."

He almost choked over the last word and averted his eyes.

"I'm sorry," Laurel said. "I know that sounds inane, but—"

"What else is there to say?" Neil looked up at her again. "I keep thinking I'll adjust to their being gone, but I haven't, not even after ten months and a new home clear across the country."

"I can't imagine a loss like that. You have to give yourself more time."

"I'm afraid it's not a matter of giving myself anything. I either go on or I die." She looked at him sharply. "Oh, I'm not suicidal. I think I was at first. Ellen was killed instantly in the car wreck, but Robbie lingered for nearly a week. The car exploded. They thought he might make it at first in spite of his burns, but infection set in. They couldn't control it; then there was renal failure."

"Oh, Neil, how awful for you."

"Yeah, it was bad." He seemed to withdraw completely into himself for a few moments. Laurel had the feeling that neither she nor any of his surroundings were real to him. He was lost to the horror of watching his son die. Then, in a flash, he returned. "I expected you to be married with a couple of kids by now."

"So did my mother." His abrupt change of tone and facial expression startled Laurel but she tried to sound casual. "So far I've left the marriage and children to my sister Claudia."

"I remember her. She won all those beauty pageants."

"She's expecting her third child in about a month. I don't think she feels like the beauty pageant queen anymore, but my parents are thrilled. They moved to Florida two years ago to be near her."

"Do you miss them?"

"Yes." The answer was automatic. She paused and responded more truthfully. "Sometimes I miss them. Most of the time I'm relieved they're no longer hovering, trying to marry me off to any single man under sixty. I think they're pretty disappointed in me."

"Join the club. Mom died five years ago, but Dad has always been horrified, no joke intended, by what I write."

"I'd think he'd be proud of your success."

"He would be if I were writing books about history or religion. That's acceptable. Horror isn't."

"I think your novels are wonderful."

He looked at her in surprise. "You've read them?"

"Every one. The plots scare me silly and I usually end up awake until morning. Your writing style is excellent—almost poetic in your descriptive passages—and your characters are so vivid I feel like I know them." Laurel realized she was gushing and ended lamely, "I've also seen the movies made from the first two books."

"There's another movie deal in the works now. I should be excited, but with all that's happened . . . Anyway, I'm flattered you like my work." He rose abruptly. "I'm going to check on Mary again."

While she sat finishing her abominable coffee, Kurt strode into the waiting room. "How's she doing?"

"I don't know yet. Neil has gone to check."

Kurt raised his black eyebrows. "Neil?"

"I ran into him in the parking lot. He's been keeping me company while I wait for word on Mary."

"What's this weirdo doing?" Kurt demanded. "Following you around?"

"Kurt, *please*," Laurel said, but it was too late. Neil had come back in the waiting room and heard him. His smile disappeared and his face closed, his gaze growing distant. "The doctor wants to speak to you, Laurel." He didn't look at Kurt. "I'll be going now. Don't worry about Mary, Laurel. I think she's going to be fine."

He turned and left immediately. Laurel was furious. She desperately needed to get an impression of Neil Kamrath's personality. Miraculously she'd had two chances today, and Kurt had interrupted both times. She might not get the opportunity again. "Notice how he always takes off as soon as he sees me?" Kurt asked.

"No wonder," Laurel snapped. "You act like a territorial Rottweiler."

"I told you I don't like the guy."

"That's your problem, not mine. *I* don't have to be rude to someone just because *you* don't like them." Laurel stalked ahead of Kurt, who looked at her with bewildered dark eyes.

The doctor told her Mary had suffered a concussion but no skull fracture. She had several contusions and lacerations, the worst being a cut on the scalp that required ten stitches. At this point they'd found no injury to the neck. She had just regained consciousness. When Kurt asked if he could question her, the doctor said he would have to wait a couple of hours until they ran a few more tests and got her settled into a room.

"How long will she have to stay in the hospital?" Laurel asked.

"Unless there are complications, she'll be going home tomorrow," the doctor told her.

When he left, Laurel turned back to Kurt. "Where's Zeke?"

"In jail on a disorderly conduct charge. Don't worry— Mary's safe from him tonight." He smiled tentatively. "You want to get an early dinner while we wait until we can see Mary?"

"I'm sorry, Kurt, I can't. I have to get back to the store. I left Penny and Norma there and I'm not sure they'll lock up properly," she lied. She stood on tiptoe and kissed his cheek. "I'll talk with you later."

2

Laurel *would* talk to Kurt later, but right now she needed to speak with Monica. She thought about stopping at home and asking Monica to come there, but this time she did fear Kurt might come by unexpectedly and she needed privacy.

She drove to the Wilson Lodge. Her last trip away from the lodge had been harrowing so she intended to leave before darkness fell. She parked and went to Monica's room. Monica opened the door almost instantly. "Laurel! I was just going out."

"Where?"

"A walk. I'm going stir crazy in this room."

"I have to talk to you." Laurel started in but Monica put a hand on her shoulder. "Let's go to the dining room. I cannot bear sitting in this room another minute."

"The dining room is too public."

"Not at this hour. Come on."

As Laurel trailed after her, she marveled at Monica's ability to command. She was thirty years old and still doing what Monica told her with barely an argument. No wonder the other Six of Hearts had always done what she wanted.

The lodge was beautifully decorated for Christmas, but Laurel found the dining room particularly exquisite. Actually there were two rooms, the first containing sofas, wing chairs, a large stone fireplace, and a dazzling Christmas tree. The hostess led them down three levels to a table in front of a huge window overlooking rolling snow-covered knolls and Schenk Lake. A buffet was being served. Laurel, too upset to eat, took very little on her plate. She couldn't help noticing that Monica heaped her own as if this were going to be her last meal. She must have fantastic metabolism to eat that way and stay so slim, Laurel thought.

Once they were seated, Monica looked at her expectantly. "What's happened?"

"Several things." Laurel glanced around to make certain no one was within earshot. "It started as soon as I left here last night."

While she told Monica about being chased down the hill and her car rammed, Monica continued to eat steadily. When she reached the funeral wreath on her door, Monica's pace slowed. By the time she'd finished with Neil Kamrath coming to the store and Zeke Howard slamming his daughter into the shelves, Monica had laid down her fork and stared.

"Laurel, my God, all of this is incredible! I've just been sitting around here taking calls from the office and watching television, and you've been through hell. You should have called me."

"So you could do what? Subdue Zeke? Anyway, I survived. What I want to know is what you think of all this."

"I think what happened last night with the car and the

wreath means you've been singled out as the next victim."

"Don't sugar-coat it, Monica."

"Are you going to tell me you don't think the same thing?"

"No. I believe you're right," Laurel said flatly. She looked out the window. A layer of snow covered the knolls. A breeze rustled the few remaining dead leaves clinging to the trees. Ducks and swans floated serenely on the gray, cold lake. The scene suddenly struck her as unbearably lonely.

"Tell me about Neil Kamrath."

Laurel pulled her gaze back to Monica. "He looks different than he did in high school. He's taller and he must wear contacts. Those awful Coke-bottle glasses of his are gone. He's very polished but sad, self-contained. I ran into him at the hospital. He was leaving after visiting his father when I arrived. He sat with me in the waiting room. He talked a bit about his wife's and son's deaths. Robbie, the child, lived a few days although he was badly burned. After they died, Neil moved to Carmel."

"Sounds like he really opened up to you."

"To a point. He's very guarded. As soon as he says something revealing, he looks like he regrets it."

"What's your impression of his stability?"

"I'm not sure. His wife and son were in a wreck. The car exploded. The wife died instantly, but the child lingered, horribly burned. I keep thinking about that—fire. It may have triggered something about Faith. He seems calm, like he's trying very hard to deal with it all, but he's clearly a deeply troubled soul."

"Zeke Howard is, too," Monica said.

"Zeke is crazy. And *strong*. And he came to the store to recite the Bible verses about destruction to *me*."

"Are you sure he wasn't just predicting damnation for everyone? He was always doing that, the damned loon. Remember how embarrassed Faith was by him?"

"Yes, but he wasn't speaking in general. He prefaced the

verses with my name. He said it twice. He was talking exclusively to me."

"Do you think he could have been driving the car that rammed you?"

"I know he drives. That's how he got to the store. But Mary also drives and she was making odd references about Faith this morning. We *must* go to the police."

Monica gave her a hard stare. *"No."*

"Why not, for God's sake? Are you blind to what's going on? What about Angie? What about *me*? You supposedly came here to *help* us."

"I did. I *am*."

"Oh, are you? What exactly have you done? We know just about as much about this killer as we did last night."

"It's only been one day, Laurel. I can't work miracles."

Laurel reached out and touched the small poinsettia on their table. "I know." She looked into Monica's vivid green eyes. "That's why I think if we don't get help, I may be joining Angie very soon."

"No you won't. We'll get to the bottom of this *without* police intervention."

"You've always been so sure of yourself, Monica. It's gotten you in trouble before."

Monica looked at her steadily. "I'm not going to the police, Laurel. Neither are the others. If you go, you go alone, and I doubt very much if they'll believe you when the rest of us claim we don't know what the hell you're talking about."

3

Denise pulled in front of the small green house and hurried up the walk. Before she reached the door, it opened. A small, blue-haired lady smiled at her.

"Sorry I'm late, Miss Adelaide," Denise said. "I got hung up at the grocery store."

"That's quite all right, dear." Adelaide Lewis motioned her inside with a slightly tremorous hand. Denise had never noticed a tremor before. "Audra has just been sharing some cookies with Hannah and me."

Denise stepped into the small, crowded living room. The scent of violet sachet was almost overwhelming. Hannah Lewis sat behind a silver tea service. She smiled weakly, looking pale beneath her carefully applied rouge. Denise knew there was three years' difference in age between the sisters. Everyone they met knew it immediately because Adelaide was quick to inform them she was the younger. Nevertheless, they seemed almost identical—frail, chatty, fluttery creatures who should have lived a century ago and insisted on being called "Miss Adelaide" and "Miss Hannah."

Audra was halfway through an oatmeal cookie. "How did it go today, honey?"

"Okay," Audra mumbled.

Miss Adelaide ran a loving hand over her piano. "She had a bit of trouble with 'Beautiful Dreamer.' I think perhaps she wasn't putting her heart into it."

Audra looked abashed. "I'm sorry."

"My dear, don't feel bad," Miss Adelaide said. "I'm sure with plenty of practice you'll turn into a perfectly competent pianist."

Competent, Denise thought in disappointment. Not gifted.

"I'll see that she practices more." A look of misery crept over Audra's beautiful little face. She hated practicing.

Denise paid Miss Adelaide. The sisters detained them in one of their long farewells, then Denise and Audra stepped outside, each taking a deep breath. "It's so hot and smelly in there," Audra complained as they got in the car.

"It doesn't smell bad. They just go a little heavy on the violet sachet. Fasten your seat belt, honey."

As they pulled away from the house, Audra said, "I don't see why I have to take piano lessons."

"When I was your age, I longed to take piano lessons but my family couldn't afford them."

"Why do *I* have to take lessons just because *you* wanted

to? I don't want to be a piano player. I want to be a doctor like Daddy."

"Your father plays the piano."

So far this argument had stopped Audra cold, but Denise didn't think her luck would continue. Audra was too smart. Soon she would point out that being a pianist had nothing to do with being a doctor.

"The sisters were all shook up when I got there," Audra volunteered, her argument temporarily defeated.

"What were they upset about?"

"They wouldn't tell me, but they were whispering about some crazy man and the Bible and Laurel and someone getting hurt. Is that your friend Laurel, the one who has April and Alex?"

Oh, Lord, what was this all about? Denise wondered, her hands tightening on the wheel. Who was the crazy man? Had something happened to Laurel?

"Mommy, I asked if that was your friend Laurel."

"I don't know. It could be another Laurel."

Audra frowned. "I sure hope Laurel's okay. I liked her a lot, and I *loved* April and Alex."

Last Christmas, when Laurel decorated for their party, she had stopped by with her dogs in the back seat of her car. Audra rushed to see them. They were too frightened to venture onto a strange lawn, so Audra climbed into the back seat and they'd covered her with kisses. Denise counted to five, knowing what could come next.

"I wish I had a dog," Audra said right on cue.

"I'm afraid of dogs."

"Mommy, we *need* a dog."

"What for?"

"To tell us if burglars are trying to get in."

"We have an alarm system."

"A dog would be better."

"Well, we'll see."

"That means no." Audra's lower lip crept out a fraction.

"Audra, please don't be petulant."

"I don't know what that means."

"Don't *pout*," Denise snapped, still wondering what the Lewis sisters were discussing.

"All I asked for was a little dog," Audra said in a tiny, heartbroken voice. Denise knew Audra was playing her better than she would ever play the piano, but it usually worked.

"Cheer up, baby. I promise I'll talk to Daddy." Audra remained silent. "Do you know what came in the mail today? A Christmas card addressed to Miss Audra Price."

Denise could tell Audra wanted to hold on to her silence, but she couldn't stand it. "Was it from Grandma and Grandpa?"

"No. C'mon, Audra, do you have a boyfriend you haven't told me about?"

Audra grinned. "Buzzy Harris."

"*Buzzy!* I certainly hope that's a nickname."

"I think so, but I don't know what his real name is. He told me I was a babe and tried to kiss me on the playground last week."

"Tried to kiss you! You didn't tell me that."

"I don't tell you *everything,* Mommy. He's real cute."

"Cute or not, you're only eight and too young to be kissing boys."

Clearly Audra hadn't even heard her. She was too excited about perhaps receiving a Christmas card from some dashing third-grade Lothario named Buzzy Harris.

Denise turned into the driveway of her two-story colonial house. She hadn't wanted to move back to Wheeling—she and Wayne clashed several times over the move before she finally relented—but she did love this house. It was imposing, twice as large as anything they could have afforded in Chicago, and Wayne had insisted it be professionally decorated. Denise worried about the expense, but Wayne was always more *dégagé* about money than she and insisted. "You didn't want to live in Wheeling, but you came because I wanted to," he'd told her. "The least I can do is give you a beautiful home in return."

Even when she'd suggested going back to work as a

nurse, he'd objected. "I know you'd rather stay home and be a full-time mom, so that's what you're going to do." How did I ever get so lucky? Denise often thought. I don't deserve Wayne or Audra, but I'll devote my life to them. It's the least I can do to make up for mistakes in the past. To make up for *the* mistake.

Audra hopped out of the car and ran for the front door, her long, wavy chestnut brown hair bouncing. Denise often thought Audra was the most beautiful child she'd ever seen. Another miracle, because Denise didn't think either she or Wayne was particularly good-looking. "Hurry up, Mommy!" Audra called as Denise lifted a bag of groceries from the back seat. "I want to see my Christmas card!"

"Hold on for a minute. It's not going anywhere."

Denise shifted the groceries to her left arm and put the key in the door. As soon as it opened, Audra dashed to the entrance hall table where Denise placed the mail. Denise carried the grocery bag into the kitchen while Audra sorted the letters. "Here it is!" she squealed with delight in the other room.

After a few moments she appeared in the kitchen doorway looking puzzled. "Mommy, I don't know who sent this. I don't even understand some of the words."

An icy finger touched Denise's spine. She closed the refrigerator door and went to Audra, taking the card from her.

On the front was a picture of an old barn layered with snow. It looked remarkably like the Pritchard barn before fire had half destroyed it. She opened the card. There was no formal printing—only a typewritten verse:

> Here for you is a happy little rhyme
> About the year's most splendid time,
> When Santa comes in the night like a wraith
> To all good girls who remember their FAITH.

Six

1

When Laurel got home, she once again cursed the garage opener that wouldn't work. She'd meant to pick up a battery on her way home but had forgotten it during the drama of Mary's injury. It wasn't completely dark. She parked as close to the front door as possible, looked around, gripped her canister of Mace, then made her dash. She had the key ready for the lock when she was pulled up short.

A large red heart blazed across the pale oak of her front door.

Laurel drew in her breath and reached out a tentative finger. Spray paint, completely dry. It could have been there for hours.

Numbly she unlocked the door and went inside. The dogs rushed to her, jumping and barking. She looked at the afghan. Once again it lay in a heap on the seat of the couch. The dogs had been at the window, watching whoever painted the heart. They'd even left nose prints on the glass.

"I wonder what Kurt is going to say when he sees *this*," she muttered. "I feel like Hester Prynne in *The Scarlet Letter*."

Laurel relocked the door, threw down her coat and purse, and went into the kitchen to make coffee. She felt cold to the bone, her hands frigid. A week ago her biggest worry had been thinking of a way to escape a trip to Florida for Christmas. Now she feared for her life. It seemed incredible, unreal. But if she wanted to make sure of its reality, all she had to do was look at her front door.

She rubbed a hand across her forehead. How much longer could she keep all of this from Kurt? How much longer *should* she? Monica said by keeping silent they were all protecting their reputations, but at what cost? Their lives?

The dogs sat looking at her expectantly. "You want dinner, don't you?"

She fixed each a can of food, fresh water, and set out a few biscuits for dessert. At least there was nothing wrong with *their* appetites. Even though she'd eaten meagerly at Wilson Lodge, she wasn't in the least hungry. Her stomach felt so tight it couldn't hold one bite of food.

The phone rang. She knew who it was before she picked it up. "Hi, Kurt."

"What are you? Psychic?"

"No. I just figured you'd had time to talk to Mary."

"You're right. She didn't have much to say. I asked her to press charges against Zeke for assault and battery."

"Good."

"Not good. She said she'd have to think about it."

"*Think* about it! I can't believe it after what he did."

"I've seen this a hundred times in domestic disputes. A man beats his wife half to death, she calls the cops, then refuses to press charges. Nine times out of ten, he turns around and does it again."

"What are the options?"

"To get a mental hygiene warrant. That would at least put old Zeke in a psychiatric ward for a while for observation and treatment."

"He definitely needs it. How is Mary feeling?"

"A lot worse than she's letting on."

"I should visit her this evening."

"No," Kurt said firmly. "You need to stay inside tonight. It's not safe for you to be out."

"But I think Zeke was the person who rammed my car and hung the wreath on my door, and he's in jail tonight."

"We don't *know* he rammed your car. We won't be checking out his car until tomorrow. For now I want you to be extra cautious. Besides, I don't think Mary feels like having company. You can see her in the morning."

"Okay," Laurel said resignedly.

"You still mad at me about Kamrath?" he asked.

"I'm sorry about that," she hedged. "I was just upset about Mary. You haven't forgotten about the party tomorrow night, have you?"

"No. I'll pick you up around eight."

"Great, Kurt. And thanks for calling me about Mary."

When she hung up, she breathed easier. Obviously Kurt wasn't planning on stopping by this evening. Maybe she could do something about the artwork on her door before tomorrow night.

Still cold, Laurel had just poured a second cup of coffee when the dogs began barking. In a minute someone knocked on the door. She hovered near it, wishing she had a peephole. After the second knock, she called, "Who is it?"

"Denise."

Laurel was shocked when she opened the door. Denise looked frightened half to death, her lips pale, her eyes wide. She started to step in, then stopped when the dogs continued barking. "Will they bite?"

"No. They don't know you and they're scared." Laurel knelt and petted each dog. "It's all right, you two. This is a friend." They quieted but continued staring at Denise. "Could you say something to them? Dogs react to your fear."

Denise looked flummoxed for a moment, then managed woodenly, "Good dogs. Pretty dogs."

Hardly inspired, Laurel thought, but some of the tenseness left their bodies. "I think we're okay now. Come in and sit down. Do you want coffee?"

"No, I'm too nervous already."

"It's decaf and you look like you could use something hot. I'll be right back."

"Laurel, please don't leave me with these dogs."

"You'll be fine." When she returned with a mug of coffee, April and Alex sat on the couch with Denise, studying her intently as she watched them gingerly. "See, I told you they wouldn't hurt you."

"Not so far, but dogs don't like me."

"That's because you're afraid of them, although why I'll never know. You've never been bitten, have you?"

"No. But when I was little I saw a movie where a person was mauled. It scared me to death. Audra loves dogs. She was talking about these two just today."

"How is she?" Laurel asked, sitting on a deep, comfortable chair across from the couch.

"Fine. Well, actually she's confused. She got a Christmas card today. She was so excited. Then she opened it . . ."

"Oh, God," Laurel gasped. "It wasn't the photograph of Angie, was it?"

"No. That would have been much worse, but this was bad enough."

Denise reached in her purse, withdrew the card still in its envelope, and handed it to Laurel. She noted the neatly typed name and address, the lack of return address, and the local postmark. "Open it!" Denise snapped. Laurel looked at her. "Sorry."

"It's all right."

Laurel pulled the card from the envelope and studied the picture. "It looks like—"

"The Pritchard barn," Denise said. "I'm sure that was no accident."

Laurel opened the card and read the verse aloud:

> "Here for you is a happy little rhyme
> About the year's most splendid time,
> When Santa comes in the night like a wraith
> To all good little girls who have the FAITH."

"Well?" Denise demanded. "Isn't it awful?"

"It's tricky. No actual threat. Nothing overtly frightening to a child."

"But frightening to *me*."

"That's the idea. What better way to scare you than to make you feel the killer is reaching out to your child?"

"Do you think that's what he's doing?"

"I think the killer is supposed to be the 'wraith' in the night, and you can't miss that all the letters of 'Faith' are capitalized," Laurel said solemnly. "Someone knew Audra wouldn't understand this but you would."

Denise put her head in her hands. "Oh, dear Lord, what am I going to do? Take this to the police?"

"Not unless you're willing to tell them *everything*."

"I *can't*. I *won't* tell them everything!" Denise raised her head, her gray eyes stormy. "And you're not going to tell them everything, either!"

Laurel's tone hardened. "Don't tell me what to do, Denise."

"If you tell them, I'll deny it. Monica will, too."

"Well, that's just great," Laurel said in disgust. "What do you intend to do? Take an unsigned Christmas card with an odd but nonthreatening verse to the police?"

"Yes."

"What do you expect them to do with it?"

"Find out who sent it."

"How?"

"Fingerprints."

"Denise, do you have any idea how many people have touched this envelope?"

"What about the card?"

"You, Audra, and I have touched it. If there were any other prints, they'd probably be smeared. If they weren't, it would still be impossible to track down the guy unless he has a criminal record, an armed service record, or worked in law enforcement or a place that requires prints for security purposes. Denise, think about it. The police aren't going to all the trouble to track down someone like that over a weird Christmas card!"

Denise closed her eyes. "Okay, I get it. What would *you* do?"

"Go to the police if I could get any of you to back up my story."

"Monica and I have more to lose than you do."

Laurel drew back. "Do you consider Crystal's and my lives so worthless?"

"No, no of course not." Denise raised her hands help-lessly. "Oh, God, Laurel, I'm so upset I don't even know what I'm saying."

"But you won't go to the police."

"Only to take the card."

"Which would be useless unless they knew the whole story, what the implications of this card might be."

"So what else can I do?"

"You know that by not going to the police, we're playing with fire, don't you? We're playing with our *lives*. You might be playing with your *daughter*'s life."

"I don't want to hear that!"

"I don't care if you want to hear it or not, Denise, it's true."

Denise shook her head violently. "No. I won't go, Monica won't go, and I don't think Crystal will go, either. She's too scared. So I'm asking you again, what else can we do?"

Laurel was furious, but she fought to rein in her emotions. Yelling at Denise would get her nowhere. She took a deep breath and said calmly, "The only option is simply to try to find out on our own who might be doing all this. I can tell you that after today, I consider Zeke Howard a definite contender."

Denise leaned forward. "Audra had her piano lesson with Adelaide Lewis this afternoon and she said the sisters were whispering about a crazy man and someone getting hurt and your name."

"It was quite an afternoon and the Lewis sisters were witnesses." She told Denise about Zeke bursting into the store shouting Bible verses and finally slamming Mary into the shelves. "She's in the hospital with a concussion and a bad cut on her scalp."

"That's terrible," Denise said a bit halfheartedly. She

barely knew Mary. "What exactly did Zeke say?"

"I can't remember all the Bible verses. God's wrath, destruction, all directed toward me. When he was shouting at Mary, though, he talked about Faith being taken before her time and that she gives him directions about how to protect himself against those who hurt her."

"Those who hurt her?" Denise echoed faintly. She took off her glasses and rubbed her eyes. "Could he know about the Six of Hearts?"

"Mary told me she kept all of Faith's things and her father has been going through them lately. Maybe there were letters or a diary. Of course, that means Mary could know, too. It seemed to me she was making some strange references to Faith this morning."

"What kind of references?"

"Just emphasizing that she'd kept *everything* of Faith's. It was probably nothing."

"I don't think we should dismiss anything as 'probably nothing,' " Denise said. "Speaking of which, why is there a red heart on your door?"

"Someone has been busy."

Denise raised her eyebrows. "You sound awfully calm."

"It's not the first time someone has been messing around here. The other night I came home from Wilson Lodge to find a funeral wreath on the door."

"Good Lord! Who could have put it there?"

"The same person who painted the heart."

"Then it couldn't have been Zeke or Mary. He's in jail and she's in the hospital."

"Denise, it's completely dry. It could have been there all day. Zeke didn't get to the store until three-thirty. He could have done it before he came, and for the first time in a year, Mary was half an hour late this morning. She could have painted it after I left for the store."

"Has Kurt seen it?"

"No, and I'm going to have a hell of a time explaining it, especially after the wreath, which he *did* see. Also, when I was coming back from the lodge, someone rammed my car. Several times. They almost made me wreck. Kurt knows about that, too." Laurel leaned forward. "Denise, I don't see how we can keep all this quiet much longer."

Denise set her untouched coffee on an end table. "I have to be going now," she said coolly. Laurel was stunned. Hadn't Denise heard anything she'd said? If so, she intended to ignore it. She stood. "You'll be by tomorrow with the decorations, won't you?"

Laurel thought of pursuing the subject of going to the police, but she knew it was useless. Denise had taken all she could handle and she was putting up a blockade as impenetrable as rock. She wasn't going to budge on this point. "Yes, Denise," Laurel said tiredly. "I'll be at your house around eleven."

Denise looked at the dogs. "Would you mind bringing them? Audra asked specifically."

Laurel smiled. "Okay, but I'm not sure I'll be able to get them out of the car. Remember last year?"

"It doesn't matter. She can get in the car with them. She loves them."

Laurel spoke gently. "You know, Denise, your family is welcome to visit anytime and Audra can play with the dogs to her heart's content."

Denise's gray eyes filled with tears. "We were so close, weren't we?" Laurel nodded and Denise reached out and touched her hand. "I promise that if we all come out of this situation alive, things are going to be like they used to be. I miss you so much."

Laurel watched Denise walk to her car, her own eyes filling with tears because she knew things could never be like they used to be for the remaining Six of Hearts, even if they did come out of this situation alive.

2

Crystal sat in her tiny living room trying to concentrate on a magazine article entitled "How to Keep Your Man Interested." According to the author, all it took was the right perfume, some tantalizing lingerie, and dreaming up a few cutesy ways to initiate sex such as leaving a seductive note saying "There's a surprise for you in the bedroom" for him to find when he came in from work.

Crystal tossed the magazine aside in disgust. Did Joyce do those kinds of things for Chuck? Did they share expensive champagne in a bubble bath surrounded by scented candles? Probably. Besides, Joyce had two athletic adolescent sons, the kind of boys Chuck always wanted, the kind she'd never been able to give him. What hurt the worst, though, was that Joyce had a beautiful daughter of seven. Crystal had seen Chuck with her at the holiday light parade before Thanksgiving. He'd held her high on his shoulders, both of them laughing and clapping. It was obvious he doted on the child, who looked like an angel. Crystal had never seen such an expression of love and happiness on his face and she'd nearly doubled over on the sidewalk from the pain.

She felt herself beginning to tremble now, the way she always did when she thought about that night before Thanksgiving. She glanced at the clock hanging on the wall across from her. Eight P.M. At least three hours before she could go to bed and hope sleep would come. It usually wouldn't without a sleeping pill. Lord, when had she started looking forward to the oblivion of sleep? How she used to love cuddling up to Chuck on the couch and watching their favorite comedies. Looking back, she realized he'd always seemed faintly restless, never as happy as she, particularly in their last year together, after the stillbirth of their daughter, after the doctor had to perform an emergency hysterectomy.

Crystal still couldn't believe Chuck was gone. Every time she came home from the grocery store or running the few errands she still bothered with, she expected to see him sitting in his favorite chair watching the sports channel on television. Sometimes she forgot and set a plate for him at dinner. He always liked her cooking. Plain and simple food. Joyce was probably a gourmet cook. No doubt she served all kinds of fancy pasta dishes and things like artichoke hearts and escargots, which Chuck would hate . . .

Oh, what was she thinking? That Chuck would return to her because he liked her cooking better? It was stupid, but then she'd never been known for her mental prowess. Not like the other Six of Hearts.

Which reminded her she had more important things to think about than cooking, or stupid magazine articles, or how soon she could go to bed and lose herself in sleep. She went to the old chest standing in the corner, opened a drawer, and withdrew the Polaroid of Angela. She shivered. What fury it had taken to beat that beautiful woman into the bloody mess in the picture, a fury that compelled the killer to keep bludgeoning the body long after Angie must have been dead.

The doorbell rang. Crystal let out a little shriek and dropped the photo on the floor. She quickly picked it up, dropping it back in the chest, slamming it shut. The doorbell rang again. And again. She stood rigid until Chuck shouted, "Crystal, I know you're in there so open up!"

He's come back! she thought joyfully. He's come back to me. I knew he couldn't stay away, not from me, not when he knows how much I love him! She wished she had on something nicer than sweat pants, that she'd bothered to put on some makeup and cologne . . .

She flung the door open and her heart fell. Chuck looked at her stonily, the clean lines of his face hard, the blue eyes narrowed. He pushed past her into the living room, leaving her standing, openmouthed, in the doorway.

"Chuck, what's wrong?" Crystal asked tentatively.

He turned. "Shut the door." For a moment she felt a prickle of fear. They'd had arguments over the years, but she'd never seen him look so coldly furious. As if reading her mind, Chuck said, "I'm not going to hurt you. I just want to talk."

She relaxed a bit and closed the door. "Do you want something to drink? A Coke? A beer?"

"Nothing." He wore a well-tailored raincoat over a navy

and white cable-knit sweater and gray flannel slacks. What
had happened to his old jeans, flannel shirts, and stained
down jacket? Crystal wondered. Gone, of course. Tossed
away as easily as he'd tossed her away. He sat down without removing his coat. "Why won't you sign the papers?"

"What papers?"

"Don't play dumb, Crystal. The *divorce* papers."

She clasped her hands. They were freezing although the
room wasn't cold. "I don't want a divorce."

"*I* do."

"I don't believe that."

"You don't? I left you months ago. I've never considered
coming back."

"That's because you're confused." She looked at him,
desperation in her eyes. He was more handsome than ever.
Her Chuck. "We've had some setbacks. Your problem finding the right job. Me losing the babies. But Chuck, we *love*
each other."

"No."

"We love each other. We always have."

"No."

"*Yes*. Since we were teenagers. We were *meant* to be
together."

"No one is *meant* to be together, Crystal. That's a lot of
romantic nonsense."

Crystal came and knelt in front of him. "It isn't nonsense
and you know it. Some people *are* meant to be together,
like us. You're not meant to be with Joyce. You were just
frustrated with our life and she came along with her money
and her kids. But we could adopt children."

"No we can't. Not with my job record."

"Oh, we can talk our way out of that. People understand—"

"Crystal, this is not about Joyce's children."

"But you don't love her."

Chuck sighed. "Crystal, stand up and stop this."

"I won't! Everything I'm saying is true. You don't love
her, you love *me*! You belong to *me*!" Chuck looked at her,

his blue eyes seeming to lose focus for an instant. He was realizing the truth of what she said, Crystal thought. "Chuck Landis, you look me right in the eye and tell me you don't love me."

His eyes refocused. He looked at her piercingly. "I—do—*not*—love—you."

Crystal sat back on her haunches, feeling as if he'd slapped her. "Chuck, there's so much between us," she persisted weakly. "So much you could never share with Joyce—"

"Stop it! What we had I don't *want* to share with Joyce." He stood, towering over her. "Sign the divorce papers."

Her throat tightened and she shook her head.

Chuck's face turned red with fury. "Dammit, you sign those divorce papers or . . ." His breath came quick and hard. "Just sign them, Crystal. For your own good sign them and have them at the lawyer's office on Monday morning. This is the last time I'm warning you."

He slammed out of the house. Crystal sat motionless on the floor for almost a minute. Then she lowered her head and sobbed as she'd never sobbed in her life.

3

Monica fixed another glass of scotch and soda and returned to her bed. She knew she'd already had too much to drink, but she couldn't sleep. The inactivity of the last couple of days was driving her crazy. She was accustomed to working twelve-hour days. She enjoyed working until she was ready to drop. It was certainly better than having all this time to think.

When she left Wheeling to go to college on scholarship, she'd expected never to return. She'd forced herself to send her great-aunt an occasional letter. The old woman sometimes returned a cold, sanctimonious little missive, always lecturing Monica about her failings. When she died ten years ago, she'd left everything she owned to charities.

Monica sent a small basket of flowers but did not attend the funeral.

Although Monica did not admit it to Crystal, Denise, or Laurel, the old lady had always been suspicious about Monica's part in Faith's death. She'd known about the Six of Hearts. Monica's fingers tightened on her glass. She'd underestimated the snooping, meddling bitch. While Monica was at school, she'd conducted daily searches of her room. She'd eavesdropped on Monica's telephone conversations. She'd played astonishingly adroit little word games in order to elicit information from her great-niece. Monica had eventually become as clever at the games as the old lady, but not before she'd accidentally given away some crucial information.

The problem was that Monica didn't know how much of that information the old bat passed on. She hadn't worried about it at the time of the woman's fatal stroke. Three years had passed since Faith's death and there had been no repercussions. Now, ten years later, things were different. Her career meant everything to her. Her career and John Tate. They were inextricably bound because no matter how good a lawyer she was, she knew in her heart she would never have achieved her impressive position in the firm at such a young age without John's help.

Impetuously she picked up the phone and dialed John's private number in his study at home. After two rings, he answered.

"John, I'm so glad I caught you," she said a trifle breathlessly. She was afraid he'd be angry. He didn't like for her to call his home.

"I just happened to be in my study getting some papers." His voice was precise, clipped, and totally without accent. He'd told her it had taken a year of training to completely free himself of the Mississippi accent he hated. Now no one could guess his roots from his speech. To her relief, he also did not sound angry. "The Goldsteins are here for dinner."

"How's everything at the office?"

"Dull without you." He'd had a few drinks himself or he would never had said anything so personal over the phone in his home. "When are you coming back?"

"My friend's funeral is Monday."

"Then we'll be seeing you Tuesday."

"Maybe. I might need another day or two."

"Why?"

"Just to tie up loose ends."

"Loose ends? You weren't Angela Ricci's lawyer."

"No." Monica suddenly felt nervous and took another sip of her drink. "I just need a couple of days."

"Monica, you haven't forgotten Kelly Kingford, have you? The trial is in two weeks."

"Of course I haven't forgotten her. I'll be ready. I always am. What about Stuart Burgess?"

"Out on a million dollars bail."

She hadn't told the others her law firm was representing Angela's ex-husband and she didn't intend to. "Has he admitted anything to you?"

"No, and if the wacko did kill Angela, I don't want to know. We'll probably have to put him on the stand and we can't suborn perjury by having him say he didn't murder her if we know he did."

"He *didn't*."

John laughed softly. "We have to do a good job for our clients, but we don't have to believe in them."

"You think he's guilty."

"Yes, but your belief in his innocence despite his having been your friend's ex-husband will help if you wrap up the Kingford mess in time to be second chair when Burgess goes to trial."

It was the chance of a lifetime. Angie was an internationally known celebrity, Stuart Burgess an eccentric millionaire. The media would be all over the case. "I intend to be second chair," she said fiercely.

"Then you'd better get back here as soon as possible."

"I—"

Monica heard a woman's voice. "Darling, you've abandoned me and our guests. Is there a problem?"

"No problem," John said hastily. "I'll be right down." After a moment, he spoke to Monica quietly. "I have to go."

"Yes, certainly." "Darling," she'd called him in her light, honeyed voice. Sweet, passive, lovely Luanne Tate, John's sweetheart from high school. He'd never leave her and his two children. "I'll be home as soon as possible," Monica said.

"Good. Got to go now."

"John," she said abruptly. "I love you."

"Uh, yeah. See you soon."

She hung up and flopped backward on the bed. He didn't say he loved you because he was afraid Luanne would hear him, she told herself. Then she laughed harshly. Sure, Monica. All this scotch has fuddled your brain, made you sloppy and romantic. John had *never* said he loved her.

But then neither had Chuck Landis. Laurel had thrown her for a loop the other night by saying Monica once had a crush on him. She'd never suspected Laurel or anyone else sensed her attraction to Chuck. She'd wanted him so badly she'd offered to let him become her first lover. She'd been so certain sex was the the way to pull him away from Crystal. She had never been so humiliated in her life as she was when he turned her down. She never told anyone she'd been besotted with a man clearly her intellectually inferior, even though savage jealousy tore through her whenever she saw him with Crystal or any other girl.

Nevertheless, her pursuit of Chuck had set a pattern she'd been following ever since. Her psychiatrist told her she only wanted men who were committed to other women because she was trying to re-create her childhood. Her father had deserted her for a woman. Ever since then she'd been trying to triumph over "the other woman," looking for a man who would choose *her,* but it never happened, not with Chuck thirteen years ago, not with five married men who followed, not with John now. John was attracted to her physically. Emotionally he *admired* her. He respected her quick mind, her legal prowess, her dedication to her work.

Admiration and respect were a long way from love, but they were all she had. She couldn't stand to lose them, which meant John could never learn about Faith Howard and the Six of Hearts.

And he wouldn't, no matter what she had to do to keep the secret.

Seven

1

Laurel spent another restless night. At two in the morning she awakened bathed in sweat, kicking under the covers. She'd been back in the Pritchard barn, reaching for Faith who swung lifelessly through the leaping flames. The dogs, alarmed by her thrashing, jumped up on the bed, licking her face as if trying to bring her back to reality.

She got up, went in the bathroom, and splashed cold water on her face. Her amber eyes were slightly bloodshot, the lids swollen from lack of sleep. "You look just great for a party tomorrow. Or rather, today, in about eighteen hours."

She'd never felt less like going to a party in her life, but she'd told Denise she'd come. Besides, maybe Neil Kamrath would be there and she'd get one more chance to talk to him.

Laurel dressed quickly and arrived at the store even earlier than usual. Until this morning she'd completely forgotten about the shattered glass shelves and the mess left after Zeke's attack on Mary. She would have to find someone to help her clean up before opening time.

She entered through the back door and walked straight into the showroom without removing her coat. Sun streamed through the front windows and she pulled up short.

All the wreckage was gone. No glass or metal. No crushed silk flower arrangements or broken ceramic bowls and vases. Only an odd navy blue throw rug on the gray-blue carpet. She knelt and pulled it aside. The smell of carpet cleaner wafted up to her and she touched a damp spot.

"We couldn't get up all the blood."

Penny and Norma stood just outside the kitchen door. "I think one more scrubbing will do it, or maybe a professional cleaning," Norma said.

"What happened to the shelves?" Laurel asked.

"My husband, Cleet, came over last night in the pickup truck and took them away. They were ruined, Laurel. Cleet said they couldn't be fixed."

"Oh, I knew that." Laurel stood. "I'll have to buy a new set. Thank you so much for cleaning and hauling away the shelves."

"We wanted things to look nice this morning."

"How's Mary?" Penny asked.

"Concussion, bad cut on the scalp. At the time I left yesterday they were going to do a couple more tests, but I think she'll be okay. If you two don't mind looking after the shop for an hour this morning, I'll run over to the hospital to see her. I didn't get to last night."

"I'm sure we can hold down the fort for an hour," Norma said. "We've got all the decorations done for the Price party tonight. You'll be going over today, won't you?"

"Yes . . ." Laurel frowned. "But someone usually goes with me to help with the decorating. I can't leave just one of you here. That's too much work."

"Cleet said he'd drive the delivery van over and help you. You'll have to tell him what to do. He's real good at taking orders." Norma grinned. "He's been taking them from me for thirty years and never realized it."

Laurel laughed. "Your family are lifesavers! I'd really appreciate his driving the van because I have to run home and pick up something before I go to the Price home. I told them I'd be there around eleven."

"I'll call Cleet and tell him to come by here about ten-thirty."

"Great. And I think we'll close around three o'clock to-day. We've been working hard."

Norma and Penny looked pleased at the prospect of an early quitting time. No wonder. Cleaning up the mess last night must have taken at least two hours.

Laurel went back to the kitchen and put on coffee. She wanted things to seem as normal as possible today. Then she looked over their orders for Saturday and Sunday and phoned her own into the wholesaler, asking if it were possible for them to deliver a bit early today because of the three o'clock closing time. At ten she left for the hospital.

Mary sat propped up in bed staring at the television. A morning talk show was on with the host gushing over an actor unfamiliar to Laurel. "Good morning, Mary."

Mary turned to her. Her eyes had a glazed look. Five small bandages decorated her face and above her left eye spread a garish purple bruise. "I didn't bring flowers because I thought you probably got your fill of them at work."

Mary forced a smile. "You're right. Besides, I'm going home in a couple of hours." Her lips trembled slightly. "Laurel, do I still have a job?"

Laurel's eyes widened in surprise. "Of course! Don't tell me you were worried about that."

"I was."

"Well, forget it," Laurel said firmly, her doubts about Mary submerging beneath her pity. "I couldn't get along without you. We'll both be tottering around Damron Floral when we're in our nineties."

Mary looked incredibly relieved. "Just like the Lewis sisters. I don't suppose they came back to buy their wreath, did they?"

"No. I think they'd had enough excitement to last a month. I may just take one to them as a gift." Laurel pulled up a chair. "How are you feeling?"

"Tired. They wouldn't let me sleep because of the concussion. I also have a few aches and pains."

"No wonder."

Mary glanced at her sharply. "Papa didn't mean to hurt me."

"That push into the shelves looked pretty deliberate to me."

"He didn't know what he was doing. I told you he's been strange lately. Old age, I guess."

"Maybe." Laurel paused. "Mary, why was he quoting all those Bible verses to me?"

"He always quotes from the Bible."

"But these verses were all about damnation and destruction, and he was directing them at *me*."

Mary's gaze dropped. "I don't know."

"What about his saying you weren't good like Faith, that you were always sneaking around at night like she and your mother?"

Mary's fingers twitched at the hem of the sheet, rubbing and twisting it. "Sometimes Papa gets me mixed up with my mother. She ran off with a man, you know. More often Papa confuses me with Faith. You were her best friend— you know she wasn't an angel. She did sneak around at night with boys and with you and the other—" She broke off. "He gets me mixed up with her."

Laurel had tensed. "You said she sneaked off with me and the 'other.' The 'other' what?"

Mary didn't look at her. "Friends. Just people she knew."

But that's *not* what you meant, Laurel thought anxiously. You were going to say "the other Six of Hearts."

2

After Laurel left the hospital, she headed for home, knowing Penny and Norma would be helping Cleet load the van and give directions to the Price home. She was extremely grateful for his willingness to pitch in and help on this hectic day.

At home she hooked April and Alex to their leashes and led them to the car. They looked at her suspiciously. Trips in the car usually meant a visit to the veterinarian. The thought immediately lowered Laurel's spirits. Their veterinarian was Victor Ricci, Angela's father. She knew he and Mrs. Ricci were back from New York preparing for Angela's funeral in less than forty-eight hours.

Laurel pushed the thought from her mind. One look at her damaged car reminded her she had her own safety to consider. She couldn't let herself become careless because her sadness was distracting her.

"Jump in," she urged the two reluctant dogs. "We're going to see a friend of yours."

After five minutes more of urging in her gentlest voice, she had both dogs in the back seat. They huddled together, looking as if they were going to their execution. She smiled as she glanced in the rearview mirror. Kurt was right—they didn't look like they would do much damage to an intruder, but she'd never admit it to him.

The Damron Floral delivery van sat in the Price driveway when Laurel pulled up. There was also a caterer's van. She knew it was useless to try to get the dogs out of the car in a strange place with so much activity going on, so she left them and went through the garage to the side door. Denise greeted her. "Cleet has already carried in most of the stuff." She lowered her voice. "I was scared when a stranger came to the door until I saw your van."

"I'm sorry, Denise. I should have called and warned you."

Audra ran up, her dark eyes alight. "Hi, Laurel!"

"Miss Damron," Denise corrected.

Laurel smiled. "I'd prefer Laurel. How are you, Audra?"

"Terrific. A couple of days ago I thought I was getting sick, but Daddy says I'm so ornery no germs can live in me."

"Wayne is a marvelous doctor," Denise said, winking. "He went to school for years to learn to make diagnoses like that one."

"Did you bring April and Alex?" Audra asked excitedly.

"I sure did. You'll have to visit with them in the car, though. They're too scared to get out."

"That's okay." Audra started to dash out the door, but Denise stopped her until the child put on her jacket. Then she shot outside and climbed into the back seat of Laurel's car.

"She's so beautiful, Denise," Laurel said.

"I know I'm prejudiced, but I think so, too." Denise paused. "But what I'm wondering is what you've done to those dogs to make them so timid."

"Daily beatings."

Denise laughed. "Oh, sure. I remember when we were kids you used to take in every abandoned baby bird and rabbit you could find. Dr. Ricci told you they wouldn't live, but they always did."

"That seems like about fifty years ago."

Denise shrugged. "Happier, more innocent times. Come in. You have to make my house look gorgeous for tonight."

Making Denise's house look gorgeous was not a hard task. This year Laurel had chosen a motif of white and gold twining vines of white silk maple leaves decorated with small golden apples down the banister of the curving staircase and across the living room mantel. Masses of white leaves, gold apples, and gilt-dipped silk poinsettias decorated the dining room table and the grand piano, and fat candles rolled in gold sparkles and surrounded by white silk leaves sat on the coffee and end tables.

When Laurel and Cleet finished, Denise looked around, beaming. "Oh, Laurel, it's wonderful!"

"I hope Wayne likes it. He might have preferred more color."

"There's plenty of color on the Christmas tree. He'll love it."

"How's the cooking coming?"

Denise grinned. "There's a minimum of cooking going on *here*. Last year I thought I'd have a nervous breakdown trying to master some of those elaborate Christmas confections, so this year I turned the food over to a caterer."

"My, *my*," Laurel drawled. "A caterer. How fancy."

"We're even having a professional bartender."

"Good heavens, and I told Kurt not to wear a tux."

"This is definitely *not* a black-tie party. I just want every-one to be comfortable and enjoy themselves, including the host and hostess who are usually harried messes dealing with food and drinks."

"Can April and Alex come, too?"

Laurel and Denise looked up to see Audra standing in the doorway with each dog on its leash. "I don't believe it!" Laurel exclaimed. The dogs were clearly nervous, nei-ther standing at full height, staying close to Audra. "How did you coax them in?"

"Just sweet talk," Audra told her airily. "I think they like me."

"They certainly must." Denise looked slightly dubious. "They're house-trained," Laurel assured her, "and they aren't destructive."

Denise smiled tentatively. "They're very cute."

"So can they come to the party?" Audra asked again.

Laurel saved Denise a refusal. "Honey, being around all those people they don't know would scare them silly. Be-sides, the party is past their bedtime." Audra's face fell. "But you can come to my house some weekend and play with them. They have lots of toys and a big backyard they'd like to show you."

Audra brightened a bit. "Can I, Mommy?"

"Sure, as long as Laurel says it's all right. We'll go in the next two or three weeks."

Fifteen minutes later Cleet left in the van and Denise and Audra, still holding the dog leashes, trailed her to the car. "Thanks so much, Laurel. You did a beautiful job."

"I'm glad you're pleased. Audra, think you can get those two in the back seat?"

"Yeah." Audra climbed in first, then urged in a crooning voice until both dogs jumped in, too. Before she climbed out, Audra leaned over the front seat and whispered to Lau-rel, "Help me talk Mommy into letting me get a dog."

"I'll try," Laurel assured her.

Denise and Audra stood in the driveway waving as Laurel drove away, but Laurel couldn't help noticing the tension behind Denise's smile. The woman was scared, just as scared as Laurel.

Eight

1

Laurel slipped into white wool slacks, pulled a white silk angora sweater laced with thin gold threads over her head, and stepped into new white and gold heels. A glance in the full-length mirror assured her the ensemble fit perfectly and looked casually festive. She wore a bit more makeup than usual, her lipstick a dark rose, her eyes accented with lavender and a touch of deep purple shadow. Even her hair was behaving for once. All in all, she felt pretty well, even in the mood for a party.

Kurt arrived at a quarter to eight. "I'm starting to look forward to what I'm going to find next on your door," he commented, staring. "A red heart? It's not Valentine's Day."

"I think Zeke might have stopped by on his way to the store yesterday," she answered offhandedly. "At least it's not as bad as a funeral wreath."

"A lot harder to get off, though. It's going to take turpentine, then the door will have to be revarnished."

He stepped inside, dressed in a charcoal gray suit and lighter gray shirt. "My goodness, you look wonderful!" Laurel exclaimed. "I didn't know you were going to get so dressed up."

"Talked myself into a new suit," he said in a slightly abashed manner. "I've been wearing that pair of dress slacks and sports coat forever."

"Well, you look quite dashing."

"I don't think I've ever been called that before. You look beautiful."

"I look okay and thank you. Before we leave, why don't you update me on Zeke Howard?"

Kurt took a deep breath. "I was afraid you were going to ask me that. He's been released."

Laurel's lips parted in surprise. "*Released!* How?"

"Mary refused to press charges of assault and battery."

"I can't believe—" She sighed. "Yes, I can believe it. I could tell when I talked to her in the hospital this morning she wasn't going to do anything. But there must be some other way to get him off the streets."

"There is. A mental hygiene warrant."

"How do you get that?"

"An application can be made to the circuit court or the mental hygiene commission for the purpose of an examination."

"Who makes the application?"

"Anyone. The trouble is we don't have a lot of witnesses. Mary isn't going to say anything. I talked to the Lewis sisters, who refuse to say a word for the record about the attack. I don't know who that young woman in the store was."

"I don't, either. But there's Penny, Norma, and me."

"Norma was in the workroom. Penny was outside."

"Then what about the other deputy and all the other people who must have seen Zeke at the sheriff's office?"

"Laurel, he was meek as a lamb as soon as we got him in custody. Just a gentle, kind old man, slightly confused by all the commotion."

"There must be something we can do!"

"Honey, even if you have a psychiatrist testifying at one of these hearings, it's still a judgment call on the judge's part. We don't have a psychiatrist, and even if we did, I'm not sure it would help. Yesterday was the first time we know of that Zeke ever acted like a danger to himself or anyone else."

"What about his ramming my car?"

"We have no proof he did that. Our examination of his car showed nothing."

"But—"

Kurt put his hands on her shoulders. "Look, Laurel, a judge would probably view his display in your store as just an aberration. Two or three more episodes and we might get him in a psychiatric institution for a month. As of now . . ." He shrugged. "I don't think we have a chance."

"Well, fabulous," Laurel said in disgust. "So this lunatic gets to run around free in spite of what he did yesterday."

"I'm afraid so. Let's just hope he does something crazy again soon."

Laurel looked at him. "The next crazy thing he does might be to murder someone." If he hasn't already, she thought grimly.

2

Around ten cars were already at the Prices' when Laurel and Kurt arrived. Tiny white lights decorated the two evergreens on the front lawn and lined the big bay window.

"I love this house," Laurel said as they parked.

"I'd hate to pay the heating bills."

"Kurt, do you always have to be so practical?"

"Well, you have to admit it's awfully big for just three people."

"Maybe they plan to have more children."

"You know what's weird?" Kurt said, turning off the ignition. "Among all you girls who were such good friends in school, there's only one child." Laurel looked at him. "Of course, if Faith hadn't died—"

"But she did," Laurel said crisply.

"That child would have been almost thirteen," Kurt went on as if talking to himself. "I'd bet it was a boy."

Laurel's heart rate accelerated. Even thinking about Faith had made her miserable for years. Now talking about her threw Laurel into a near panic. "Let's go in. I'm cold."

She nearly jumped from the car and hurried up the front

walk. "Hey, wait a minute," Kurt called. "Trying to leave me behind?"

She'd already rung the doorbell and Wayne was opening the door by the time Kurt caught up with her. Wayne, five feet ten, slightly stocky with a round face and thinning brown hair, beamed at her. "Laurel! You look wonderful. So does the house. You did a great job. Hello, Kurt. You two come on in out of the cold. We've got some of the best eggnog in the world to warm you up."

He took their coats. Several people were gathered in the living room and music poured from the stereo. Laurel was relieved it wasn't Christmas carols. Hearing them over and over for weeks could be wearing. Instead, the sounds of soft rock filled the room. Denise came to greet them. She wore a long red and green plaid hostess skirt and a white silk blouse. "Everyone loves the decorations, Laurel."

"I'm glad."

"Wayne says you have some extra special eggnog," Kurt said.

"It's on the dining room table. Why don't you get a couple of glasses for you and Laurel while I talk to her for a minute."

"I guess females never outgrow girl talk."

"No sexist remarks from you tonight," Laurel warned. "And make sure my eggnog—"

"Is nonalcoholic," Kurt finished. "Yes, ma'am."

As he left them, Laurel asked softly, "Is Monica or Crystal here?"

"Crystal is. I didn't think she'd come and she's nervous as a cat. I believe this is her first social event in a year. She looks dreadful. Something else must have happened but I haven't been able to get a word alone with her."

"I was certain Monica would be here."

"If I know Monica, she'll wait to make an entrance. No sign of Neil Kamrath, either. Any word on Mary and Zeke Howard?"

"They've both been sprung," Laurel told her. "Mary was discharged from the hospital and she wouldn't press charges against her father so he's out of jail."

"You're joking! He's running loose? Can't anyone do something?"

"Kurt already explained the process. Getting him committed, which is what he needs, would be incredibly complicated."

Kurt returned with her eggnog. "Lots of calories, no alcohol."

"Just how I like it."

Audra appeared in a red velvet dress. "Hi. Are April and Alex asleep?"

"Yes. They get up early and go to sleep early."

"I get to stay up later because of the party." Audra wiggled her finger for Laurel to bend down while Denise talked with Kurt. "Mommy wants me to play the piano, but I don't want to," Audra told her confidentially. "I'm terrible. I'll just *die* if she makes me play."

She looked so distressed Laurel couldn't help taking pity on her. "Maybe I can help you out. I'll suggest your daddy play something."

Audra brightened. "Would you? That'd be great."

"What does he like to play?"

Audra pursed her lips. "Lots of times he plays classical stuff I don't like. But his favorite *fun* thing to play is 'Great Balls of Fire.' Mommy gets embarrassed when he does it in front of people, but he *loves* it. So do I."

"I'll make a special request, then."

"I need to talk to you!" Crystal suddenly whispered in Laurel's other ear, making her jump.

Denise was right—she did look dreadful. Her eyes were rimmed with dark circles and she'd slathered unflattering makeup shades on pale, dry skin. She wore burgundy knit slacks too small to accommodate the weight she'd gained, a striped ski sweater, and no jewelry except for her wedding ring. Her short dishwater blond hair lay lank against her head. It was impossible to believe that just fifteen years ago she'd been the slender, golden blond, baby-faced head cheerleader everyone found so adorable.

"How are you, Crystal?" Kurt asked.

"Okay." She gave Laurel an appealing look.

"Still driving that old red Volkswagon?" Kurt persisted. "You'd better get rid of it before you have serious problems."

"I *have* serious problems."

"What? Alternator? Brakes?"

It was obvious Kurt wasn't going to give up. "I don't mean problems with the car," Crystal snapped. "If you've talked to Chuck lately, you know what problems I'm having."

Kurt looked like he'd stepped on a land mine. "I'm sorry things aren't going well," he said lamely.

"Not going well! That's an understatement!" Crystal reached out and clutched his arm. "You and Chuck are best friends. Can't you do something?"

"Do something?" Kurt echoed, his cheeks reddening as Crystal's voice rose.

"Yes. Talk to him."

"I have talked to him."

"But did you *really* talk to him?" Crystal had drawn several people's attention. Laurel was certain she'd downed more than one drink. "Have you told him how awful that woman is for him? She's old. She's spoiled. Chuck's just a plaything for her. She doesn't love him like I do—"

Denise interrupted. "Have you tasted some of the candied cranberry and raisin tarts yet, Crystal? It's absolutely delicious."

"I'm not hungry and I'm trying to talk to Kurt."

"Well, I *am* hungry," Kurt said. "I'll try some of those tarts, Denise."

He fled toward the dining room table where a buffet was set up. Instead of staying to talk to Laurel, Crystal followed in hot pursuit, warming to her subject. Denise rolled her eyes. "Oh, no."

"Kurt will shut her up," Laurel assured her. "She's going to lose it if she doesn't let this thing with Chuck go, though."

"Do you think she ever will?"

"I don't know. Looks like she'd have more pride."

"I think she led a charmed life for so long she's having trouble accepting that she can't have everything her way. Besides, this murder business is taking its toll."

"On all of us," Laurel said. "Still, we should make more of an effort to be Crystal's friends and drag her out of that house. I know she feels abandoned by everyone."

"I told you I intend to make some changes in *my* life," Denise commented. "I have more free time than you do. I'll make Crystal my first project."

Laurel joined Kurt at the buffet table. Cyrstal lingered, but she'd quieted although she still looked anxious. Laurel wondered if she ever relaxed these days.

The doorbell rang a couple more times and two other couples arrived. The third ring was answered by Denise. Laurel had her back to the door but Audra, standing beside her, widened her eyes and muttered, "Wow!"

Laurel turned. Monica strode into the room. She wore an emerald green Far Eastern–style gown with cap sleeves, a mandarin collar, heavy gold embroidery, and slits three-fourths of the way up her thighs. The dress was so tight it left no curve of her well-toned five-foot-ten-inch frame unrevealed. Her eye makeup was heavy, exotic, yet perfect for her. Her hair lay in gleaming strands almost to her waist and her perfect teeth shone between crimson lips. She looked like an exotic bird amid a flock of brown wrens.

"Hi, folks," Monica said gaily. "Sorry to be late."

Everyone stood speechless for a few moments. Laurel had a brief mental flash of Scarlett O'Hara arriving in her skin-tight, sexy red sequined and feathered gown at sweet Melanie's sedate party. Denise was the first to react, coming forward with a forced smile. "Hello, Monica. We'd nearly given up on you."

"Oh, you know I never miss a party." No, Laurel thought, Denise and I didn't know that and no one else here has ever even met you except for Kurt. "Thanks so much for inviting me."

Denise began making rounds, introducing Monica to everyone. "Is she a movie star?" Audra asked Laurel in awe.

"No, honey, she's a lawyer in New York."

"Do they all dress that way?"

"Not when they go to the office."

"I think she looks cool. I wonder if Mommy would let me have a dress like that."

"I doubt it," Laurel said. "Besides, you're much prettier the way you are."

Kurt sidled up to Laurel. "Does Monica look as out of place as I think she does?"

"She's probably forgotten she's in Wheeling, West Virginia, not Manhattan. But she does look beautiful."

"And knows it. Look at her, taking control of the whole room."

Laurel nudged him playfully in the ribs. "I think she intimidates you. Always did."

"She *doesn't* intimidate me. I just don't like her."

After about twenty minutes, Monica unobtrusively cornered Laurel. "Denise tells me Zeke's free as a bird."

"Unfortunately. I wish the law weren't so difficult."

"If it weren't, I wouldn't make the salary I do."

"And you would love your work so much. I really don't see you doing my job."

"Oh, I don't know. Arranging flowers must be relaxing."

Laurel started to snap back that there was a lot more to running Damron Floral than daintily arranging flowers all day, but Monica was scanning the room, paying no attention to her. She probably hadn't even realized how belittling her comment was. Sensitivity had never been one of Monica's strong points.

"Mary is fine, not that you asked," Laurel said tartly. "She was released from the hospital today."

Monica's attention whipped back to her. "With Zeke free, we have two of our possible killers on the loose," she whispered. "Damn."

Crystal joined them. Although she had a drink of what

appeared to be straight bourbon in her hands, she didn't look any calmer. She immediately hissed, "Someone's been in my house. I went to the grocery store this afternoon and when I got back, I found some things missing."

Monica's gaze shot to her. "What things?"

"A porcelain figurine. My *yearbook*."

Laurel's breath left her. "Your yearbook?"

"Yes. The one with the memorial page dedicated to Faith."

"Did you leave your door unlocked?" Monica asked.

"Of course not! With all this going on? Do you think I'm crazy?"

"And there was no sign of breaking and entering."

"No."

Laurel frowned. "What was the figurine like?"

"It was a gift from my grandmother—lady carrying an umbrella and wearing a long, frilly gown. It was beautiful and valuable and Faith always loved it."

"Oh, God," Laurel moaned. "Now I vaguely remember it. It came from France. Didn't you have a name for it?"

"Bettina." Crystal took another sip of her drink. "Monica, have you found out anything yet?"

"No, although I'm seriously considering that Zeke Howard might be our culprit."

"Zeke!" Crystal squawked before Monica and Laurel shushed her. "How could Zeke kill someone who lived in New York?"

Monica sighed. "Crystal, you persist in thinking New York is halfway around the world. Manhattan is just a little over four hundred miles from Wheeling. You can drive it in six hours."

"But Zeke's an *old* man."

"He's barely seventy and he's not an invalid."

Laurel nodded. "He can also drive and he's crazy. Didn't anyone tell you what happened at my store yesterday?"

"Yes, Denise did."

The doorbell rang again. In a moment, Neil Kamrath

walked hesitantly into the room. Laurel glanced at Kurt. His face grew still and white. Even Crystal drew back slightly, as if in distaste. Only Wayne and Monica seemed genuinely pleased to see him. Wayne clasped his hand in a hearty shake and Monica mumbled, "My goodness, you were right, Laurel. He *has* improved with age," before she put on her dazzling smile and walked with a seductive sway toward Neil.

Crystal shook her head. "Monica and Faith. They never met a good-looking guy they didn't like."

Introductions were being made. Laurel could tell Neil's smile was forced and it completely disappeared when he met Kurt's hard stare. Laurel's temper rose. Kurt knew nothing about her suspicion that Neil might have killed Angie. Maybe, like many people in this town, he blamed Neil for Faith's death. But even though he thought she committed suicide, certainly Kurt realized one person isn't responsible for another taking their own life. If he didn't, his immature thinking was not only disappointing, it was downright annoying. Kurt was not a stupid man, but he was acting like it.

Fearing his chilly welcome might send Neil out the door in ten minutes, Laurel went up to him. "Hi, Neil. I'm glad you decided to come."

He smiled warmly. "I wouldn't have without your encouragement."

"I'm glad I had so much influence."

"Well, it doesn't seem appropriate for me to be here when my father's dying."

"Wayne said he's in a coma," Laurel reminded him gently. "He wouldn't be aware of you even if you were sitting by his bed. Besides, your life has to go on, Neil."

He looked at her gravely. "That's what everyone kept saying after Ellen and Robbie died. I didn't necessarily believe it then, and I'm even less sure now."

"Neil—"

"Never mind." He smiled. "Talk about a party pooper.

I'll try to work up a little Christmas cheer, although it's hard with your boyfriend glaring at me."

"Kurt's a good man, but he can be stubborn and irrational. Just ignore him."

Laurel glanced up to see Denise urging Audra toward the piano. I promised Audra I'd help, Laurel thought. "Excuse me, Neil," she muttered.

"Now, honey, everyone would enjoy hearing you play 'Jingle Bells.' "

"But Mommy, I don't want to."

"I think she looks a little tired." Denise glanced at Laurel in surprise. "And flushed." Laurel put her hand on Audra's cool forehead. "You do feel a bit warm."

Denise's look of surprise turned to one of anxiety. Oh, this isn't fair, Laurel thought guiltily, but Audra's big brown eyes were filled with gratitude.

"Warm!" Denise repeated, putting her own hand on Audra's forehead. "I think you're right. Wayne!"

Audra rolled her eyes at Laurel. In a moment Wayne stood beside them. "What's the problem?"

"Laurel thinks Audra might have a fever. You check and I'll get the thermometer."

Denise disappeared. Wayne touched Audra's forehead, then grinned. "Talked Laurel into saving you from playing, didn't you?"

Audra nodded. "I'm sorry," Laurel said. "I was only trying to help."

"Quite all right," Wayne told her. "I keep telling Denise that forcing children to play when they don't want to makes them hate the piano even more." Denise reappeared with the thermometer. "Sweetie, I think she's okay," Wayne told her, "but it's past her bedtime and she didn't feel well a couple of days ago." He kissed Audra's cheek. "Off to bed with you."

Audra looked disappointed, but it was a trade-off. Bed or concert. Laurel thought she'd prefer bed.

Fifteen minutes later Denise returned from upstairs. The noise level had increased as several guests made frequent trips to the bartender. Laurel saw that Neil looked as if he were ready to depart when Monica descended on him, all flashing eyes and long, exposed legs. Laurel wasn't sure if Monica's intent was to glean information or flirt.

A woman whose name Laurel didn't remember cornered her to harangue about how overpriced she thought the Flower Basket was and hint that she might consider throwing a little business toward Damron Floral. Laurel knew this business would probably amount to two or three orders a year, for which she was supposed to simper with happiness. The woman seemed insulted by her tepid reaction and moved away.

Laurel glanced at Kurt talking animatedly with a striking young blonde. Crystal sat by herself eating chocolate walnut bread and looking desolate. Denise was in earnest conversation with a dark-haired woman who appeared about eight months pregnant. Just like Claudia, Laurel thought. My sister is supposed to give birth in a few weeks and I'm not excited. I don't even want to go see her at Christmas. What's wrong with me?

The room suddenly seemed smoky, close, and loud. She'd suggest going home, but she had the odd feeling that if she left, so would Neil, and Monica might not have the chance to get valuable information from him. Besides, Kurt looked like he was having a marvelous time with the blonde. She supposed she should be jealous, but she wasn't.

Abruptly she found herself reaching for Wayne's arm as he walked by. "I know Audra didn't want to play, but how about you? I'd love to hear a few songs."

Wayne looked pleased. "Is this a genuine request, or are you just being polite?"

"I'm just being polite," Laurel said lightly.

"Oh, well, I don't care. You made the mistake of asking."

He walked to the piano and Laurel clapped her hands for attention. "Tonight the gifted hands of our favorite surgeon will turn to his second greatest talent as a pianist." A lot

of people laughed, clapped, and walked toward the grand
piano.

"My repertoire is limited, so I don't take requests,"
Wayne said solemnly. "I only play what I know. I'll start
out with something nice and easy. 'Even Now' by Barry
Manilow."

Laurel had only heard him play once and had forgotten
how good he was. Even his voice was good—not polished
and professional, but good. Denise stood behind him, casually sipping eggnog, but her eyes gleamed. How lucky
she'd been to find him, Laurel thought. Denise, Wayne, and
Audra made as perfect a family as one could imagine.

When he finished, someone yelled, "Bravo! More!"

Wayne ducked his head. "If you insist." He started
"Every Little Kiss" by Bruce Hornsby. Someone began
clapping along, and in time the living room was filled with
the sound of the piano, Wayne's voice, and nearly everyone
clapping.

By the end of the song, most of the guests were in high
gear. A few freshened drinks, some moved away from the
piano while others drew nearer. Laurel didn't even see
Kurt. By now the living room was crowded by people ready
to cut loose and really have fun.

Laurel raised her voice over the din. "I know you don't
like requests, but I'm going to make one anyway. How
about 'Great Balls of Fire'?"

Denise threw her a playful glare. "Audra put you up to
that, didn't she?"

"She just said it was one of Wayne's favorites, and I'm
dying to see if he can do the mule kick with the bench."

"Denise won't let me," Wayne laughed. "But I'll do the
rest with every bit of Jerry Lee's spirit I can manage."

In a moment mild-mannered, plump, balding Dr. Wayne
Price turned into a rock star with a vengeance. A few people were so carried away they began dancing. Laurel
couldn't take her eyes off Wayne's flying fingers. Jerry Lee,
you don't know it but you've got some real competition in
Wheeling, she thought in delight, feeling young and happy

for the first time in weeks. From nowhere an unfamiliar man grabbed her and began whirling her around the living room.

Wayne was winding the song to a dramatic close when suddenly a woman screamed. Apparently some of the guests either didn't hear her or thought she'd just gotten carried away because they kept dancing and clapping. Wayne, however, lifted his hands from the piano keys and jumped up so forcefully the bench went flying backward. His eyes were fastened on the curving staircase.

Laurel pushed her partner away and swung around. On the staircase stood Audra in pink pajamas. She gripped a slender plastic fashion doll and below her huge, terrified eyes a wide piece of silver duct tape covered her mouth.

By now most people realized something was wrong, becoming motionless and staring at the child. Wayne and Laurel bolted across the living room, reaching her at the same moment.

Gently Wayne pulled the powerful tape from his daughter's chalky face. "My God, honey, what happened?" he whispered.

"A ghost came to my room," Audra said in a flat voice. "A ghost in a long white gown with long curly red hair. The ghost put a hand over my mouth, then the tape. It said my mommy didn't deserve to have me. Then it gave me this."

She held out the doll to Laurel. It had long red hair and was naked except for a heart locket on a chain hung around its slender neck.

Denise rushed up, enfolding her rigid child in her arms. "Sweet Jesus," she gasped. "What's happened?"

Laurel took the locket from the doll's neck and turned it over, although she really didn't have to. She recognized it but read the engraving anyway. "F. S. H. Faith Sarah Howard." She looked at Denise. "This is the last gift Faith's mother gave her before she vanished."

Nine

1

Laurel wasn't aware of Kurt crowding in beside them until she heard his voice. "Audra, where did the person go?"

"It wasn't a person. It was a ghost. It said so."

"In a man or a woman's voice?"

Audra looked uncertain. It was her first expression except for stark fear. "I don't know. It sort of whispered."

"Where did it *go*?" Kurt persisted.

"Out of my room. Down the hall."

"The back stairs!" Laurel said.

While Denise and Wayne cuddled their terrified daughter, Laurel led Kurt to the kitchen. It was empty. The back stairs were against the west wall, the bottom step about ten feet from the back door, which stood open nearly an inch. Kurt grabbed a towel off the counter, grasped the doorknob with it, and pulled the door open. The small back porch was dry under its roof. The remaining snow on the back lawn bore a multitude of footprints.

"What do you think?" Laurel asked.

"I think our 'ghost' is long gone."

"But who—"

"Mary or Zeke. Who else would have Faith's locket?" A muscle flexed in Kurt's jaw. "I'm going to call the city police and tell them to get over here while I go out to see the Howards."

"Shouldn't you wait here for the police?"

"If I wait, Zeke or Mary could destroy evidence. Besides, we dealt with Zeke before."

"And got nowhere."

"We did the best we could," Kurt said harshly. "And I'm damn well going to find out if either one of them have come here and terrified this child."

When they returned to the living room, half the guests were gone. Wayne was saying good night. Laurel didn't see Denise or Audra and guessed she'd taken the little girl back to her room. Crystal and Monica lingered near the piano. "Will you two meet me at my house so we can talk?" Laurel asked.

Crystal looked fearful. Monica's eyes hardened. "You're going to badger us about going to the police, aren't you?"

"I'm not going to *badger* you. I'm going to appeal to your good sense. Monica, you're a lawyer. What would you advise a client in these circumstances?"

"To keep his mouth shut." Monica set down her drink. "I'm leaving now. Crystal, unless you want to get yourself in a hell of a lot of trouble and make sure you lose Chuck for good, I suggest you do the same."

Laurel touched Crystal's icy hand. "Crystal, *please* . . ."

"I . . . I can't." Crystal's gaze dropped. "I'm sorry. I know you're disappointed in me, but Chuck—"

"Chuck is *gone*," Laurel said roughly. "Keeping quiet about Faith's death won't bring him back to you but it might get you killed."

"I *won't* talk to the police. I *can't!*"

Crystal rushed toward the front door, tears running down her cheeks.

2

Laurel knew talking to Denise was hopeless. Even if she agreed it was time to go to the police, she was too upset over Audra to do anything tonight. Besides, Laurel had already made up her mind.

Kurt dropped her off at home before heading for the Howard house. As she fitted her key in the lock, she looked at him. "Will you stop by after you've seen Mary and Zeke?"

"If we have to bring one of them in, it could be late."

"I don't care. I really need to talk to you."

He looked at her piercingly. "Are you *finally* going to tell me what the hell has been happening for the past week?"

She paused. "Yes, Kurt. I'll tell you everything."

He kissed her on the forehead. "Good. I hate it when you shut me out, especially when I know you're scared or unhappy. We've been friends since you were seven."

"I was forced on you by Faith."

Kurt smiled. "Chuck and I weren't the pushovers we seemed. We may have been only eight, but we knew a couple of good-looking girls when we saw them." Laurel laughed, thinking of herself with her tangle of unruly hair and missing front teeth. "I'll be back as soon as I can."

Laurel had left two lamps glowing in the living room. April and Alex raised their heads and looked at her sleepily from their cushions in front of the fireplace, so apparently nothing had happened during the evening to upset them. Denise had been the victim tonight, although Laurel would rather have come home to find some harmless decoration on her door than to see Audra so frightened. Whoever had dressed up as a ghost to frighten a helpless little girl needed to be flogged, Laurel thought fiercely.

Could it have been Zeke or Mary? Laurel wondered as she put more logs in the fireplace. It would have been so easy to come in the kitchen door, slip up the back stairs, and disappear unnoticed since the caterers had simply delivered the food earlier, not stayed to serve.

As the fire grew, Laurel sat down on the couch, thinking. There was so much commotion in the living room, it would have been just as easy for a guest to slink away for a few minutes. She closed her eyes, trying to picture the scene. Had she seen Neil Kamrath? No. She was sure of it. Had he taken advantage of the confusion to escape as he'd clearly intended to do earlier before Monica cornered him?

Or had he gone outside where he had a robe and wig stashed, then gone upstairs?

She drew up her legs and wrapped her arms around them. The thought of Neil dressing up in a robe and wig and carrying around a doll wearing Faith's locket seemed absurd, but Audra and Denise had been horrified, and horror was Neil's stock in trade. Didn't he make his living by dreaming up scary senarios?

But she'd been the one who argued fervently with Crystal and Kurt about the difference between imagination and reality. Just because a writer's topic was horror didn't make him crazy.

Laurel wasn't sure how long she'd sat staring into the flames, her thoughts racing, when Kurt knocked on the door. When he walked in, she saw that his cheeks were pink from the cold and the slacks of his new suit were damp and dirty above his dulled shoes.

"What happened?" Laurel asked.

"When I got to the house, no one was home. Lights on, but no one came to the door. I was getting ready to leave when I heard Mary calling, 'Papa! Where are you?' I went toward the voice. I found her half frantic. She said she went in to check on Zeke to see if he was sleeping okay and he was gone. We searched the woods and finally found him sitting against the trunk of a tree, talking."

"Talking to whom?"

"To Faith and Genevra. I didn't remember, but Mary said Genevra was her mother."

"Yes. What was he saying?"

"Something about Genevra not deserving her children, about Faith being taken unfairly, a lot of stuff like that."

"Kurt, Audra said the *ghost* said her mother didn't deserve her."

"I know."

"Where is Zeke now?"

"At home in bed."

"At *home!*"

"Laurel, I can't arrest someone for sitting in the woods

talking to themselves. There wasn't any evidence. Of course by the time I found him at least an hour had passed since someone scared Audra. But get this—Mary wouldn't let me search the house without a warrant. She was adamant."

Laurel raised an eyebrow. "Sounds like she has something to hide."

"I thought so, too. She told me to leave so she could call a doctor for Zeke."

Laurel suddenly became aware of how exhaused Kurt looked. "Sit down. Do you want something to drink?"

"A beer."

She hurried into the kitchen and retrieved a can and a glass, although she knew he'd probably ignore the glass. When she came back in the living room, he'd slipped off his wet shoes, his head propped against the back of the couch, his legs stretched toward the fire. "Your poor suit," she murmured.

"Think the dry cleaners could do anything with this mess?"

"I'll take the slacks to the place I use. They work miracles."

"Great. I'd hate to see my new suit ruined after one wearing." He grinned. "My mother never even got to see me in it."

"We should have taken a Polaroid before we left this evening." A Polaroid. The picture of Angie's battered body. There was no putting this off any longer. "Kurt, I said I was going to tell you what's going on." He looked at her seriously. "It all began thirteen years ago with the death of Faith Howard."

Her heart pounded as she told the story, starting with the formation of the Six of Hearts, their growing interest in witchcraft, and finally the night when Faith, drunk and reckless, had stuck her head in a noose and slipped off the bale stool. The fire. Then their flight from the barn. Finally their silence.

She'd expected a look of disbelief or even horror on

Kurt's face. There was nothing but a tightening of his jaw, a slight twitch under his left eye. "Kurt, what are you thinking?" she asked in a small voice.

"I'm not thinking," he said stonily. "What does all this have to do with what's going on now?"

He looked at her as if he didn't know her, didn't *want* to know her, and for a moment she felt as if she couldn't go on. But she had to.

The next part of the tale came out almost without emotion. She told him about the evidence found in Angie's house—the six and the heart drawn on the mirror in blood, the judgment card beside her body. She told him about the photos she, Monica, and Crystal had received, getting the Polaroid of Angie to show him. "Then there was the ramming of my car, the funeral wreath, the heart painted on my door. Crystal says someone has been in her house and taken her yearbook and a valuable figurine Faith always loved. Finally there was tonight with Audra. Denise, Crystal, and Monica don't want to tell the police about Faith's death. They said they'd deny everything if *I* told, but I can't sit back and let a child be terrorized or risk someone else being killed."

Her hands were icy and trembling when she finished. Kurt finally switched his dark gaze from her face to the fire. His body was totally motionless. Laurel waited as long as she could, then finally burst out, "Say something!" He remained silent. "Kurt, if you want to tell me I'm a horrible human being, a coward, a liar, if you just want to *yell* at me, do it! But *please* don't sit here like the Sphinx. Your silence is driving me crazy."

"Seems to me you understand silence pretty well."

She'd begged him to talk. His words felt like a slap in the face, but he was right.

"I know we were wrong, Kurt, and I'm not going to excuse us by saying we were young and scared. We were, but we all knew better. What we did was wrong, but we *didn't* kill Faith. It was an accident."

"You all got her drunk and talked her into doing something stupid, and it cost the life of her and her baby."

They hadn't talked Faith into anything. Everyone except Monica had tried to dissuade her from putting her head in the noose, but Laurel wasn't going to make excuses. Kurt wasn't in the mood to listen anyway.

"What are you going to do?" she asked softly.

"There's nothing I can do for Faith and the baby."

"I know that, Kurt. I meant about this killer who seems to be trying to avenge her."

"I don't know yet. I'll try to get more information from the New York police department, although I don't expect them to be too cooperative, especially since Monica was privy to information she shouldn't have had. But they might be interested in what I have to tell *them*." He sighed. "I have to go."

He slipped on his shoes and walked stiffly to the door. Laurel followed. "Kurt, will I hear from you tomorrow?"

"I don't know," he said absently. "Good night, Laurel."

He didn't touch her, never even met her eyes. She'd taken him for granted for months, but as she watched his back retreating toward his car, her throat tightened. She felt as if she'd lost her best friend.

Ten

1

Laurel didn't try sleep in bed. She covered herself with the afghan and curled up on the couch. As soon as Kurt left, April and Alex joined her, burrowing under the afghan, snuggling as close to her as possible. She knew her white slacks and sweater would be covered with dog hair in the morning, but it didn't matter. A cleaning bill was nothing in comparison to the comfort they offered.

"Denise, Crystal, and Monica are really going to be mad at me," she told the dogs. Talking to them as if they were people had become a habit for the last couple of years after she'd begun living alone with them. Alex tilted his head, seeming to give her his full attention. "But I had to tell Kurt. I know everyone will be shocked about how Faith really died. She was my best friend—it might even affect business. Dad will be furious. But I'd do it again. Talking to Kurt was no mistake. I should have told him as soon as I heard about Angie's murder . . ."

She continued to mumble to the dogs until sometime in the middle of the night she fell asleep. Bright sunlight streaming through the front window awakened her.

Laurel looked at her watch. Eight-fifteen. She hadn't slept this late for months. The dogs were already up, staring at her expectantly. "Breakfast is late, isn't it?" she asked in a voice thick with sleep.

She threw off the afghan and stood up. Although the couch was long and comfortable, she felt stiff. If only she could take the day off and relax. But this was one Sunday she couldn't stay home. Because of the uproar with Zeke and Mary on Friday and her early closing time yesterday, she had a few orders left to fill for the Angela Ricci visitation tonight.

A hot shower, a couple of aspirin, and a cup of coffee made her feel almost human again. Dressed in jeans and a heavy red sweater, her hair tied back carelessly with a ribbon, she went to her car and once again inspected the damage, looking at the battered bumper and slightly buckled trunk lid. Kurt had said he would take the car around to mechanics for estimates. She didn't think she could expect that favor now.

She left home at ten and put on a pot of coffee when she reached the store. Her eyes seemed grainy from all the sleep she'd lost this week, but she wasn't hungry. She felt an odd mixture of relief that she'd told Kurt and misery over his reaction. He didn't understand. Isn't that what Monica had predicted? That *no* one would understand? That the remaining Six of Hearts would become pariahs in the town? She'd probably been right, but that didn't change Laurel's mind. She'd done the right thing, no matter what the consequences.

Laurel had been working for about an hour, sticking flower stems in Instant Oasis, the damp green base used in all fresh arrangements. She was just adding leather leaf into a basket of carnations, gladiolas, and daisies when she heard someone tapping on the front door.

It's Sunday morning, she thought irritably. Couldn't the person see the hours painted on the door or the Closed sign?

Maybe it was Kurt, she thought suddenly. Quickly she wiped her damp hands on her jeans and ran to the front door.

Neil Kamrath peered through the window at her.

Laurel hesitated. Did she want to be alone in the store with him? For all she knew he'd murdered Angie. But his smile was disarming and it was daylight. She saw a couple walking across the street. Certainly Neil wouldn't risk doing anything violent with witnesses around, and it was a great chance to talk to him.

Slowly she unlocked and opened the door, looking at him questioningly. "Hi, Laurel," he said pleasantly. "I called your home a while ago. I thought you might be here." She continued to stare at him, trying to make up her mind about letting him in. "I really need to talk with you," he said, ignoring her bad manners. "May I come in?"

Laurel hesitated, then stepped back, opening the door wider. A vampire can't come in unless you invite it, she thought inanely, then wondered why she'd come up with that piece of important information. She'd probably read it in one of Neil's books.

"Do you usually work on Sunday?" he asked.

"No. I gave everyone an early quitting time yesterday, which would have been fine if the wholesalers had delivered early as I requested. Unfortunately, they were late and not all the orders are filled for Angie's visitation tonight."

"I see." He made a wry face. "I think I'll skip the visitation. Judging by the reaction I got when I walked into the party last night, my name is still mud in this town."

"Not with everyone."

"Then why are you standing stiff as a ramrod, not even giving me a little smile?"

Because this is the first time I've been alone with you, she thought. "I guess I'm still a little shook up about that doll business last night."

"That's what I wanted to talk to you about."

"Oh?"

He nodded. "I saw something that's been bothering me." Laurel looked at him questioningly. "Oh, not who scared the little girl, but I saw the doll. Or, more important, what was on the doll."

"The locket?"

He nodded. "A week after Faith died, I went to the Howard house to see how they were doing. Zeke wasn't home. Mary came out on the porch and started screaming like a banshee at me. She said neither she nor her father wanted

to see me. She said she held me responsible for Faith's
death. She threw my class ring at me. I said I thought Faith
had been buried with it. She shrieked that she'd never let
Faith be buried with anything of *mine*. 'The only piece of
jewelry buried with my sister was the locket my mother
gave her,' she said. 'It meant more to her than even a wedding ring from you would have.' "

Laurel frowned. "Mary said the locket had been buried
with Faith?"

"Yes. At the visitation Faith was in a closed coffin, as
I'm sure you remember. The condition of her body . . ."

Laurel's stomach wrenched. "I remember." She glanced
away. "But obviously the locket *wasn't* buried with her.
The necklace on the doll *was* Faith's. I've seen it hundreds
of times."

"That's what I wanted to confirm with you. I didn't get
as close a look at it as you did last night."

Laurel frowned. "Neil, I didn't see you when Wayne was
playing the piano, right before Audra came downstairs. I
thought you'd left."

"No. I was edging toward the door, but I hadn't made it
outside when the little girl came down the stairs. I didn't
leave until you read the initials on the locket. Then I bolted.
Emotional reaction, I guess. The poor little kid looked terrified."

Did she believe him? Yes. He must have been there. He
knew *she* had held the locket in her hand and pronounced
it Faith's. "Neil, when you got outside, did you see anyone
running away from the house?"

"No." He took a deep breath. "You must wonder why
I've come to you like this. It's because I can't confront the
Howards and I don't want to go to the police. Thirteen
years ago they suspected me of murdering Faith."

"Only briefly."

"Still, your friend Kurt's attitude toward me is typical of
the entire police department's. Even Crystal looks at me
like I'm a madman."

"Crystal is a bit fragile right now. Three miscarriages, a

stillbirth last year. Then Chuck leaving. Everyone pretty much ignores her irrational reactions and mood swings."

"I've never said more than ten words to her—I don't care what she thinks of me. But I wonder about the Howards. Mary works for you. You know her well and you care about her. I'm sure you don't want to say anything negative, but I've still got a big problem with what happened last night. Let's say Mary lied to me and Faith wasn't buried with the locket. That means Mary has had it all along. So what the hell was it doing on that doll?"

"Someone wanted to scare Audra."

He looked impatient. "Yes, but why?"

"I don't know," Laurel said stiffly. "Audra didn't even know Faith."

He stared at her. She had the feeling his smoky blue eyes were seeing right into her brain. "This isn't the first weird incident that's happened, is it? That's why Monica was giving me the third degree, even asking exactly when I'd arrived in Wheeling. I got the feeling she was trying to track my movements, especially around this time last week." He blinked twice. "Around the time Angela was murdered!"

Great, Monica, Laurel thought in annoyance. The subtle inquisitor.

"I'm right, aren't I?" Neil demanded.

God, why had she let him in? What was she supposed to do now? Go on playing dumb and enrage him further? Or pretend that he was a trusted friend whom she wanted to take into her confidence? She made an instant decision.

"Neil, if you have some time, I'd like to talk to you."

"You mean question me some more?"

"No, I mean tell you some things—things that are going on now, things that happened a long time ago. Come back to the kitchen and let's sit down. This is a long story."

After she poured each of them a cup of coffee, she started just as she had with Kurt, explaining about the Six of Hearts, the increasingly disturbing games they'd played, and finally describing the night in the Pritchard barn. She paused after that while Neil gazed out the window. His hand had tightened on his coffee mug and his face turned pale. Finally he muttered, "I always knew Faith wasn't the suicidal type."

"She wasn't."

He pinned her with his gaze. "Did you know about her pregnancy?"

Laurel shook her head. "She never said a word to me. She'd been acting odd for a couple of weeks—"

"Odd?"

"Moody. One hour quiet, withdrawn, even depressed, the next almost boisterous. That's how she was the night of her death. She'd barely said a word all evening, then she was gung ho to go to the Pritchard barn. She insisted on putting her head in that noose, even though most of us were trying to stop her."

"*Most* of you. Let me guess who encouraged her. Monica."

"Monica really wanted Denise to do it. Denise refused."

"And if she hadn't, she'd be dead instead of Faith," he said coldly.

"Not necessarily—"

"And when Faith died, you all kept your mouths shut."

"Neil, we were afraid people would think we'd gotten drunk and murdered her. At the very least we might be charged with manslaughter."

"That's Monica talking, even then. All I know is that you kept quiet and let me take the blame, let everyone think Faith had committed suicide because she was pregnant with my baby and I wouldn't marry her!" He stood, towering over her, his face red with anger. "Damn you, Laurel! Damn all of you and your sick little club. I hope you all get exactly what you deserve!"

Laurel thought he was going to strike her. Time slowed for her as she mentally and physically braced for the blow. He raised his hand, glared at her with the desperation and fury of a man driven to the edge, then turned on his heel and stalked from the kitchen.

When Laurel heard the front door slam, she let out her

breath. She ran to the door, locked it, and looked through the front window. There was no sign of Neil.

Abruptly she realized she was trembling and sank to the floor, crying as she hadn't cried for years.

2

Laurel still hadn't heard from Kurt when she slipped on a navy blue dress and gold button earrings. In twenty minutes she was leaving for Angie's visitation. She'd thought she'd be going with Kurt.

Her hopes lifted when the phone rang. They abruptly plummeted when she heard her mother's voice. "Laurel Damron, why didn't you call me about Angie? My goodness, how many nights has that girl stayed under my roof? You two were friends since grade school and I have to hear about her murder on television!"

"I'm sorry, Mom. Things have been hectic around here."

"Too hectic to give me a ten-minute phone call?"

Meg Damron could harangue for an hour straight when she was in the mood, and she was definitely in the mood. "Mom, I didn't want to upset you."

"But I left four messages! Don't you ever check your machine?"

"You know I've always been careless about that. I'm really sorry. How's Claudia?"

The change of subject worked. "We had a false alarm yesterday. Spent hours at the hospital. Claudia got rather . . . well, rude with the doctor when he wouldn't do a cesarean and get the whole business over." I'll bet she was rude, Laurel thought, grinning. Claudia had a lightning temper and an extensive vocabulary of expletives. Laurel could just imagine the scene she'd created. "Your father got upset and told her if she got pregnant again, we were moving back to West Virginia. I was angry with him for losing his temper with her, but it did quiet her a bit."

It threw her into a sulking spell, Laurel thought. She genuinely wished she liked her sister, but she didn't. She

HERR MEMORIAL LIBRARY

wanted all good things for Claudia, but she couldn't stand
to be around her for long, and she knew the feeling was
mutual.

"Now tell me how this awful thing happened to Angie,"
Laurel's mother said abruptly.

"I don't know any more than you do. I was just getting
dressed to go to the visitation tonight."

"And there are no flowers from your father and me!"

"Yes there are, Mom. A huge basket. I wouldn't forget
something like that."

"Good. Oh, Angie's poor parents. They adored her.
Spoiled her rotten, of course." Laurel rolled her eyes. No
one could have been more spoiled than Claudia. "They
spent a fortune on all those singing and dancing lessons."

"Well, they paid off. She was a Broadway star."

"Yes." Meg Damron sighed. "Sometimes I wish Claudia
had taken that route." Impossible, Laurel thought. Angie
had phenomenal talent. Claudia only had good looks.
"How's Kurt?"

"He's fine. I'm expecting him any minute," Laurel lied,
wanting to cut the conversation short. She could *not* talk
about Kurt. "I have to go, Mom."

"All right. We'll be seeing you in a few days. Give the
Riccis your dad's and my heartfelt condolences."

"I will, Mom. Talk to you soon."

Laurel drove to the funeral home without even turning
on the radio. Usually she enjoyed singing along as she
drove, but not tonight. She dreaded this visitation even
more than she thought she would. After the scene with Kurt
last night and the one with Neil today, she wanted nothing
more than to be alone. When she pulled into the funeral
home parking lot, she thought of simply going home again.
If she went to the funeral tomorrow, that would be
enough . . .

Someone tapped on her car window. She jumped before
looking around to see Denise. Laurel opened the door and
stepped from the car.

"How could you?" Denise exploded before Laurel shut the door.

"How could I what?"

"Tell Kurt about Faith. He came to my house today. Thank God Wayne was out with Audra. Laurel, I just can't *believe* you went to the police!"

"After what happened last night to your own *daughter?*" Laurel flared. "Good Lord, I'm surprised *you* didn't go to them. How could you possibly think of keeping quiet after what someone did to Audra?"

"Don't you dare imply I'm a bad mother because I didn't go to the police about something that happened thirteen years ago!"

"I'm not implying you're a bad mother in general, but you're not showing good judgment at the moment. Denise, we're not really talking about Faith's death. We're talking about what's going on *now*." She took a deep breath, trying to quell her anger. "What did you tell Kurt?"

"That I didn't know what you were talking about. I never heard of the Six of Hearts and I certainly wasn't around when Faith killed herself."

Laurel's jaw dropped. "You lied about *all* of it?"

"You're damned right I did. I told you I would. So did Crystal and Monica."

"Do you mean that Kurt talked to the three of you and you *all* lied?"

"*Yes.* We did exactly what we told you we'd do. We *can't* have our lives ruined because of a thirteen-year-old accident." She turned her back on Laurel. "I'll *never* tell," she flung over her shoulder. "Never!"

Laurel watched her stride to her car. "Denise, you'll live to regret this," she called. "At least I hope you'll live."

3

Twenty minutes later Laurel emerged from the funeral home. The place had been packed, mostly with people Laurel didn't know. Monica stood near the family and gave

Laurel a look that could melt glass when she drew near. Laurel stiffened her spine and ignored her, holding out her hand to Mrs. Ricci.

"I'm so sorry," she said, thinking how empty the words sounded. The woman, who looked ten years older than she had in the spring when Laurel last saw her, grasped her hand.

"I know you are, dear. It's such a tragedy. Our beautiful Angela and we can't even open the casket. Did you know that ex-husband of hers sent flowers? Orchids. Son of a bitch!"

"Now, Gina," her husband said mildly.

"Well, he is. He did it, but he hired some fancy New York law firm that will get him off—Goldstein and Tate or something." Laurel's gaze snapped to Monica, who was edging away. "It's the O. J. Simpson case all over again!"

Dr. Ricci, whose soothing manner made him such a successful veterinarian, placed his hand on his wife's arm. "Gina, please don't upset youself. If Stuart is guilty, he'll pay."

"I told her not to marry him," Mrs. Ricci continued, beginning to cry. "I begged her . . ."

Dr. Ricci threw Laurel an apologetic look and led his sobbing wife away. Laurel signed the guest book, glanced at the cherry wood coffin with its blanket of red roses, and slipped out the door. The crowd, the overwhelming scent of flowers, the sight of Gina Ricci's raw grief next to her husband's quiet devastation, and the knowledge that Monica's law firm was defending Stuart Burgess, a fact she'd carefully omitted from her seemingly boldly honest meeting with the other Six of Hearts, had been too much. Laurel felt light-headed, almost sick. All she wanted was to get home as quickly as possible.

Getting home did not bring the peace she thought it would, though. In the two years since her parents had gone to Florida and she'd moved back into their house, Laurel had relished her privacy. Her apartment in town was tiny, the walls like paper. She could hear neighbors on both sides, and there always seemed to be someone around, watching every time she went to her car. Here she had no near neighbors, she could have pets, and she could make as much noise as she wanted without worrying about disturbing anyone.

But lately she'd felt lonely in spite of the dogs. Tonight she felt desolate. She knew without a doubt Kurt would not be dropping by. Mary would not be calling to discuss any special orders for tomorrow. And even though she hadn't been close to Denise and Crystal for years, she had at least known they wouldn't refuse to speak to her if she phoned. She suddenly felt more alone than she had in her entire life.

Laurel tried to watch a Sunday evening movie that was supposed to be the uplifting story of a woman dying of cancer who finds what life is truly all about in her last month of life. Laurel found it unbearably depressing. She turned off the television and picked up a book. The reviews called the novel "spellbinding." She'd been drudging through it for over a month, never once finding herself anywhere near spellbound.

Finally she tossed down the book, went to the stereo, and slipped in a CD. She lay down on the couch, pulling the afghan over her, and drifted along with the strains of "Moonlight Sonata." After a few moments she could see Faith and Angela dancing. Faith's father thought all dancing was a sin, but Faith wanted desperately to be a dancer. So many Saturday afternoons when Laurel's parents were at the store, they'd come to her house and Angie taught Faith what she'd learned in ballet class that week.

Now, behind closed eyes, Laurel could see them spinning in slow motion to the haunting music. They were both tall and graceful, one with long, glossy black hair, the other with shining copper curls that fanned out behind her as she floated in eternal youth and timeless perfection.

Then Faith looked at her, her azure eyes bright, her smile enigmatic. "Laurel," she said softly. "You can stop all this death because you *know*. You're the only one. You *know*."

Laurel jerked to a sitting position, her eyes darting

around the empty room. What the hell was that? She hadn't been asleep. At least she didn't think so. Was there such a thing as a waking dream?

But more important, what did it mean? Faith and Angie had danced, but Faith had never uttered those words to Laurel. "You can stop all this death because you *know*." Knew what? The truth about how Faith died? "You're the only one." She wasn't the only one. Angie, Monica, Crystal, Denise, and she had all known. And now Kurt and Neil also knew how Faith died. Could the imagined words mean she knew why Angie had been murdered? She thought she did. Retribution. But she didn't know who killed Angie.

The music ebbed on hauntingly, filling the shadowy room. "Laurel, you're losing your mind," she muttered, throwing off the afghan and sitting up. But she couldn't shake the vision. She also couldn't shake the feeling that either Faith, from beyond the grave, or more likely her subconscious, was trying to tell her something.

Laurel turned off the CD and walked down the hall. When she moved into the house after her parents left, she'd taken their bedroom. It was larger and had more closet space. Her old bedroom now served as a guest room, but nothing had been changed since she left it years ago for college. She flipped on the light. The yellow walls needed to be painted—they'd dulled over the years. Laurel remembered Claudia asking why she wanted a yellow bedroom. "Because it looks like sunshine," Laurel had answered. Claudia turned a disdainful back. "Pink is more flattering to the skin." Laurel couldn't have cared less what color looked best with her skin. She wanted a cheerful bedroom.

She went into the room and ran a hand over the white and yellow quilted bedspread. On the wall hung a print of Van Gogh's *Sunflowers,* a photo of her beloved Irish setter Rusty who'd died many years ago, and a poster of Tom Selleck during his *Magnum, P.I.* days. Heavens, what a crush she'd had on him. She laughed aloud at the memory of the sacred time each Thursday when she watched the show religiously and had a fit if her father blundered through the room talking, drowning out any of Tom's precious words. It seemed so long ago.

A cedar chest rested under a window, its top covered with stuffed animals from her childhood. A polar bear, a Siamese cat, a tiger, a dog, and her favorite, a little melon-colored teddy bear she'd named Boo Boo after the character in the Yogi Bear cartoon series. How old had she been when she got Boo Boo? Three? Four? His synthetic fur was worn, but his eyes still gazed at her brightly.

On her dresser sat a battered pink jewelry box holding a few pieces she'd abandoned during her teenage years. Beside it was an old-fashioned alarm clock and an empty navy blue cologne bottle she'd thought elegant. In the corner sat her desk. Usually she did her homework sprawled on the bed, but her mother had insisted both girls have real desks. It bore a goosenecked lamp, a globe, a dictionary and thesaurus, and a blotter with a few scribbles. She touched the blotter, running a finger over badly drawn flowers, cats, and a heart with L. D. + T. S. (Laurel Damron + Tom Selleck). Then she noticed that in the corner was a small but perfect drawing of a baby. She hadn't done it.

She frowned, sitting down at the desk, lightly touching the drawing. Suddenly she remembered the week before Faith died. She'd spent Saturday night with Laurel. They'd listened to tapes, tried different hairstyles and makeup, the usual routine. But Faith had seemed different. She wasn't really having a good time. She was *trying* to have a good time and Laurel sensed it. She'd asked what was wrong until Faith finally snapped at her, then apologized.

They went to bed around midnight. Laurel recalled waking up hours later. Faith sat at the desk, the goosenecked lamp on. "What are you doing?" Laurel had mumbled. "Nothing," Faith answered. "Go back to sleep." Laurel was so sleepy, she'd done exactly as she was told. She hadn't thought of that incident for thirteen years, not until this moment. What was Faith doing? Drawing the baby? Probably. But that wasn't all. She'd been writing. Laurel could see her clearly now. But what had she been writing?

Laurel flipped through every page of the blotter, searched every drawer, even looked under the lamp and the globe. No folded sheets of paper. Faith hadn't been writing something she'd hidden for Laurel to find. But the tiny drawing of the baby showed what was on her mind. So what did she write? A note to Neil? Perhaps a plea for marriage?

From another room the phone rang. There was no extension in her old room and Laurel hurried out, a tingle of relief running through her. It was after eleven. This had to be Kurt.

But it wasn't. Her "Hello" was followed by a slight pause before a male voice said, "Laurel, I'm sorry to disturb you so late. This is Neil Kamrath."

Eleven

1

Laurel's mind went blank for a moment. Was he still angry? Had he called to continue his tirade? But his voice sounded calm, even polite. Finally she managed, "Yes, Neil."

"I wanted to apologize for my behavior this morning."

Laurel swallowed. "It was certainly understandable."

"So was your silence thirteen years ago. You were only seventeen."

"Seventeen, not seven. We were mature enough to do the right thing, but we didn't."

"It's always easy to look back and know what was the right thing to do. At the time it isn't so easy."

Why was he being so nice? Laurel wondered uneasily. Kurt couldn't seem to forgive her and he'd suffered none of the fallout from Faith's death. Neil, on the other hand, had been treated like a leper.

"I do want to assure you, Neil, that if there had been *any* suspicion of you, we would have come forward."

"You would have. And probably Angie. The others—I don't think so. Anyway, apologizing is only part of the reason I called," Neil went on. "You said you were going to tell me about things that are happening now and things that happened a long time ago. I stormed out on you right after you told me about Faith's death. I didn't give you a chance to tell me what's going on now."

So that's why he was being so civil. He wanted information. Should she tell him everything? All along she'd thought he might be the possible murderer of Angie, the person who sent the photos, the one who tried to ram her car. But now she realized her suspicion had been almost a game. She hadn't known Neil well in high school, but she'd been fascinated by the things Faith told her about him—his intelligence, his creativity, even his aloofness. Later she'd been mesmerized by his books, and after she'd talked with him at the hospital, his kindness and obvious pain over the death of his wife and son touched her deeply. This morning, though, he'd genuinely frightened her. He wasn't just a sensitive, hurt soul. He was a man capable of rage. Now he wanted details about present events. Was *he* playing a game, only trying to find out how much she knew, what she suspected?

"Laurel, are you still there?"

"Yes," she said slowly. Even if this were a game, she'd go along with it, she decided. Maybe his reactions to her narrative would reveal something.

She told him everything from the heart and the number and tarot card at the scene of Angie's murder to her harrowing ride back from Wilson Lodge with someone trying to push her off the road to the funeral wreath and the heart painted on her door. "The other day Audra received a Christmas card with a weird verse on it." She quoted it. "And I don't have to tell you what happened at the party."

Neil was silent for a moment. Then he breathed, "Someone is after the Six of Hearts."

"Somebody already got one."

"So you think this is all about retribution for Faith's death?"

"Don't you?" she asked carefully.

Another beat of silence. "Sounds like it. But why after all these years?"

"I don't know. Mary said her father had been going through Faith's papers lately. Maybe she wrote down something about the club and Zeke figured out we were with her when she died. Either Zeke or Mary."

"Maybe," he said slowly.

"You sound doubtful. Even *you* mentioned that Mary lied about the locket."

"Yes. Both of them could want revenge for Faith's death. Who else might want revenge?"

Laurel licked her dry lips. She was getting into dangerous territory. "I . . . I don't know."

"Yes you do," Neil said evenly. "Faith isn't the only one who died that night. You're thinking maybe the father of the baby wants revenge."

"Uh, well . . ."

"Which means you suspect me." Laurel cast frantically in her mind for an inoffensive answer. There was none. "Yes, Neil, I've thought of that."

"That's why Monica was questioning me at the party."

"Yes."

"I'd like to be angry that anyone would suspect me of murder, but it's not the first time. Some people thought I killed Faith."

"Not for long. You had a rock-solid alibi."

"Thank God. But I don't this time. I could have done any of the pranks you talked about. Hell, I could even have killed Angela. I was in Wheeling when she died. New York is no great distance. I could have driven there and back in one night." Laurel couldn't answer. "But I didn't."

Silence spun out while Laurel tried to analyze his tone. Not nervous. Too calm?

"Laurel, I understand why you think the person you're looking for might be the father of Faith's baby. It's a logical assumption. That's why I'm going to tell you something I've never told anyone. I was *not* the father of Faith's child."

Shouldn't she have expected this denial given the direction of the conversation? Wouldn't any man say the same thing to divert suspicion from himself? "Neil, after Faith died and everyone thought she'd committed suicide because you wouldn't marry her, why didn't you ever say it wasn't your baby?"

"Because I didn't know it wasn't mine. I should have

known because she never said a word about being pregnant to me. I had no idea. But when I heard she was, I assumed it was mine."

"I don't understand."

"Four years ago I found out I'm sterile."

"Sterile!" Laurel burst out in spite of herself. "Neil, you had a son with Ellen. What about Robbie?"

"I married Ellen six weeks after she gave birth to Robbie and I adopted him. Her ex-husband didn't want children and divorced her when she got pregnant. She thought he'd come back to her after he saw the baby, but he didn't, so she agreed to marry me and give her baby a father."

"But how did you find out you were sterile?"

"Ellen wanted more children. We tried for two years and nothing happened. We went through a battery of tests. It didn't take long to find out the fault was mine. I had mumps when I was a kid. The doctor said they can cause sterility. That was when my marriage began to fall apart. It was also when I realized I couldn't have been the father of Faith's baby."

Very convenient, Laurel thought cynically. Also very hard to prove. But he sounded so sincere. And if he were lying, why hadn't he done it thirteen years ago? Even now he wasn't denying he'd had sex with Faith. In fact, he said that at the time of her death, he believed he *was* the father of her baby.

"Laurel, I know you probably don't believe me," he said. "I'm not asking you to cross me off your list of suspects. All I'm asking is that you keep an open mind, not so much for my sake as for your own. There's someone out there who *was* the father of Faith's child, someone who could know about the Six of Hearts." He paused. "Someone who could do to you what he did to Angela."

2

A lazy, lovely snow began around seven A.M. Laurel had been awake for around an hour and now sat at the table in the glass-enclosed breakfast nook, sipping coffee and watching April and Alex frolic. Being taller, April looked more graceful than her brother, who tended to lower his head and plow forward like a charging bull.

Laurel smiled. She wished she could get as excited about playing in the snow. Instead, all she had to look forward to was a funeral. At least the snow was light and shouldn't interfere too much with the service at eleven.

She fixed the dogs their Alpo but skipped any breakfast for herself. Just the thought of food nearly choked her. She showered, put on a sedate black suit, black boots, pulled back her hair in a black bow, and left for the store.

"You're not going to work today, are you?" Norma exclaimed when she and Penny found Laurel in the workroom.

"I'll take time off for the service, but I'm really better off keeping busy."

"Well, do it behind the counter," Norma ordered. "You don't want to mess up that nice suit back here."

"Will Mary be in today?" Penny asked.

"I'm not sure. I told her not to come back until she's feeling one hundred percent fine. I doubt if she's there yet."

"I hope they put her father away for a long time for what he did," Penny said.

Laurel looked at her. "As a matter of fact, he was out of jail Saturday afternoon and causing more trouble Saturday night."

Penny's eyes widened. "You're kidding!"

"I wish I were." Laurel sighed. "I get very frustrated with the law sometimes."

"Don't we all," Norma agreed. "I sure hope they find who murdered your friend."

"So do I," Laurel said vehemently.

Later she couldn't concentrate on the funeral mass. She studied the large crowd. She recognized a few celebrity faces from the entertainment world, the governor of West Virginia, and a handsome man who sat with the family. Judson Green, Angie's fiancé. Laurel remembered his picture from the newspaper. It certainly hadn't done him justice. What a great life had been snatched from Angie.

Laurel also saw the blue-haired Lewis sisters, who never missed a local funeral. Near them sat Monica. Denise was seated by Crystal. Laurel caught Denise's eye and smiled. Denise gave her a flat, cold look and turned her head. It doesn't matter, Laurel thought staunchly. I did the right thing.

She followed the entourage to the cemetery. The snow still fell desultorily, as if its heart weren't really in it. Not as many people came to the cemetery as to the church. Once again, Laurel found herself unable to concentrate on the priest's words. Pictures flashed in her mind. Their fourth-grade teacher losing her temper with Angie because she kept making everyone giggle and sending Angie to the blackboard to write "I will be serious" fifty times, and how Angie laughed afterward because the teacher never noticed she'd misspelled "serious" every time. Angie singing "These Dreams" in the talent contest. Angie teaching Faith to dance a *pas de deux* to "Moonlight Sonata."

Dancing in slow motion. Faith looking at Laurel. "You're the only one. You *know*." The intensity of her azure eyes. Laurel shuddered.

"Cold?" a woman whispered.

Laurel nodded, then looked at the woman. It was easy to see she'd once been a beauty. Now in what Laurel guessed to be her late sixties, the woman had skin that was pale and webbed with fine wrinkles. Her blue eyes were slightly dulled, and her white hair was pulled back in a severe French twist. Not every older woman could have looked attractive with the stark hairstyle, but her classic features did not require curls.

Laurel realized with a start the service was over. People gathered around the Riccis. Some formed small groups, others made their way to their cars. No one approached her and she turned away, feeling oddly disoriented, partly ashamed that she hadn't shed a tear, partly relieved that the ordeal was over. She pulled her coat more closely around

her and started in the direction of her car. As she plodded
through the snow, she suddenly realized how close she was
to Faith's grave. She hadn't visited it since the day of
Faith's funeral. Her footsteps slowed. Did she want to go
there, especially today?

She was already walking in that direction before she'd
consciously made up her mind. Big flakes of snow fell on
her face, and caught in her lashes as she climbed the knoll
where Faith rested. She buried gloved hands in her pockets
as her heart beat harder. What did she expect? she asked
herself. Faith to pop up and point an accusing finger at her?

As she neared the grave, Laurel saw a figure bending
over it. She squinted through the snow. It was a woman in
black. A woman with upswept white hair.

"Hello!" Laurel called, recognizing the woman who'd
stood beside her at Angie's gravesite.

The woman looked up, then began to run in the opposite
direction with amazing swiftness. Surprised, Laurel slowed.
What was wrong with the woman? *Who* was the woman?

Laurel picked up speed again, watching the woman disappear over the top of the knoll. She wiped a gloved hand
over her eyes, brushing the snow away. When she reached
Faith's grave, she knelt. The simple gray stone looked little
and bleak, almost lost in the blanket of snow. But against
it, red as blood, rested six carnations tied with a red ribbon
from which dangled a small red plastic heart.

Twelve

1

For the second time in the last week Laurel vowed to get a cell phone for the car as she pulled up at a curb and climbed from the car, sloshing through dirty road snow to reach a public phone. She called the store and told Norma and Penny she would be returning later than she'd expected. Then she headed out of town to the Howard house.

Laurel had only been to Faith's house once although it was not too far from her own. Long ago Zeke insisted on meeting Faith's new best friend. Even then his hair had been bushy and white and he'd looked at everyone accusingly as if they'd committed some horrible deed. Laurel had been scared to death of him, but apparently her sedate appearance and shy manner reassured Zeke. Laurel remembered Neil saying Zeke had only allowed Faith to date him because his parents were part of Zeke's congregation and Zeke had considered him "safe." She guessed Zeke had considered her safe, too.

The house was old, two-story, and covered with peeling white paint. One green shutter hung loose from an upstairs window. For the first time, Laurel thought about the Howards' finances. Zeke used to be a handyman. He was quite skilled, but eventually he lost jobs because he couldn't confine his preaching to his church meetings. Everyone he worked for was treated to a long sermon, and when he wasn't preaching, he was belting out hymns at the top of his voice. Eventually no one would hire him. The Howards now subsisted solely on what Mary earned at Damron

Floral, which wasn't a generous salary. Laurel's father hadn't raised wages for four years, even though the store was doing better than it had in the past decade. As Laurel climbed the rickety front steps, she decided to change that situation, no matter what her father said. Everyone at Damron Floral deserved a raise.

She knocked on the door. In a moment Mary appeared. The bruise above her eye had turned a glorious mixture of purple and green. Her freckles stood out starkly from her parchment-colored skin, and her lips were colorless. Dark circles lay under her eyes. She wore an old blue chenille robe that had seen far too many washings.

"Hello, Laurel," she said dully. "I've been expecting this visit."

"You have?"

"Yes. You've thought it over and come to fire me after what Kurt told you about Papa the other night in the woods. You think he's crazy and he might come back to the store and do more damage."

"Mary, I won't deny I think your father needs psychiatric help, but I certainly didn't come here to fire you." She paused. "I do need to talk with you, though. Privately."

"Oh." Mary seemed taken aback. "Then come in. Papa's asleep."

"Are you sure?"

"Yes. The doctor gave him something strong."

Laurel stepped into a small, dreary room. She remembered the yellow wallpaper with little blue cornflowers. Twenty years ago she'd thought it was rather pretty. Now it was faded and bore water stains near the windows. The rug was worn bare in spots, the wooden tables scratched, the chairs and couch sagging.

"Can I get you some tea or something?" Mary asked as Laurel sat down in an armchair. A spring jabbed her in the right buttock and she tried to shift subtly so as not to insult Mary about the state of the furniture.

"Nothing to drink, thanks. I just need to ask you a few questions."

"You sound like Kurt."

"I'm not the police, Mary. Just your friend."

Mary smiled slightly and sat down on the couch. "All right. Ask away."

"When Kurt was here the other night, did he tell you what had happened at the Price party?"

"Yes."

"Even about the locket on the doll?"

Mary looked away guiltily. "Yes. He made quite a point about the locket."

"Well, last night I talked with Neil Kamrath." Mary tensed. "He called me about the locket. He said you told him years ago the locket had been buried with Faith. Yet there it was on the doll. We both saw it."

Mary drew a deep breath. "I lied to Neil. Faith wasn't buried with the locket. Papa wouldn't let her wear any jewelry, especially something from my mother. She always carried it in her purse, then put it on when she got away from home."

"But she didn't have it on the night she died."

"It disappeared about a week earlier."

"A week."

Mary looked at her earnestly. "Yes, Laurel. It just disappeared. At first Faith thought Papa found it, but he never mentioned it. She was upset when she couldn't find it. It meant so much to Faith."

She looked like she was telling the truth, but if Faith were so upset, why hadn't she mentioned the missing locket to Laurel? She wouldn't keep pushing Mary, though. "All right. Will you talk about your mother with me?"

Mary drew back. "My mother! What does she have to do with anything besides the locket?"

"I'd just like to know more about her."

Mary's fingers twitched on a ragged lace doily on the arm of the couch. "I'm not comfortable talking about her. Papa never let us mention her."

"You're twenty-six, Mary. You may talk about anything you want. Please. I have a really good reason for asking."

"Well . . . she was only a teenager when she got married. She and Papa lived in Pennsylvania then. Her name was Genevra. She had Faith when she was eighteen. Me four years later. When I was two, she ran away. After that, we moved here."

"Why did your father choose Wheeling?"

Mary's foot jiggled. "He lived here when he was a boy. He liked it and knew some people."

"Tell me more about your mother."

"She was lots younger than him. She was very beautiful, like Faith. I found a picture of her a long time ago."

"May I see it?"

"When Papa found out I had it, he burned it."

"Has your mother ever contacted you in all these years?"

"N . . . no."

"Which means yes."

"Well, it was a *long* time ago. I was only five or six."

"Where was she?"

"I don't know."

"Didn't the letter have a return address or a postmark?"

"I don't remember. I told you, I was really young."

"Did she contact Faith?"

"Yes."

"More than once?"

"I don't know." Mary rubbed a hand across her forehead. "That's a lie. They wrote to each other all the time. Faith begged me to write to her, but I wouldn't. Papa said she was a sinner. I always tried to do what Papa wanted me to, but I never told him that Faith wrote to her. I wanted to please both of them."

"How did Faith keep your father from intercepting the letters?"

"Someone here in town rented a post office box for Faith. I don't know who it was."

"Really? When did the communication stop?"

Mary looked at her as if she were stupid. "When Faith died."

"Not until then!" Laurel exclaimed. Mary nodded. "Faith

never told me anything about her mother except that she had run off with another man and she didn't blame her."

"You know how Faith was about men. I guess she *would* understand."

It was the first time Laurel had ever heard Mary sound critical of her sister. Yes, Faith liked boys, maybe too much. But as far as she knew, Mary had never even been on a date. Did she isolate herself from men because her father had spoken so harshly of Genevra all these years? And before his mind began to slip and he'd decided Faith was some kind of angel, he'd probably said the same things about her, or even worse. After all, she was pregnant when she died. Had he convinced Mary that Faith and Genevra were two of a kind? "Mary," Laurel asked softly, "where *was* your mother when Faith died?"

"Why are you asking me all these questions about my mother?" Mary flared. "She doesn't have anything to do with anything! She's probably dead by now."

"Oh, no."

Mary frowned. "What do you mean? How could you possibly know anything about my mother?"

"Because I'm almost certain I saw her at Faith's grave today."

2

"I think we should go home," Denise said. "The snow is getting heavier."

"Oh, Mommy, no!" Audra wailed. "I see the lights every year!"

Denise turned up the windshield wipers a notch. Traffic crawled toward Oglebay Park. She was still furious with Laurel, still shaken by the funeral, and she was catching a cold. The last thing she wanted to do was drag through the park, but she and Wayne had been going out of their way to please Audra after her awful experience less than forty-eight hours ago. She still had to sleep with her light on and wanted Denise to stay with her until she drifted off. Tonight, while Wayne was at the hospital with an emergency, Audra had insisted she wanted to see the Festival of Lights at Oglebay Park as Denise had promised.

"Did you come up here every year when you were a little girl?" Audra asked.

"They didn't have the light show then."

"Gosh," Audra breathed. "There *were* Christmas trees back then, weren't there?"

"Yes, dear," Denise said dryly. "The celebration of Christmas began shortly before my birth."

"That's good."

Denise gave her a sidelong look to see if she were kidding. She wasn't. "Are you cold?"

"Nope."

"I'm freezing. If we wait until tomorrow night, Daddy can come with us."

"He'll prob'ly have another emergency. Besides, we're almost there."

Denise sighed. An hour, she thought. In an hour I'll be back in my nice warm house with my cold pills and my spearmint tea. Maybe there will even be something good on television.

"Was Laurel at the funeral today?" Audra asked abruptly.

"Yes."

"I know she didn't bring April and Alex, but she said I could go over and play with them at her house."

"Yes," Denise said neutrally. At the moment she couldn't imagine paying Laurel a visit under any circumstances.

"Mom, she said I could come over."

"I *know*." Denise felt a headache forming behind her eyes and her neck stiffening. "We'll just have to pick a good day." Which won't be soon, she thought.

Audra leaned forward and turned on the radio. A rap song blasted through the car. Denise winced and turned off the radio. *"Mommy!"* Audra wailed.

"I can't stand that stuff."

"I want to hear music."

Denise pushed in a CD. In a moment the Carpenters were singing Christmas songs.

"Oh, *wow*," Audra grumbled. "That's about a hundred years old."

"Not quite and it's very pretty. Quit complaining." Audra began fumbling with things on the seat. "What are you looking for?"

"My camera." Wayne had bought her a disposable camera for her trip to the light show.

"Audra, you can't get any good pictures with all this snow."

"We always take pictures."

"Not in the snow. You'll just get a blur. For heaven's sake, we have a videotape of the light show."

"It's not the same. *Where* is my camera?"

She began rummaging again. Denise clenched her teeth. This wasn't going to be a good evening. Audra was still in high gear after the Christmas party scare. Denise herself felt terrible. Nevertheless, she'd come this far. She wouldn't turn back for home now. Audra would have a fit.

Who's the parent here? Denise could hear her mother saying. Be quiet, Mom, she answered mentally. You have no idea what I'm going through. It won't kill me to indulge her for a couple of days, especially since I'm the one responsible for her being terrorized.

They passed through Ornament Way, where on either side of the road giant Christmas tree ornaments hung suspended from towering candy canes. Audra was already squealing with delight as Denise stopped at the donation booth.

"I'm gonna take every picture on the roll of film," Audra announced. "How many is that?"

"Twenty-seven. And if you insist on photographing everything, roll down the window before you take a shot. Otherwise all you'll get is splatters of snow on the glass."

"I know," Audra said in the beleaguered tone she'd recently adopted that indicated Denise was always stating the obvious. Denise's teeth clenched. She knew children had to grow up and assert their independence, and that she'd probably used the same tone with her own mother, but Audra was only eight. It was too soon.

"Audra, I want you to *stop* talking to me that way," she snapped.

"What way?"

"You know."

Audra sighed gustily. Maybe I'm being overly sensitive, Denise thought. My nerves are strung tight. I'd better cool it.

"Are you cold?" Denise asked again.

"No, I'm *fine*. But how come you keep rubbing your neck?"

"It's a little stiff." Actually, it was rigid. "Look, honey, there's the Christmas Express."

The display featured a full-sized train that seemed to be moving along.

"It's beautiful!" Audra cried, rolling down the window. Cold air and snowflakes poured into the car as Audra snapped a picture.

"Okay, we're past it. Roll up the window. It's freezing."

Audra closed the window. "Mommy, can we listen to other music?"

"No, I like this." Audra sighed again. "I'm sorry. I just can't stand that stuff you listen to."

"Okay," Audra said in a deflated tone.

"Look, here's the Waving Snowman."

Audra rolled down the window again. More cold air. More snow. Denise sneezed and her nose started to run. Her throat was beginning to hurt. "Audra—"

"I know, I know, roll up the window."

They passed the little girl with the hobby horse, then the animated equestrian.

"That guy with the horse is Buzzy's favorite," Audra informed her.

"Who's Buzzy?"

"Buzzy *Harris*. My boyfriend. I *told* you."

"And I told you that you are too young for a boyfriend."

Denise felt rather than saw Audra roll her eyes again. "He hasn't been kissing you, has he?"

"Mommy!"

"You told me he tried to kiss you. I will not have some little boy slobbering all over you—"

"He doesn't kiss me and he doesn't slobber. What's wrong with you, Mommy? How come you're being so mean tonight?"

"I'm not mean. I just don't feel well—"

"Look, here's Cinderella!"

Denise glanced at the glittering lights forming the huge, turreted castle, the horses leading Cinderella's magnificent carriage, the big orange pumpkin looming ahead, a reminder of passing time.

"This is my favorite display!" Audra gushed.

"Take a picture."

"Pull over so I can get a good one."

"I'll block traffic."

"Not if you pull over far enough. Mommy, *please*."

Denise felt as if someone were pounding on her head with a hammer. The tension of the last few days had been unbearable. The beautiful house of cards she'd built for herself over the last thirteen years was about to come tumbling down, and she had so much to lose. Wayne. Her precious Audra.

The little girl opened the door and stepped out into the show. "Audra, get back in the car!"

"I wanna get closer to the lights."

Denise's frustration and fear ignited. "Audra Price, I said get back in the car this instant!" she screeched in a voice she hardly recognized as her own. The child looked at her in shock. "You heard me!" Denise ranted, appalled at her own tone but unable to stop herself. "Audra, right *now* or I swear I'll—"

Audra's face crumpled and she bolted away from the car, her small booted feet throwing up a skim of snow in front of her.

"Oh, God, what have I done?" Denise moaned as she

opened her door and circled the car, following the silhouette of the fleeing girl. "Audra?" she called. Because of her cold, her voice emerged raw, almost threatening. No one would be reassured by that rough sound, Denise thought, but she couldn't do anything about it. "Audra!" she shrieked again. Dammit. Why had she kept carping at the child? Why was her voice so awful? Why had she even come out here tonight?

The displays were so large they had to be set far back from the road. Denise caught a glimpse of Audra in the glow of the yellow, green, and red carriage lights, then she was gone. The snow abruptly picked up speed, peppering Denise's face, covering her glasses. She stopped, took them off and wiped them dry on a tissue in her pocket, but a moment after she put them on again, snow speckled them. She took them off and stuck them in her pocket. Her extreme nearsightedness turned everything into a blur. Blind with the glasses, blind without them, she thought in disgust. Why was she one of the few people in the world who couldn't wear contacts?

"Audra!" Nothing. She plowed ahead. "Audra, I'm *so* sorry. Please forgive me." Denise began to cry. She stumbled and almost fell. She turned and looked back at the road. A steady stream of headlights drifted along, their glow diffused by the snow and her weak sight. Still, she could make out her own headlights, stationary beside the road. Looking the other way, she saw multicolored lights of the Cinderella display looming over her. She'd always known the displays were tall, but actually standing beside one was almost frightening. The red turrets of the castle looked gigantic. She suddenly felt small and helpless.

She trudged on through the snow, following a trail of footprints. "Audra!" she shouted. "Audra, don't do this!"

Her curly hair twisted into a hundred corkscrews. I probably look like Medusa, she thought. Tears and snow froze on her eyelashes. Her teeth chattered. The trail circled the display and she rushed ahead. She hadn't worn boots. Her shoes were filled with snow and she couldn't feel her feet anymore. "Audra! *Please* come back!" Her voice cracked but she kept trying. "Audra, I'm sorry."

She stood behind the display now, glancing over her shoulder. What looked beautiful from the road now took on a surreal quality. Blinding lights hulking over her from behind. Utter darkness ahead. She knew she was invisible from the road.

A footstep crunched in the snow. She whirled, at first seeing nothing. "Audra!" she cried, brushing frantically at her eyes. "Aud—"

The first blow caught her along the collar. She heard bone cracking and staggered but somehow kept her footing. "My God!" she gasped, clawing at her injury, not sure what was really happening. Then she felt the warm blood seeping below her sweater.

Denise turned and tried to run. A second blow to the back of the head brought her to her knees. She began crawling, her fingers digging for solid earth and finding only lacy snow. "No," she quavered. "No, please—"

Another blow to the neck. She went facedown in the snow. "Audra," she mumbled, blood pouring from her mouth onto the pristine, fluffy white. "Run, baby. Run away . . ."

Her body was numb but she could still feel the cold wetness under her cheek, the blood running into her eyes, blinding her. She lay shuddering, her last vision that of a beautiful little girl with long, curly brown hair and huge eyes the color of dark chocolate laughing up at her. "Audra, I love you," she whispered as the last blow crushed her skull.

Thirteen

1

Laurel was dreaming of Faith. They were little girls with flowers in their hair, but instead of daisies, Faith wore a crown of red carnations. She danced to "Moonlight Sonata" slowly, gracefully. When she finished, she looked at Laurel and said, "You're the only one. You *know*."

Ringing. She moaned as Faith drifted away, still saying "You *know*." "I know *what*?" Laurel cried. Ringing. Weight on her body. Something warm on her face. She opened her eyes. April sat atop her, licking her cheeks, and the phone rang insistently.

"I'm awake, April," she muttered, struggling under the dog's weight. "Move over, puppy."

April sat solidly on her abdomen, clearly frightened by all the muttering and thrashing Laurel had done earlier. She stretched her arm as far as she could, reached the receiver, and finally got it to her face. "Hello."

"Laurel. Kurt."

"Kurt." Laurel looked at the clock. Twelve-thirty. "What's wrong?"

"There's no easy way to tell you this." He drew a deep breath. "Denise Price is dead. She's been murdered."

Laurel felt as if every drop of blood in her body gushed to her lower extremities. Her head swam, her vision darkened. Her mouth opened but nothing came out.

"Laurel, are you there?"

"Yes." Her voice was little more than a whisper. "How?"

"She took Audra to Oglebay to see the lights. For some

reason the kid got out of the car—we don't know why because she's barely speaking. Apparently Denise went after her. She was beaten to death behind one of the displays."

"Beaten? Like Angie?"

"Yes."

"Oh, God, Audra didn't see Denise being murdered, did she?"

"We don't know. She's in the hospital in shock. We do know she saw the body and it was bad. There's not much left of Denise's face."

"Oh, no," Laurel moaned, feeling as if someone were plunging a knife into her stomach. What a horrible image for anyone to see, but Denise's own daughter . . . Laurel fought to catch her breath. "Kurt, was there anything on or around the body?"

He paused. "I shouldn't be telling you this, but yes. There was one of those magic cards you told me about."

"Tarot cards. It was the judgment card, wasn't it?"

"I wouldn't know one card from the other. But there was also a heart and a six."

"Where?"

"She had on a light gray coat. They were drawn on the back in blood."

"Kurt—"

"I have to go now. I thought you'd want to know." His voice grew harsh. "Maybe this could have been prevented if—" She heard him draw a ragged breath. "Oh, to hell with it. Good-bye, Laurel."

She held on to the receiver after Kurt hung up. She felt paralyzed. Saturday night Denise had been throwing a Christmas party in her beautiful home. Two nights later she was dead. Not just dead, *murdered*. Bludgeoned like Angie. And Audra had seen her.

The dogs began to bark. Laurel tensed. What did they hear? An intruder? Had someone come here to kill her the way they had killed Denise?

Someone knocked on the door. Laurel still clutched the receiver, huddling in her bed. Someone knocked louder.

Well, good heavens, she thought, a killer wouldn't bother to knock. Or would he if he were a friend . . .

Pounding again, then someone yelled, "Laurel, it's Monica! Open the damned door!"

There was no mistaking *that* strong, husky voice. Laurel slowly felt life coming back into her. She finally put down the receiver and threw her leg over the side of the bed, grabbing for her heavy terry-cloth robe. In a moment she opened the front door. Monica stood tall and serious in tight jeans, boots, and a leather jacket. "Will those dogs bite?" she asked abruptly.

Laurel looked at April and Alex, who had backed off and were staring warily at Monica. "Not unless you make any sudden moves," Laurel said dryly, already knowing April and Alex were not going to warm up to Monica.

Monica strode into the room. "Denise is dead."

"I know. Kurt just called me. How did *you* know?"

"I'm staying in Oglebay Park. Police are everywhere. It's pandemonium out there. It didn't take me long to find out what happened."

No, it wouldn't, Laurel thought. The police could warn her away from the scene until they were blue in the face, but it wouldn't stop Monica. Sometimes Laurel thought nothing could stop the force that was Monica Boyd. "Kurt said the tarot card was beside her body, and a six and a heart drawn on the back of her coat in blood."

"I figured so."

"Oh, my God, what about Crystal?" Laurel exclaimed suddenly. "We have to find out if she's all right!"

Laurel started for the phone but Monica held up a hand. "I already called. She's safe at home having hysterics."

"Maybe she should be here with us."

"She's in no condition to drive and I'm in no condition to listen to her weep and wail."

"You *must* be shaken if you're here. Yesterday and this morning you wouldn't speak to me."

Monica ignored her. "Do you have any scotch?"

"No, just beer."

"Well, any port in a storm."

Laurel got her a can and a glass. Like Kurt, Monica didn't bother with the glass. She took a long drink, then winced. "God, why don't you get something decent?"

"Because I don't drink."

"You should. Liquor makes long, lonely nights bearable." Monica sat down on the couch, crossing one ankle over a knee and staring into the empty fireplace. "I guess I didn't help much by coming to Wheeling."

"We should have gone to the police."

"You *did* go to the police. What good did it do?"

"I told Kurt night before last. There wasn't enough time for them to do much."

"And you blame me."

"No, I blame *me*. I'm a grown woman. I should have done what I thought was best from the beginning."

"Oh, stop trying to be noble, Laurel. It's annoying. The truth is you do blame me, just like you did thirteen years ago when I talked you into keeping your mouth shut about how Faith died."

Laurel's temper rose along with her voice. "Yes. I wanted to blame you then. I want to blame you now because it's so easy to blame someone else. But I'm not being noble. *I* should have done something. *That* is the truth and if you find it annoying that I don't think you're omnipotent, responsible for my, Crystal's, and Denise's actions, that's too damn bad. We all acted foolishly." Monica stared straight ahead, unresponsive. "But there is one thing I *do* hold you responsible for," Laurel went on. "Why didn't you tell us your firm is defending Angie's ex-husband?"

"Look, Laurel, I don't decide what cases the firm handles."

"That's not what I asked."

"Okay. I didn't tell you because I thought you'd jump to conclusions."

"What kind of conclusions? That pinning the murder of Angie on someone else would ensure Stuart Burgess is acquitted? That would be quite a coup for your firm."

"Well, we know Stuart didn't kill Denise."

"Do we? He's out on bail."

"And being watched."

"Oh, come on, Monica. You've pointed out a couple of times how close New York is to Wheeling. Are you going to tell me Burgess, with all his resources, couldn't possibly come here and make it back to New York undetected?"

"Maybe, but why would he?"

"Because he knew about Faith and the Six of Hearts and he wanted it to look like Angie was killed by someone seeking revenge."

"Nonsense."

"Is it?"

Monica drained her beer. "Could I have some more of this nectar of the gods?"

"It's in the refrigerator," Laurel said coldly, her mind racing. As Monica left the room, she thought of a terrible scenario. What if Monica were making it look as if someone seeking revenge for Faith's death had killed Angie? Wouldn't the death of Denise convince police that this was the motive? After all, Stuart Burgess didn't even know Denise. And what about the heart and the six and the tarot card at the scene of Angie's murder? After murdering her, could Stuart have called someone, had them tamper with the scene, plant evidence that would connect that crime with another, maybe one planned for the future? Who could have come up with such a scheme? Someone clever, ambitious, cold? Monica had been in New York when Angie was murdered. She'd been in Oglebay Park when Denise was murdered.

When Monica came back in the room and settled on the couch, Laurel tried to act natural although she felt as if every nerve in her body was thrumming. "Monica, when you came to Wheeling and told us the details of Angie's murder, did you think any of us would go to the police?"

"No." She gulped beer. "Well, maybe you. You were the one who fought hardest to tell the truth thirteen years ago."

"Then why did you tell me? Why did you tell any of us and risk someone going to the police?"

Monica jiggled her foot. "Laurel, I'm not completely hard-hearted. I couldn't leave the three of you in ignorance, sitting ducks just waiting for the killer."

"I see."

"It's true. What are you implying was my real motive?"

"I don't feel like explaining myself right now."

"And I don't feel like listening to any more of these veiled accusations. I've had a lot of scotch and this beer isn't sitting too well on top of it." Monica stood. "I'm going."

"I want to ask you one question."

"All right. One."

"Will you have anything to do with Stuart Burgess's defense?"

Monica tucked her long hair behind her ears. "No." She looked closely at Laurel. "What are you smiling about?"

"About how cocksure you are." Laurel shook her head. "You've never realized, have you, that I *always* know when you're lying."

"Is that so?"

"Yes. You're lying now. You *will* have something to gain if Stuart Burgess is found innocent."

"Certainly, Laurel. When the firm wins, so does everyone who works there."

"Oh, Monica, please! I believe your interests are a little less altruistic. I think you have a whole lot to gain from Burgess's acquittal."

Monica's eyes narrowed. "You might be going down a dangerous road with all your speculations. I've never known you to be so confrontational."

"For thirteen years I've lived in shame and fear. I don't think I realized until recently just how reclusive I've become. I haven't had close female friendships, and the one man I was truly serious about I sent away because I couldn't bring myself to tell him the truth about Faith. I'm not going to live that way anymore, Monica. Maybe I am being confrontational. Maybe I'm even being foolhardy voicing all my doubts, but I'm tired of trudging around with a load of guilt on my shoulders. I'm sick of sitting here being quiet and watching my own back, guarding my own reputation. I'm going to do everything I can to find out who killed Angie and Denise, and to protect Crystal and myself. *Everything.*"

The corner of Monica's lip lifted in a half-grin. "You're not worried about protecting me?"

"If there's one thing you've always excelled at, it's protecting yourself."

Monica looked at her oddly for a moment, then laughed. "You're right, Laurel. I don't need anyone. I never have."

As she walked toward her car, Laurel could hear her still laughing.

2

Laurel sat up the rest of the night, listening to music, pacing, trying to cry in order to release some of her pent-up emotion, but the horror was too new. She kept seeing Denise in her plaid hostess skirt smiling as she stood behind Wayne playing "Great Balls of Fire." Her gray eyes had warmed with pride as she looked at her husband. Those eyes would never warm again, not with pride, not with love, not with the simple joy of being alive.

Laurel knew if her mother were here, she would already be whipping up the traditional tuna casserole and Jell-O mold to take to the Prices' tomorrow. Laurel hated both dishes. Besides, God knew how many of those delicacies the Prices would receive. She'd pick up a nice tray at a deli, although she doubted if Wayne and Audra would have much appetite. The food at homes of the bereaved were mostly for guests.

And what about her own Christmas plans? Day after to-morrow she was supposed to close the store and fly to Flor-ida. The fact that she hadn't wanted to go anyway had nothing to do with her decision. She picked up the phone at seven o'clock and called her mother.

"This is a surprise hearing from you so early in the morn-ing," Meg Damron said. "How was Angie's funeral?"

"Sad, like all funerals, but quite the affair. The governor was there and a few celebrities." She took a deep breath and said hurriedly, "Look, Mom, I'm not going to be able to come down for Christmas."

"What!" her mother burst out. *Why?*

"Because . . . well, there's been another death. Denise Price. She used to be Denise Gilbert."

"Denise! Of course I remember Denise. What hap-pened?"

"She was . . . murdered last night."

"Murdered?" her mother repeated slowly. "Where? How?"

"At the Oglebay light show. She was beaten to death."

Laurel could almost feel her mother struggling with the concept. At last she said, "At Oglebay? That's unthinkable! Nothing like that has *ever* happened there. Beaten to death?"

"Yes. Behind one of the big displays."

"Oh, my God! *Beaten* to death! Just like Angie. You, Denise, and Angie—you were all friends. Is there a con-nection?"

"I don't know," Laurel hedged. "I don't think Angie and Denise have even seen each other for years."

"But the coincidence . . ." Her mother's voice trailed away, then came back full force. "I want you to close the store and the house and come down here today!"

"I can't, Mom."

"You can and you will!"

"Mom, Denise left a little girl. She's only eight and she saw the body—"

"And I assume she has a father and other family to look after her. You *aren't* staying."

"I *am*."

"Laurel, for heaven's sake, why are you being so stubborn? You know your father and I can't come back. Claudia needs us—"

"I know she does. I want you to stay in Florida with her. But my place is here."

"Why?"

"I don't want to argue and I can't go into all the details, but I won't be coming for Christmas."

"Do you know how worried I'm going to be about you?"

"Don't worry."

"That's easy to say. As if Hal and I don't have enough on our minds with Claudia and all the squabbling she's been doing with your father. I don't know what's come over her. I also don't know when the baby is coming." Her mother sounded as if she were going to cry. "Laurel, I think you're being incredibly inconsiderate."

"I'm sorry you feel that way but I'm doing what I need to do. I'll be fine, I promise."

When she hung up, Laurel murmured, "I only hope that's a promise I can keep."

3

Laurel called Norma. "Do you still have the spare key to the back door of the store?"

"Certainly. You don't think I'd lose a store key, do you?"

"No. I don't know why I even asked. I don't suppose you've heard about Denise Price, have you?"

"No. Who is she?"

"She is . . . was a friend of mine. She was murdered last night."

"What?" Norma squawked. "Murdered!"

"Yes. I don't want to go into details right now, but could you and Penny handle the store for me this morning? I was up all night and I just don't think I can make it."

"Of course you can't! Oh, Laurel, I'm so sorry. First Angela Ricci and now this lady. Lord, Lord, what is this world coming to?"

"I don't know, Norma, I really don't know."

"Well, you stay home and get some rest. Penny and I can handle everything *all* day."

"I can't thank you enough. I can tell you that after the first of the year I intend to give everyone raises."

"Oh, honey, that's not necessary," Norma said, but she sounded pleased. "You take care of yourself today and don't worry about one thing at the store."

Laurel wouldn't have to force herself not to think of the store. At the moment the running of Damron Floral seemed like one of the least important things in her life. Her main concern was trying to prevent more murders.

"And how do you intend to do that, Wonder Woman?" she asked herself sarcastically. The idea that she—shy, quiet, troubled Laurel Damron who had run home from college to hide behind the counter of her father's floral business—could root out and expose a killer seemed ludicrous, the stuff of young teenage dreams. But what was her alternative? To flee to Florida? To slink around in fear until the murderer got her or Crystal?

No. It was time to emerge from her carefully constructed shell and face not only the past but the future. She could no longer live with the feeling that people had died because of what she should have done, what she *could* have done if she'd only had the nerve.

An hour later she was dressed in jeans and a heavy sweater. As she pulled on a jacket, she decided to take the dogs with her. Leashes attached, they trundled through the snow to the car.

Laurel didn't know why she had an overwhelming desire to see the Pritchard barn. She'd gone by it several times since the night Faith died, each time wondering why the owners left it standing. The fire that night would have completely destroyed it if the sleet hadn't been so heavy and the wood already damp from all the snow. The family who owned the farm let the wreckage stand, although each year took its toll on the structure. Five years ago the family moved away. They'd never had any luck with the place, nor had anyone else who'd owned the farm since the early Pritchards. Each year everything from unusually heavy spring rains to midsummer heat waves and droughts to hordes of destructive insects ruined the crops. Laurel didn't believe it would ever be used as a farm again. A few years from now it would probably be the site of a shopping mall.

As she drove down the rutted road she and the other Six of Hearts had traveled that awful night thirteen years ago, she remembered the tales she'd heard about the Pritchard farm all her life. Supposedly right before she was hanged, as she stood with the noose around her neck with the preacher entreating her to repent, Esmé Dubois cursed not only the people who'd found her guilty of witchcraft, but the land and everyone who set foot upon it. Strangely enough, during the nearly three hundred years following Esmé's death, the inhabitants of the farm had suffered an unusually large number of deaths and accidents. In the mid-1800's there had even been a murder when the owner found a field hand making love to his daughter. He'd stabbed the field hand to death with a pitchfork. The girl, it was whispered at the time, had a miscarriage and ran away, never to be heard from again. The owner spent the next twenty years in prison while his wife and three young sons lost the farm and ended up destitute. In the 1930's the four-year-old son of a farmer riding the tractor with his father fell backward, landing under the set of razor-sharp disks. In the sixties a man had caught his coat sleeve in a corn husker and been pulled into the machine. Hours later his young wife found the shredded remains of his body and nearly lost her mind with grief.

A place of death, that was the Pritchard farm. The darkness started with the deaths of the Pritchard children blamed on Esmé Dubois and ended . . . She thought of Faith, but the darkness didn't end with Faith's death. The darkness still lingered over everyone who came in contact with the farm, especially the barn. It certainly still lingered over the Six of Hearts, who'd sneaked out here when they were heedless teenagers and dabbled in the occult.

Laurel had never really believed in the power of the occult, not when she was young and they were playing Monica's games, not even now. Still, the history of the Pritchard farm could have a powerful effect on a more impressionable mind than hers, maybe so powerful it would lure someone into making it look as if Faith were reaching beyond the grave, using a living agent to avenge her death.

She pulled as near to the barn as possible and coaxed the dogs from the car. She held their leashes, even though she knew it wasn't necessary. In strange territory, the dogs would stay as close to her as possible.

She crunched through the snow, looking at the landscape. Snow dusted the trees, every limb covered with white, looking lacy against a low pewter sky. A few evergreens drooped beneath the weight of the snow, and in the distance Canadian geese floated peacefully on a big pond as if the weather were a pleasant seventy degrees.

The remains of the old barn loomed ahead, snow piled on its peaked roof, the rough, unpainted boards of its walls dismal and neglected. She could barely see the farmhouse in the distance, but she felt as if she were being watched from it. That was quite possible. Abandoned so long, it had surely become a haven for vagrants. She didn't worry about them in the barn—no one would choose to live in that half-destroyed building with its dirt floor when they could stay in the house, even if the house had no heat or running water and most of the windows were broken. A slight mist hung over the farm, making the air heavy, threatening more snow by afternoon. A sharp wind blew up, tossing her curly hair to one side and making her shiver. She could never remember seeing a more desolate place than the Pritchard farm. It seemed unreal, like something out of a frightening fantasy.

Laurel stopped in her tracks. What was she doing out here? What had drawn her to this place? The unlikely notion that because the trouble had started here, the solution lay here, too? Had her resolution in the long, shadowy hours of night to find the murderer eclipsed her good judgment, her sense of reality? Maybe it wasn't even safe to be out here alone. She reached in her pocket and felt the canister of Mace. It wasn't very reassuring. She'd never considered buying a gun and two weeks ago would have said the idea was ridiculous. Now it didn't seem ridiculous at all. With a murderer on the loose, it certainly made more sense than exploring with Mace and two timid dogs.

April and Alex seemed to read her thoughts and agree. She had to pull on the leashes to get the dogs into the barn, where they pressed against her legs for reassurance.

Laurel looked around. Near the front of the barn only a few hand-hewn supporting posts, charred and gray, stood alone. She walked farther into the barn, pulling the dogs along. Stalls where long-dead animals had once spent their nights still stood, filthy and stripped of even the smell of cows and horses. Snow feathered through holes in the roof. An ancient pitchfork leaned against a wall. Was it the one the farmer had used to kill the field hand so long ago? Laurel wondered. Had the young couple been found here, in this barn? Near the pitchfork lay a moldering blanket. From behind it she saw a rat watching her closely. God, how many more of them were in here? Maybe hundreds.

She was turning to go when something caught her eye. A bale of straw sat in the middle of the floor. Faith had stood on one just like it. Instinctively Laurel looked up, then gasped.

A hangman's noose dangled from a tie beam—a noose fashioned from new rope.

Suddenly the dogs began barking uproariously. Several pigeons flapped noisily up from the loft, flying crazily under the roof, looking for escape holes. The rat and two of its friends skittered across the floor, heading straight for Laurel. She let out a strangled cry and whirled.

Ten feet behind her stood Neil Kamrath.

Fourteen

"Neil!" Laurel managed in a tone at least an octave higher than normal. "What are you doing here?"

"I might ask you the same question." He walked toward her and, to her surprise, both dogs stood firm. Alex actually growled. "Am I about to be attacked?"

"I'm not sure." Laurel was certain he was in no danger, but it was best not to say so. "I just felt an urge to look at this place. I don't know why."

"Me, too." Neil wore jeans and a suede jacket. He calmly lit a cigarette while her heart trip-hammered. Had he followed her here? There was no one to help her if he meant to do her harm. She tried to casually put her hand in her pocket for the canister of Mace. Dammit. The lid wasn't even off. She could be dead before she got it out of her pocket, uncapped it, and pointed in the direction of his eyes.

She looked around. "There were rats running right toward us."

"They're hiding now. This place must be filled with them. Rats *will* attack, but not unless they're cornered." He looked up at the noose. "I suppose you saw this." Laurel was having trouble getting her breath. "What do you make of it?"

"I don't know. The rope is new."

"It's a threat, Laurel."

She looked at him steadily. "To whom? Who could know I'd come out here?"

"Maybe it wasn't directed at you. Maybe it was meant for Crystal or Monica."

"Crystal is too frightened to come here. I don't think Monica is haunted by this place. She wouldn't come." He took a puff of his cigarette and she said, "You followed me here, didn't you?"

"Yes." He looked neither embarrassed nor menacing. "I had a feeling you might come here after Denise's murder."

"How did you hear about that? It happened too late to make the morning newspaper."

"I heard at the diner where I had breakfast. I don't have all the details, but I do know she was killed like Angie. Beaten to death."

Laurel nodded. "A horrible way to die."

"Are there any good ways?"

He seemed so calm, talking softly, smoking nonchalantly. Dangerous or not, suddenly she was wildly irritated with him. "Why did you follow me?" she blurted. "So you could see my reaction to the rope?"

He looked genuinely surprised. "You think *I* put that up there?" Laurel was silent. "God, I believed you were one of the few people in town who don't think I'm a wacko, but I see I was wrong."

Oh, no, Laurel thought. The last thing she needed to do was make him angry. "I don't think you're a wacko—"

"Don't explain. If I were in your place, I'd be scared, too." He dropped the cigarette and ground it out with his shoe. "I didn't mean to frighten you, Laurel. In fact, I followed you out here because it's not safe for you to be in this secluded place by yourself considering all that's going on. Now that I've seen the noose, I know I was right to come. Whoever killed Angie and Denise has been out here."

Laurel swallowed. "So you came here to protect me?"

He smiled. "I'm not the scrawny, helpless kid you knew in school. I'm no superhero, but I'm a great shot and I'm pretty good at boxing and karate." He paused. "Does Kurt know you're out here?"

She hesitated. Should she lie and say yes? She still didn't

know how safe she was around Neil. Her hesitation answered his question, though. "He doesn't."

The edges of Laurel's teeth touched together. What did
that mean? That Neil felt free to do whatever he wanted,
knowing she might not be found for days?

"I think we'd better get out of here," he said as if reading
her mind. "This place gives me the creeps and that noose
tells me it's definitely not a place we should be."

"Yes." Laurel heard the relief in her voice. She was sure
he heard it, too. "I should go home."

"Laurel, I really need to talk to you." She glanced at him
warily. "Would you consider meeting me at McDonald's
for a cup of coffee?"

Well, there was certainly nothing threatening about that
suggestion. But still . . . "I have the dogs with me. They
panic when I leave them alone in the car."

Neil glanced at them. "I'm sure you don't want to invite
me home for coffee. I don't blame you. We'll get coffee at
the drive-thru window, then I'll join you in your car in the
parking lot where you're in view of dozens of people.
Okay?"

What did he want to talk about? Denise's death? Faith?
Curiosity overrode her desire to get away from him.
"Okay."

"Good. I'll walk you to your car. I'm parked right behind
you."

Quite a bit of deserted land to cover with a man she was
afraid had murdered Denise last night. But what choice did
she have? As they crossed the stubbly field leading to the
road, Laurel couldn't shake the feeling that someone in the
house watched them. After a moment she asked, "Did you
see anyone around the farmhouse when you drove up?"

The wind blew his sandy hair across his forehead, making him look younger. When he was in school, his parents
made him cut it so short she never realized it had natural
wave. "I didn't see anyone, but I have the feeling someone
is in there. I've heard some of what my grandfather would
call hobos take refuge in the house during winter."

"Yes," Laurel said vaguely.

"But that's not what you're worried about, is it? You're afraid the person who put up that noose is in the house." Laurel nodded. "Do you want to go check it out?"

"No!" Wait, she thought. What happened to her determination to find the killer? That determination didn't include going into a deserted house with one of her suspects, she thought. "I'm cold and God knows what we'll find in there. It could be the person who put up the noose, or it could be several vagrants who'd gang up on us."

Neil grinned. "You're not a liberal who believes the homeless are just hapless victims of the system who don't mean anyone any harm?"

"I'm sure many of them are. I'm also sure some would slit your throat for a dollar. I don't like to think in generalizations."

"Very wise, Laurel. Generalizations can get you in trouble. So can thinking you can solve all problems by yourself, no matter how serious they are."

Laurel looked at him sharply. "Are you referring to anything in particular?"

"A couple of things." He pointed. "There are the cars. Meet you in ten minutes."

April and Alex were grateful to climb onto their warm blanket in the back seat. Alex, with his short hair, was shivering.

Neil had already maneuvered a turn and was heading away from the farm by the time Laurel got behind the wheel. Was she making a mistake by meeting him? she wondered. No. They would be in a public parking lot and she might learn something important from him.

When she reached McDonald's, she ordered coffee for herself and Chicken McNuggets for the dogs. She pulled into a space. While she poured creamer into the hot coffee, Neil tapped on her window. She motioned for him to get in.

"McNugget fans?" he asked as Laurel fed bits of the chicken to the dogs.

"Fans of just about everything. I try to watch their diet carefully, but every once in a while they need a treat."

"What are their names?"

"The long-haired one is April. The other is her brother, Alex."

"She's beautiful. He's cute. He's also got a powerful set of jaws."

"I know. Dr. Ricci thinks there must be some pit bull in his background. It's always hard to tell with mixed breeds, especially when there are different fathers involved, as in this case."

"My son Robbie had a dog. A mixed breed. Apollo. Robbie was crazy about him."

"Do you still have him?"

Neil took a quick drink of his coffee and stared straight ahead. "No. He was killed in the car wreck. When Robbie was lingering, so burned, in such pain, he kept asking about Apollo." A wry, bitter smile twisted his lips. "He asked more about Apollo than his mother. I told him the dog was fine. I lied to my son on his deathbed."

"It was the right thing to do," Laurel said softly.

"Maybe the only right thing I did for a long time." His face hardened. "Ellen and I were separated at the time of the wreck. If we hadn't been and I'd been driving . . ."

"There could still have been an accident."

"She was an alcoholic, Laurel. That's why we separated. I wouldn't put up with her drinking anymore."

"So you left her?"

"No. She kicked me out because I kept nagging her to get into rehab. I should have taken Robbie with me when I went. Instead I left him in her hands and look what happened. She was driving drunk. At least she died instantly. As usual, everything was easy for her. But poor Robbie . . ." His voice thickened and Laurel sensed not only his great sorrow but his anger. He sounded as if he hated Ellen. She probably would too if their positions were reversed.

"Neil . . ."

"I'm sorry," he said curtly. "I didn't ask you to meet me

so I could pour out my troubles." She sensed the Herculean effort he was putting forth to pull himself together. "I wanted to talk to you about Angie's and Denise's murders."

"All right, but answer one thing for me first. How did you know I might go to the Pritchard farm this morning?"

"You're still uneasy about my following you, aren't you?"

She looked directly into his eyes. "Wouldn't you be uneasy if someone were following you?"

"Yes. But let me explain. I haven't been following you until today. It's just that you're the only one I can talk to about all this—Faith, the unborn baby, the whole thing. You told me about the weird stuff found at Angie's murder scene pertaining to the Six of Hearts. When I heard about Denise's murder this morning, I came to your house to talk to you. Then I was worried I might frighten you, turning up at your door so early when you don't know me well and you live alone. I pulled off the road and was thinking about just waiting and catching you at work when you pulled out of your driveway and headed in the opposite direction from the store. I had this strange feeling you were going to the farm, and I knew you shouldn't be out there alone. After I saw that noose in the barn, I knew I'd done the right thing by not letting you go out there alone."

The explanation sounded plausible. His voice sounded sincere. The expression in his eyes was earnest. Laurel decided to believe him.

"All right, Neil. I understand. But I'm sure I don't know much more about Denise's murder than you do."

"Was there a six and a heart and a tarot card?"

"Yes. That much I do know."

"Damn. Not much doubt about a connection, then, is there?"

"I'm afraid not."

He stared ahead, quiet for a moment. "Did you talk to Mary about the locket?"

"Yes. She admitted that she lied to you. She said her father wouldn't let Faith wear it. She always put it on *after* she left the house. He would never have allowed her to be buried with it, even if it hadn't disappeared a week before she died."

"Disappeared?" he repeated skeptically. "That's convenient."

"I know. Faith never said anything to me about losing her locket."

Neil reached for two McNuggets and gave one to each of the dogs. April took hers delicately. Alex nearly relieved Neil of a forefinger and thumb. Laurel was surprised when he laughed. It was a deep, heartfelt laugh that chased the sadness from his eyes. "You don't fool around, do you, Alex?"

"He's never certain where the next meal is coming from."

"I'm sure that's a valid worry. They look neglected." Neil took a drink of his coffee. "Did you learn anything else from Mary?"

"Well, yes, something really interesting. She said Faith communicated with her mother by letters until the time of her death. Zeke wouldn't allow communication, so someone rented a post office box for Faith."

"The Lewis sisters."

Laurel gaped. "The *Lewis* sisters!"

He nodded. "Didn't you know they're Genevra's aunts?"

"Genevra's *aunts*. Faith never said a word to me about that."

"She didn't mean to tell me. She was drunk on wine at the time."

"Drunk!"

He looked at her and smiled. "You thought the night she died was the first time she'd had alcohol, right? Wrong. We were the typical repressed teens, Laurel. We drank, we smoked, we had sex. We probably would have done drugs if we could have afforded them. But she wouldn't have wanted you to know all that. Your opinion was too important to her."

"Why didn't she ever tell me about the Lewis sisters?"

"Zeke didn't want her having anything to do with them. She tried to keep the relationship a secret and so did they, to protect her."

"But she never even said anything about writing to her mother!"

"She was scared to death someone would tell Zeke."

"Me? She thought *I* would tell Zeke? That's crazy."

Neil shrugged. "Laurel, you were her best friend, I was her boyfriend and wildly in love with her, but I wonder how well either of us really knew Faith. She lived in a world of secrets. I don't suppose you have any idea who the father of that baby could have been."

"I've wracked my brain, Neil." She didn't tell him she still wasn't sure he was telling the truth about being sterile. "Faith and I talked about boys all the time—you know how teenage girls are—but she *never* mentioned an involvement, or even a crush on another boy."

Neil looked into his cup. "I've wondered if . . . well, Zeke is such a nut and Faith was so beautiful . . ."

Laurel's eyes widened. "Oh, God, you don't mean incest! Neil, that's revolting!"

"But possible."

"*No.*" She closed her eyes. "Oh, what am I talking about? I don't know." She opened her eyes and looked at him intensely. "But there is someone who might."

"Mary?"

"No. Genevra Howard."

"Faith's mother? But we have no idea where she is. I never did. She might even be dead."

"She's not dead. She's very much alive and in Wheeling. At least she was yesterday. Neil, she stood beside me at Angie's funeral."

Fifteen

1

Neil looked stunned. "How do you know it was Faith's mother?"

"She looked like Faith. Much older than Genevra would be, as if she'd had a hard life, but the features were unmistakable. And she left flowers at Faith's grave."

"You sound as if you didn't talk to her."

"No, not really. As I said, she stood next to me. I might not have paid any attention to her if she hadn't asked if I were cold. Then *I* decided to visit Faith's grave. Before I reached it, I saw someone placing red carnations. When I called out, she looked at me and ran. That's all. I went to the grave. Neil, she'd left six red carnations with a red plastic heart attached."

Neil looked at her steadily for a moment. Then he muttered, "Oh, shit."

"That's what I thought. Neil, we've got to find her, but I have no idea where to look."

"Don't you? Where would you go if you were she?"

Laurel shook her head slowly, then closed her eyes. "The Lewis sisters!"

"Exactly."

"But if she doesn't want to be found, they won't tell me anything. Besides, she might have left after the funeral."

"That's true. I suppose it's too much to ask that Mary communicated with her, too."

"Yes. Unlike Faith, Mary always did what Zeke told her.

She still does. Neil, didn't Faith ever give you a clue about where her mother was?"

"No. Faith never talked about her mother except to say that she wasn't the person Zeke claimed."

"Obviously Faith loved her mother very much, but there's no denying Genevra deserted the family."

"There's also no denying that Zeke Howard is a lunatic. I think he always has been, although he used to be able to hide it better than he does now."

"But Faith wasn't frightened of him."

"I think she was scared senseless of him but she wouldn't admit it. I do know she hated him."

"And now he thinks she's his guardian angel. That's ironic."

"Maybe he feels so guilty about her he's completely re-fashioned their relationship in his mind." Neil drained his cup. "I guess we've traded all the information we have for now. I'm going to work on tracking down Genevra Howard this afternoon."

"And I'm going to the Prices'. Did you know Audra was hospitalized?"

Neil looked concerned. "She wasn't attacked, too, was she?"

"No, but she saw her mother's body. She's in shock."

A look of genuine anguish passed over Neil's face. "I'll pay Wayne a visit, but I really don't think I can bear seeing another child in a hospital bed . . ."

Impulsively Laurel put her hand out and touched his. "I don't think Wayne would expect you to visit her. She doesn't even know you. He'll understand."

Neil smiled. "How come you seem so much more human than Monica and Crystal, or even Denise? No wonder Faith thought so much of you. She told me one time she'd trust you with her life."

Laurel was so taken aback she could only blink at him for a moment. Then she said huskily, "And look what happened when she was with me."

"It wasn't your fault, Laurel. If my guess is correct, you

didn't want the two of you to be in the barn that night. And you tried to save her."

Laurel hesitated. "What makes you say that?"

"In the hospital waiting room the other day you pushed up your sleeves. I saw the faint burn scars on your arms and hands. I didn't think much about it at the time. Then you told me how Faith really died and that you were there. The fire. You don't have to be a genius to realize you must have reached into the flames trying to save her. I know none of the others would have done it." He ran a finger lightly down her cheek. "I agree with Faith. Her life *was* safe in your hands. Even now you're trying to help her."

Laurel's mind jumped to her waking dream of Faith, so beautiful, looking into her eyes and saying, "You know, Laurel. You *know*." What did she know? How could she help?

When she came back to the moment, Neil was climbing out of the car without even a good-bye.

2

Laurel watched Neil drive out of the parking lot. Then she fed the dogs the rest of the McNuggets, drank her cold coffee, and left for home.

April and Alex had clearly enjoyed their adventure, particularly the food, but when she opened the rear door of the car, they both jumped out and ran directly to the house. "No place like home, huh, guys?" she laughed as she unlocked the front door. Inside they made a beeline for their cushions in front of the fireplace. Laurel knew they would appreciate a fire, but she intended to leave soon and never left a fire untended.

Twenty minutes later she entered a local deli and ordered a huge platter of cold cuts, potato salad, and coleslaw. When it was ready, she went to the Price home.

The driveway was parked full of cars. Laurel sighed. She thought it must be so hard on bereaved families to be inundated with people, to force themselves to be polite and sociable when probably all they wanted to do was crawl into bed and cry. But "paying respects" was a custom Laurel had grown up with. She would have felt as guilty about not coming as she did about inflicting herself on Wayne.

He opened the door looking like a different man than the one who'd welcomed her to the party. His skin was pasty, his sparkling dark eyes dulled and almost lost in shadowy hollows, and his whole body seemed shrunken.

"Wayne . . ."

He squinted at her, as if the light hurt his eyes. "Laurel, how kind of you to come."

She walked into the house. People were clustered in the living room. "I'll just take this tray back to the kitchen."

Wayne nodded vaguely. Laurel went to the kitchen where two women who looked to be in their mid-thirties nearly pounced on her. "Oh! More food." One looked closely at the platter. "*Cold* cuts. How clever of you to choose something easy. Jane and I were up half the night baking a ham and cherry and apple pies and banana bread." Laurel pretended not to notice the intended insult to her unambitious offering.

"Isn't this just *awful?*" the one named Jane piped. "Denise and I were *so* close. And poor Wayne—he's just shattered. I heard there was nothing left of Denise's face—"

"I heard that, too!" the other added avidly. "Someone said it was done with a tire iron and there were at least twenty blows. She was just beaten to a pulp. There will have to be a closed coffin, of course. Have you heard any more details?" she asked Laurel.

"I don't know anything," Laurel muttered, her stomach clenching. She felt like picking up her metal deli tray and hitting the egregious pair over their stupid heads with it. "I have to go."

"Who *is* she?" Laurel heard one ask as she turned and rushed from the kitchen.

"I don't know. I think I saw her at the party. I can't say much for her manners. She probably just came to find out

what she could. She didn't even *cook* anything, for God's
sake."

Laurel was surprised when Wayne stopped her in mid-
flight from the kitchen to the front door. "Come upstairs
with me," he said softly. "I want to talk to you."

Laurel saw people in the living room curiously watching
them climb the spiral staircase together. Wayne led her into
a large blue and white bedroom and closed the door. She
knew what was coming before he uttered the words.

"Laurel, do you have any idea who might have done
this?"

What do I say now? she wondered. Tell him that yes, I
think it's someone seeking revenge for the death of Faith
Howard? No. That was out of the question and she truly
didn't know who committed the murders of Denise and
Angela. "No, Wayne, I don't know who killed Denise."

"She changed so much this past week. Nervous, short-
tempered, having nightmares, not eating. Something was
troubling her, but she wouldn't say what. Do you know
what she was so upset about?"

"Angie's death," Laurel said quickly. "She and Angie
weren't close anymore, but you know how childhood
friendships are. You've spent so many formative years together, made so many memories . . ."

Laurel knew she was doing nothing except spouting cli-
chés, but Wayne didn't seem to notice. Or maybe he just
wasn't listening.

"She never talked about you girls very much," he said.
"I never even heard of Monica until the party, but I guess
you were good friends."

"At one time, yes. But that was a long time ago."

Wayne paced restlessly around the room, picking up a
silver-backed brush. "My mother's. She gave it to Denise."

"It's lovely."

"My parents loved Denise. They're dead, you know.
They were older when I was born. I wish they were here,
though. I need them so much."

"Where are Denise's parents?"

He smiled wryly. "One of those seniors tours of Europe. In the winter, can you imagine? I thought they were crazy to go, but Denise's mother was determined. She said the rates were better than in summer. She gave me an itinerary, but it's all screwed up. I can't find them. They don't even know their daughter is dead."

"Wayne, how is Audra?"

"She and Denise were both flirting with the flu last week. All that exposure last night broke the rest of Audra's resistance. She's not in good shape today. I wish to God someone had put her in a warm car or taken her to the lodge. She might not have gotten so sick. She also might not have seen—"

He made a strangling sound and Laurel was beside him in an instant, holding his head against her shoulder. "Wayne, I am *so* sorry."

"I just don't understand," he sobbed. "I know something was wrong, something other than Angie's death. Denise wasn't sleeping well. Did I tell you that?"

"Yes."

"She kept tossing and muttering about a barn and a fire and faith. Faith? What was she talking about?"

"Faith Howard was a friend of ours. She died when she was seventeen."

Wayne drew back, staring at her. "She's the one that locket belonged to!" Laurel nodded. "How did she die?"

"Suicide," Laurel said promptly. "She hanged herself in a barn. Then the barn caught on fire. That was what was on Denise's mind, probably because of Angie. The three of us were good friends."

He stared at her with baffled eyes. "I never *heard* of Faith Howard before the night of the party. Why wouldn't Denise have told me about her?"

"Because she was devastated by Faith's death. I guess it's just something she didn't want to talk about."

He shook his head. "No. No, it isn't making sense. Why didn't Denise ever mention Faith? Why wasn't she closer to you after we moved back here? What the *hell* was that scene at our party about? What nut came into my house pretending to be a ghost and frightened my baby?"

"I don't have any answers, Wayne." It was a lie. She did have *some* answers, but she knew how desperately Denise wanted to keep the truth about Faith's death from Wayne. She wanted it so desperately she may have died because of it. The truth would come out someday, but now was not the time. Wayne was clearly a wreck. She didn't know him well, but Denise had seemed convinced he couldn't handle the truth about Faith's death. It had been an accident, but the Six of Hearts had kept the details of Faith's death a secret. Wayne might react as Kurt had done if he learned that his wife had participated in Satanic rituals, even if she were just a kid, and then withheld important information from the police. That's what Denise had feared most— Wayne's total disillusionment with his wife. The least Laurel could do for Denise at this awful time was to keep her secret. "I'm sorry, Wayne," she said in a dry, wooden voice, "but I've told you all I can."

3

After Laurel left the Price home, she went to work. She was surprised to see Mary in the workroom. "Are you sure you're up to this?" Laurel asked.

"Oh, yes." Mary smiled. "We thought it was best if Penny manned the counter. I don't want to scare anyone with my appearance."

She still bore some noticeable bruises, but she seemed in good spirits. "I'm sorry about your friend."

"Oh, good Lord, that's all people have been talking about today," Norma broke in. "You didn't tell me any details this morning, Laurel. That poor woman. She had a little girl. How *is* she?"

"She's in the hospital suffering from exposure and shock. She saw her mother's body."

"Oh, how awful!" Norma's eyes filled with tears. "Sometimes things like this make you wonder if there really is a benevolent god looking out for us."

"Of course there is!" Mary flared. "He looks after *good* people."

"And you think that woman wasn't good?" Norma snapped.

"She must have done something to deserve what she got."

"And what about that little girl?" Norma demanded. "What did *she* do?"

"I don't know," Mary floundered. "Sins of the father."

"Oh, hogwash!"

Laurel raised a silencing hand. "Ladies, please, lower your voices." I sound like one of the Lewis sisters, she thought as Mary and Norma stood glaring at each other. "I don't think anyone really knows why these things happen. I mean . . . well, it's just so hard on the family."

"And the friends." Norma was instantly contrite, patting Laurel on the back. "You've been through a lot lately, honey. Why don't you go home and get some rest?"

"No, I think I'd be better off here." Mary was jabbing daisy stems into Instant Oasis, obviously still angry. "I haven't done much designing for a few months. I'll work back here until closing time. Do we have many orders?"

"More than you can shake a stick at," Norma informed her. "Mostly Christmas stuff, thank goodness."

Laurel knew what she meant. The orders for Denise's funeral hadn't begun to come in yet. They would tomorrow when the funeral arrangements appeared in this evening's newspaper.

While she worked, Laurel tried to keep her mind off Denise, but it was difficult. She kept asking herself if going to the police sooner would have made a difference. She also worried about not being honest with Wayne. But what would that have accomplished? It wouldn't help either one of them figure out who murdered Denise.

After work, when everyone had gone home, Laurel placed a quick call to Kurt. She got his answering machine.

Maybe he wasn't home yet. She'd try again later. She had
to tell him about seeing Faith's mother and about the noose
in the Pritchard barn.

It was six when she left the store and drove to the hospital. She didn't know if Audra was allowed visitors, but
she at least wanted the child to know she'd stopped by. She
was surprised when a pretty, dark-haired nurse said she
could see Audra for a few minutes.

Audra lay propped on pillows, deathly pale, her brown
hair spread around her mournful little face, her eyes fixed
blindly on a cartoon show rattling annoyingly on the television opposite her bed.

"Audra?" she said gently. "Audra, it's Laurel." No response. She neared the bed and held out a bud vase. "April
and Alex each sent a pink rose with some baby's breath.
They thought you might like pink roses."

The child's big brown eyes moved for the first time. She
reached out a tentative finger and touched a petal. "Pink
roses are my favorite." Her voice was scratchy. "Did they
come with you?"

"They would have, but dogs aren't allowed in hospitals."
Laurel put the roses beside Audra's bed and sat next to her.
"How are you feeling, honey?"

"Not so good." A tear trickled down her cheek. "My
mommy's dead."

Laurel's throat tightened as she hugged the child who
felt so slight in her grasp. "Your mommy is in heaven,
honey. Heaven is a wonderful place with pink roses and
puppies and kittens and big, fluffy clouds and beautiful angels."

"Are you sure?"

"Absolutely."

Audra suddenly went into a coughing jag, then moaned
slightly. Laurel wiped her nose with a tissue and gave her
a drink of water. "Are you warm enough?"

"I'm way too hot. Could you take the blanket off?"

"I don't think we should do that. It's your fever making

you hot. Just try to hang on. You'll feel better in a couple of days."

"No I won't. I'll never feel better. Laurel, I heard a nurse in the hall say it's my fault Mommy's dead."

Laurel's anger ignited so violently it shocked her. "That's ridiculous! Who said that?"

"A tall nurse with lots of yellow hair. She said if that little brat had stayed in the car, nobody could've killed Mrs. Price."

"That is *not* true."

"But it is. Mommy was grouchy and I got mad and ran out of the car. I wanted to scare her." Tears brimmed in Audra's eyes. "Instead she got killed and it's my fault."

Laurel's instinct was to coo and comfort, but something told her that wasn't the way to approach Audra. She was a tough, smart little girl. Logic would appeal to her more than coddling. "Audra, did you kill your mother?"

The child's eyes widened. "No! Honest!"

"Then her death is *not* your fault. Her death is the fault of whoever killed her. Doesn't that make sense?"

"Kind of. But I was out there running around . . ."

"Did anyone try to kill you?"

"No."

"That's because they weren't after you. Whoever it was wanted to hurt your mommy and if they hadn't done it that night, they would have done it some other time. I'm not just trying to make you feel better, Audra." She looked straight into Audra's bloodshot eyes. "I *know* what I'm saying. Do you believe me?"

Audra frowned, still sniffling. "Well . . . I guess."

"Good. That nurse doesn't know what she's talking about. *I* do, so you *have* to believe me. You also have to believe that your mother is in a beautiful place and she's looking down on you and loving you just as much as ever."

"But I'll never see her again," Audra quavered.

"Yes you will, sweetheart. I guarantee it. Now you just concentrate on getting well. April and Alex are looking forward to seeing you as soon as you get out of here."

"Really?"

"My word of honor. You're their favorite person."

"Except for you."

"That's just because I'm the one who feeds them."

Finally Audra smiled slightly. "Give them kisses for me."

"I will," Laurel promised.

When Laurel left Audra's room, she went to a phone in the hospital lobby and called Kurt's number. Still the answering machine. She looked at her watch. Six forty-five. She knew he was home by now. Maybe he was still so mad at her he just wasn't answering her calls. But she had to talk to him.

Ten minutes later she pulled up in front of his apartment house. She remembered her last trip here. She'd been frightened senseless by whoever had chased her down the hill, trying to push her car off the road. Kurt hadn't been home, but he'd certainly been angry with her for coming there instead of going to police headquarters. He'd been right. It was a stupid move. But this evening was different.

Laurel entered the building and tapped on his door. No answer. She tried again. Right on cue, Mrs. Henshaw threw back her door and stepped into the hallway. "You after him again?" she asked rudely.

Laurel tried to hold on to her temper. It seemed she'd been losing it all day. "I really need to speak with Kurt and I can't seem to reach him by phone."

"Thought you was his girlfriend. Looks like he's avoidin' you."

I will not get mad, Laurel said to herself as she looked the woman up and down. She wore double-knit pants strained at the seams in the hip and thigh area, a sweatshirt with sequined poinsettias stretched across her ample bosom, dirty running shoes, and a green velvet clip-on bow in her salt-and-pepper hair. She also had a rim of chocolate around her mouth and Laurel heard a television game show playing noisily in the background. Bells and whistles were going off while the audience clapped wildly.

"Mrs. Henshaw, has Kurt been in this evening?"

"How would I know? What do you think I am? A snoop or somethin'?"

"I just thought you might have heard him."

"Can't hear anything in my apartment with the door shut."

"You heard me knocking on his door."

"You was poundin.' "

"No I wasn't."

"Well, I don't know nothin' about him." A slightly crafty look passed over her round, boneless face. "I'm manager of the buildin', though. I've got keys to all the apartments. If it's *real* important . . ."

"It is," Laurel said firmly. Kurt was avoiding her, but he had to know a few things she'd found out. "I'm going in for just a moment to leave him a note," she told Mrs. Henshaw. "If you see him later, will you tell him I was only here for a couple of minutes?"

Mrs. Henshaw retrieved the key and gave it to her with a conspiratorial wink that sent waves of dislike through Laurel. "Sure I'll tell him. You can count on me."

Laurel didn't like counting on Mrs. Henshaw for anything, but she had no choice. The woman had seen her. No doubt she would report to Kurt as soon as he set foot on the upstairs landing.

Laurel had been in Kurt's apartment a couple of times, and then only briefly. It was utilitarian, almost Spartan, with only a vinyl-covered couch, a couple of cheap, scratched tables, a small bookcase, and a worn recliner chair lined up opposite the television in the living room. Only a double bed and a walnut-veneer dresser occupied the bedroom. "I don't need much and I'm saving money for my dream house," Kurt explained the first time she was here and had badly concealed her surprise at the barren look of the apartment.

Right now Laurel wasn't at all concerned about his furnishings or lack of them. She glanced at his answering machine. The red light did not blink, which meant he'd listened to and erased her two earlier messages. She picked up his receiver, dialed her number and code. There were no messages on her machine. He hadn't returned her calls.

Okay, fine, Kurt, she thought. If he didn't want to talk to her, she wouldn't force him.

Looking around, she saw no notebooks in the living room—nothing but a scratch pad beside the phone. A pencil lay beside it. She picked up the pencil and began to write, immediately breaking off the lead point. She fished in her purse for a pen. She got out "Dear Kurt, I" before it went dry.

"Oh, for heaven's sake!" she muttered. She looked around the room. On the bookshelf sat a cup full of pens and pencils. As she went for one, she couldn't help noticing Kurt's scant library. No one could accuse him of being an avid reader. He owned two of Mickey Spillane's Mike Hammer novels, three of Ed McBain's, Benchley's *The Deep* and *White Shark,* Ken Follett's *The Key to Rebecca,* a Clive Cussler, and a book of Shakespeare's sonnets.

Laurel did a double-take. A book of Shakespeare's sonnets? Could it be a leftover from high school? If so, Kurt hadn't kept any of the other books they'd read in school. Besides, their senior English class Shakespeare book had contained plays as well as sonnets.

Overcome by curiosity, she withdrew the book. It was bound in brown leather, obviously a fairly expensive edition. A bit of dust on the top showed that it hadn't been read for a while, which didn't surprise Laurel. She couldn't imagine Kurt lounging in his easy chair reading Shakespearean sonnets.

She opened the cover, then the flyleaf. The book was inscribed in a beautiful, sloping hand:

All days are nights to see till I see thee,
And nights bright days when dreams do show thee me.

A couplet from one of the sonnets. The book had been given in love. But it wasn't the book so much as the giver that left Laurel breathless. Beneath the inscription she read:

All my love,
Faith

Sixteen

1

Laurel sat back on her heels. Why on earth would Faith give Kurt a book of Shakespearean sonnets? Well, it didn't take much thought to figure that out after reading the inscription. Faith loved Kurt. Laurel closed her eyes. Faith loved *Kurt*? They'd been friends since they were seven and Faith had swung on the ivy vine into the tree house. Kurt and Chuck, Faith and Laurel. They'd been inseparable that summer, but gradually drifted apart as they got older. Faith had never dated Kurt. She'd never dated anyone except Neil.

At least openly. Hadn't Neil said he was the only guy Zeke would let her go out with because his parents were members of Zeke's church? Laurel thought about Kurt's animosity toward Neil lately. Was it only because he thought Neil was strange, or was it because he'd once considered Neil a rival, another of Faith's lovers? And what about the night of the Price Christmas party? Kurt had been talking about Faith and her baby. What had he said? Laurel dredged up the memory: "That child would have been almost thirteen . . . I'd bet it was a boy." He sounded strange, wistful and removed, almost as if he'd forgotten she were in the car.

Neil said he couldn't be the father of Faith's baby. If Laurel chose to believe him, then someone else had to be. Could it have been Kurt? Is that why he was so furious with her when he found out how Faith died? Was he merely disappointed in her lack of truthfulness, or was he livid over losing the girl he loved and his child?

Suddenly the apartment seemed oppressively small and airless. Laurel grabbed a pen from the cup and wrote briefly on the scratch pad: "I have some information that might interest you. Please call me. L." She'd intended to explain about Faith's mother and the noose in the barn, but she couldn't bring herself to stay in the apartment that long. She placed the piece of paper in his chair where he'd be sure to see it, dashed from the apartment, and knocked on Mrs. Henshaw's door. "Here's the key," she said hurriedly.

"Find what you was lookin' for?" Mrs. Henshaw asked, smirking.

"I left a note," Laurel said curtly. "Thank you for the key."

As she ran down the steps, she was aware of Mrs. Henshaw watching her from a crack in her door.

2

Laurel drove straight home, trying to recover from the shock of what she'd found in Kurt's apartment. When she turned into the long, dark drive leading to her house, she was glad she'd remembered to pick up a battery for her garage door opener. When she pressed it, the door slid up. She pulled in, closed the door, then emerged from the car and went into the house via the side door.

Both dogs eagerly awaited her. "I know. Dinner is late," she told them. "You're probably both on the verge of starvation. Speaking of starvation, I haven't eaten anything all day. I feel like I'm going to faint."

She fixed the dogs' food first, then rummaged in the refrigerator until she found a package of hot dogs. She stuck three in the microwave, then wrapped them in bread, ketchup, and relish and wolfed them down with unladylike speed. Still hungry, she next turned to the freezer, withdrew two Fudgesickles, and dispatched them just as quickly. "I have to remember to go to the grocery store," she said aloud

as a cramp clenched her stomach when all the food landed
with a thud. She went to the couch and lay down, feeling
like a five-year-old who'd eaten too much birthday cake.

A few minutes later, as her stomach was beginning to
calm, the phone rang. Laurel picked it up and Kurt barked,
"What do you mean coming into my apartment when I'm
not home?"

"Well, pardon me, but you won't answer my phone calls.
I was only there about ten minutes. Didn't your resident
hall monitor inform you?"

"Yes, but she said it was a lot longer than ten minutes."

"Oh, big deal. Besides, she gave me the key. Calm down.
I didn't go through your underwear drawer or anything."

"Very cute. What do you want?"

"First of all, I'd like for you to stop acting like a jackass."

"Thank you."

"You are and you know it." It was hard to keep her voice
even. If Kurt *had* been the father of Faith's baby, he'd let
Neil take all the blame, but he was treating her like a criminal. "Okay, you're mad because I didn't tell you how Faith
really died. I made a terrible mistake. Don't you dare tell
me *you've* never made one."

He was quiet for a moment. "What did you want to tell
me, Laurel?" he asked in a more civil tone.

"First, Genevra Howard, Faith's mother, was at Angie's
funeral."

"Faith's *mother*! Did you talk to her?"

"No, not really."

"But she said she was Faith's mother."

"No. She looked like Faith and she left flowers on Faith's
grave."

"That's it?"

"Kurt, she left six red carnations with a red plastic heart
attached." He was silent. "Don't you think it's important
that a woman who disappeared over twenty years ago, who
didn't even come to her own daughter's funeral, suddenly
showed up at Angie's? And what about the flowers on
Faith's grave? Didn't you *hear* me? I said *six* red carnations

with a red plastic *heart* attached. The Six of Hearts."
"It's pretty odd *if* it was really Faith's mother who left
the flowers." His voice sounded hollow. He doesn't want
to believe me, but he does, Laurel thought. Why doesn't
he want to believe Faith's mother might be here? Is he
afraid of what she knows?
"There's something else, Kurt," she said in a rush. "I
went out to the Pritchard farm yesterday and—"
"What the hell did you do that for?" he exploded.
"I don't know," she floundered. "I just wanted to see it.
I went into the old barn and there was a hangman's noose
dangling from a beam."
"A *noose?*"
"Yes. It was made from new rope."
"A *noose?*"
"*Yes,* Kurt, a *noose.* Like the one Faith put her head in
that night."
"Jeez!" He sounded natural for the first time during the
phone call, animation replacing cold anger. "I'll go out
there and take a look. But you stay away from there. You
shouldn't have gone there in the first place. You shouldn't
be anywhere alone. Look at what happened to Denise."
"Denise wasn't in a secluded spot."
"Well, not technically, but no one could see her from the
road."
Laurel swallowed. "Kurt, this has been bothering me. Do
you think Denise suffered or did she die quickly?"
"It's too early to have the medical examiner's report."
"But you saw the body. What would you say?"
He paused. "Laurel, I'm no expert. There was a lot of
blood." He drew a breath. "I don't think she died after the
first blow. There were signs that she tried to get up on her
knees, tried to crawl . . ."
"Oh," Laurel gasped. "I don't want to hear any more."
"You asked."
"I know. I wish I hadn't. There were two female ghouls
masquerading as friends at the Price home this morning
who just couldn't get enough details. It made me sick."

"There are a lot of people like that."

Laurel could feel herself calming down a bit. Besides, she didn't want Kurt to think she'd seen the book of sonnets and had any idea of his connection with Faith. "Kurt, I'm sorry I came into your apartment without an invitation, but I really needed to talk to you."

"You could have called me at the office or come in," he said stiffly.

"Yes. . . . well, I . . ."

"You don't want to talk about any of this in public. You still don't want anyone to know how Faith died."

And you don't want anyone to know you were involved with her, Laurel almost snapped, but caught herself. Besides, he was right. She still didn't want the whole town to know the truth. But there was more. She'd always thought of Kurt as a confidant, someone on whom she could depend. After seeing the book of sonnets and the declaration of love from Faith in his apartment, though, she wasn't so sure how far she could trust him anymore.

"At least you know that Faith's mother might figure into all this. And the Pritchard farm definitely needs to be checked out."

"Laurel, I'm going to say this again. I don't want you to go out there or any other place where someone can get at you without being seen. You're very lucky you didn't run into anyone this morning. The killer no doubt put up that noose and might be staying around the place. Are you sure you didn't see anyone?"

"No," she said aloud. Silently she added, I didn't see anyone except Neil Kamrath watching me look at the hangman's noose.

3

When Laurel hung up, she couldn't help thinking how different her conversation with Kurt had been than one just last week. They'd never been overly romantic, their conversations were not laced with longing and endearments, but there had always been a closeness. That closeness was gone forever. It was what she had feared when she broke off her engagement to Bill Haynes five years ago, and she still believed he would have reacted to the truth exactly as Kurt had.

She had just put on a kettle for tea when the phone rang. She answered, hoping it wasn't her mother demanding she come to Florida.

"Laurel, I'm so glad you're home!" It was Neil.

"What's going on?" she asked, her interest piqued by the excitement in his voice.

"I've found Genevra Howard."

"What? Where?"

"Just where I guessed she'd be."

"With the Lewis sisters."

"Yeah. I parked down the street and waited all afternoon until I saw a woman matching your description come outside and fill a bird feeder."

"Did you talk to her?"

"No. I didn't want to scare her."

"Did you go to the door after she went in the house?"

"No." He sounded slightly embarrassed. "I used to take piano lessons from Miss Adelaide when I was a kid, but you know how she and her sister are. They act like every adult male is out to ravish their maidenhood."

Laurel burst into laughter. Both sisters were in their early eighties without an ounce of flesh to spare, but they'd always clung to each other, fluttering and cringing away from men as if they were dewy Victorian belles. Laurel often thought that in secret they probably lived on a diet of torrid romance novels.

"I have an idea," she said. "They barely know me, but I'm female. I'd been planning to take them a wreath as a gift because they were in the store trying to select one when Zeke came in and put on his sideshow. I'll run to the store, get a wreath, then meet you outside their house. We'll simply be a young couple bringing them a wreath."

"Laurel," Neil said slowly, "they *do* know me. They

think I'm the father of Faith's baby. They won't let me inside the door."

"Oh." Laurel bit her lip. "Neil, you look so different now than you did as a teenager I don't think they'll recognize you until we're inside. Then they'll probably be too polite to throw you out. I don't want to go alone. Please meet me there."

"Okay, we can give it a try. Do you know where they live?"

"Yes. I'll meet you in about half an hour."

She turned off the stove, grabbed her jacket, and headed for the store. As she remembered, the sisters had been torn between a pine and a cedar wreath. She chose the largest wreath she had left, pine decorated with small pieces of wax fruits and tiny, foil-wrapped packages and finished off with a large red velveteen ribbon.

When Laurel pulled up in front of the Lewis sisters' house, she stood by the car for a minute, looking down the dark street. She didn't see the white Buick Neil had been driving earlier. Then she saw him emerge from a dark Mercury Marquis. "Different car," she commented as he drew near.

"Dad's car. Old as hell, but it runs fine. It hasn't been driven for a month, though, and needed some road time. Nice wreath."

"Big and probably not what they wanted, but at least it might get us in the door."

She rang the bell. In a moment the curtain drew back a fraction and she caught a glimpse of blue hair. She counted to ten and rang the bell again. The porch light went on and slowly the door opened.

"Miss Lewis?" Laurel wasn't sure which sister was looking at her warily. "I'm Laurel Damron from Damron Floral. You were in my store last Friday when that awful scene occurred with Zeke Howard. You left without a wreath. I wanted to bring you one as an apology for the terrible distress you suffered."

The·woman relaxed slightly and managed a small smile.

"My dear, that's so kind of you, but it really isn't necessary."

"It would please me if you'd accept the wreath. If you don't like this one, I can get you another."

The woman's faded blue eyes studied the wreath. "It's simply beautiful. It was our favorite but a bit beyond our finances. I really can't accept."

"I insist. I see you don't have a hook on your door. We'll come in and hang it for you." Laurel was already stepping into the house with unaccustomed pushiness. "Where are my manners? Miss Lewis, this is Neil Kamrath. He used to take piano lessons from you."

"Oh, not me," the woman fluttered. "I'm Miss Hannah."

A woman seated on an old-fashioned settee immediately stood. "I'm Miss Adelaide. We look very much alike, but I'm three years younger than Hannah. I remember you, Neil. What a fine young man you've grown into! Did you ever master Tchaikovsky's 'Song of the Swan'?"

Neil looked slightly taken aback by her cordiality. "Good heavens, what a memory!" he exclaimed. Miss Adelaide beamed. "No, I'm sorry to say I never learned to play it well. Music isn't my forte."

"Oh, well, very few have the calling. I've heard you write stories."

"Yes, ma'am, I do." He looks totally cowed by these two fragile old ladies, Laurel thought with amusement. In a minute he's going to start shuffling his feet and sprout a cowlick.

"I'm sorry to say I haven't read any," Miss Adelaide went on. "Hannah and I lean toward the classics. Mr. Charles Dickens is a favorite." I'll bet, Laurel mused. No doubt they'd read their share of Dickens, but she was sure the sisters also possessed a large library of bodice-rippers.

"That's all right, Miss Adelaide," Neil said. "I doubt if you'd care for my work, but it earns a good living."

"Well, now, isn't that just fine?"

They all stood looking at each other for an awkward

moment. Oh, no, Laurel thought. It can't end like this. We haven't found out a thing. "I brought a heavy-duty hook for the wreath," she said hurriedly. "Would it be all right if Neil hangs it? It's getting *so* near Christmas."

The sisters looked at each other. "Certainly," Hannah said. "How kind of you. I'll get a hammer."

"Can you do this?" Laurel whispered as Adelaide scurried out of the room behind her sister.

"I'm capable of doing more than hitting computer keys," Neil retorted.

"Don't get your feathers ruffled. Not all men are handy with carpentry."

"Hanging a Christmas wreath is hardly carpentry."

The sisters returned with a huge hammer. "Is this one all right? We have another somewhere. We could look for it."

"This one will be fine," Neil said, looking at the hammer dubiously.

When Neil went to the door, hook and unwieldy hammer in hand, Miss Adelaide motioned to the settee. "Sit down, my dear. Would you care for tea?"

"No—" Laurel caught herself. Tea could draw out the visit. "Well, yes, tea does sound lovely."

Both sisters went to the kitchen again. A great deal of muttering and clattering went on. Neil turned to Laurel and grinned, murmuring, "What a production over tea, not to mention that I could knock the whole damned house down with this monster they call a hammer."

Twenty minutes later Neil had the wreath in place and the sisters walked in carrying a silver tea service and a plate of lemon cookies. They first oohed and aahed over the wreath, then set about the elaborate ritual of serving tea. Laurel thought of her own style—pouring boiling water over a tea bag and dumping in a packet of artificial sweetener—and thought she'd never drink tea again if it involved all this ceremony. When at last everyone had been served, Miss Adelaide asked, "How is Mary Howard?"

"All right," Laurel said. "She had a nasty cut on the back

of her head and a concussion, but she's fairly well recovered. She was back at work today."

"Oh, that's fine! Honestly, I thought I would faint when she crashed into those shelves. That awful man. He should be locked up."

"The police tried, Miss Adelaide, but there are so many legal technicalities," Laurel said. "One of the problems was that Mary wouldn't file a complaint against him."

"I can't imagine why. That man is a cruel, unbalanced detriment to society who should *never* have been allowed to run loose," Miss Hannah burst out. "He was *always* crazy!"

"Now, Hannah!" Adelaide said, faint alarm in her eyes. "You mustn't upset yourself. Your heart, you know."

"There is absolutely nothing wrong with my heart and Zeke Howard *is* crazy. Has been since he was a child."

"You've known him since he was a child?" Neil pounced.

"Oh, yes," Hannah went on heatedly. "He used to live here in Wheeling. He was a close friend of our younger brother, Leonard. And what my brother did—"

"Hannah!" Adelaide cried. "Please watch what you're saying!"

"I get tired of watching what I say!" Hannah spluttered. "When I saw that maniac push poor Mary into those shelves, I felt like killing him myself. How in God's name Leonard could have done what he did—"

"What did he do?" Laurel asked breathlessly.

The regal white-haired woman from the cemetery entered the living room from the hall. "He forced me to marry Zeke Howard when I was only seventeen years old."

4

Laurel and Neil both stared at her. Miss Hannah made helpless fluttering motions with her hands while Miss Adelaide stood abruptly, banging her knee into the coffee table and nearly overturning the tea service. "Genevra, dear, don't you think you should be resting?" Adelaide asked.

Genevra Howard smiled. Her smile was so much like
Faith's that for a moment Laurel felt the past and the present blending together. "I believe these people want to talk
to me."

"No they don't, dear," Adelaide assured her. "They just
brought a Christmas wreath. Mr. Kamrath here used to take
lessons from me."

"Neil Kamrath," the woman said gently. "You dated my
daughter."

"Yes." For a moment Neil looked as if he were going to
flounder, unable to talk to this woman he'd been seeking.
Then he recovered himself. "How did you know we dated?"

Laurel realized he knew the answer to his question, but
he didn't want the Lewis sisters to know Faith had confided
in him about the post office box.

"My daughter wrote to me. She admired you very much."

Laurel noticed Neil's weak smile. She was sure admiration wasn't the primary emotion he'd wanted Faith to feel
for him.

Hannah looked up at Genevra. "If you don't want to keep
where you're staying a secret, which you obviously don't,
you might as well sit down and have some tea and cookies."

"I'd like that." Genevra wore a long pink robe tied at the
waist. She was tall and her thick white hair hung below her
shoulders. Her delicate skin bore a cobweb of fine wrinkles,
but her eyes were a lovely, if slightly faded, blue-green,
her lips touched with faint pink lipstick. She must have
been absolutely beautiful when she was young, Laurel
thought. As beautiful as Faith. Now she had a thin, atten-
uated look and a sweet but removed manner, almost as if
she weren't completely aware of those around her. She
reached for tea with her left hand. Laurel saw that she wore
no wedding ring.

"I heard Zeke caused quite a commotion in your store,"
she said to Laurel.

"He was frightening. At first he just quoted Bible verses,

then he pushed Mary into a set of glass shelves. I was scared to death for her, but as I'm sure you know, she's fine now."

"I know because you've told me," Genevra said. "Unlike Faith, Mary doesn't communicate with me."

Miss Adelaide's face set in disapproving lines. "Mary is a sweet girl but she doesn't have a mind of her own like Faith did."

"No, Faith was her own woman," Hannah agreed. "Spirited, much as I was when I was young."

Adelaide cast her an astonished glance. Laurel doubted if either sister had ever been what could be called "spirited."

"Mrs. Howard, why did you run away from me at Faith's grave?" Laurel asked bluntly.

Genevra looked into her eyes. "I came here because Adelaide and Hannah told me what happened to Mary. I wanted to keep my presence a secret because I hoped to get a casual chance to know Mary without her knowing who I was. If she knew I was here, she'd avoid me. If Zeke knew . . ." She shivered.

"I noticed you left six red carnations on Faith's grave," Laurel said.

"Faith loved red carnations."

"And the red plastic heart attached to the flowers?"

Genevra smiled her placid smile again. "It's a key ring. Faith sent it to me a long time ago. She said she had one and she wanted me to have one, too, because it had a special meaning."

Laurel's scalp tingled. She certainly wasn't going to ask what that special meaning was. Even if Genevra knew about the Six of Hearts, she didn't want her to admit it in front of the Lewis sisters.

Neil leaned forward. "Mrs. Howard—"

"Please call me Genevra. I hate being Mrs. Ezekial Howard."

"I understand," he said gently. "Genevra, you can tell me

to mind my own business if you like, but where have you been for nearly twenty-five years?"

Laurel felt the Lewis sisters stiffen, but Genevra merely took a sip of tea and looked at Neil calmly. "I've been in a mental institution. I was committed when I was twenty-three for killing my infant son."

Seventeen

1

Utter silence fell over the room. Miss Hannah's hands locked on the arms of her chair. Neil's teacup froze halfway to his mouth. After a moment when Laurel was certain her breath had stopped, Miss Adelaide looked around brightly and said, "Lemon cookie, anyone?"

Later Laurel thought if she'd seen that moment on television, she would have laughed, but there was nothing laughable about the shock on Neil's face or Miss Adelaide's desperate attempt to bring things back to normal.

"I've been locked away too long," Genevra said. "I've said something awful and ruined the evening."

"You just surprised us," Laurel said in a composed voice that didn't sound like her own. "Neil and I had no idea."

Genevra shook her head. "As close as you were to Faith, she never said anything? Or did she repeat Zeke's story that I'd run off with another man?"

"She never said you ran off with a man," Neil told her. "She just didn't say that you'd—"

"Murdered my son," Genevra finished for him.

"Oh, Genevra, dear, please stop saying that," Adelaide said in distress. "It sounds so terrible and you know it's not true."

"I *hope* it's not true," Genevra said.

"Would you mind telling us what happened?" Laurel asked softly, praying the Lewis sisters wouldn't interfere and send her and Neil straight out the door. But they seemed too flustered to do much except stare.

Genevra began speaking in a firm, even voice. "You know that Zeke has his own religion and he's very fervent about it. Long ago, when he lived in Wheeling as a boy, he made friends with my father, Leonard Lewis. My father was . . . well, very devoted to Zeke and his religion—"

"Leonard was unbalanced," Miss Hannah interrupted. "Our parents couldn't handle him so they simply let him go his own way unchecked. It was a great mistake. He only got worse. He moved to Pennsylvania shortly after Zeke did. Much later he married some unfortunate young girl who died giving birth to Genevra, leaving poor Genevra to be reared by Leonard. Considering that Leonard left here over fifty years ago and never came back, not even for one visit, most people still living don't remember him or even knew his daughter was Faith's mother."

"My father promised Zeke that if he had a daughter she would become Zeke's wife," Genevra went on. "I was that unlucky daughter."

"But it wasn't the middle ages," Neil said. "He couldn't *force* you to marry Zeke."

"I had a very strange childhood. Repressive, they said in the hospital. I didn't go to school. I was home-taught. I didn't really know what life was like for regular children. I only knew what life was like in my father's delusional world, and I was terrified of him. He was very physically abusive—not sexually, but he kicked and hit and he often locked me in a closet without food for two or three days at a time when he felt I'd been bad. As I said, I was afraid of him. Terrified. I didn't want to marry Zeke, but my father said I had to or suffer punishment as I'd never known before. I was only a frightened teenager. I thought of running away, but I believed my father had the power to find me anywhere. Besides, I had no money, no knowledge of how to get along in the world, so I did as he ordered. I was afraid not to."

"I had Faith when I was eighteen," she continued. *Eighteen!* Laurel thought. My God, the woman was only forty-eight. She could have passed for sixty-eight. "Zeke was pleased that I could produce a healthy baby, but he was disappointed that the child was a girl. Four years passed before I conceived again. Those were four very difficult years. Zeke was always raving that I was out of God's favor and that's why I couldn't conceive. He was also getting stranger, keeping me almost a prisoner in the house so I wouldn't have a chance to do wrong and displease God, preaching at me constantly. When I had a second baby, it was Mary. I'm sure you can imagine his reaction."

She took a deep, slightly shaky breath. "Less than a year later I gave birth to a boy, Daniel. He was premature and had respiratory problems. All the children were born at home, you understand. They had none of the benefits of hospital births. I was so worried about Daniel, but Zeke would never let me take him to a doctor. He said God would look after him. Daniel cried constantly, couldn't keep down milk—he was miserable and so was I. I suppose I had a breakdown. I really don't remember much about that time."

Her gaze grew distant. "Then one morning I was sitting in the rocking chair. It was a beautiful spring morning, I do remember that. A soft breeze was blowing. I was so tired. I'd been up all night with Daniel. I'd put him in his crib just about an hour earlier. At least I think it was an hour. It's all so vague. Then Zeke came in holding Daniel. He was dead. Zeke screamed that he found the baby lying on his face and there was a pillow over his head." She shuddered. "Zeke wouldn't stop screaming. He laid Daniel on the couch and hit me. He kept hitting me. Mary was shrieking. Little Faith was pummeling her father's legs, trying to make him stop. I was afraid he was going to turn on her. 'You killed the baby, didn't you?' he kept yelling. 'You're crazy and you killed my boy child because he made so much noise. Admit it!' Finally I did. He called the police."

"It was probably sudden infant death syndrome!" Laurel exclaimed.

Genevra smiled gently. "I'd never heard of such a thing."

"But you didn't deny that you'd killed Daniel?" Laurel gasped.

Genevra shook her head. "I told the police I did it. I wrote a confession. I don't remember writing it, but I saw it later. I said I'd deliberately smothered my baby because I couldn't stand his crying anymore. There was a trial. My lawyer used the insanity defense and I was found guilty. I've been in a sanitarium in Pennsylvania until just a few weeks ago, around Thanksgiving."

"But she did *not* kill that baby," Miss Hannah insisted. "I know my niece. She wouldn't hurt a soul."

"Of course she wouldn't," Adelaide agreed. "That's what I told Faith when Zeke brought the girls back here. Faith had loved her mother so much and Zeke had told her all those awful stories about Genevra. He'd told her she *murdered* Daniel but that she was to say Genevra had run off with another man and deserted her. Faith never believed any of it. She was aptly named. She had faith in her mother. That's why Hannah and I rented a post office box for her so they could write to each other. We wanted her to know her *real* mother, not the creature Zeke invented."

"We tried to do the same with Mary," Hannah said, "but she would never listen to us or to Faith."

"Mary was only a baby herself when I was sent away," Genevra said defensively. "She didn't have any impression of me besides what Zeke told her. Faith was older and we'd been *so* close. I adored her."

"She adored you," Neil said.

Genevra smiled. "That means so much to me. I know how much she cared for you, too."

Faith's baby, Laurel thought. Did she dare bring that up in front of the Lewis sisters? It didn't seem appropriate, but they might not get another chance to talk to Genevra.

She cleared her throat. "Faith was pregnant when she died—"

"She was *not!*" Hannah flared.

Adelaide's clouded eyes snapped wide. "A vicious rumor! Not true, absolutely not true! Faith knew right from wrong and Neil was such a good boy!"

At first Laurel had been a bit puzzled by how nice the sisters were to the man who supposedly seduced and impregnated their niece. Now she understood. They didn't believe Faith had been pregnant. But Genevra? Laurel glanced at her. She was sipping tea, looking as if she were in another dimension.

"Then you don't believe Faith committed suicide because she was pregnant?" Laurel ventured.

"That's ridiculous!" Hannah huffed. "Adelaide and I don't know exactly what happened in that barn, but we know Faith didn't commit suicide. She was too full of life, too excited about the future. Isn't that right, Genevra?"

Genevra Howard blinked at her aunt, slowly turned her head and gave Laurel an unnerving, cunning smile. "My daughter did *not* commit suicide."

2

Neither Laurel nor Neil pressed the subject further. Miss Adelaide abruptly asked if Laurel had been a friend of Denise Price's. When Laurel said yes, the woman looked as if she were going to cry. "I give little Audra lessons. I'm afraid she's not very talented, but she's a dear thing. Mrs. Price seemed so nice, too. I don't suppose the police have any leads about who could have done this awful deed."

"No, they don't," Laurel said. She looked directly at Genevra. "But her murder was exactly like Angela Ricci's. We were all friends in school, you know—Angie, Denise, Faith, and I."

Genevra yawned politely behind her hand. "I hope you'll excuse me. I seem to tire easily these days. Good night. It's been so nice talking with you."

"Good night," everyone murmured as the woman rose and drifted away. The sisters seemed flustered by her behavior, but they weren't going to comment on it. Hannah forced a smile. Adelaide turned the subject back to Audra. "How is the little girl?"

"Audra is in the hospital. She was already getting the flu and being out on such a cold night looking for her mother—"

"What?" Adelaide cried. "The police made the child search for her mother?"

"Oh, no," Laurel corrected. "Audra had been in the car with Denise taking a tour of the light show. She got out and went running toward one of the displays to take a picture. Denise went after her. That's when Denise was attacked. Audra didn't see the murder, but she did see her mother's body. Between that and the snow, she got very sick."

"Oh, dear Lord!" Adelaide fanned herself as if she were going to faint. "I didn't know all that. That dear child! That poor woman! Oh, this is dreadful . . ."

"I'm sorry I've upset you so," Laurel said sincerely. "I assumed you knew. Audra will be all right. I've been to visit her in the hospital."

"Oh, I suppose I should go, too. The dear thing. And I was rather sharp with her during her last lesson."

"Now, Adelaide, settle down," Hannah said sternly. "You wouldn't be a good piano teacher if you didn't point out mistakes or let children know they aren't practicing enough. Isn't that right, Neil?"

"Yes," he said gently. "And I'm sure you weren't harsh, Miss Adelaide. You never were with me, now matter how abominably I played."

"Oh, I hope not. Dear me. I feel awful."

"Perhaps we should go," Laurel said quickly. "We've taken up your entire evening and upset you on top of it all."

"Oh, no you didn't," Adelaide said kindly. "It's just the state of the world. Sometimes I just think I can't stand all the frightful things that happen. Poor Genevra. And Faith. And Mrs. Price and Audra."

Hannah nodded at them. Laurel and Neil stood quickly. "We'll be leaving now. I do hope you'll feel better tomorrow," Laurel said.

"She will," Hannah said firmly. "A good night's sleep makes a new woman of her. And thank you so much for the wreath."

"Yes, thank you," Adelaide said faintly.

"You're very welcome. I hope you enjoy it."

Once they were outside in the biting cold, headed for their cars, Laurel said, "I thought I'd feel triumphant after learning so much. Instead I feel terrible for upsetting Adelaide."

"Hannah's right. She'll be fine. They didn't live to be this old by collapsing over every little thing." Neil smiled. "Under all that artificial Southern gentility they are two tough broads."

Laurel laughed. "Somehow I've never thought of the Lewis sisters as 'broads.' "

"Neither have I until just now." Neil put his hands in his pockets. "Want to meet at our favorite restaurant and talk over what we've learned?"

"By favorite restaurant I assume you mean McDonald's."

"Of course. Only I think we'd better go inside. It's a cold night."

Laurel thought for a moment. She still worried slightly about meeting with Neil, but once again he'd not suggested coming to her home. He seemed to be going out of his way to make her feel comfortable. "Okay. Meet you inside in fifteen minutes."

3

It was almost ten when they converged at McDonald's. Both ordered coffee and an apple pie. At this time of night the coffee was strong and bitter, the apple pies soggy after too much time under the infrared lights. As if I didn't do a number on my stomach earlier, Laurel thought as they sat down at a booth away from any other customers. Nevertheless, she quickly took a sip of the coffee.

"Well, I don't know where to start," Neil said in a weary voice. "We thought we'd tracked down a woman who'd run off with her lover twenty-four years ago. Now we know she's been in a mental institution for killing her baby."

"What do you think of her story?" Laurel asked. "Do you believe she's innocent of murder?"

Neil frowned. "You know, she never really protested her innocence. She kept saying she didn't remember. Then she said Zeke screamed at her and hit her until she claimed she *had* killed the baby. Even if the child had died of sudden infant death syndrome, I can understand her saying anything at that moment to make Zeke stop hitting her or keep him from turning on Faith, but why the confession to the police?"

"Because she was afraid and confused?"

"Afraid and confused enough to write a confession claiming she killed her own baby? And what about the pillow over the child's head?"

"According to her, Zeke is the one who said there was a pillow over the baby's head. Anyway, I suppose after all she'd been through—life with her father, five years with Zeke, the death of her baby—she might have been emotionally battered enough to say anything to the police."

"It's also possible all that history with her father and Zeke pushed her to the point where she *could* kill her baby. Laurel, did she act normal to you?"

"Sometimes. She's well-spoken. She has a good vocabulary, her sentences flow smoothly. And she seems very calm." Laurel and Neil looked at each other and said simultaneously, "Too calm."

Laurel grinned. "We sound like people on a bad television show. Still, it's true that sometimes she seemed totally removed from what she was saying as if it'd had no effect on her."

"And what about her reaction to the talk about Denise's murder?" Neil asked. "She *yawned*."

"I know. Weird." Laurel paused. "Neil, do you think she believes Faith was pregnant?"

"Yes. I don't know why I think so. Maybe because she was so quiet when Adelaide and Hannah were vehemently defending Faith's virginity. There was absolutely no expression on her face."

"What does that prove?"

"Nothing. It's just that I got the impression it wasn't one of those times she'd zoned out on us. Her lack of expression seemed deliberate." He raised his hands. "I told you it was just a feeling."

"Neil, if she *does* believe Faith was pregnant, she doesn't think you were the father. Otherwise she wouldn't have been so polite to you."

"Maybe not. She could have been playing cat and mouse with me, watching to see if I squirmed. But I'll tell you one thing—I'm damned sure she knows about the Six of Hearts."

Laurel nodded. "I think so, too. Faith didn't want anyone to know that her mother was in a mental institution, but being locked away made Genevra a safe confidante. Who would she tell? And if she *did* tell about this secret club, who would believe her? Unless Faith confirmed it, it would be considered just the ramblings of a deeply disturbed woman. But I'm sure the heart key ring Faith sent her mother means she told Genevra all about us."

"Yeah. And there's another thing. Genevra *knows* Faith didn't commit suicide. Did you see that creepy smile she gave you when she said so?"

"It was worse than creepy." Laurel took the last bite of her soggy apple pie. "Neil, what if she *is* insane? What if the baby didn't die of SIDS?"

"And Faith told her about the Six of Hearts and she figured out you might be linked to Faith's death?" She nodded and Neil looked at her solemnly. "Then we might just have been sharing tea and cookies with a murderer."

Eighteen

1

The next morning Laurel was waiting for the coffee to finish brewing when the phone rang. She sighed and picked up the receiver. "Hi, Mom."

"It's not your mother, it's Crystal." Her voice was high-pitched and tense. "I tried to get you all day yesterday and last night, but there was either no answer or a busy signal."

"I was out most of the day—"

"It doesn't matter. Oh, Laurel, I know you've heard about Denise!"

"Of course."

"Is that all you can say? 'Of course,' like it doesn't matter?"

Laurel looked out the window at a squirrel darting into a hole in a hickory tree. "Crystal, I told *all* of you what would happen if we didn't go to the police."

"Oh. You *told* us so. Does that make you proud of yourself?"

"Crystal, don't be absurd," Laurel said angrily. "I think you have a hell of a lot of nerve to call me and say something like that when *none* of you would back me up when I did what you all knew was right."

"Confessing to Kurt didn't help anything."

"I'll tell you the same thing I told Monica. We should have gone to the police immediately. We didn't give them enough time to do much. Now, why are you calling? To bitch at me because Denise was murdered in spite of my telling Kurt the truth?"

"No." Crystal's tone was apologetic. "I had no intention of bitching at you. You know how I am. When I get upset, my mouth just runs away with me. I only wanted to talk. I'm horrified and I'm *scared*. There are only three of us left. Laurel, who could be doing this?"

The coffee was finished. Laurel put the receiver between her shoulder and her ear and poured milk into the mug, then coffee. "I don't know."

"I think Neil Kamrath."

"I don't believe so. I've talked to him a lot the last few days. I just don't see him murdering Angie and Denise."

"So you think Mary or Zeke murdered them?"

"*Or* another member of the Howard family." Laurel felt slightly squeamish telling Crystal about Genevra being in town, but she believed strongly that the woman was a likely suspect and Crystal a potential victim. She told Crystal the story of Genevra Howard.

For a moment Crystal seemed speechless. Then she said in genuine wonder, "All these years Faith's mother was in an asylum for murdering her own child and she just got out?"

"Yes."

"My God, Laurel, is this whole town full of lunatics?"

"They seem to be confined to the Howard family."

"You sound like this is a joke."

"I don't mean to sound that way. I'm scared, too."

"Do you think Faith was crazy?" Crystal asked in a whisper.

"No, I don't. I don't even know if Genevra is. Maybe she was falsely accused—twenty-five years ago they didn't know as much about SIDS as they do now. She could simply act strange because she's had such an awful life and been confined for so long."

"And Mary?"

"Mary lives with Zeke. Anyone who had to live with him would act odd from time to time."

"Well, I still think Neil Kamrath is weird and Monica says Angie's ex-husband is a wacko."

"Is that why she's defending him?"

"What?"

"The law firm Monica works for is handling Stuart Burgess's defense."

"*What?*" Crystal's voice had risen to a squeak. "But someone else in the firm. Not Monica herself."

"I doubt if she's the main lawyer. Probably John Tate is. But she's his assistant or whatever they call people who help the primary counsel."

"I wouldn't know. And I have trouble believing it."

"Have you talked with her about Denise?"

"Yes. She's upset, but she handles things differently than we do."

"I'll say." Laurel took a sip of her coffee. "Look, Crystal, I want you to promise me you'll be extra careful."

After a pause, Crystal said without sarcasm, "You sound like my mother."

"Frankly, I don't trust Monica anymore. I'd rather you didn't tell her that. In fact, just to be safe, I'd rather you weren't around her. I don't want to lose you, too."

Crystal said haltingly, "Laurel, I can't believe you care so much about my welfare."

"Why not? We've been friends most of our lives. Did you think I stopped caring about you the night Faith died?"

"Not that night, but afterward. I mean, I'm sure not the privileged, pretty girl I was in high school."

"And you think friendship is based on money and looks?"

"Some friendships. Some marriages."

"Crystal, I am *not* Chuck."

"Do you think if I were the way I used to be—pretty with money and able to have children—Chuck would come back to me?"

Laurel closed her eyes briefly. "Thinking like that is pointless. Things *aren't* the way they used be, Crystal. And frankly, if it were the money and the ability to have children that attracted Chuck to you, then it wasn't really love."

"But most men want their own children."

"Joyce's children aren't his, and you said he's crazy about them. Crys, I don't mean to be cruel, but it's over with Chuck. You have to accept it. There are other men out there who can appreciate you. Chuck Landis doesn't. Let go of him. End this mess and start living again."

"It's just so hard," Crystal said meekly.

"I know it must be, but you have to do it. Besides, you have something more important to worry about right now. Your life. Not just the quality of your life, but your actual *life*. You do want to live, don't you?"

"Yes, I guess."

"You guess? You do. I know it. So do as I say and be careful until we can find this nut." She glanced at the clock. "I have to get to work, Crystal. If you want to talk more, call me tonight."

When Laurel hung up, she wondered if she'd come on too strong about Chuck. She knew how desperately Crystal loved him and wanted him back. She also agreed with Crystal that Chuck didn't love Joyce. He was attracted to her money, her children, and possibly her strength—not quiet strength of character, but her simple pushiness, her ability to get what she wanted for herself and those she called hers. Crystal didn't have that kind of strength. She needed someone to look after *her*, but that person certainly wasn't Chuck and never had been.

Oh, well, right or wrong, she said what she felt. Maybe she'd hurt Crystal's feelings about Chuck, but at least she'd reminded Crystal to stop concentrating on her marital situation and look out for herself.

Laurel arrived at the store a few minutes late. Mary was friendly, but it was hard for Laurel to act normal around her after all she'd learned last night. On the day Laurel visited the Howard house, Mary had sat on her couch with seeming sincerity telling Laurel her mother was a "sinner" because she'd run off with another man. She knew quite well where her mother had been all these years. Faith never revealed her mother's whereabouts, but she hadn't lied as Mary had done so easily.

How many other lies had Mary told her? Laurel wondered as she tried to concentrate on placing her order for the day with the wholesaler. And if Mary could lie so easily, so convincingly, what else might she be capable of doing?

2

"Where have you been?" Joyce asked when Chuck walked in, his cheeks red from the cold.

"Doing a little last-minute Christmas shopping." He placed a couple of small packages under the heavily decorated tree and shrugged out of his suede jacket. "Where are the kids?"

"The boys are at Sammy's. Mollie is at her ballet lesson."

"I can't keep up with them since they're out of school on Christmas break. What've you been up to?"

Joyce finally looked up from the hardcover novel she'd been reading. Her face was pale, her dark eyes stormy. "I spent an hour on the phone with my charming ex-husband."

"Gordon talked for an hour without the kids here?" Joyce nodded. "What's up?"

"He's going to sue me for full custody of the children."

Chuck's handsome face went blank for a moment. Finally he registered shock. "*Full* custody! How can he do that?"

"My living situation. Chuck, we've been living together for six months while Gordon is respectably remarried. To make things worse, you're unemployed. His wife is a kindergarten teacher. She even teaches Sunday school. She's a damned saint!"

Chuck sat down beside her. "Honey, I'll be employed as soon as the deal for the car lot goes through. Didn't you explain to him that these things take time?"

"He knows that. He also knows *I'm* buying the lot for you."

"What's that got to do with anything?"

Joyce slapped shut her novel. "Chuck, employment isn't the big issue. We're not married!"

"We will be as soon as I get divorced."

"And when will that be?"

"As soon as Crystal signs the papers."

"I *know* that much. But when is she going to sign them? She's had them for months."

"I talked to her."

"And you told her to have the papers at the lawyer's Monday morning. This is Wednesday afternoon. I called him half an hour ago. He still doesn't have them."

Chuck put his arm around her rigid shoulders. "Sweetheart, this has been a tough week for Crys."

"Crys is *always* having a tough week."

"I mean it, Joyce. Monday was Angie Ricci's funeral. I know she went. Then Monday night Denise Gibson was murdered."

"Gibson? Oh, Dr. Price's wife. I always forget you went to school with these people."

You always forget I'm fifteen years younger than you, Chuck thought, anger flickering through him. You always forget I had any life before you met me.

Joyce let out a small, gusty sigh. "Well, anyway, I understand that Crystal's friends have been dropping like flies the past few days—"

"That's a helluva thing to say!"

Joyce flinched at the tone of his voice. "You're right. I get nasty when I'm mad. I *am* sorry about the Price woman and especially about Angela Ricci. She *was* somebody. I saw her on Broadway once. But their deaths don't have anything to do with Crystal not signing the divorce papers. Like I said, she's had those papers for months."

"I'll talk to her again."

"Talk to her? *Talk* to her?" Joyce stood up. Her ash blond hair was pulled back in a simple ponytail and she hadn't dressed with her usual care, a simple, baggy sweater hanging over a pair of loose slacks. She wasn't worried about showing off her carefully maintained figure today. "Talking to her won't do any good. She doesn't take you seriously."

"What do you expect me to do?"

"Act like a man!"

"Act like a man?" Chuck jumped up, furious. "What do I usually act like?"

"When it comes to Crystal you act like a boy! A guilty little boy!"

"A boy!" Chuck raised his hand and Joyce dodged backward.

"Don't you *ever* hit me," she hissed. "If you do, I will never speak to you again."

Chuck immediately lowered his hand. He'd always had a quick temper and Crystal tiptoed around it. Joyce wouldn't, but he couldn't push her. No matter how angry she made him, he had to control himself around her because she held all the cards. "I'd never hurt you."

"That's not what you looked like a minute ago."

Chuck forced himself to swallow his anger. He said meekly, "I'm sorry. I really am. This situation is just—"

"Impossible." Joyce turned away and walked to the Christmas tree where she began toying with ornaments. "Chuck, I want you. I want to marry you, I want to sleep with you every night, I want to set you up in a good business, I want *you* to be the male influence in my boys' lives. Gordon is such a sanctimonious little twerp." She turned and looked at him. "But as much as I want you, I won't lose my children for you."

"Maybe if I move into an apartment for a couple of months, Gordon will settle down. Then we won't be living together."

Joyce closed her eyes in exasperation. "And Crystal will take it as a sign that you're losing interest in me and she'll *never* sign the divorce papers. No, Chuck, you have to do something. *Fast*. Otherwise . . ."

Chuck looked around at the beautiful living room. This house was four times larger than the houses he'd shared with his parents and with Crystal. He thought about the car lot that this summer could be his. He thought about his new

Corvette in the driveway. Finally, and most wrenchingly, he thought of the three children he'd come to think of as his own. He couldn't lose all of this because of Crystal, whom he'd come to hate. He just couldn't.

"Don't worry, Joyce," he said, pulling her reluctant body into his arms. "We're going to be together as soon as possible. I'll see to it."

3

Laurel was in the kitchen taking two Excedrin when she heard the bell on the front door ring again. She glanced at the clock. Four-fifteen. Thank goodness. Forty-five minutes until closing time. It had been a busy day, the wholesalers had run short on gladioli, which she desperately needed for all the orders coming in for Denise's funeral, and she'd lost too much sleep lately. Now she felt as if an ice pick were lodged behind her eyes.

She walked into the display room to see Kurt standing impatiently at the counter. She smiled and said, "Hi!"

He glared and said, "I need to talk to you."

Laurel halted. "Couldn't this wait until tonight?"

"No. I have something to do. Besides, you're kind of hard to catch at home these days. Or should I say *nights*?"

Chatter in the workroom stopped. The women were tired. All they needed was a scene to liven up things. All Laurel needed was a scene to drive the ice pick deeper behind her eyes.

"Norma, would you cover the counter if anyone comes in?" she called.

"Sure."

Laurel looked at Kurt. "Let's go in the kitchen." He strode ahead of her. She closed the door. "Do you want coffee? It's probably awfully strong by now. There might be a Coke in the refrigerator."

"I don't want anything to drink. Just sit down."

She sat as ordered and looked him straight in the eye. "I

know someone else hasn't been murdered or you'd be a
little kinder. What is it?"

"I hear you've been spending a lot of time with Neil
Kamrath lately."

"And how did you find out this juicy bit of gossip?"

"You were seen at McDonald's. *Twice*."

His face was red. He looked absurdly indignant. Laurel
gasped and clapped a hand to her chest. "My God, how
compromising! I'm so humiliated! Why, if this gets
out . . ."

Kurt scowled. "Knock off the comedy routine. I'm serious."

Laurel couldn't stifle her laughter. "I know you are—
that's what's so funny. You aren't jealous so what is this
all about?"

"It's about your safety. I've told you I don't like Kamrath."

"And because you don't like him, I'm not safe with
him?" Suddenly Laurel was angry. "Kurt, you've barely
spoken to me since I told you about Faith's death. Now
you stomp into the store and embarrass me in front of my
employees because you've heard I was at McDonald's with
Neil. McDonald's, of all places! Who the hell do you think
you are?"

"I'm someone who cares about you and doesn't want to
see you hurt by that freak."

"Freak? Why is he a freak? Because he's not a huntin'
and fishin' and beer-drinkin' good ol' boy like you and
Chuck? Well, let me tell you something. Chuck has devastated Crystal and you haven't done wonders for my feelings the last few days, either."

"Chuck and I are nothing like Kamrath. He's weird, Laurel. He's dangerous."

"Dangerous? Because he writes horror novels?"

"No. I've been doing some checking up on him."

"Kurt—"

"Don't tell me it's none of my business. We've had a
murder here and there was one in New York. You and I

know they're connected, they're both related to Faith Howard. Kamrath is a suspect."

"Unofficially."

"Yeah, unofficially, but still . . ."

"Okay," Laurel said stiffly. "What awful thing did you
find out about him?"

"He beat his wife. She had to get a restraining order."

"He *beat* Ellen? I don't believe it."

"Believe it. She reported two incidents but didn't press
charges. Finally he pushed her down the stairs. She had a
broken rib and eye damage. *That* time she still didn't press
charges but she did get the restraining order. She told him
if there was one more incident, she *would* press charges.
Two weeks later she died."

"In a car wreck." Laurel's mouth had gone completely
dry. "Ellen died in a car wreck."

"She was driving a car that was missing a nut on one of
the steering tie rods." Laurel frowned. "Put simply, the
steering mechanism had been tampered with. She had no
control over the car."

"And you think Neil had something to do with that?"

"His father-in-law did. The police were convinced
enough to do a full-scale investigation."

"And obviously found nothing to incriminate Neil."

"Nothing solid enough to hold him on."

"Kurt, his *son* was in that car. He adored the child. You
think he wanted to kill him, too?"

"The kid was supposed to be spending the weekend with
a friend." Kurt looked at her grimly. "Laurel, Kamrath is a
violent man. He might be guilty of murdering his wife and
child."

Laurel felt perspiration popping out on her forehead as
her headache intensified. "Even if Neil did tamper with the
car, which I find impossible to believe, why would he kill
Angie and Denise?"

"Because he's a nut who only cared about one person in
his whole life besides himself—Faith Howard."

"That's not true."

Kurt smacked his hand on the table. "What is *wrong* with you? I'd expect this kind of stubborn thinking from Crystal, but you've always been so sensible. For God's sake, you barely know the guy. You've known me most of your life but you'd rather believe him than me. I don't get it."

"Maybe because I'm not sure I *do* know you."

"What does that mean?"

"What if I tell you I know who the father of that baby was, and it *wasn't* Neil?"

Kurt gave her a sour look. "And just who do you think was the lucky guy?"

She spoke evenly although her heart pounded. "The day I was in your apartment I saw the book of Shakespeare's sonnets. It was inscribed 'Love, Faith.' She gave you that book. She was in love with you. You were the father of that baby. Not Neil, *you!*"

Kurt met her accusing gaze without flinching. "I think that guy must be a better hypnotist than a writer because he's sure got you mesmerized." He shook his head. "I came here to warn you. That's all I can do. If you end up like Angie and Denise—"

"It won't be on your conscience," Laurel snapped. She shoved away from the table, setting it rocking. "I think you'd better go now. I'm tired of your evasions and I'm tired of your insinuations about Neil."

Kurt slammed out the back door without a word while Laurel stood trembling, her body wracked by violent chills.

Nineteen

1

Laurel felt shaken to the bone when she got home. She hadn't realized until the last week how placid her life had been for years. College and a degree in business had gone smoothly. She'd come home "just until I decide what to do" and ended up staying. Her romance and breakup with Bill Haynes five years earlier had seemed earth-shattering at the time, but compared to what had been happening lately, it was nothing. In fact, at the moment she could no longer clearly picture Bill's face. Good Lord, Laurel, she thought as she walked in the front door, tossed off her coat, and kicked off her shoes, are you losing your mind? You thought you wanted to spend your life with him. Now you can't remember what he looked like. If all this mayhem doesn't stop, by this time next week you won't be able to find your way to the store.

She fed the dogs and gave each a rawhide chewbone to work on. The bones were always a special treat and she felt she hadn't spent enough time playing with them lately. While they gnawed assiduously, she searched the refrigerator for food. Because she'd planned the trip to Florida, she'd let supplies dwindle to nearly nothing. Before all the trouble she'd always done the shopping on her way home from the store. Now as soon as she left Damron Floral, she made a beeline for the safety of the house.

Finally she decided on canned chicken noodle soup. She wasn't very hungry anyway. Certainly not like last night when she couldn't seem to get enough food.

Ten minutes later she sat over the hot soup thinking about the things Kurt had said about Neil. Certainly he wouldn't lie about Ellen getting a restraining order against Neil or about the formal police investigation of the wreck that killed her. But could that investigation have simply been routine? What about the restraining order?

She put down her spoon. Even if everything Kurt said were true, he hadn't explained the book of sonnets from Faith in his apartment. He hadn't denied being the father of her child. She'd thought before that maybe he hated Neil so much because Neil was a rival for Faith's affection. But Faith had never talked about Kurt with any particular interest. She and Faith had been best friends. Wouldn't she have picked up on *something* special about Faith's feelings toward Kurt if they were more than casual friendship?

Which brought her back to Neil. It wasn't impossible to check on his story that Robbie had been her first husband's child whom Neil had adopted if she had access to adoption records, which she didn't. Ellen's parents would know, but she couldn't possibly call them. She didn't even know who or where they were. And even if she did, Ellen's father obviously hated Neil. Could she get a truthful answer from him or his wife?

She put her head in her hands. "Oh, God," she moaned, "this is just too hard to figure out. I don't know who to believe, Kurt or Neil." But the true paternity of Faith's baby wasn't really the issue. Finding the killer of Angie and Denise was, and that might not have anything to do with Faith's pregnancy.

Laurel finished her soup and washed the pan and bowl, looking out the window over the sink. Light snow was beginning to fall again, feathering down in big, fluffy flakes. She probably wouldn't have been able to get to Florida tomorrow as planned anyway. If this weather held, there would be no flights.

When she'd finished the dishes, she decided a fire would be nice. She walked into the living room and saw one lonely log waiting for the fireplace. She sighed. She could skip the fire or she could go outside and get more wood.

Her desire to cuddle up with the dogs in front of a fire won out. She threw on an old jacket and went out the kitchen door to the back porch.

A strong north wind blew snow onto the covered porch. Laurel shivered and lifted a piece of wood off the top of the stack, then another. That should be enough to keep the fire going for a couple of hours. Then she planned on going to bed early.

She was turning back toward the door when she saw something white from the corner of her eye. She blinked, then peered intently into the darkness. Although officially the backyard of the house was half an acre, no houses were near hers. She'd considered having the yard fenced in when she got the dogs, but as they grew up they showed no tendency to wander away from the house and she never bothered. So what she looked at now was half an acre of lawn with a few trees and a single dusk-to-dawn light blending into acres of woods beyond.

What had she seen? Merely a flash of light on the snow, she decided. Wind chilled the right side of her face. Her eyes were filling with tears from the cold when she caught another glimpse. A dog? An opossum or a groundhog? Whatever it was, it turned and headed for her.

A thrill of fear ran down Laurel's neck. A groundhog or opossum would run from her, not to her. Besides, she'd seen stray animals out here before, but they didn't move like this thing. It seemed to be half running, half crouching. And for some reason, she couldn't move.

Suddenly April and Alex burst through the dog door, barking furiously. Laurel cried out and dropped the wood. The dogs stopped abruptly at the edge of the porch. Laurel looked into the yard. Whatever it was back along the edge of the trees had also stopped. They all stood frozen in place for a moment. Then the dogs charged off the porch, kicking up snow as they raced across the yard. With a wraithlike movement, the thing moved back into the trees.

The dogs were still in pursuit when Laurel found her

voice. She began yelling for them. Dear God, what *was* that thing? It was too big for April and Alex to take on. They were gentle, inexperienced fighters. They could so easily be killed.

"April! Alex!" she shrieked. "Come here!" Her heart sank when she heard the sounds of snarling and then a yelp. "April! Alex! Come back to me *now!*" She tried to whistle but her lips were too stiff from the cold. "April—"

Abruptly the dogs appeared under the dusk-to-dawn light. Laurel knelt and held out her arms. Both dogs dashed to her. Alex was limping, but she didn't see any blood. He breathed heavily and snuggled as closely to her as he could. April stood a little apart. She held something in her mouth. "Drop it," Laurel said gently. This was one of the few commands the dogs understood. "April, *drop* it."

Obediently April dropped something onto Laurel's lap. She picked it up, studying it under the porch light.

It was a scrap of white cotton cloth stained with a few drops of blood.

2

This probably wasn't a good idea, Joyce thought as she walked up Crystal's driveway. She'd left her car by the side of the road, not wanting to give Crystal any warning. After all, she hadn't even told Chuck what she intended to do. He would be offended that she didn't think he could handle the situation on his own. Crystal was certain to run to Chuck and claim Joyce had tried to intimidate her. Well, so what? Chuck might bluster, but she could handle him. Joyce knew he did not want to lose her and all she could do for him. Crystal? She was a spoiled little bitch who'd always gotten her way by manipulating, playing helpless, crying like a pathetic child. But tears and entreaties wouldn't work with Joyce. Crystal didn't have her fooled for a minute. She could whine all she wanted but Joyce wouldn't feel an ounce of sympathy for her.

Snow blew on her. Why had she worn her newest cashmere coat when it was snowing? It wasn't as if she cared about making a good impression. She didn't care how she looked in front of Crystal. She should have worn her lined raincoat.

God, what a crummy little house, she thought. How could Chuck have lived here for so long? Of course the house he'd grown up in hadn't been much better. He'd never had a taste of the good life until lately.

The lights were on but when Joyce knocked on the door, no one answered. She tried again. Nothing. Well, she'd expected it. She reached in her purse and dug around until she found a metal key ring holding two keys. Chuck's keys to the house. She opened the door and yelled, "Crystal?" She smiled, thinking, Trapped like a rat! She went farther into the house. "Crystal!"

Two lamps burned in the tiny, ragged living room. Joyce stood still, listening. No sound of human movement. Still, Crystal must be here. Her car was in the driveway and the lights were on. Would the idiot actually cower and hide from her?

Annoyed, Joyce stalked through the little house. The kitchen had worn linoleum and a plethora of samplers, baskets, and embroidered pot holders hanging on the walls. The red light on the coffemaker glowed. She went down the hall and entered a small bedroom with a white chest of drawers and a crib with a mobile hanging above it. Chuck said Crystal had her first miscarriage eleven years ago. Had this room been furnished for that baby or only last year when they awaited the arrival of their stillborn daughter?

Joyce shook off the thought. She didn't want to feel sorry for Crystal. On down the hall was a small bathroom done in shades of pink and black with, oh, God, flamingos on the shower curtain! Joyce shook her head and smiled. For someone who'd grown up in a moneyed home, Crystal had dreadful taste.

Joyce's opinion was reinforced when she saw the "master bedroom." The pink theme continued with pink fuzzy throw rugs, which were really bath mats, cheap mass-produced pictures of huge-eyed children and kittens, heart-shaped pillows on the bed, and lacy doilies on the dresser. Had her masculine, virile Chuck spent years sleeping with Crystal in this child's room? Joyce wondered. Of course he had, but she didn't want to think about that, didn't want to picture him making love in this pitiful little room, conceiving children that would never live. No, vapid Crystal could never have satisfied the man Joyce knew. She had nothing to be jealous about where sex was concerned.

When Joyce walked out of the bedroom, she stood still for a moment. The tiny house was immaculately neat. It was also empty.

Joyce entered the living room again. Well, where the hell was she? She had to be around or the coffeemaker wouldn't be on. Joyce went to a window and looked out. There was a one-car garage attached to the house, but nearly a hundred feet away was a double garage Chuck told her he'd built and used to work on cars while between jobs. A light glowed through the windows. Crystal must be in the garage, Joyce thought.

She started out the front door, then paused. The snow was coming down harder. She knew there was a second driveway leading from the garage to the road, but the path from the house to the extra garage was narrow and rutted, trees crowding close on either side. She saw a plaid coat and a pair of rubber boots sitting beside the door. Quickly she slipped off her cashmere coat, put on the plaid coat and pulled the rubber boots over her leather pumps.

I should just go home, she fumed as she stepped out in the snow. If I'd known this was going to be so much damned trouble I wouldn't have come tonight. Then she remembered her ex-husband Gordon's phone call that morning. He'd been livid, spluttering his outrage. After their divorce two years ago, he'd moved to Boston. For the past six months he hadn't realized Chuck was living with her. Then he'd received an anonymous letter from someone in Wheeling. Joyce thought the person was probably Crystal. At the moment Joyce wasn't really angry over the letter.

It was just a catalyst. This situation could have drifted on for months. Gordon's call had merely spurred her into action.

Lord, this place was primitive, Joyce fumed silently, appalled. Chuck told her that Crystal's family had been rich. She barely remembered the Smiths and she knew they weren't what she considered rich, but they'd certainly been comfortable. She could even recall her own parents and Gordon talking about what a shock it was when they were killed in the plane crash and everyone learned they were bankrupt. What a blow that must have been to Crystal, Joyce thought. Her whole life she'd been emotionally and financially indulged. Then suddenly she had nothing. Nothing except Chuck, whom she'd married a year before her parents' deaths. He'd stuck by her a long time, especially when all Crystal could do was drag him down. But now it's my turn, Joyce said to herself. I deserve Chuck after all those dull years with Gordon and Chuck deserves a better life than he's ever had. She'd make Crystal see that tonight, even if it killed her.

She wiped snow off her face and cursed as she turned her foot in a rut. She stopped to rub her ankle. That's when she heard a rustling in the trees. She looked at the garage. No door stood open, but maybe Crystal had come out without Joyce seeing her. "Crystal?" she called. Silence. Just the wind in the trees, she decided.

Joyce took a couple of steps forward, wincing as pain shot up her leg. Oh, hell, had she sprained her ankle? *Why* had she come here? She'd just go home—

She thought of Gordon again. No. She'd come here to talk to Crystal, and goddammit, after all this trouble she *would* talk to Crystal.

Something rustled in the brush again. Joyce stopped. Any kind of animal could lurk around here. She was no expert on wildlife, but didn't opossums and groundhogs come out at night? Would they attack a person? What if it was a skunk and she got sprayed? That would just make the whole damned evening. Maybe it was a deer. But deer didn't eat meat, that much she knew, so she wasn't about to become dinner for some huge-antlered male deer, whatever they were called. A big dog? Joyce hated dogs and they hated her. She hoped it wasn't a dog.

Get to the garage instead of standing here trying to figure out what kind of animal might be stalking you, Joyce thought furiously. The more trouble she went to, the more her temper grew. She hobbled a few feet farther. Rustling. Much closer. Joyce managed one high-pitched squeal before something crashed against the side of her head. She fell heavily to the left. Her arm broke the fall, but the force of the blow blinded her. Or was it blood running into her eyes that turned the world black? She rubbed her hand over her face. Wet. Wet with snow or blood?

Before she could even try to look at her hand, something struck her along the jaw. She cried out, pushing her battered face into the snow, trying to fasten her hands over her head to protect it. Something slammed down on her neck. Feeling abruptly left her body. Feeling, but not awareness. She heard heavy breathing, muttering. She also heard a slight whistling sound as an object swept through the air, striking her paralyzed body time after time. Finally she heard her own labored breathing growing raspier, almost grinding, until at last it stopped.

Twenty

1

Laurel hustled the dogs inside as quickly as possible, locked the door, slid the lock panel down on the dog door, then checked every door and window in the house. Finally she inspected each dog carefully. Neither had bite marks but Alex whimpered when she ran her hand over his left hip. No blood, just pain. He'd been kicked, she thought. Some big animals kicked, but nothing that resembled what she'd seen in the woods. It was a person.

As she tossed newspaper in the fireplace as kindling for her single log, she wondered what the presence of the person meant. At the very least it was meant to frighten her. At the worst? It had been coming toward her. What if the dogs hadn't run outside?

They sat on the floor beside her in front of the fireplace. "Where did all this bravery come from?" she asked them. They looked anxiously into her face. They were breathing heavily, frightened, but they'd still come to her rescue. She would never have believed it. "I'm very proud of you," she told them. "But if anything else happens, you let me take care of myself, okay?"

But could she have taken care of herself? She was weaponless and she had no fighting skills. The person who had killed Angie and Denise had been armed, strong, and vicious.

A few days ago she would have immediately called Kurt. Now she wouldn't think of asking for his help. Still, there

HERR MEMORIAL LIBRARY

might be evidence outside. Footprints. Blood. She had to call the police.

In twenty minutes two deputies arrived. Laurel was glad Kurt wasn't one of them. She explained what happened. They looked at her skeptically and she could tell they thought she'd panicked at the sight of some small animal. Then she told them about the funeral wreath, pointed out the red heart spray-painted on her door, and showed them the piece of white bloodstained cotton April had brought back. "Don't try to tell me a groundhog was wearing white cotton," she said to the youngest, cockiest deputy named Williams, whom she knew Kurt didn't like. "Thinks he knows everything," Kurt had complained. Laurel agreed. Williams literally swaggered and talked to her as if she were a fool. Thank goodness his partner had more sense. He searched the area and reported back to her that there were a few footprints in the snow although the dogs had churned up a lot of it. "The footprints disappear in the woods, Miss Damron. There are a lot of evergreens back there that protected the ground from the snow."

"Would you guess the ones you saw to be a man's or a woman's prints?" Laurel asked.

"About a size eight," Williams said with authority. "A woman."

The other deputy looked exasperated. "We're not sure of the exact shoe size. I'd guess larger than eight. Could be a man or a woman in boots."

"Or a woman with big feet," Williams put in. "Look, Miss Damron, it was probably just a prankster but you got spooked because of the murder lately. Just keep your doors locked and relax. You'll be fine."

Laurel didn't appreciate being dismissed so lightly. Maybe it was because the police got so many false alarms, but they couldn't ignore the fact that a woman had been murdered two days ago. Perhaps that was the trouble. Maybe women who lived alone had been calling in over every noise, real or imagined.

Still, after they left, Laurel couldn't stop thinking about

the incident. She looked again at the piece of white cotton. Audra said the "ghost" that had come into her room wore white. Was this nut actually dressing up to scare people? Audra was one thing. She was eight. But had someone donned a white robe and come crouching toward *her*, a thirty-year-old woman? Yes. And who would do that?

The first name that popped into her head was Genevra Howard. It was so easy to imagine a woman recently released from a mental institution wearing a white robe, pretending to be or imagining herself to be a ghost. It was something right out of *Jane Eyre*. But not as absurd as it might seem at first considering the circumstances.

Laurel wanted to find out if Genevra Howard had been at the Lewis sisters' all evening, but what excuse could she use? Oh, hell, what did it matter? she thought after turning over several possibilities. This was too important to sit around wasting time figuring out how to be diplomatic.

She looked up the Lewis sisters' number in the phone directory. In a moment the phone was ringing before a fragile voice said, "Hello?"

"Miss Adelaide?"

"No, Miss Hannah."

"Oh, Miss Hannah, hello. This is Laurel Damron."

"Why, hello, Miss Damron. Adelaide and I have so been enjoying our wreath. Thank you again."

"You're very welcome. And please call me Laurel. Miss Hannah, I'm going to ask something that may strike you as none of my business, but I have a good reason for asking. Has Genevra been home all evening?"

There were several beats of silence and Laurel thought Miss Hannah was indeed going to say it was none of her business. Instead the woman said, "When Adelaide and I rose this morning, Genevra was gone. Clothes, toiletries, everything."

"Oh. But I thought she was going to stay around and try to befriend Mary."

"So did we, dear. We just don't understand."

"Did she leave a note saying where she was going?"

"No. She has a little apartment near . . . well, where she was staying before." The mental hospital, Laurel thought. "We've called but there's no answer. She's had plenty of time to get back . . ."

"I'm sure you'll hear from her soon, Miss Hannah."

"Do you think so?"

"Oh, yes. She was probably just overwhelmed with being out in the world. She might even have been afraid of running into Zeke."

Anyone who knew Laurel well would have heard the insincerity in her voice, but Miss Hannah said hopefully, "Why, I hadn't even thought of that! I'm sure that's all it was—a little case of nerves. She's been through so much. Oh, Laurel, you've made me feel much better."

"I'm glad. I hate to be rude, but I really have to go now."

"But why did you wonder if Genevra had been here all evening?"

"Good-bye, Miss Hannah. Merry Christmas."

She hung up before the woman could ask any more questions and she had to tell more lies. The truth was she didn't believe for a moment Genevra was on her way back to Pennsylvania. She thought the woman had been in her backyard less than two hours ago.

Laurel paced restlessly around the house, flipping on the television but not paying much attention to the national news. World problems seemed so unreal when she was in immediate danger herself. She knew she wouldn't get any sleep tonight. Day after tomorrow Damron Floral would close for Christmas. She wished it were closed tomorrow. Of course as the manager she had the power to close whenever she wanted, but Denise's visitation would be tomorrow night and she had a lot of orders to fill. Orders to fill. How businesslike she sounded, but thinking about making floral arrangements was better than thinking of going to the funeral visitation of another friend, another one who would rest in a closed coffin because she'd been mutilated by a maniac.

Laurel leaned forward and put her head in her hands.

Good Lord, what was happening? Faith's death was an accident but the repercussions had already destroyed two women. Two good women. How many more would be claimed before this madness ended?

The phone rang. Now what? she thought. Had word of her prowler filtered back to Kurt? Her mother? Miss Hannah?

She was totally unprepared for the raspy, sexless voice on the other end. "Your friend Crystal needs you. She's in trouble. Deadly trouble." The line went dead.

Laurel sat dumbfounded for a moment holding the receiver. Who in the name of God was that? Was it a prank?

Quickly she looked at the notepad beside her phone and dialed Crystal's number. Three rings. Six rings. Twelve rings. She hung up. What should she do? Sit here safe and cozy and tell herself it was a cruel joke, or risk going to Crystal's funeral next week?

She called the police. "Williams here," the crisp voice said.

Oh, great, she thought. The smartass. She took a deep breath and told him what had just happened.

"Having an exciting evening, aren't you, Miss Damron?" he commented with ill-concealed humor.

"This is serious," she snapped. "I can't get an answer on the phone at Crystal's house."

"Well, now, isn't it just possible she went out for the evening?"

"Possible but unlikely. Are you going out there or not?"

He sighed. "I think this is just a practical joke," he said. And you're a hysterical fool, Laurel could feel him thinking. "But if it'll make you feel better, we'll take a run past there in a little while."

"In a little while!" Laurel said loudly. "Crystal could be in trouble *now!*"

"Just calm down, Miss Damron. I told you we'll check it out and we will."

"But *when* . . . oh, never mind," Laurel said in frustration. "Please get there as soon as you can."

Which given his attitude could be an hour. And what do I do in the meantime?

She checked her purse for the canister of Mace. "This doesn't look too threatening," she muttered. She went to the kitchen and searched the drawers for the largest butcher knife she could find. She held it up, feeling like the teenage heroine in a horror movie. Jamie Lee Curtis in *Halloween*. "I swear I'm going to buy a gun and learn how to use it," she said aloud. "It's ridiculous for a woman living alone to be so damned defenseless."

Armed with her knife and her Mace, she pulled on her coat and looked at the dogs. No, she wouldn't take them. They'd saved her earlier this evening, but she'd been terrified for them. That concern might distract her tonight, when she needed to be alert. "You two stay here," she said as they looked at her expectantly. "Hopefully I'll be back in less than an hour."

As she drove through the snow toward Crystal's house, she wondered if Crystal had it in her to fight back if attacked. She'd always seemed so gentle, so childlike. Long ago Laurel had thought they'd been aptly named. Crystal was as fragile as fine glass. Inside, Laurel was as tough as the plant for which she'd been named—the mountain laurel with its heavy, hard wood.

When she finally reached the narrow road that led to Crystal's house, Laurel noticed a white Lexus parked by the side, just off the pavement. It appeared to be empty. Maybe someone had car trouble, she thought. But the closest house from which to make a call was Crystal's.

She pulled slowly into Crystal's driveway. There sat her little red Volkswagen. Lights burned in the house. Laurel turned her engine off and sat for a moment. Had the call been a ruse to get her here? Was she being incredibly reckless? Yes. So what would she do?

She blew the horn. If Crystal came to the door safe and sound, she would know the call was a prank, talk to Crystal for a few minutes, then scuttle back home, knowing Deputy Williams would be laughing at her when he finally made his way out here to check on Crystal for himself.

But Crystal didn't come to the door. Laurel blew the horn again. Her eyes fixed on the door, she waited anxiously. Nothing. Oh, God, what now?

"Now you take up your weapons and go in," she said aloud. "I hope Crystal appreciates this because I am scared to death."

She opened the car door and ran to the front door of the house. She started to pound on it, but realized if Crystal were in any shape to answer, she would have come when Laurel honked the horn. The knob turned easily in her hand. An unlocked door, not a good sign. She stepped into the living room. "Crystal?" Quiet. The smell of strong, bitter coffee wafted from the kitchen. Laurel went in and saw perhaps an eighth of an inch of black gunk in the bottom of the pot. She turned it off.

Laurel made a quick tour of the house. There were no signs of a struggle. The only thing out of place was an expensive black cashmere coat lying on the couch. It certainly wasn't Crystal's.

"I should just go home," Laurel muttered when she caught a flash of light through a living room window. The garage light. What on earth would Crystal be doing in the garage on a cold night like this?

The garage was an uncomfortable distance from the house. The path to it was lined with trees. Laurel wanted to walk out there about as much as she wanted to walk over hot coals. But she wouldn't have any peace of mind until she knew Crystal was safe.

Holding the butcher knife and the Mace, feeling like an idiot but also so frightened she was trembling, she went back outside, leaving the door to the house open. Snow fell on her face and her bare head, the dampness making her hair curl tighter. She walked slowly along the path. The wind had picked up. Tree branches groaned above her head. She'd forgotten to put on boots and snow came over the tops of her shoes.

Laurel was halfway to the garage when she heard a

branch above her head cracking. She looked up and saw the narrow branch falling. She ran, her feet sliding on the path. The branch crashed to the ground behind her. She looked back, then toppled over something lying on the path. She screamed as she went down but still remembered to toss the knife to the side so she wouldn't fall on top of it. She landed on knees and hands and whipped around, grappling wildly for the knife even before she looked at what she'd fallen over. Her hand closed over the wooden handle. She tried to scramble to her feet, but she slipped on the snow and fell again, this time landing against the mound. It was motionless.

Drawing a deep breath, Laurel fought down her rampaging terror. She'd been floundering for at least a minute and the mound had remained perfectly still. Her heart pounding, she reached out and touched it. A plaid coat. *Crystal*'s plaid coat.

Tentatively she put her hand on what she now realized was a shoulder. She rolled over the body. Beneath matted brownish hair was the crushed, bloody face of a woman.

"Crystal!" she screamed. "Oh, God, I was too late!"

2

Laurel clambered to her feet and stumbled sobbing back to the house. She slammed the door behind her, locked it, and ran for the phone. By now she knew the number of police headquarters by heart. "Williams here."

"Good God, are you *still* there?" Laurel shouted.

"Who is this?"

"This is Laurel Damron. I called you an hour ago and asked you to check on Crystal Landis—"

"Now, Miss Damron, we're pretty busy tonight," he said in a patronizing tone. "I told you we'd take a spin by there as soon as we could."

"She's dead."

"What?"

"She's *dead*, dammit! I came to her house because I

knew you wouldn't and she's dead . . . beaten to death,"
Laurel choked. "Is Kurt Rider there?"

Williams sounded slightly flustered. "I don't think so . . .
no."

"Well, get him. I should have called him in the first
place. He would have done his job. Oh, God . . ."

"Calm down, Miss Damron. We'll be right there."

Laurel hung up then looked at the receiver. It was
smeared with blood. She held up her hands. Blood all over
them. She didn't remember touching the battered face, but
it could have been on the coat. That ugly plaid coat Laurel
thought looked like a horse blanket. She wished she could
see Crystal walking into the store in her ugly coat again.

Still crying, occasionally hiccuping from the emotion and
shock, Laurel went into the kitchen and turned on the fau-
cet. There was no bar soap—only dishwashing liquid. She
soaped, rinsed, soaped again, paying special attention to her
nails. Anything to keep her mind off what had just happened.

What if she'd come immediately after the phone call?
Was Crystal already dead, or could she have prevented the
murder? How? With her Mace? Her butcher knife? Why
hadn't she called Kurt? Simple pride. Pride that might have
cost Crystal her life.

Laurel turned off the water and reached for a towel. As
she slowly dried her hands, she heard a noise at the front
door. A click, as if the lock were opening, then a faint groan
of hinges that needed oil.

She froze. It wasn't the police. They couldn't have gotten
here this fast. Besides, they would have arrived with much
more fanfare. Cold air wafted in from the living room. The
door closed.

Laurel stepped to the kitchen table and picked up the
butcher knife. She moved soundlessly to the living room,
her breath coming so hard and fast she was afraid she might
faint.

In the glow of the lamplight she saw a woman staring in

puzzlement at the black cashmere coat on the couch. She looked up and Laurel stifled a scream.

It was Crystal.

3

Crystal's eyes batted wide. "Good Lord, Laurel, what's wrong?"

Laurel dropped the knife. "You're alive!"

Crystal's horrified gaze flew to the knife on the floor. Then she looked back at Laurel and said in a thin, wary voice, "Of course I'm alive. What made you think I wasn't?"

Laurel rushed to her and enfolded her in a hug. "I don't think I've ever been so glad to see anyone. It was so awful . . ."

She pulled back. Crystal was here, alive and healthy, but someone lay beaten to death on the path.

"Laurel, what is going on?" Crystal demanded.

"Where have you been?"

"Next door, baby-sitting."

"Alone, at *night,* after Denise—"

"The little Grant girl is terribly sick. They had to take her to the emergency room. The baby was asleep and the Grants asked if I could come over and watch him. I just slipped over . . . it's so close, Laurel, and it was an emergency."

"That's why your car is in the driveway."

"Yes. I told you they're right next door." Crystal frowned. "Laurel, why did you think I was dead? And how did you get in here? I'm sure I locked the door."

"The door wasn't locked. Crystal, sit down."

"You've got bad news," Crystal said in alarm.

"Yes. So sit down and brace yourself. The police will be here soon."

"The *police!*"

"Crystal, listen to me. I got a call. Someone told me you were in trouble—deadly trouble. It was a terrible voice, grating, raspy. I couldn't even tell if it was a man or a woman. I called the police, but they didn't sound like they were in any hurry to get here, so I came."

"You came to help me when you thought there might be a killer here? Laurel, I—"

Lights flashed in the driveway and in a moment someone pounded on the door. Laurel opened it. Williams stood in front of her. "You've found the body of Crystal Landis?"

"What?" Crystal cried. "I'm not dead! I'm right here!"

Williams's eyes narrowed as he looked at Laurel. She gazed back stonily, keeping her voice even. "There *is* a body on the path between the house and the garage. I assumed it was Crystal. The face is so mutilated I couldn't tell who it was."

Williams still looked at her suspiciously, but he told her and Crystal to stay in the house. "I don't want you messing up evidence if there really *is* someone there," he said.

As he walked down the path, Crystal asked in a shaking voice, "Who do you think it is?"

"I don't know, but she was wearing your plaid coat. I couldn't tell much about her hair."

"Was it dark?"

"No. More like yours." Laurel looked at the cashmere coat on the couch. "Does that belong to you?"

Crystal reached down and touched the fine cloth. "You think I own a coat this nice?"

"No, I didn't think so. But it was in here when I arrived, which means the woman took it off and put on your plaid coat."

"But I'm telling you I locked the door!"

"Well, she got in somehow." Laurel stared at the coat. "Crys, does Chuck still have a set of keys to this house?"

"What? I don't know. Maybe. But what does this have to do with Chuck? This isn't *his* coat."

"What kind of car does Joyce drive?"

Crystal frowned. "Joyce? I don't know. I've never been good with makes of cars. It always drove Chuck crazy. It's white. Something expensive."

Laurel sat down beside Crystal. "I saw a white Lexus parked by the side of the road when I came here. Add that to a set of keys to this house with a woman who has an expensive coat and hair the color of yours. Who does it sound like?"

"I don't know, Laurel . . . it could be—" Crystal broke off. "Oh, my God! Joyce!"

Twenty-one

1

"Crystal, I think we'd better call Monica."

Crystal blinked at her. "Why? What does this have to do with her?"

"If it *is* Joyce, you need a lawyer."

"A lawyer! What do I need a lawyer for? I haven't done anything!"

"Crystal, who has a better motive for killing Joyce Overton than you?"

Crystal opened her mouth, closed it, then turned so pale Laurel thought she was going to faint. "But we don't know if it *is* Joyce—"

"I think it is and if I'm right . . . Crystal, I'm calling Monica. If Williams gets back here before Monica does, you don't say one word to him, do you hear me? Not *one* word."

"But I didn't do anything," Crystal repeated in a wispy voice.

"Not a word and I mean it!"

Laurel hated to lash out at Crystal, but she thought it was the only way to get through to her. She didn't seem to realize the seriousness of the situation. She looked like she hardly knew where she was.

Luckily Monica was in her room. "Monica, it's Laurel. I need for you to get to Crystal's house as soon as possible."

"What's wrong?"

"There's a dead woman on Crystal's lawn and I think it's Joyce Overton."

"Who?"

"Chuck's girlfriend."

"Wow. You really know how to get my attention."

"Now is not the time for your deadpan humor. Get over here. Crystal needs some legal advice in a hurry."

"Be right there," Monica said and hung up. Thank God I didn't have to argue with her, Laurel thought as she sat down beside a shaking Crystal. Williams would be back any moment and in fifteen minutes heaven knew how many policemen would be here, badgering Crystal, who had no more idea how to handle a situation like this than a child would.

When she looked away from the phone, Crystal sat huddled on the couch. Laurel went to her. "Monica is on her way."

"I need a drink."

"I don't think that's a good idea. When the police question you, you don't want to be breathing alcohol fumes all over them."

"I thought you told me not to say anything to them."

"Not until Monica gets here. She'll tell you which questions to answer."

Crystal gnawed on a thumbnail. "Maybe it isn't Joyce."

"Maybe not. Still, there will be questions."

"If it *is* Joyce, Chuck will think I killed her out of jealousy."

"What Chuck Landis thinks is the least of your worries, Crys. Forget about Chuck."

Williams walked inside without knocking. "I've already radioed for help," he said, his young face taut. He's scared, Laurel thought. He's never been faced with something this serious and it's taken the swagger right out of him. "I found the body. Any idea who it might be?"

"No," Laurel said.

"Joyce Overton," Crystal blurted at the same instant. Laurel glared at her.

Williams looked at Crystal and asked, "Who is Joyce Overton and why do you think it's her?"

Crystal looked fearfully at Laurel and huddled even deeper into herself. "I don't know."

"You don't know what?" Williams barked. "Who Joyce Overton is or why you think it's her?"

"I'm not going to talk to you."

Williams assumed his tough-cop face. "Lady, you *have* to talk to me!"

"Not without the presence of her lawyer," Laurel said.

"Her *lawyer*! What do you have to hide, Mrs. Landis?"

"Nothing," Crystal mumbled.

"Then what's all this about not talking to me without a lawyer? It makes you sound guilty as hell!"

Crystal cringed. "Stop trying to intimidate her," Laurel said in a firm voice. Inside she felt like Jell-O. She was only repeating lines she'd heard on television. "By law she doesn't have to talk to you without an attorney present." Please let Monica get here soon, she prayed. I might only be making things worse.

More lights flashed in the driveway. Unfortunately they were colored lights. Police cars, not Monica. Williams opened the door and Laurel heard men's voices. Kurt's? No. Soon it seemed as if there were lights everywhere, men in uniform tramping around, phone calls. At last Laurel heard Monica's husky voice. "I am Mrs. Landis's attorney. Either you let me in or I'll have a talk with your superior you'll regret for the rest of your career!"

In a moment she strode into the living room wearing tight black velvet slacks, a gold silk blouse, and a black leather jacket. Her hair fell over her shoulders and large hoop earrings dangled beneath. She looked beautiful. She also looked daunting. Laurel noted with amusement that some of the deputies stood back, obviously slightly awed as she swept past them.

She turned and looked at them sternly. "I want you to be very careful with the crime scene."

"We don't take orders from you," Williams ventured. "Besides, we know what we're doing."

"Yes, I'm sure you do," Monica said deprecatingly. "I want you to look for a heart and a six drawn in blood near or on the body. Also look for a tarot card. And I think it would be a good idea for you to get Kurt Rider out here. He worked on the Denise Price scene and he *does* know what *he's* doing. Now, I need to speak with my client alone."

Some of the deputies gaped at her. They weren't as accustomed as big city cops to an aggressive female attorney, especially one who looked more like a fashion model or movie star than many of the local female lawyers with their conservative suits and hairstyles.

"When did you become such a fan of Kurt's?" Laurel muttered close to Monica's ear.

Monica winked at her. "He'll tell you what they find. These other hotshots won't." She raised her voice. "Are you all right, Crystal?"

"No. There's a dead person in my yard."

"Well, that does put a dent in the evening, doesn't it?"

Crystal looked at her, aghast. "How can you joke about this?"

"I can joke about anything." Monica sat down close to Crystal on the couch and spoke softly. "What have you told the police?"

"Only that I think the body might be Joyce Overton. Actually it was Laurel's idea. I haven't even seen the body."

Monica looked at Laurel. "A white Lexus like Joyce's is parked beside the main road before you turn into Crystal's lane," Laurel said.

Monica nodded. "I saw it."

"Also, Crystal was next door baby-sitting. The door was locked, but the woman had been in here. That's her coat. I think she probably used Chuck's keys to the house."

"Good guess. But why would she leave her coat in here? It's freezing."

"She's wearing Crystal's coat. The light is on in the spare garage. I think she was on her way there. Maybe she thought her coat was too nice to wear in this weather."

"Crystal, why is the garage light on?" Monica asked.

"I've been so scared I leave lights on all over the place

at night. Lights were on in the house and in the garage. I
didn't want someone hiding out there."

"Did you ask Laurel to come here? Why was she the one
to see the body?"

Laurel told her about the call she'd received, reporting it
to the police, then coming here herself. "When I didn't find
Crystal in the house, I thought she was in the garage because of the light. I literally fell over the body."

Monica looked back at Crystal. "Can you prove you were
next door baby-sitting?"

"Of course. The Grants called me. It was an emergency,
you see."

"Okay, let's talk to the cops," Monica said. "Don't be
scared, Crystal, but if I tell you not to answer a question,
don't. Got it?"

Crystal nodded and the interrogation began. Meanwhile
a deputy found a black purse that had slipped under the
couch. He opened the billfold and boomed, "Driver's license says Joyce Overton."

Laurel closed her eyes. So she'd been right. When she
opened them, she saw Crystal shivering, her face white to
the lips. Then Crystal's gaze flew to the doorway.

Chuck Landis stood there, his own face red with fury,
two deputies holding him back as he shouted, "Crystal, you
bitch, what in the name of God have you done?"

2

Laurel didn't know what would have happened if Kurt
hadn't arrived at that moment. He was Chuck's best friend,
and after jerking him outside for a severe talking-to, he
brought him back into the house and nearly pushed him
into a chair. "Now you sit there and stop acting like a crazy
person long enough for us to ask a few questions," Kurt
told him. "Otherwise I'm hauling you in for attempted assault."

"I never touched her," Chuck muttered.

"But you touched a few people outside. I'm serious, Chuck. I'll do it and you know it."

Chuck looked at him sulkily, then sat glaring at Crystal, who hung her head. "Where's the sheriff?" Chuck asked.

"Handling the press."

"Already?" Laurel asked. "Do they have ESP?"

"No, police scanners," Kurt said. He pinned Chuck with his piercing gaze. "Okay, did you know Joyce was coming out here?"

"No."

"Then what are you doing here?"

"She left two hours ago and didn't say where she was going. It got to be way past Molly's bedtime and Joyce wasn't back. She's *always* there to tuck in Molly. Then I discovered my keys to this house were missing. I just put two and two together."

"How did you know she was dead?"

Chuck looked at Kurt incredulously. "Hell, there are police cars all over the place. I was trying to come in and one of your guys told me a woman had been murdered."

"And you didn't assume it was Crystal?"

"Just as I got to the door I heard someone yelling out that the driver's license said Joyce Overton. Then I saw Crystal sitting here."

"Why would Joyce have come here?"

"Probably to talk to Crystal about the divorce. Crystal wouldn't sign the divorce papers. Joyce's husband called her this morning threatening to sue for full custody of the children because she was living with me. She's been a wreck all day." He glowered at Crystal. "Why couldn't you just sign the damned papers? Why did you have to murder her?"

Crystal's eyes filled with tears. "Chuck, I *didn't*. I wasn't even home. Laurel, tell him about the call."

"What call?" Chuck demanded.

"Someone called me to say that Crystal was in trouble. Deadly trouble, they said. I came here. *I* found the body."

Kurt looked at her. "Who called?"

"I have no idea. The voice was so gravelly I couldn't even tell you if it was a man or a woman."

"What time?"

"Around seven, maybe a little before. The evening news was on."

Kurt stared deeply into her eyes. I have more to tell you, she screamed inwardly, wanting him to know about Genevra Howard and that she thought this whole thing had something to do with the Six of Hearts murders. Miraculously, he seemed to get her message. He rose abruptly. "Chuck, you sit still. Williams, you watch him. I'm going outside for a few minutes."

Williams obviously didn't like being told what to do, but he said nothing. Laurel had a feeling Kurt intimidated him. Under these circumstances, she had to admit the warm, friendly Kurt she'd always known *did* seem intimidating.

Williams continued to question Crystal. With her safely in Monica's hands, Laurel unobtrusively watched Chuck. He shifted restlessly in his chair. His gaze went from deputy to deputy and there was something besides grief in it. Anxiety? Apprehension? What would he have to fear from the police if they thought Crystal killed Joyce?

Joyce's car was not in the driveway but Crystal's was. Joyce was wearing Crystal's coat. They were about the same height with the same hair color. It was a bad night—visibility was terrible in the snow. Chuck said Joyce's husband had called this morning threatening to sue for custody of the children. "Why couldn't you just sign the damned divorce papers?" he'd asked Crystal. Laurel barely knew Joyce, but she'd seen the woman with her children a couple of times. It was clear she adored them. No matter how young and sexy Chuck Landis was, Laurel didn't believe Joyce would give up her children for him. And if she wouldn't, what would that mean for Chuck? The end of a very good life.

It had been so long since she and Faith were close to Chuck that Laurel felt as if she no longer knew him. He certainly wasn't the daredevil kid with the gap-toothed

smile and eyes full of anticipation of what wonderful things
life had in store for him. Years of failure and disappointment must have taken their toll. Was it conceivable that in
his desperation to hang on to Joyce, his last hope, he re-
sorted to murder? Could he have killed Joyce thinking she
was Crystal? Did this really have nothing to do with the
murders of Angie and Denise?

Chuck turned his head and gazed at her, his brilliant blue
eyes looking as if he could read her thoughts. She felt color
flood her cheeks. She shifted her own gaze, feeling guilty
but knowing she would have to tell Kurt her suspicions.

Kurt came back into the house. She wanted to jump up,
drag him into a bedroom, and tell him she thought Chuck
had killed Joyce by mistake. Then Kurt looked at her, his
face grim, the muscle beside his jaw twitching. He gave
her a brief nod and instantly she knew.

They'd found the six, the heart, and the tarot card.

3

Kurt followed Laurel home at ten-thirty. Things were still
a mess at Crystal's, but Monica said she would stay with
her and Kurt had done all he could for the moment. He
walked her to the door and she was surprised when he
accepted her invitation to come in.

"Want a beer?" she asked.

"I'd better not. I'll be working all night on this. We've
got to get the alibis."

"Crystal's and Chuck's."

"Yes, unfortunately." He sat down heavily, looking tired
enough to drop.

"Where were the six and the heart?"

Kurt glanced away, rubbing a finger over an eyebrow.
"Carved on her abdomen."

Laurel gasped. "*Carved!* The murderer hasn't done *that*
before."

"Maybe we're not dealing with the same murderer."

"A copycat?"

"Someone who wanted to be rid of Joyce and decided to make it look like the Denise Price murder."

"But there was nothing in the papers about the six or the heart on Denise."

"You told Crystal about it, didn't you, Laurel?"

"Yes," she said quietly. "How could I not when I thought she might be a potential victim?"

"I understand. That's why I told you about it."

"And Crystal could have told Chuck." Kurt nodded. "It makes things complicated. But Kurt, Joyce wasn't one of the Six of Hearts."

"But she *was* someone Crystal would have been glad to see dead."

"Well, out of the picture," Laurel said. "But don't forget Joyce's car was out of sight, she came out of Crystal's house wearing her coat, her hair is almost the same color—"

"I know all that, Laurel. It's very possible the killer mistook Joyce for Crystal. In fact, that's easier for me to believe than that Crystal lured Joyce out there, got Joyce to put on her coat, then took her outside and beat her to death."

"That is ludicrous. So you think it might have been Chuck?"

"It's whoever killed Angie and Denise."

"You don't think that could be Chuck?"

"No." He closed his eyes. "God, I don't know. Maybe, although I don't know why the hell Chuck would want to kill Angie or Denise."

"Then *who?*"

"If I knew that, this mess would be over."

Laurel sat down beside him. "Kurt, I found out something important, something about Faith's mother," she said earnestly. "I think it could be the key—"

"Faith's *mother?*" Kurt repeated. "Tell me."

Without mentioning Neil's participation, Laurel told Kurt about her visit to the Lewis sisters' house, meeting Genevra Howard, and the fact that Genevra had spent over twenty

years in a mental institution for killing her infant son and
had only recently been released.

Kurt's face slackened as she talked. "Did she seem crazy
to you?"

"Odd. One minute she'd be perfectly normal, the next
minute she'd get this strange look on her face. And she
gave me this godawful smile and said she knew Faith didn't
kill herself. She also left six red carnations with a red plastic heart attached on Faith's grave. She said the heart was
part of a key chain Faith had sent her. I'm sure she knows
about the Six of Hearts."

"And doesn't believe Faith's death was suicide, which
means she might know—"

"That we were partially responsible."

"Is she still at the Lewis house?"

"No. She left this morning before the sisters got up. They
have no idea where she is. Kurt, I don't think she's stable.
I even think she might have been here earlier this evening."
She told him about the figure in white that had terrified her
earlier. "I know you won't believe it, but the dogs rescued
me. They actually attacked."

"You're right," Kurt said dryly. "I don't believe it."

"Well, Alex was kicked in the hip and April brought
back a piece of bloodstained white cotton." She got the
cloth, which she'd laid on the mantel.

Kurt looked at it closely. "Can I keep this?"

"Sure. Maybe you can get a blood type."

"With our luck it'll be the dog's blood."

"Neither of them was bleeding."

"Okay. What about the call you got? Can you tell me
anything more about the voice?"

"It was deep and raspy. I couldn't tell if it was male or
female."

"Any background noise?"

Laurel thought a moment. "Not that I can remember."

Silence fell between them. It wasn't a comfortable silence like they used to share. At that moment Laurel knew

that whatever had been between them besides friendship was irrevocably gone.

"Well, I'd better get back to Crystal," Kurt said. He smiled at her. "Be sure to lock all the doors."

"I will."

"I know you won't get a good night's sleep, but try."

"I will."

He grinned. "And tell the dogs my opinion has changed. I'm proud of them."

Laurel smiled. "I'll tell them. Good night, Kurt." As she watched him walk to the car, she thought, Good-bye, Kurt. It was nice while it lasted.

Kurt had said she wouldn't get a good night's sleep. She doubted if she would get any sleep at all. But around midnight she drifted off out of sheer exhaustion. Before long she heard chanting: "Hail, the Lords of Darkness. In the name of the rulers of earth, king of the underworld, rise to this place . . ." She was aware of being doubled over on the cold floor, her eyes shut. Slowly she opened them. Shadows leaped. Girls holding hands went in a circle. Their feet. Her blurry vision made it seem at first as if there were hundreds of feet. Then they individualized. Some loafers. Some flat-heeled lace-up boots. A pair of water-spotted tan suede boots. Fire. Fire running across the floor, the bale of straw igniting. Screams. Milling around. Pain in her hands and arms. A blast of cold air and being propelled through the dark, wet night.

Laurel woke up kicking and gasping. The dream. Again. And once again April and Alex had gathered around her, licking her face, trying to free her from her distress.

She sat up in bed. The dream had been more detailed this time. She didn't remember ever dreaming about feet and shoes.

"Wonderful," she said aloud, brushing her damp hair away from her face. "The dream isn't going away. It's just getting worse."

Twenty-two

1

Laurel arrived at work on time although she was dead tired. Norma had already started coffee. "One more day," she told the woman who'd brought in home-baked blueberry muffins. Laurel bit into one and closed her eyes. "Scrumptious."

"I heard on the news about that Overton woman," Norma ventured. "She was living with your friend Crystal's husband, wasn't she?"

"Yes. She was murdered at Crystal's house and naturally the police are suspecting Crystal, which is ridiculous."

"Well, I'm not going to ask you a lot of nasty details. I can tell you were up late and had a hard night. I swear, I don't know what's happened to this town. You'd think it was New York City or Los Angeles—murders everywhere."

"I know. It's strange, isn't it?" Laurel said vaguely.

"This will be a Christmas I won't forget. We haven't done one wedding, do you know that? Just funeral after funeral. I don't know what happened to 'good will toward men.'"

"I don't believe murderers think in those terms."

"I guess not, but I don't understand how *anyone* could go walking around like a normal person after beating a woman to death."

"A normal person couldn't."

Norma shook her head. "Oh, listen to me! I said I wasn't going to talk about this and I can't shut my mouth." She patted Laurel on the shoulder. "You eat two or three of those muffins, honey. You're getting way too thin."

Even though her stomach growled, Laurel couldn't force down more than one muffin. Tonight was Denise's visitation. God, how could she go through it? She didn't even know what was going on with Crystal and Chuck. Had either been arrested? And what about Joyce's children? Had they been told? Was the ex-husband who twenty-four hours ago threatened to take them from Joyce now on his way to get them?

Around ten o'clock Wayne Price walked in looking gray, drawn, and ten pounds lighter than the night of the party. "Hello, Laurel," he said, even his voice sounding thin and shaky, like that of an old man.

"Wayne!" She started to follow with the traditional "How are you?" but that would be a stupid question. "Is there something I can do for you?"

"Two things. One, I wanted a second opinion. I told you daisies were Denise's favorite flower and you said you'd make a casket blanket mostly with daisies and a few other flowers mixed in for color. Do you think people will believe I'm being cheap, having daisies instead of roses?"

Laurel smiled at him gently. "No, Wayne, I don't believe anyone would think that, but even if they did, does it matter? You've ordered what you think Denise would have wanted. That's what's important."

"Yes, I suppose you're right. I gave her a corsage of daisies to wear last Easter and she loved them."

"I remember. How's Audra?"

"That's the other thing I wanted to talk to you about. I know you and Denise weren't really close lately and I feel nervy asking this of you . . ."

"Wayne, what is it?"

"Audra gets out of the hospital this afternoon. Of course she can't go to the visitation. I could leave her at home with one of Denise's other friends, but . . . well, she's so upset and there's no adult she seems to take to like you. You and your dogs."

"You want me to come and stay with her during the visitation?"

"Well, actually I wondered if she could stay at your house. People come by after the visitation and I don't want her around any of that confusion, considering the circumstances of Denise's death and Audra's illness. You know how it is—people rehash the murder details even when you ask them not to. And she said you invited her over sometime. I know it's a lot to ask, but . . ."

Laurel reached out and touched his hand. "Wayne, I'd be delighted to have Audra tonight."

"Really? I'm not spoiling plans? It means you can't go to the funeral home."

"I think Denise would prefer I look after her little girl than go to the funeral home and I didn't have other plans. What time do you want me to pick her up?"

"I'll bring her by about six, if that's all right. She's still on a couple of medications. I'll explain the dosage. I can pick her up by ten or ten-thirty."

"Wayne, that's rather late and it's so cold. Why not let her spend the night?"

"The *whole* night?"

"Oh, you'd probably rather have her at home."

Wayne frowned. "No, you're right. It would be better for her to get an uninterrupted night's sleep. It's very kind of you to offer."

"I have to warn you, Wayne. I don't have much experience with children. I hope I don't do anything wrong."

Wayne managed a smile. "Kids are tough little characters. They don't break easily. I have complete faith in you."

"I'll see you tonight, then. Tell Audra that April and Alex will be thrilled to see her."

Laurel had been aware of Norma coming into the display room to check an order. As Wayne wandered out the door, she looked up at Laurel, tears in her eyes. "That poor man. I just don't understand life." Mary entered the room. Norma glared at her. "And don't you dare lecture me about God's will and sins of the father! I don't want to hear it!"

Norma stalked into the kitchen, sniffling. Mary looked at Laurel, blank-faced. "I wasn't going to say anything. I feel sorry for Dr. Price."

"She's upset." Laurel stared at Mary's smooth, untroubled face. "How is your father?"

"Much better, Laurel," she said with too much enthusiasm. "Really, this new medicine the doctor put him on is doing wonders."

"Good." Mary turned to go back to the workroom and Laurel couldn't resist adding, "I didn't know the Lewis sisters were your great-aunts."

Mary stopped in her tracks. Her body stiffened. When she turned, her face looked frozen. "How did you know that?"

"I visited them the other night. They told me they were your mother's aunts. I didn't know your father spent his childhood in Wheeling and was best friends with their brother, Leonard."

"They were in a chatty mood." Mary's voice sounded sandpapery. "What else did they have to say?"

Laurel was irritated because of the lies Mary had told her and blurted out, "I met your mother."

Color drained from Mary's face. "You met my mother?"

"Yes. I know everything—about the baby, your mother's stay in the . . . hospital. She said she came back because she wanted a chance to talk to you. Have you seen her?"

Mary's lips parted. The color that had so abruptly faded flooded back into her cheeks. "No, I *haven't* seen her and, if I did, I wouldn't talk to her. If Papa knew she was here—"

"She left," Laurel said quickly. Her purpose in bringing up Genevra was to see if Mary had any idea where her mother could be. Her tone was sincere. Laurel didn't believe she had seen Genevra. But she'd forgotten the threat posed to Genevra by Zeke. She wasn't sure about Genevra's stability, but she knew Zeke was insane. Insane and violent. She might just have put Genevra in danger. "Your mother left the Lewises' yesterday morning."

"Where did she go?"

"They have no idea."

"Oh." Mary looked shaken.

"Since she's gone, it might be best if you didn't mention her visit to your father," Laurel went on nervously. "After all, it could upset him and you said he's doing so much better."

"Yes, you're right," Mary said slowly. "I won't tell him. I just hope she doesn't come back. I don't know how Faith could have ever written to her all those years. She's evil, and evil should be destroyed."

"Destroyed?" Laurel repeated cautiously. "You believe your mother should have been destroyed?"

"She *killed* an innocent!"

Laurel was taken aback by Mary's vehemence. "What if it was an accident, Mary? What if your baby brother died of sudden infant death syndrome?"

"*No.* Papa said she *killed* him. I believe in an eye for an eye."

"You're a Christian. What about 'turn the other cheek' or 'vengeance is mine, sayeth the Lord'?"

"I know what my papa told me and he says she *killed* Daniel."

Norma came out of the kitchen, her eyes red, a few muffin crumbs clinging to her mouth. "Don't tell me someone else got murdered!"

"No, Norma," Laurel said. "We were just having a philosophical discussion."

Norma gave Mary a hard look. "I don't know anything about philosophy. I've got work to do."

When Norma went back to the workroom, Mary said in a pathetic voice, "She doesn't like me anymore."

I don't like you as much as I used to, either, Laurel thought, but she tried to keep her expression neutral. "I told you she's just upset. We're all tired. We'll feel better after a few days off."

"I won't feel different about my mother," Mary said stubbornly. "I won't feel different about anyone who takes the life of an innocent."

"Was Faith an innocent?" Laurel blurted.

Mary gave her a long, measuring look. "Faith wasn't perfect, but she became my mother after my real mother killed her own baby and was sent away. Faith loved me and looked after me and made me as happy as any child could be living with the burden of guilt we had to bear because of our mother. I loved her more than anything in the world. I would have done anything for her. *Anything*." Her eyes grew hard. "I'm going back to work now and I don't ever want to talk about any of this again."

2

Part of Laurel felt enraged at Mary's cheeky response. She didn't like being told off by an employee. At the same time, she thought she had it coming. Mary's relationship with her mother was absolutely none of Laurel's business. Normally she would never have pried into such private territory, but she was afraid either Mary or her mother might be the murderer and she was trying to get information. Still, if Mary were innocent, she had every right to respond as she did.

Usually Mary, Penny, and Norma chattered in the workroom. Today the room was heavily silent. There were even few customers. Most people had already picked out their floral Christmas decorations. Laurel glanced at her watch. Ten-thirty. Six and a half hours until closing time. It seemed like six and a half days.

She was walking around the display room, taking inventory of the depleted Christmas stock, when Neil Kamrath walked in. "Your cupboards are just about bare," he said amiably.

"That's good. Perfect would be having *no* Christmas stock left at closing time today."

"Are you going to join your family for Christmas?"

"No, not this year. Even if it weren't snowing, there's too much going on."

Neil walked near and lowered his voice. "I heard what happened last night. Want to talk about it?"

"Not really," she said coolly. A restraining order. A police investigation of his wife's death to make sure it really was an accident.

Neil's smile faded. "Laurel, what's wrong?"

"Another murder."

"I mean between us. I'm getting frost bite just standing near you."

Laurel looked into the smoky blue, pain-filled eyes, the closed look on his face just like the first time he'd walked in the store to order flowers for Angie's funeral. "Okay, Neil. But let's get out of the store. There's a place down the street where we can get coffee."

She told the others she was going out for twenty minutes. Shortly afterward she and Neil sat in the same cafe where she and Crystal had drunk vanilla coffee a few days ago and discussed the photos they'd received of Angie and Faith. She and Neil both ordered cappuccino and croissants. "I've been living on coffee, pastry, and hot dogs for over a week," Laurel commented. "A green vegetable would throw my poor stomach into shock."

"You have to eat somewhat sensibly, Laurel. After Ellen and Robbie died, I lived on coffee and the nearest thing I could find that didn't require cooking. A couple of months later a doctor told me if I didn't start eating right, I'd get rickets."

"Rickets! I didn't think that disease existed anymore."

"It does if you don't eat right." He went back to the counter, ordered orange juice, and set it down in front of her. "Drink every drop. You need vitamin C."

She smiled and drained the small glass. "I feel like a new woman."

"I knew it." His gaze grew serious. "Now why don't you tell me what's wrong?"

She drew a deep breath. "I had a talk with Kurt about you. He told me some things about your marriage."

She felt him retreating emotionally although his expression didn't change. "You had him check me out?"

"No." She couldn't help grinning. "It seems we were spotted in McDonald's not once but *twice* and he took it upon himself to do a background check."

Laurel could tell Neil was trying to hang on to his haughty aloofness but he couldn't. He laughed softly. "Sometimes I forget what life in a small town is like. Did he know what we ate at McDonald's?"

"Probably, but he didn't comment on that part."

"He stuck to information about my marriage. What about it?"

"Well, first that Ellen had to get a restraining order against you because you beat her twice and once pushed her down the stairs, breaking a rib and doing eye damage."

Neil closed his own eyes. "Laurel, I told you Ellen was an alcoholic. She was always falling and in the later years, when things weren't going well with us, she started blaming me, especially for the tumble down the stairs. She couldn't admit she was drunk. It was easier to claim I'd done it."

"But certainly the doctors in the emergency room could see she was drunk. And what about the police?"

"Laurel, Ellen's father is a judge on the Virginia State Supreme Court. To say he has clout is an understatement, and he never admitted Ellen was an alcoholic. If he'd worked with me instead of against me, things might have turned out differently for Ellen and me. What else did Kurt have to say?"

"The car wreck that killed her and Robbie. Kurt said there was a police investigation because the steering had been tampered with."

"Look, Laurel, Ellen ran the car over a curb and hit a telephone pole. She was arrested for driving under the influence. Two weeks later, after the car had been repaired, she was behind the wheel again even though she'd lost her license for the DUI charge. That's when the fatal wreck happened. The police determined there *was* a faulty steering mechanism—something about a loose nut on a tie bar—I don't really know much about cars. It was Ellen's father who claimed I'd tampered with the steering. The police thought the nut hadn't been put on properly at the garage when the car was fixed a few days before. Nevertheless, she was drunk when she had the wreck. Besides, Robbie was in the car."

"Kurt said he was supposed to be spending the weekend with a friend."

"That was Kathy's son. Ellen changed her mind about letting Robbie stay. Kathy called me because Ellen was drunk when she called. There was nothing I could do, but I *did* know Robbie was with his mother that weekend. Good God, Laurel, do I seem like the kind of man who'd beat his wife and tamper with her car, especially when there was a chance my son might be riding with her?"

Laurel stared into her cup for a moment. "No. You seem like a man tormented by grief."

"Well, it's true I wanted out of the marriage because Ellen refused to get help. The environment she created was terrible for Robbie. I had some crazy notion I could get full custody of him, although I'm sure my father-in-law would have effectively blocked any attempt I made." His voice tightened. "Anyway, all I can do is swear to you that I never hit my wife and I didn't tamper with her car so she'd wreck and be killed."

Laurel bit her lower lip. "I know. Deep down I knew it all along."

"Are you sure?"

"Yes. It's just that everything has been so strange lately, so awful. I suppose you start doubting everyone."

"Especially someone you don't know very well."

"In some ways I feel as if I do know you well. Maybe it's because I've read your books."

He grinned. "Great. I write horror."

"You write about normal, decent people getting caught up in horrible circumstances."

"Not too different from what's going on around here except that our killer is real, not some creation of my imagination."

"Yes." She took a sip of her cappuccino. "I'm not going to Denise's visitation tonight. I'm looking after Audra as a favor to Wayne. He doesn't want her exposed to any of the funeral trappings, especially after she's been so sick."

Neil nodded. "Wayne's a good man. He's doing the right thing."

"I've never taken care of a child before except for my niece and nephew, and I'm not convinced they're completely human."

Neil burst out laughing. "Shades of *Rosemary's Baby* and *The Omen*?"

"Exactly." She rubbed at her tired eyes. "I'm sure something terrible will happen to me for saying that, but I can't help it. All they need is some old-fashioned discipline. Let me amend that. A *lot* of old-fashioned discipline."

"Rearing children isn't easy. Sometimes disciplining them hurts you more than it does them."

"I suppose." She sighed. "I keep thinking about Joyce Overton's children. At least Audra comes from a stable home. Joyce was divorced. From what I've heard the kids were crazy about Chuck. Now they'll lose both of them."

"What do you think really happened at Crystal's?"

"I think the killer mistook Joyce for Crystal. The tarot card was there. The six and the heart had been carved into her abdomen."

"*Carved!*" Neil said in a low, horrified voice. "That's more brutal than the others. Why carved?"

"I don't know. Maybe because the coat Joyce was wearing—Crystal's coat—was so garish the symbols wouldn't have shown up if they'd been written in blood on the back, like with Denise. It's just a guess. By the way, Genevra Howard is missing. At least as of yesterday. We can't rule out that she's the killer and dealing with an escalating psychosis."

Neil shook his head. "Oh, God. Do you think Mary knows where she is?"

Laurel huffed. "Just mention Genevra to her if you want to get an earful about sin and how killers of the 'innocent' should be destroyed. She sounds increasingly like her father."

Neil tapped his fingers on the table. "You don't think it's as simple as Chuck killing Joyce by mistake?"

"Oh, I haven't ruled that out. Crystal could have told him about the tarot card and the symbols. He might have planned to kill Crystal and make it look like another Six of Hearts murder. When he realized his mistake, he simply went through the ritual as planned to divert suspicion from himself."

"Unless he's been the killer all along."

"I just can't imagine that, Neil. What is his motive?"

"You and Faith were always close to him and Kurt. Maybe it's got something to do with delayed grief over Faith."

Laurel shook her head. "Grief over Faith when he'd just latched on to his idea of heaven with Joyce? I don't think so. Besides, Faith and I were close to Chuck and Kurt when we were *children*." She lowered her gaze. "Actually, that's not the complete truth. Maybe I shouldn't be telling you this because I know you loved Faith, but I found a book of Shakespearean sonnets in Kurt's apartment. They were from Faith and signed with love." She looked up at him reluctantly. "I believe Kurt was the father of Faith's baby."

3

Kurt couldn't stop thinking about Genevra Howard. Faith had been in touch with the woman all her life, but she'd never said anything to him, and not to Laurel. Instead, she'd let everyone think Genevra had simply abandoned the family. Well, maybe he understood. It was better than having people know her mother was in a mental institution for killing her baby.

Now the woman was missing. He'd talked with the Lewis sisters this morning, which sent the two elderly la-

dies into stuttering, fluttering terror. He'd tried to soothe
them, but a visit from the police about their recently institutionalized niece had been too much for their genteel ex-
istence. He'd left them white and trembling, clutching at
each other.

So far the alibis for Crystal and Chuck had checked out,
however tenuously. The Grants said they'd called Crystal
at six-thirty. She'd rushed over to baby-sit while they took
their three-year-old to the emergency room. At seven-thirty
they'd called Crystal to report that the child was being admitted to the hospital and they would be home soon. Crystal
had answered promptly, and Laurel said Crystal arrived
home shortly after eight.

The Overton children had been at a neighbor's. The eldest, fifteen-year-old Alan, claimed he'd come back to his
house at seven to get a CD computer game and Chuck was
home. All three children returned home shortly around
eight, Molly's bedtime. They said Chuck seemed agitated
because Joyce had left two hours earlier without saying
where she was going and had never returned home. Saying
he had a feeling where she might be, he left the little girl
in the care of the boys and apparently went directly to Crystal's.

The police didn't know yet exactly when the murder had
been committed. The cold weather made time of death
harder to determine, and in real life pathologists were never
able to be as precise as they were on television or in the
movies. They did know the call to Laurel had been made
from the cellular phone in Joyce's car. The killer had left
blood on the receiver, but Kurt was certain the blood was
Joyce's and would tell them nothing about the killer.

Snow had been falling heavily since yesterday. The temperature hovered around thirty-five degrees. Kurt couldn't
imagine anyone lingering around the Pritchard farm in this
weather, but he also couldn't forget Laurel's report about
the hangman's noose in the barn. He'd promised he'd check
it out, but he'd done nothing. He didn't for a minute believe
that the noose had been put up by pranksters, not now that

he knew the truth about how Faith died. He had a feeling the murderer was making the Pritchard farm a sort of second home.

It would be the perfect place to hide, he reasoned as he neared the place, his wipers sweeping steadily across the windshield to keep it clear. The farm was secluded and considered by many, mostly kids, to be haunted. He remembered when he and Chuck were ten and had decided to spend a night in the old barn to catch sight of the ghost of Esmé Dubois. They'd sneaked out of Chuck's house and caught a ride with one of Chuck's dad's friends who was slightly drunk and seeming to be getting a big kick out of their planned adventure. They ignored his snickering and stupid jokes, rolling their eyes at each other over his ignorance. They carried sleeping bags, crosses (Chuck said they worked just as well on ghosts as on vampires), a vial of holy water Kurt had snatched from the Catholic church, and a camera so they could catch Esmé on film before they recited the Lord's Prayer, banishing her to the netherworld and freeing Wheeling forever from the haunting by the witch. They knew their pictures would be in the newspaper, they might have to appear on talk shows, and they could even be called to other cities to rid them of their ghosts, but they were up to the task.

They'd come on a crisp autumn night, set up their "equipment," and ate potato chips and drank Cokes until after midnight, when they dozed off. Chuck awakened Kurt with an ear-shattering shriek. Kurt looked up and saw a huge hulk looming over Chuck. Both boys fled the barn screaming at the tops of their voices, waking up the family who at that time lived at the farm.

Furious, the farmer had stalked out of the house with his shotgun and found the quaking boys. They jabbered out their story of the monster that had almost devoured them. Using his own strong flashlight, the farmer heedlessly entered the barn while the boys huddled together, terrified. In a moment the farmer led the hulking shape toward them and shined the flashlight on its face. "Here's your monster, boys," he said as the Holstein looked at them with big, melting brown eyes. "It's called a cow and her name is Bessie. Now I'm drivin' you two home, and if I catch you out here again, I'm gonna skin you alive!"

Frightened and humiliated, they slumped in the truck seat until the farmer dropped them off at Chuck's home. They crept inside only to find Chuck's mother waiting up for them. The final indignity of the night was when she spanked both of them with a wooden paddle as if they were little kids. Kurt threw back his head and laughed at the memory. "And thus ended the illustrious career of Rider and Landis, Ghosthunters," he said aloud.

But Faith hadn't been scared away from the place. Not Faith or Laurel or any of the other Six of Hearts. A bunch of teenage girls had made the rotting, spooky old barn their clubhouse. Clubhouse. That sounded too innocuous for the use they were making of it. Practicing Satanic rituals. He didn't have any trouble picturing Monica dabbling in the occult, but Laurel and Crystal? It was remarkable that you could think you knew a person so well when you didn't really know them at all.

Well, his failure to understand those girls wasn't really his concern right now. He'd always known he wasn't the most perceptive person around. He was a step above Chuck. He was several steps below Neil Kamrath and that made him mad. No matter how smart the guy was, Kurt was convinced he was a creep. His romance with Laurel was over—she wasn't the sweet, open, innocent woman he'd thought would make a good wife and mother—but that didn't mean he wanted her mixed up with a nut like Kamrath.

Kurt jounced down the rutted road. The farm looked abandoned, desolate, even forbidding. It was no wonder rumors of it being cursed had finally overcome the place.

He drove as near to the old barn as he could, then walked through what had once been a cornfield. The remaining stubble was frozen and jabbed at his feet, even through the thick soles of his shoes. Only half of the old barn remained.

He stepped inside. The front part, which was roofless, bore a thick layer of snow. The old dump should have been torn down years ago, he thought.

He walked farther into the place and immediately saw the bale of straw in the middle of the floor, just as Laurel had described. His gaze traveled upward. There it dangled, the hangman's noose. A breeze blew up, sending it swinging. Had a noose swung that way the night Faith's neck was in it? He closed his eyes. He'd seen some terrible sights, especially lately, but Faith hanging there on fire was one he couldn't face.

Kurt wandered around the barn. No footprints in the fresh snow, no signs that anyone had been in here within the last twenty-four hours. There was nothing but some aged, rusting farming equipment and a few birds huddled pathetically on the beams.

He walked a few hundred feet to the "new" barn, built over a hundred years ago. Inside he saw no structural damage, but it was obvious the barn hadn't been used for a long time. All the animal smells were gone. This had once been the home of Bessie, the heifer that had nearly scared the life out of him and Chuck. He imagined poor old Bessie had gone to cow heaven years ago.

Near the back he found a few rakes, hoes, shovels, and an antique tractor he was surprised hadn't been hauled off long ago. He also found a few old blankets and signs of a fire in the middle of the room. Maybe vagrants had taken refuge here, maybe kids like him and Chuck, sitting around a campfire telling stories. But in spite of the crumbling equipment, there was nothing ominous about the barn. It had a completely different feel from the other one, or maybe it was just his imagination.

Kurt left the barn and plodded toward the house. In the distance he could barely see the outline of the farm pond where Mrs. Pritchard drowned back in the eighteenth century. He saw a couple of Canadian geese floating on the cold water, but most wildlife had abandoned it. Untended, the pond had become covered with water lilies and algae.

It would take dredging and a lot of work to restore it to its former beauty.

The farmhouse had once been white. Now at least a third of the paint had peeled off. Several windows were broken out and the porch swing hung by one chain, the wind sending the lower end scraping back and forth over the battered porch floor. On either side of the steps sat large pots in which he pictured red geraniums. Now they held beer cans and cigarette wrappers. Yes, this was the place where vagrants sought refuge on cold nights, a place that once had been a real home.

He hesitated at the door. Undoubtedly some of the people who came here had been unfortunate enough to lose their own homes and merely wanted to find a place to escape the elements. Others probably had less savory histories and motives. Besides, he'd come here thinking he might find the person who'd brutally murdered three women.

He withdrew his gun before he opened the door and stepped into the house. It was not much warmer inside than out. Slowly he walked into the living room. The wallpaper had once sported red roses, but moisture had made the color run, making the walls look like they were streaked with old blood. More blankets were piled in front of the fireplace, which showed recent signs of a fire. The dust on the floor was scuffed although there were no clear footprints.

Kurt walked through the downstairs, his gun drawn. Everywhere were signs of human habitation, but he couldn't tell if someone had been here days ago or weeks ago. More beer and soda cans sat on the kitchen counter, and even a pizza box and wrappers from fast food restaurants, all gnawed on by mice. The sink was rust-stained and filthy.

He checked all the downstairs bedrooms and found similar signs of filth and decay. Here and there lay a dead bird that had flown in through a broken window and gotten trapped. He also saw a few rotting rat carcasses and wondered if they'd been poisoned.

Something creaked overhead and he jerked to attention.

Quickly he backtracked down the hall until he reached the stairs. He clicked off the safety of his gun and started up the steps slowly. The dust was badly scuffed on them. Someone had gone up and down them frequently and not long ago. Pieces of paper littered the stairs, mostly crumpled newspaper pages. Near the top of the stairs he stopped. Here a newspaper lay spread out. The stairs were so close to the front door Kurt knew he would have noticed the newspaper if it had been in this position when he came in the house.

He bent down and read the headline: Local Girl Found Hanged. He read the first couple of lines describing the discovery of the partially burned body of Faith Howard, seventeen, hanging in the Pritchard barn.

The paper was thirteen years old and in perfect condition, Kurt thought, his breath quickening. This newspaper had been treasured, saved to remind someone in particular of what had happened to Faith.

A whisper of movement from above sent a prickling along his neck, a sudden chill, a certainty that he was not alone. He stood up in time to glimpse a figure in a white robe with flowing red hair holding a tire iron. In a rush of motion, before Kurt could even raise his gun, the tire iron crashed against his skull.

Kurt tumbled noisily to the foot of the stairs and lay motionless. The figure wafted down the steps, leaning down to stare at his quiet face with the streak of blood oozing down his temple. A finger dabbed at the blood and drew on the floor, forming a bloody heart and a six. Then, slowly, the figure raised the tire iron again.

Twenty-three

At four-thirty they had completed and delivered all their orders, Norma and Mary were still not speaking, and Laurel was exhausted so she declared the store officially closed for Christmas half an hour early. On her way home she stopped for groceries because Audra would be spending the night. She couldn't expect the child to eat the way she had this past week.

Snow fell steadily as she loaded her grocery bags in the car and started for home. The roads were slightly slick and Laurel drove slowly, wishing darkness didn't fall so early in winter. The long lane to her house, which she usually thought beautiful with all the tree limbs coated with snow, now looked lonely, even scary. After the murders, she wondered if she would ever find winter nights beautiful again.

Laurel pulled into the garage and shut the door behind her. These days, like Crystal, she left the garage light on so she wouldn't have to step from the car into darkness. The dogs were waiting on the other side of the door for her.

"Guess what, guys?" she said as they bounded after her into the kitchen. "We're having company tonight. One of your favorite people—Audra."

They sat looking at her expectantly, at this moment more interested in their dinner than a prospective guest whose name they didn't yet recognize. "I know. Alpo time. You both look famished."

Laurel had just finished feeding the dogs when someone knocked on the front door. Wayne stood on the other side

holding Audra, who was dressed as if she were going on
an expedition to the North Pole. Wayne was clearly being
overprotective, but Laurel understood. "Hi!" she said cheer-
ily. Both managed weak smiles. "Come in."

"I hope we're not early," Wayne said.

"You're right on time. How are you feeling, Audra?"

"Okay. And thank you very much for letting me stay the
night."

She'd been coached, sounding like a formal little adult.
"It's my pleasure, Audra. The dogs are just finishing their
dinner in the kitchen if you'd like to go see them. Right in
there."

Audra's smile brightened as Wayne set her down and
she headed in the direction Laurel was pointing. Laurel
turned back to Wayne. "How are *you?*"

"Not too well. I don't know how I'm going to get
through this evening." He set down a small suitcase. "I
finally tracked down Denise's parents, but they can't get
here until tomorrow. They're furious with me, as if it's my
fault Denise's mother screwed up the itinerary."

"That's their primary reaction? Anger at you?"

"I don't think the situation has really sunk in with them.
It's easier to get mad at me than accept that their daughter
has been murdered."

"Will they be back in time for the funeral?"

"I think so."

"Wayne, this is probably none of my business, but do
you think Audra should attend the funeral?"

He shook his head. "Absolutely not. Even if it weren't
her mother being buried tomorrow, she's just not well
enough. I'll find someone to stay home with her."

"Why don't you let her stay with me? People will be
coming back to the house after the funeral. You don't want
her around all that commotion, all that talk about the murder."

"No, I don't. But don't you want to go to the funeral?"

"Well . . . I . . . ."

"Of course you don't. Who *wants* to go to a funeral?

People do it out of respect for the family—either that or curiosity. Your offering to look after Audra shows more affection and respect for Denise than going to the funeral. Yes, I would really appreciate your looking after Audra if you're sure you don't mind."

"I would enjoy it."

He gave her that weak smile again, bent and opened the suitcase. "Audra's medicine is in here. There's just an antibiotic, cough syrup, and some Tylenol. She's been having headaches. I've written down the dosages. If you have any questions, call me."

Audra came back into the living room, both dogs scampering after her. "Daddy has to leave now," Wayne said, sweeping her into his arms. "You be a good girl."

"I will, Daddy. And will you give Mommy my special flowers?"

Yesterday Wayne had called the store and asked if Laurel could put together a wicker basket of spring flowers as Audra's offering. Mary had designed it with daisies, violets, pansies, and moss roses interspersed with babies' breath and tied with a pink ribbon. Laurel thought it was one of the loveliest arrangements Mary had ever done.

"Certainly I'll give her your flowers, sweetheart," Wayne said.

"And they're very pretty," Laurel told her. She found her purse and withdrew a Polaroid. "We took a picture."

Audra looked at the photograph. "Oh, they're beautiful! All the flowers Mommy had in her garden."

Wayne nodded and Laurel could tell he was unable to speak. "We'd better let your daddy be on his way," she said quickly. "He should drive slowly on slick roads, and you and I need to decide what to have for dinner."

Wayne gave his daughter a final, hard kiss and hurried out the door as if he didn't trust himself to say anything. Audra looked at Laurel. "I don't really know what a visitation is."

"It's when people go to the funeral home to say goodbye to the person who died."

"Oh." Audra's big brown eyes clouded. "I didn't get to say good-bye to Mommy."

Laurel sat down on the couch and patted the spot beside her. Audra joined her. "Don't worry about it, honey. You don't really have to say good-bye. Your mommy will always be alive in your heart, and you can talk to her any time in your prayers."

A bit of gloom left Audra's face. "*Any* time?"

"Absolutely."

"That's good 'cause I'm gonna have lots to tell her." She paused. "Laurel?"

"Yes?"

"I'm starving."

Laurel laughed. She didn't underestimate Audra's pain or devastation over losing her mother, but children had such a charming way of throwing off their troubles, even for a little while. "I'm really hungry, too. Any requests?"

"Pizza!" Laurel had imagined fixing healthy things for the child in her charge. "Hospital food is yucky and Daddy said when I got out I could have a nice big gooey pizza."

"Okay. You tell me what toppings you want and I'll call the pizza shop."

Forty-five minutes later, as Audra downed her sixth piece of pizza loaded with enough toppings to clog Laurel's arteries for the next year, Audra said, "My boyfriend, Buzzy Harris, called me up today and said another lady got murdered just like my mommy."

"Well, isn't Buzzy a fountain of information?"

"Huh?"

"Maybe Buzzy shouldn't be telling you things to upset you."

"He didn't want to upset me. He thinks we should find the killer as soon as I get well."

That's what Monica had wanted to do, Laurel thought. Denise had scoffed at the idea of amateur detectives, but she wouldn't consent to go to the police. And now she was dead.

"I think tracking down killers should be left to the police," she told Audra. "They're the experts."

"They didn't find who killed my mommy."

"They will."

Audra looked soulfully at her plate for a moment and Laurel braced for another comment about Denise's murder. Instead Audra asked, "Can April and Alex have some pizza?"

The dogs had been sitting stolidly on either side of Audra, avidly watching each bite that went into her mouth. "They can each have a couple of bites of crust. The toppings might upset their stomachs. And just drop the crust into Alex's mouth. He likes fingers."

Audra giggled and carefully tore off four pieces of crust, explaining to the dogs why that's all they could have. Afterward she sat back, puffed out her cheeks, and said, "I think I'm gonna pop."

"Me, too. How would you like to have a big fire in the fireplace and watch TV?"

"Neat! There's a *Peanuts* special tonight."

"Good. I love *Peanuts*. Why don't you take April and Alex in the living room? I'll clean up in here and be in there in about four minutes."

Cleaning up after pizza was easy. Shortly afterward she found Audra curled up on the couch with April and Alex. Laurel had never seen the dogs bond with anyone like they did with Audra. She was telling them a story about a beautiful princess named April and a handsome prince named Alex. Both dogs looked at her as if they were following every word.

Laurel built a fire. "We never had fires at my house," Audra told her.

"Well, they can be messy. You have a fancy house. I don't. A little smoke doesn't bother me."

The four of them cuddled under the afghan and watched the *Peanuts* special. By the time it was over, Audra was yawning ferociously. "I think it's bedtime for you, little one," Laurel said. She gave Audra her antibiotic and took her into her old room. "There is where I slept when I was growing up."

"It's pretty. I like all your stuffed animals."

"Would you like to sleep with one?"

"Yeah!" Audra went straight for raggedy old Boo Boo Bear. "I like this one."

"That's Boo Boo and he was my favorite, too."

"Are there any *real* bears this color, sort of orange-red?"

"I don't think so. Whoever made him got creative with the dye for his fur. Now, let's get your pajamas on and then into bed with you."

Ten minutes later she pulled the covers up to Audra's chin. "Comfy?"

"Yes. But can I have a night-light?"

Laurel walked over and flipped on a night-light with a seashell cover. "Okay?"

"Great."

Laurel kissed her. "If you want anything, just call out. I'll be right down the hall."

"Okay. Sometimes I have bad dreams."

Tell me about it, Laurel thought. "If you do, wake me up. Good night, sweetheart."

She wanted to make a couple of calls, so she closed Audra's door. The child didn't object since she was guarded not only by Boo Boo, but April and Alex. When she went in the living room, she looked at the time. Nine-thirty. Monica should be back from the visitation by now and Laurel wanted to get a clearer perspective on Crystal's situation than she knew Crystal could give her.

No one answered in Monica's room. Maybe she'd gone home with Crystal, but she didn't want to call there. She was concerned about Crystal, but she didn't want to deal with Crystal's high-strung reactions tonight. She tried Kurt's number but got only the answering machine. She was too embarrassed to say she was calling to get information she knew she had no right to have and hung up quickly.

The fire had died and she suddenly felt cold. She tiptoed

in to check on Audra. The child slept deeply, clutching Boo
Boo Bear, with April and Alex planted on the bed on either
side of her. Alex was snoring, but April looked at her. "Little guardian angels," Laurel whispered. "Take care of her
tonight."

Before Laurel climbed into bed, she stood gazing out the
bedroom window at the snow still falling heavily. The yard
looked so cold and lonely with only the dusk-to-dawn light,
considerably weakened by the white veil. It seemed impossible that summer would ever come, that the lawn would
be alive with green grass and multicolored flowers and daylight would last until nine o'clock.

Laurel got in bed, and pulled the comforter close. She
didn't know why she felt so chilled tonight. She used the
remote control to turn on the television. She watched old
situation comedies for a while, then dozed off, the television still going.

Soon she was in the barn again. Sick. Cold. Leaping
shadows. Chanting. "Hail the Lords of darkness." The
shoes going round and round. Fire. Faith hanging. Screams.
Screams.

Laurel jerked awake. She *had* heard a scream. She threw
off the comforter and was jumping out of bed when she
heard a door opening, then footsteps running down the hall.
Audra appeared in her doorway and streaked to the bed,
April and Alex pounding along behind her. "Honey, what's
wrong?" Laurel cried, opening her arms for the child.

"My mommy's dead!" Audra sobbed, clutching Boo Boo
and burying her face against Laurel's shoulder. "It was
snowing and I was running and there were lights everywhere and I saw somebody following Mommy—" She
heaved a deep breath, then hiccuped.

"Audra, it was just a dream," Laurel said, holding her
tightly. April and Alex panted anxiously, sensitive to Audra's distress.

"I know it was a dream but somebody hit Mommy *real*
hard over and over. I *saw* her with blood all over her and
in the snow and—"

"Audra, remember how I told you your mother is in a beautiful place?" Laurel asked quickly. "It's true. You forget about that night in the snow."

"I *can't.*"

"Yes, you can if you try. Don't let that be your last memory of your mother. Concentrate on the happiest times you had together."

Audra shuddered and looked off in the distance. "Like when we went to Disney World last summer and Mommy screamed and laughed on the rides?"

"Yes. That's good," Laurel said in relief. "Audra, why don't you sleep with me? It's such a big bed and I'm lonely."

"You are? Okay," Audra sniffled. She scooted under the covers and April and Alex promptly jumped up. Good thing this is a king-sized bed, Laurel thought as the dogs stretched out. Audra, on the other hand, squeezed as close to Laurel as she could. Laurel was around children so seldom she'd forgotten how small and fragile they felt. How desperately Denise must have wanted to protect this vulnerable little girl. Laurel hugged her.

"You hug just like Mommy," Audra said.

"That's good. I know your mommy gave good hugs."

"Were you and my mommy friends when you were my age?"

"Yes, we were. We met when we were in the same third-grade class."

"So *long* ago," Audra marveled, making Laurel feel ancient. Suddenly she asked, "When you get to be a grown-up like you, do you stop having bad dreams?"

"No, I'm afraid not."

"What do you have bad dreams about?"

Oh, Lord, if you only knew, Laurel thought. "Dogs."

"I love dogs, but Mommy never let me have one." She sighed. "Will you tell me a story?"

Laurel began a rambling tale about a little girl who lived in the forest and could talk to all the animals. She had no idea where she was going with it, but she knew it didn't matter. Audra was yawning and her eyes were half-closed. In a minute they closed completely. Laurel continued in a soft voice until seconds later when Audra's long lashes fluttered. "Boo Boo rattles and he has a tear in his side. I didn't tear him, honest." Then her eyes closed firmly as she lapsed back into what Laurel hoped was a peaceful, dreamless sleep.

Laurel gently extricated her arms from around Audra. In sleep the child had released Boo Boo and the teddy bear rolled over to Laurel. She picked it up, smiling at it in the semidarkness created by the light of the television screen. Poor old Boo Boo. He'd been through a lot. She squeezed him the way she used to do. Something made a noise. She squeezed again. It sounded like paper being crushed. What had Audra said? "Boo Boo rattles and he has a tear in his side."

She reached over, turned on the soft blue hurricane lamp beside her bed, and inspected the teddy bear. His right side was intact. The seam along the left side was split about two inches. His stuffing hadn't fallen out because a safety pin held together the two edges of material. She hadn't put in the safety pin. She'd barely touched Boo Boo for years, but if she'd known he was torn, she would have mended him.

Laurel took out the safety pin and inserted careful fingers, not wanting to make the tear larger or pull out stuffing. Almost immediately her fingers touched paper. It was folded into a small square. She pulled it out, laid down Boo Boo, and unfolded the paper. Her eyes widened when she saw a title written in Faith's ornate, sloping handwriting:

In the Event of My Death

Twenty-four

1

Laurel's gaze flew to the date written in the upper right hand corner of the paper. December 10. Faith died on December 17. This had been written one week before her death, the last night she spent in this house. Laurel's mind flashed back to Faith's odd mood, her forced gaiety that frequently lapsed into cold, distracted silence. She'd thought Faith was mad at her. But could the silence have been fear? She'd awakened in the night to find Faith writing at her desk. Is this what she'd been writing and then hidden in Boo Boo?

Laurel's hands shook. Finding this note was like receiving a letter from the grave. She sat up in the bed and began to read:

Dear Laurel,

Soon it will be no secret that I'm going to have a baby. I probably should run away, but doing that would mean I have to leave the man I love. He says he's too young to get married, too young to handle the responsibility of a wife and a baby. He wants me to get an abortion. He nearly forced the money on me last week, but I won't take it. He's furious. I can't help it. I love him. I won't give up his baby.

But Laurel, I'm really writing this because I'm scared. My mother says she always had a touch of clairvoyance. I think I do, too, and I have a feeling of doom. My locket is missing. I've always felt I was safe if I had my locket.

I talked to one of those phone psychics yesterday. She said someone is burning black candles against me, which means they want to hurt me. She said they have something of mine, like a piece of jewelry. She couldn't have known my locket was taken. I believe her. I believe I'm in danger. I believe I will die soon. If I do, I want you to know someone wants me dead. I can feel it.

Laurel, you're my oldest, dearest friend. If I die soon, and it isn't an accident, find the killer of me and my baby. I know you can do it.

Love always,
Faith

Laurel's heart pounded when she put down the paper. No wonder Faith had acted so strange those last weeks of her life. Not only was she pregnant, she was afraid she was going to be murdered. Why hadn't she told someone? Because she thought no one would believe her, the daughter of a religious fanatic and a mother institutionalized for killing her child? Of course few people knew about Genevra, but Faith had probably lived in fear that the Lewis sisters might tell. "Faith, why didn't you say in the letter who the father of the baby was?" Laurel muttered. "Did you tell anyone? Your mother?"

She felt as if her head were spinning. Someone had been murdering the Six of Hearts. Could that person be the father of the child? Why? The father obviously hadn't wanted Faith or the baby.

Suddenly a possibility flashed across her tired mind like a comet, a possibility that led to another and another so quickly Laurel put her head in her hands, feeling as if it were going to burst. "I know. Dear God, Faith, you were right. I've known all along. I just didn't remember."

She reached for the phone beside the bed. It was a cordless phone and she'd carried the receiver into another room. Damn.

She crept out of bed, pulling her robe around her. Alex, as usual, was so soundly asleep he looked as if he were sinking into the mattress. Even April didn't raise her head as Laurel slipped from the bedroom. She went to the living room, not bothering to turn on lamps. She'd lived in this house most of her life. She could walk around the rooms blindfolded. She reached the end table and picked up the phone receiver. No dial tone. The phone was dead. That was odd. Had the snow brought down phone lines? She'd try the kitchen phone.

As soon as she stood, she noticed something wrong with the room. The corner. It didn't look right. The angle seemed off. Or was it just moonlight reflecting off the snow in a peculiar way? She stepped away from the couch, never taking her eyes off the corner. She caught a twitch of movement. It wasn't a trick of the light. Someone was in here with her. Her mouth went dry. "Who's there?" she asked, barely above a whisper. A shadow separated itself from the wall. Her heart slammed against her ribs and she whirled. She had to get to the bedroom where Audra slept and lock the door.

But she'd only managed three steps before something cracked against her skull, sending her into oblivion.

2

Laurel was first aware of pain in her head. She reached up and felt something damp and sticky on her temple. When she pressed, the pain stabbed.

Slowly she opened her eyes. All she saw was darkness, but she knew she was lying in a fetal position in a small space—a small, cold place. And she was moving. Tires hissing on snow sounded under her right ear. Good Lord, she was in a car trunk!

How long had she been in here? How badly was she hurt? Where was she going?

Audra! She raised her head and hit it on the trunk lid. What had happened to Audra? Oh, God, Wayne had left the child with her so she wouldn't suffer the emotional discomfort of the visitation. Instead he'd sent Audra right into the arms of Denise's killer.

Laurel felt the car slowing, turning, then beginning to jolt over a rough road. Her body bounced painfully against the hard floor of the trunk. Whoever had stuffed her in here hadn't bothered putting a coat on her. She wore only a thin, silky nightshirt and a velour robe, no shoes. She was freezing, particularly her feet. How long was this ride going to last? Her right hip would certainly be bruised from the constant slamming against the trunk floor.

But a bruised hip was the least of her problems. She knew this was meant to be a death ride. The killer had her and certainly didn't intend to return her home safe and sound. But why hadn't she been killed in her living room, beaten to death like Angie, Denise, and Joyce?

The car slowed again and stopped. Nothing happened for a couple of minutes. Then she heard a car door open.

"I don't want to go!" Oh, God, Laurel thought. Audra. "I *won't* go!"

A low voice, harsh, unrecognizable. "If you don't, I won't let Laurel out of the trunk and she'll smother. Do you know what it's like to smother to death?"

More moments of silence. Then the door slammed. A key scratched in the trunk lock. The lid opened and a beam of light blinded Laurel. Snow fell off the back of the car into the trunk. More blew in from outside.

"Get out."

Laurel wiped at her eyes and squinted upward. Audra watched her anxiously. The other face was partially hidden by a parka hood.

"Get *out!*"

"All *right*." Laurel pushed herself up, blinking rapidly. Then she moved her stiff legs.

"Hurry up!"

"I'm hurrying. These aren't the most comfortable accommodations, you know. I hurt."

"Do you think I care?"

"No, I don't." Laurel scooted around, threw her legs over

the bumper, and pushed. A shock went through her as her bare feet sank two inches in the snow. She pulled herself up straight, glaring. "Satisfied?"

"Very." A brisk wind blew back the parka hood and Crystal's hard, pale face stared at her. "Now *walk*."

Twenty-five

1

Laurel wasn't surprised to see Crystal. In the moments before the shadow moved in the living room she'd realized Crystal was the killer. "What if we don't go with you?"

Crystal raised a gun and pointed it at her. "Then this."

"I thought you were afraid of guns."

"You thought a lot of things about me." Crystal glanced at the gun. "Glock Model Nineteen Compact. Nine millimeter, ten rounds. It was my father's. I could never afford anything so nice."

"I'm impressed," Laurel said calmly, although everything inside her quivered. "I suppose your father taught you how to shoot, too."

"Of course he did. I'm a little rusty, but at close range, I'm still pretty good."

"Laurel?" Audra quavered.

"It's okay, honey. She's not going to shoot anyone." Crystal's eyes narrowed and she knew Crystal would shoot *her* in an instant. She'd only been trying to soothe the child. "Where do you want us to go, Crystal?"

"The barn." Laurel looked around, confused. "Don't tell me you didn't realize we're at the Pritchard Farm."

"It was a little hard to tell. I was in the trunk, remember?"

"Don't get smart with me." She waved the flashlight beam forward. *"Walk."*

"She doesn't have any shoes," Audra said.

Laurel looked at her. The child was dressed in the boots,

jacket, gloves, scarf, and hat she'd worn when Wayne dropped her off. In spite of her extreme fear, she felt a degree of relief. At least Audra was protected from the cold. Clearly Crystal didn't mean *her* any harm. But why had she brought her at all?

"Laurel doesn't need shoes," Crystal said roughly. "Pretty soon she won't feel the cold at all."

Audra's eyebrows drew together. "What do you mean?"

Laurel assumed a reassuring voice. "She means I'll be warm soon."

Like hell, she thought. Crystal means I'll be dead.

They began trudging through the snow. Crystal walked behind Audra and Laurel, shining the flashlight ahead. Audra reached out and took Laurel's hand in her warm gloved one. Crystal said nothing. Laurel squeezed Audra's hand and tried to flash her a smile when the child looked at her.

"Crystal," Laurel asked, raising her voice above the wind, "how did you get into my house tonight?"

Crystal didn't answer for a moment. Then she laughed. "I crawled through the dog door. You forgot to put the lock panel on, and I'm not a big person."

Oh, God, Laurel thought angrily. She'd been thinking about making Audra comfortable, not securing every possible entrance to the house. How damned stupid of her. "Weren't you afraid of the dogs? After all, you did tangle with them last evening when you paid a visit in that ridiculous white robe and wig."

"You didn't think it was so ridiculous then. You should have seen your face. You were *terrified*."

"Until the dogs came out."

"That surprised me. One left a nice bite on my leg and took a piece of my robe. But they're not attack dogs. I knew I could fend them off if I had on enough clothing to protect me. But as it turned out, I didn't have to worry. They were shut in your old bedroom with Audra."

Laurel was appalled. "You came in the house that long ago?"

"Patience is a virtue. I spent quite a bit of time in the basement being very quiet, waiting for you to go to sleep. Then Audra came tearing into your room. That's when I slipped into the living room. I'd already cut the phone line."

"But what about when you took Audra and me out? The dogs. What did you do—"

Audra pulled on her hand. Tears ran down her face. "She sprayed something in their eyes when they went after her. It hurt them so much. They yelped and cried. I *hate* her!"

"You do *not* hate me!" Crystal snapped. "It was just the Mace good old Monica instructed us to get. But don't get all upset, Laurel. I shut them in the bedroom. *They'll* be fine in the morning."

But *you* won't be, her unsaid words told Laurel.

"Crystal—"

"Shut up and *walk!*"

Laurel's hair hung in damp ringlets. Snow stung her cheeks and she had to keep her head bent downward to protect her eyes. And I used to like the feel of snow on my face, Laurel thought wryly. She was certain she couldn't feel her feet anymore until she stepped on a frozen cornstalk. Pain shot up her leg. She let out a little cry and bent to grab her foot. Crystal kicked her and she fell, rolling sideways.

"Stop it!" Audra screamed.

"I'm all right," Laurel gasped. She was terribly frightened but she didn't want Audra to see her fear. She climbed to her feet as quickly as possible, brushing snow off her robe, clasping it around her. "I'm tough as nails, Audra. It takes a little more than a spill in the snow to get to me."

"Please give her shoes," Audra begged.

"I don't have any extras. Keep walking."

Laurel's teeth chattered. Her back muscles were rigid with cold and she was beginning to worry about her feet. She'd been almost grateful for the pain of the cornstalk. It meant she still had feeling. But what about fifteen or twenty minutes from now? Would she be suffering from frostbite?

She could lose her toes or even her feet. If you live that long, she thought dolefully.

Audra clung to her hand, sniffling. "Don't cry, honey," Laurel said. "The tears are freezing on your face."

"I can't stop."

"Crystal," Laurel called, "I know you care about Audra or you wouldn't have bundled her up this way. Don't make her go through this. She's been very sick."

"I won't let her get sick again. You'd better just worry about yourself."

Through the blowing snow Laurel could see the hulking shape of the old barn. Dear Lord, this place had haunted her for thirteen years. Was it to be her last sight before she died?

"Why are we going here?" she asked.

"I thought you liked this place. I put up a reminder of Faith for you a few days ago."

"The noose?"

"Yes. You had a little tryst with Neil in the barn."

Laurel gasped. "How did you know I saw Neil?"

"I know everything that goes on here. It's not like I have a lot to do at home anymore." Laurel felt something jab her back. The gun. "Stop babbling and get in the barn."

Audra looked fearfully at Laurel. "I don't want to go in there."

"We have to. It's just a big, empty building."

"Not so empty," Crystal said. "Go on."

They walked into the roofless portion. Snow fell as heavily as outside, but in the back half of the barn Laurel spotted the glow of a kerosene lamp. She hadn't seen one lighted since the awful night Faith died and the memory sent her spiraling back in time. The cold. The darkness. The surreal setting that made the whole scene seem dreamlike, other-worldly.

"Go back farther, toward the lamp," Crystal ordered.

Laurel couldn't move. She felt as if her body were covered by a veil of ice. Then came the awful jabbing in her back again. The gun. She didn't think Crystal meant to kill her now and not by shooting her, but she also knew Crystal was strung tight and probably not nearly so skilled with a gun as she boasted. She could very easily shoot Laurel, or even Audra, by accident.

Laurel pushed her wet hair behind her ears and wiped a damp arm of her robe across her eyes. She moved forward. Under the roof, the glow of the lamp seemed brighter. She saw the bale of hay, the hangman's noose, and Monica, hands and feet bound with rope, mouth covered with silver duct tape, standing bound to a joist supporting the rotting wall.

"Monica!" Laurel cried. Monica wore a coat, but her hair was wet and she shivered violently. Her eyes darted frantically above the tape. "How long has she been out here?"

"Since shortly after Denise's visitation," Crystal said calmly. "She came back to my house to talk about my *case*. She was almost certain I was going to be arrested any time for Joyce's murder. You got the call from Joyce's cell phone at seven. At seven Chuck was home. That oldest boy of Joyce's swore to it. That's why I had to move fast, get everything done tonight."

"What are you going to do with Monica?" Laurel asked.

"Exactly what *she* did to Faith. Hang her. Set her on fire. She's escaped her punishment for a long time."

The circle. The chanting. The shoes. The fire. Laurel closed her eyes for a moment. Then she opened them and said slowly, "Monica didn't kill Faith. *You* did."

Monica's eyes flew to Laurel's face and Crystal went rigid. "Monica killed Faith with her Satanic ritual."

Laurel drew a deep, freezing breath that hurt her lungs. "Oh, no she didn't. If the devil was here that night, it was in the form of you."

Crystal looked at her piercingly. "What the hell are you talking about?"

Laurel was shuddering all over, both from cold and from fear, but she hadn't descended into blind panic. She believed if she kept talking, kept telling everything she remembered, she could get Crystal flustered and somehow overpower her, in spite of her weakened condition and lack of a weapon.

"I've dreamed so often of the night Faith died, so *damned* often," she began. "I know why now. I was trying to remember something, something that only came to me tonight when I found a letter Faith left for me."

"A letter?"

"Yes. She must have thought I handled the teddy bear often, but I rarely touched it."

"The teddy bear?" Crystal smiled. "The cold must be getting to you. You're rambling."

"No I'm not. That night, thirteen years ago, the wine made me so sick. I couldn't be part of the circle because I was going to throw up, remember? Most of the time I had my eyes closed, but there was a moment, one crucial moment, when I opened them."

Crystal raised her eyebrows. "Well, don't keep me in suspense. What did you see?"

"Everyone thought because Faith was drunk and dizzy, she slipped off the bale of straw and kicked over the kerosene lamp, starting the fire. But that's not how it happened. The sequence is wrong." She saw that she had Crystal's full attention. Crystal was even breathing harder.

"You had on suede boots that night," Laurel went on. "You were always so well dressed in those days when your family had plenty of money. The boots were expensive. I thought they were so pretty. And as everyone went around in a circle, chanting, their eyes closed, I saw you *purposely* kick over the kerosene lantern. The straw on the floor caught fire, then the bale of hay Faith was standing on. She panicked, kicked, and fell off. That's when her neck snapped."

Crystal made a little huffing noise. "You *were* drunk. So drunk you were hallucinating."

"I wasn't drunk—just sick. I *know* what I saw, Crystal. What's the point of denying it now that you've kidnapped Monica and Audra and me? You're going to kill us anyway."

"Not Audra!" Crystal snapped as Audra whimpered. "Don't listen to her, sweetheart. I won't hurt a hair on your head."

"But you're going to kill Monica and me."

"Well, I have to, now." Crystal sounded almost petulant.

"You killed Faith because she was pregnant with Chuck's baby, didn't you?"

Crystal glared at Laurel. "It *wasn't* Chuck's. It was Neil's, everyone knows that."

"Neil loved Faith. He would have married her. Her letter to me said the father wanted her to have an abortion. For a while I thought maybe Kurt was the father, but I know he's always hated the idea of abortion. Besides, Faith said the father tried to force money for the abortion on her, but she wouldn't take it. Kurt didn't have any money."

"Neither did Chuck."

"No, but you did. Chuck had to tell you about the baby, didn't he? He had to tell you because he needed money. You gave it to him. But Faith refused to get an abortion."

"She wanted him for herself!" Crystal stormed. "*My* Chuck."

"*Your* Chuck was having sex with someone else."

"Once! He explained it. He was drunk and she seduced him. She'd try anything to get him. After she got pregnant, she threatened to tell *everyone* Chuck was the father. My parents would have cut me off without a dime if I'd married him."

"So you decided murder was the only answer."

"She was a poor little slut, the daughter of a crazy man. She'd only drag him down. I told him, but—"

Laurel pounced. "But what? He was going to marry her anyway?"

"*No!*"

"You were afraid the whole mess would come out, your family would cut you off, and he would marry Faith instead of you. Chuck is a fortune-hunter, but he's not a killer. He didn't ask you to murder Faith for him. How could he have possibly guessed such an opportunity as our night in the barn could crop up? He *couldn't*. But when you saw it, you jumped at it. Did he know what you'd done?" Crystal's lips narrowed. "You said after the stillbirth of your last baby, when you were sedated, you babbled things about 'Faith' and the 'fire.' That's when he began to suspect, didn't he?"

"He married *me*, not Faith. He loved *me*."

"He couldn't very well marry Faith if she were dead. Besides, you had money back then."

Crystal's face tightened. "Money didn't matter to Chuck. Look how long he stayed with me after we found out my parents died bankrupt."

"But you were pregnant. Then you lost the baby. Then another and another. Maybe it was guilt that kept him with you or maybe just lack of opportunity—at least until after the last loss, when he got suspicious about your part in Faith's death. Then Joyce Overton came along, and he dumped you quick enough."

"You *bitch*!"

Audra cringed but Laurel held tightly to her hand. She was afraid if the child's terror overwhelmed her and she ran, Crystal would shoot her.

Laurel glanced at Monica. She was shuddering violently. She must have been out here for hours, and Laurel was certain if she stepped on that frozen cornstalk now, she wouldn't feel it. She didn't dare look at her feet because they would probably be blue.

"Why, Crystal?" she asked, trying to keep her increasingly raw voice firm. "Why did you kill Angie and Denise? Why do you want to kill Monica and me?"

"Because the Six of Hearts ruined my life!" Crystal screamed. "Everything was wonderful for me. Then you lured me into that club. You forced me to take part in all those Satanic rituals. You made me dabble in evil. Evil! And who suffered? Any of you? No. *Me*. Only *me*!"

In spite of her fear and dropping body temperature, Laurel glared at Crystal. "What in the name of God are you talking about?"

"Everything has gone wrong for me. My parents died.

The money was gone. Chuck flunked out of college. He couldn't hold a job. I lost four babies. *Four*. And after all that, Chuck left me like some old dog he'd drop off at the pound." She drew a long, shaking breath. "I was trying to hold on to my pride, my sanity. Then Angie called and begged me to come to New York for a visit. And I did."

"You went to New York?" Laurel asked in surprise.

"Yeah. No one knew. Why would they? I didn't have any friends around here who kept up with me, even after everything I've been through."

Laurel felt a little rush of shame. Maybe none of this would be happening if she'd reached out to Crystal sooner. Then her shame vanished. Crystal had killed Faith thirteen years ago. It wasn't neglect that motivated that murder. The instinct to get whatever she wanted, even if she had to kill for it, had been present in Crystal even then.

"So you went to New York."

"Yes. Angie looked gorgeous. She was the star of a hit play. She'd divorced a rich man who made her a wealthy woman. She was engaged to another rich man, this one as handsome as Chuck. Judson Green. I never met him, but I saw his picture, I heard her on the phone with him. She only lived in part of her house, but it was beautiful. She took me to fancy restaurants, introduced me to her high-class friends. You should have seen how they fawned over her! But the way they looked at me . . . like I was a bag lady. One night at a cocktail party I wore my good black dress and pulled up my hair. I thought I looked sophisticated. Then a guy asked me to get him a fresh drink. They thought I was the maid! Angie *laughed* when I told her. Damn her, she *laughed*! When we got home and I was crying, she turned all sympathetic and said it was a shame everything had turned out so rotten for me. She just kept hammering away. 'Why do I have so much when you've lost it all?' she said about five times. 'It's *tragic*, Crystal. Of course I never believed Chuck would stay with you so long after your parents' money was gone. But you're better off without him, honey. He didn't really love you. Everyone knew that.' "

Crystal's voice had begun to shake with rage and grief. "When I saw all she had, all she was in spite of what she'd done with the Six of Hearts, I felt sick. I felt . . . murderous." She paused, her voice drifting away. "I couldn't let her live. I just couldn't."

"But if Judson knew you were visiting her when she was killed . . ."

"He was on a business trip when I stayed with her. I asked her not to mention my name. She just said 'an old friend from Wheeling' was visiting. She hinted it was a man. She got a big kick out of him being jealous. You know how she was—always playing games. I sat and watched her flirting with him on the phone, wearing her exquisite negligees just to get my goat, flashing that huge diamond engagement ring around. I watched and I planned. While I was there, I had copies of her keys made. Two weeks later, when I knew Judson was going to be gone on another trip, I went back. It only takes four hours to get from here to Manhattan, you know."

"So you killed her and you mailed the Polaroids of Angie and the photos of Faith from New York."

"Yes. I even sent a set to myself. My mailman is so damned nosy. He goes through all my mail. He could swear *I* got an envelope of photos from New York if it was necessary."

Laurel hesitated. Should she bring up this next subject in front of Audra? She had to. She needed to buy time. "And Denise?"

"Looking at Angie just got me started. She wasn't the only one who'd done well for herself in spite of everything. There was Denise married to a successful doctor. Living in that big house. Having *her*." Crystal stepped closer and touched Audra's cheek. The child flinched. "I lost all my babies, *all* of them, but Plain Jane Denise gave birth to this *beautiful* little girl, this angel. Audra should have been mine. She *will* be mine."

So that's why she'd taken Audra, Laurel thought. She intended to keep her. "I'm not yours!" Audra cried.

"Quiet, baby," Crystal said gently. "You'll be happy with me. I'm a born mother."

Audra shook her head vehemently. "You killed my mommy! And you're the one that came in my room dressed like a ghost. I remember your voice. You're mean!"

Crystal's eyes hardened. Laurel didn't want her angry with the child. She was unstable enough to do anything, even to this little girl she supposedly wanted. "So you blame the Six of Hearts for the troubles you've suffered," she said quickly.

Crystal's gaze shifted to her. "My troubles all started that awful night. That's why I always put the six and the heart and a judgment card near the bodies. So the rest of you would know you hadn't escaped judgment for what you'd done."

"What *we'd* done!" Laurel cried. "You're the one who deliberately kicked over the lantern."

"But I wouldn't have done it if all of you hadn't pulled me into that awful club. Satanic rituals. Calling up spirits and devils."

"So that's your argument?" Laurel asked. " 'The devil made me do it'?"

"Don't make fun of me!" Crystal snarled. "There *is* evil in the world and it overcame me because I wasn't as strong or as smart as the rest of you. You all knew that. You should have protected me!"

"You, the person who has killed four women and managed to cover her crimes, isn't strong and smart?"

"I wasn't strong and smart *then*, not when I kicked over the lantern. It was an impulse, an evil impulse, caused by demons Monica called forth!"

"Bullshit!"

Everyone jumped as Monica's voice rang out. Somehow she'd managed to get the tape loose from her mouth. It dangled from one cheek. "In the first place, I didn't call forth any demons, you idiot. Didn't you know I was just making up those chants? I don't know anything about Satanism, demonology, or witchcraft, white or black."

"That's not true!" Crystal shouted. "The chants were real!"

"No they *weren't*. But even if they were, they have nothing to do with what you've done. You've never wanted to take responsibility for anything that goes wrong. Even when we were in school you blamed your low grades on teachers' dislike, not on the fact that you never studied. When you lost that stupid cheerleading contest, you said it was because a girl on the other team was sleeping with a judge. Now you commit *murder* and blame it on demons I called forth with a bunch of mumbo jumbo. It was *jealousy!* You killed Faith, Angie, Denise, and even Joyce out of jealousy!"

"It's not that simple!"

"Isn't it? You just said you saw all that Angie had and snapped. The same thing happened with Denise. Faith was pregnant with Chuck's child and you were afraid he'd marry her instead of you. Later Joyce got Chuck. By the way, how did you pull off that one? Call her and ask her to come to your house?"

Crystal's mouth twisted slightly. "No. I *was* baby-sitting. Then I remembered I'd rushed out in such a hurry I hadn't turned off the coffeemaker. I was on my way back over to the house when I saw her go in. First she takes my husband, then she just uses his keys and walks into *my* house like it's her own. I was ready for her when she came out dressed in *my* coat."

"Then you called me from the cell phone in her car," Laurel said.

"Phone records, again," Monica said. "She had to make it look like the killer was afraid of going back in Crystal's house after he realized he'd made a mistake and killed someone else. After all, Crystal might walk in on him."

"Why did you call me at all?" Laurel asked.

Crystal looked at her. "*I* didn't want to be the one to find the body. It was so much better to have you find it, then see my shock when I came in the house and didn't seem to know why you were there or what was going on."

"The police searched your place, Crystal. They didn't find any clothes with blood or a murder weapon," Laurel said.

Crystal smiled slightly. "The Grants had a dog that died a couple of years ago. It had a nice big doghouse at the back of their yard. I stashed my clothes and the tire iron there. The rest of the time I kept my robe and wig and tire iron at the Pritchard farm. It seemed only fitting since this is where all the trouble started." A look of regret crossed her face. "I had no idea Chuck would turn up at our house that night, or that Joyce's children weren't home all evening to give him a perfect alibi. I never wanted him to be a suspect. I don't want to hurt him, you see. I just want him back."

"But you weren't afraid of becoming a suspect?"

"I thought I'd be cleared immediately. But Monica said the police are still suspicious of me. They think because I was just next door, I had plenty of time to kill Joyce and be back at the Grants' to get their call at seven-thirty." She shrugged. "The police are right. That's why I had to act quickly. I don't have time to be arrested."

"How did you know she was with me?" Laurel asked.

"Wayne told me at the visitation. I did go, you know, just like I did to Angie's. It was the proper thing to do."

"You mean it *looked* like the proper thing to do."

"Not just that. It was sort of fun to know they were lying in those closed caskets, never able to enjoy their wonderful lives again, while I was moving around talking, full of life, full of hope."

"You make me sick," Laurel spat.

"You should be nicer to me. I *had* planned to spare you."

"To what do I owe that honor?"

"Because your life wasn't a whole lot better than mine. Thirty. One big, broken romance. Finally another, obviously going nowhere. No children. Living in your parents' house running their crummy little flower shop. You're not even beautiful. Just a plain woman living alone with her two mongrel dogs. Pathetic, really." Crystal paused. "But you were always nice to me."

"Apparently not nice enough."

"You were until you started messing around with Neil Kamrath. Even I can see his attraction to you. He's famous, probably wealthy. And then you began asking too many questions, taking your job as amateur detective a little too seriously. You're shrewder than I thought. You would have figured out things eventually."

"But you tried to scare me earlier."

"I had to. I couldn't make you seem like the only Six of Hearts who wasn't being terrorized so I started out by driving an old Chrysler New Yorker Chuck left in the garage out to Wilson Lodge and ramming your car on the way home. It's what I brought you here in." Crystal sighed and rubbed a hand across her forehead, as if she were clearing her thoughts. "I'm getting really tired of all this explaining. I'm cold, the child's cold. I think it's time to get on with things."

2

Neil rolled over, punched his flabby feather pillow, and looked out the window at the snow. Or what he could see of it. His father had been too cheap to buy storm windows. Cobwebs of frost grew, blocking his view. He'd offered a hundred times to refurbish the old house, but his father refused to take money from the "trash" Neil wrote. His mother had sat here with him in this damp, cold place with her arthritis getting worse every year until she'd become a cripple. Then she died quickly in her sleep, no doubt in a bed as uncomfortable as this one. When his father went, Neil didn't intend to sell the place. He would take the few mementos in it that mattered to him, then have the house demolished.

But it wasn't thoughts of his parents, his dreary childhood, or his plans for the house that kept Neil awake.

Something was wrong, something he couldn't put his finger
on. It wasn't that Laurel hadn't attended Denise's visitation.
Wayne explained she was taking care of Audra, which Neil
thought was a good idea. Not seeing Kurt had seemed a bit
odd because Kurt knew the Prices. But it wasn't that, either.
It was something someone had said, something strange,
something "off," something that didn't add up. What the
hell was it?

He tossed to the other side, beating on the pillow again.
Good God, how long ago had geese lost these feathers?
The turn of the century? He liked thick, fluffy pillows. He
liked the sound of the ocean over the cliffs beside his house
in Carmel. Dammit, he liked his house with all its windows
and bright spaciousness. Minimalist, the decorator had
called it. A perfect place for a woman and two frisky dogs.

Wait a minute, Kamrath, he thought. Just because he'd
always liked Laurel and now found her the warmest, most
interesting woman he'd ever known didn't mean anything.
She was attached to Kurt Rider. Besides, his wife and son
had been dead less than a year. Still, the only times in those
ten months when he'd felt really alive were his meetings
with Laurel. He grinned. Two scandalous meetings in a
fast-food restaurant. There was their talk at her shop, and
another at the little café down the street. Then there was
their rip-roaring evening at the Lewis sisters' house when
they had met Genevra Howard. That had been shocking and
disturbing. It had also been exciting.

Funny, he thought. In some ways he felt like he knew
Laurel better than he'd ever known Ellen. Ellen was like a
spun-sugar figure—all pretty and dainty on the outside, hollow on the inside. But she had produced a miraculous child,
a child Neil would miss until he died.

Who was it at the visitation who sympathized with him
over the loss of Robbie? he wondered suddenly. He
squinted, trying to see her face. "Always so tragic," she'd
said. "Sometimes I think it's worse on the father than on
the mother. Why, I remember . . ."

Neil sat bolt upright in bed. *That's* what he had been

trying so desperately to recall! He reached for the phone and dialed Laurel's number. No answer. He glanced at his watch. Eleven-thirty. Laurel wouldn't be running around with Audra at eleven-thirty. Something was wrong. He hated doing it, but he rang Monica's room at the Wilson Lodge. Once again he got no answer. In dread, he looked up Crystal's number and called. The phone rang in an empty house.

"That does it," Neil said, climbing out of bed. "I can't just lie here all night worrying. I have to do something, but I'm not sure what."

3

Crystal walked over to Monica, withdrew a knife from her coat, and began sawing at the rope around her wrists. "Don't think because you're bigger than I am, you can overpower me," she warned Monica. "I've got a gun."

"You would never have gotten me in that car trunk without it," Monica said bitterly.

Crystal severed the rope. Monica rubbed her wrists. Crystal gave her the knife. "*You* cut the rope on your ankles." She pointed the gun at Monica's head. "And don't try any heroics. Two shots and you and Laurel will both be dead."

"You'd actually kill us in front of Audra?" Laurel asked, noticing how weak her voice was growing. She wouldn't be able to talk much longer.

"She'd forget in time. Children are very resilient."

"Maybe it's better you never had a child," Monica snapped. "You don't have a clue about how children's minds work."

"Shut up!" Crystal hissed. "As if *you* with your fancy career and your men and your life in New York would know *anything* about kids."

"This might come as a surprise to you, Crystal, but career people in New York City actually have children and do a good job of raising them."

Laurel didn't know if Crystal heard the apprehension in Monica's voice, but *she* did. Monica's doing the same thing I've been doing, she thought. She's trying to get Crystal unfocused, flustered, so we can overpower her. The problem was she didn't believe either of them had the strength to overcome Crystal. Laurel was beginning to feel terribly sleepy, even fuzzy, and she knew by the way Monica sawed clumsily at the rope around her ankles that she too was losing her battle with the cold.

"Hurry up!" Crystal prodded.

Monica looked up at her. "Why don't you just shoot me and get it over with?"

"Because that's too easy. You forced *me* to take part in your Satanic rituals. Now I'm going to force *you*."

Monica sighed. "Crystal, how many times do I have to tell you the rituals weren't *real*. And no one forced you to do *anything*."

"You *did*. I was scared not to do what you said."

"Oh? Tell me, what did you think would happen to you?"

"I . . . I didn't know. You seemed so powerful, so capable of anything."

"*I* seemed capable of anything?" Monica managed a ragged laugh. "God, Crys, you really *have* gone around the bend."

"The rope is cut. Quit stalling." Crystal put the gun against Monica's temple. "Get over there, step up on the bale of straw, and put your head in the noose. Just like Faith did."

Twenty-six

1

After he got in his car, Neil's first impulse was to drive to police headquarters. But what would he say? "No one I call is home?" That should electrify the cops, he thought wryly. Most of them probably held the same view of him that Kurt Rider did, anyway. He was just some nut who wrote ghost stories and was probably trying to stir up some publicity for himself. No, he had to have a little more to tell them if he expected any action.

So, where should he start? With Laurel, of course. It was her failure to answer the phone that disturbed him the most. He drove to her house, cursing the snow, the slick roads, the rental car that didn't handle like the Porsche he'd left in California. It didn't even handle as well as his father's old boat of a vehicle, but he'd brought it because it had a cellular phone.

He pounded on Laurel's front door. There was no answer and the door was locked. He walked around the house. As he neared the back, he heard the dogs barking. He tracked the sound and pecked on a window. A dog nosed open the draperies and looked out at him. It was the long-haired female, but something was wrong with her face. The eyes—they were inflamed, pouring water. When he circled the house, he'd spotted a dog door: He went back to the main door, tried it to find it locked, and knelt at the dog door, calling to them. He could still hear their frantic barking, but they didn't come near the door. They were shut in a room. He considered crawling through the dog door, but he was too big. He walked back to the front of the house, muttering angrily to himself. Laurel and Audra could be inside the house hurt, or even worse. He considered finding a rock and throwing it through the front window. Then he saw a splash of color beneath a layer of snow near the driveway. He stiffened, his first thought that he was seeing a bloody body. He rushed to it.

Reaching down, he started to laugh in relief. It was a teddy bear. A melon-colored teddy bear, not much more than a foot long. But where had it come from? The house. But why was it here?

He picked up the bear and walked back to the driveway, studying the snow. Blurred tire tracks lay in front of his car, but they didn't go all the way into the garage. He shuffled around to the side of the garage and looked into the uncovered window. Laurel's Cavalier. He went back and studied the car tracks, then saw a patch of snow that looked as if it had been churned up by some kind of struggle.

Suddenly Neil was certain Laurel and Audra had been taken away in another vehicle, a full-sized car, and not too long ago judging by the width of the tracks and their depth in the snow. Either Audra had left the teddy bear in the yard as a message or she'd dropped it and not been allowed to pick it up. He knew who had taken them. He just wasn't sure where.

2

"Unless you want to carry me over to that bale of straw, you'll have to wait a minute," Monica told Crystal.

"Why?"

"Because my legs have gone numb. Let me get the blood flowing again."

"It's a trick."

"Oh, dammit, Crys, what difference does a few seconds make?" Monica fired back. "After all, you've been planning this for months, haven't you?"

"Only since I went to see Angie."

It's my turn, Laurel thought. Monica was clearly exhausted, her husky voice rough as sandpaper. "All these
years I've thought so often about that night here with
Faith," she said. "How about you, Crystal? Did you keep
picturing it like I did?"

Crystal looked at her in confusion, as if Laurel had just
presented her with a difficult math question to answer. "I
don't know. I guess I did sometimes."

"I dreamed about it. None of us ever talked about it. I've
always wondered if anyone else dreamed about it, too."

"I don't dream," Crystal said flatly.

"I dream," Audra volunteered.

Crystal's face softened. She lowered the gun from Monica's temple as Audra grabbed her attention. "What do you
dream about, sweetheart?"

"Mostly about good things, like having a puppy or playing the piano as good as my daddy. But sometimes I have
bad dreams. I had a bad dream tonight. I went to Laurel's
room. She said even grown-ups have bad dreams."

"You won't have bad dreams when you're with me,"
Crystal said firmly. "We're going to have such a good life,
Audra, although I think I'm going to change your name to
Bettina. Do you like that name?"

Audra opened her mouth. Laurel knew she was going to
protest. She squeezed the child's hand. Crystal seemed
completely caught up in her and took another step in Audra's direction. She didn't even notice Monica moving toward her slowly and silently. "It's a beautiful name," Audra
said obligingly. "Lots better than Audra. How did you think
it up?"

Bless you, Audra, Laurel exulted silently. Just keep her
focused on you.

"When I was little, my grandmother read me a book
about a girl named Bettina. Later she gave me a lovely
porcelain figurine and I named her Bettina. I told people
she'd been stolen, but she wasn't. She's safe, hidden in the

old farmhouse here. When you're my little girl, I'll give her to you."

"Really?" Audra beamed.

A board creaked. Crystal whirled to see Monica lifting a hand, ready to land a karate chop on Crystal's wrist, making her drop the gun. She was a second too late. Audra screamed at the explosive sound of the gunshot. Then Monica fell.

3

Neil wasn't about to call Wayne Price at this point and tell him he thought Audra had been kidnapped. Instead, he tried to figure out where Audra and Laurel could have been taken. He sat in the car for five minutes, thinking. There had to be a logical place, one that wouldn't easily spring to mind if the police were searching for someone. It would be somewhere away from town, somewhere secluded.

Somewhere that had special meaning for the killer.

He hit his forehead with the heel of his hand. "Idiot, where else?" he yelled at himself. He started the car and backed out of the driveway, then headed for the Pritchard farm as fast as the slick roads would allow, constantly picturing that hangman's noose he'd seen in the old barn. Dear God, he prayed, don't let someone be putting that to use.

Ten minutes later Neil turned into the rutted lane leading to the farm. A couple of times the car skidded perilously close to the edge. With each slide his breath nearly stopped. If he slipped into a ditch, he'd never get the car out without the help of a wrecker, and he didn't have time.

The wind blew harder, slanting the snow. His windshield wipers worked at top speed, but still it was hard to see. This was the kind of night he'd create for a scene in one of his books—the kind of night that never had a happy ending.

As he drew near the farm, he saw two vehicles ahead. He pulled up to the first one and looked at it closely. A dark blue Chrysler New Yorker, an older model, ten years on it at least. It was empty and covered with a light layer of snow. He pulled forward about thirty yards. The second car huddled under a blanket of snow. It must have been here for hours.

Leaving his own car running, Neil got out. A blast of cold air hit him so hard it nearly knocked him sideways. Bitter snow strafed his face and he had to shield his eyes. Bracing himself, he walked to over to the second auto. No one appeared to be inside, but he couldn't tell much about the car itself except that it had a strange mound of snow on top.

He used his sleeved arm to brush aside the mound of snow on the roof. Lights. Emergency vehicle lights. "Oh, God," he muttered, frantically wiping away more snow. As the car emerged, his mouth went dry. It was black. The side bore the insignia of a badge with "Ohio County Sheriff's Department" written inside. A police cruiser.

Stumbling, Neil ran back to his own car, jumped in, and picked up the cell phone. Now the police would listen to him.

4

Audra continued to shriek as Monica slowly collapsed on the cold dirt floor. "Shut her up!" Crystal shouted.

Laurel knelt and put her arms around the little girl. "Hush, baby. Don't scream anymore. It just makes her madder."

Audra immediately stopped screaming but she drew long, shuddering breaths and Laurel's stomach clenched when she heard a slight rattle in the child's chest. She'd barely escaped pneumonia earlier in the week. What would tonight do to her?

Crystal bent over Monica. "It's just her shoulder."

"Are you sure?" Laurel asked, shaking with cold and shock. "Is she breathing? Is she conscious? How bad is it?"

"Do I look like a doctor?" Crystal flared. "She's breathing. I told you it's just her shoulder."

"Crystal, you have to stop the bleeding."

Crystal looked at her as if she were crazy. "*Why?*"

Laurel cast frantically in her mind for an excuse. "Because you wanted her to die like Faith did. That can't happen if she bleeds to death."

Crystal's gaze darted around the room. For the first time she didn't look sure of herself. She seemed like the slightly inept, vulnerable Crystal Laurel had always known. "What should I do?"

"Apply pressure to the wound."

"How? *You* do it." She stood up looking at Monica as if she were some kind of disgusting insect.

"Stand here while I help Monica," Laurel told Audra.

"No," Crystal said. "She comes with you. I don't want her to run off."

Audra clung to Laurel's hand as they walked to Monica's body. My feet are completely numb, Laurel thought. My body doesn't even feel like it's my own anymore. Monica and I might possibly have overpowered Crystal before, but I don't know how we can do it now.

As they neared Monica, Audra gasped. She wore a white dress coat, the coat she must have worn to Denise's visitation, and blood spread across the right shoulder.

Laurel knelt, unbuttoned the coat, and turned to Crystal. "I need something to press against the wound."

Crystal looked affronted. "Well, *I* don't have anything."

Audra took off her wool scarf. "Here. It's not dirty."

Laurel smiled at her. "Thank you, honey." Did I have her bravery and presence of mind when I was eight? Laurel wondered. No. She's more like Monica. She'll grow into a strong young woman.

Laurel pressed the wool against the small wound in Monica's shoulder. She wondered if the bullet had gone straight through flesh and muscle or whether it had hit bone. It seemed to her the flow of blood was slowing, but maybe it was only being absorbed by the wool of Audra's scarf. In a moment, Monica's eyelids fluttered. "Monica, can you hear me?" Laurel asked anxiously.

"I can hear you," Monica answered weakly. "But I feel like hell."

"Don't talk like that in front of Bettina," Crystal snapped. "Sit up, Monica."

Laurel looked at her pleadingly. "Oh, Crys, can't she just rest?"

"She's got an eternity to rest after this. Get *up*!"

Laurel and Audra helped Monica to her feet. Her face hadn't an ounce of color except for her burning green eyes. She staggered but regained her footing.

"How do you like not being in charge?" Crystal asked her. "Now *I'm* the boss."

"I was never the boss."

"Yes you were. You made us all dance to your tune."

"Oh, God, Crys, when are you going to stop blaming me for everything that's happened to you?" Monica asked.

"Never. You're all responsible, but you the most. I explained that to you, but you never listened to anyone else in your whole life."

"You're wrong, Crystal. I listened to my father. He was the most important person in the world to me and he threw me away, just like Chuck threw you away. I went to a woman who didn't want me and let me know it every day of my life. Yes, I enjoyed being leader of the Six of Hearts. It was the only time I felt like I had any control, that anyone *really* listened to me. And I enjoyed scaring you all with that occult nonsense. But I *never* meant for anyone to get hurt. And Crystal, *I* didn't hurt anyone. *You* did."

"Shut up." Crystal's face took on that strange, hard look again. "You're on your feet. Climb up on the bale of straw."

"Crys, she's wounded," Laurel tried.

"She won't be in pain much longer. Go on, Monica." Monica closed her eyes briefly. Then, pressing Audra's scarf to her shoulder, she stepped onto the bale. "Now put your head in the noose."

"Crystal?" Audra ventured.

"*Mommy*," Crystal corrected.

Audra's lips parted but she forced out, "M-Mommy, please don't do this to her. It'll make me cry."

"I cried the first time it happened. I cried for days. But then I stopped. So will you. Monica, I said to put your head in the noose." With a resigned expression, Monica used her left hand to slip the noose over her head. Crystal moved the kerosene lantern about a foot away from the bale of straw, then took Laurel's hand. In the other she held her gun. "Now, Bettina, you hold Laurel's other hand. Then we'll do the chant."

Laurel, who now felt on the verge of collapse, moaned. "Oh, God, Crystal, not that."

"Yes. It has to be just like before."

"I don't even remember the chant."

"I do. I've said it every day since Faith died. I'll go through it once, then you repeat, just like we did that night. You either do it, or I'll shoot you." And she will, Laurel thought fearfully. "Ready?"

Crystal began pulling them around in a circle, repeating the words Laurel now vaguely remembered:

"Hail, the Lords of Darkness. In the name of the rulers of the earth, the kings of the underworld, rise to this place. Open the gate and bring forth your faithful servant, Esmé Dubois, who died for doing your work among the God-worshipers. Azazel, Azazel, scapegoat released on the Day of Atonement, its destination hell. Appear before us, Esmé and Azazel. Appear before the Six of Hearts, your modern-day servants. Let us bask in your glorious presence."

The lantern created jumping shadows, hollowing eye sockets and cheeks. Wind whistled around the old barn. Audra looked terrified. Monica and I might deserve this, Laurel thought, but not Audra.

Crystal looked around at them. "Now, you begin to chant, too."

She began circling, chanting. Audra said nothing, but Laurel joined in. She was so dizzy and weak she could hardly stand on feet she couldn't feel anymore. Audra flashed her a look that clearly said "traitor" because the child thought she was cooperating completely. Actually, she had a plan. A poor plan, but better than nothing. By holding Crystal's hand, she had some control over her movements. Maybe if she could muster enough strength, she could keep Crystal from kicking over the lantern or knocking Monica off the bale of straw.

They began to circle again. "Hail, the Lords of Darkness. In the name of the rulers of the earth, the kings of the underworld . . ."

Thirteen years ago. The cold. The dancing shadows. The chant. Laurel looked up at Monica. She was swaying, just as Faith had done. But this time Laurel wasn't sitting helpless on the floor.

Laurel thought she heard something outside, something above the wind. Imagination. Wishful thinking. Then she heard something again. Someone running in the snow? A muffled voice. Audra's gaze flew to hers. She'd heard it, too.

They finished the chant. Thirteen years ago they had finished the chant together once before the fire. That meant—

Summoning all her strength, Laurel jerked on Crystal but she was too late. Crystal's booted foot suddenly shot out and she kicked over the lantern. Audra screamed as fire ate the straw on the floor, making its way to the bale on which Monica stood.

Between the kick and the jerk Laurel had given her, Crystal was off balance. She staggered backward and fired the gun. This time Laurel and Audra both screamed.

Monica flung herself violently to the right and at first Laurel thought she'd been hit. Then she saw the fire licking at the bale, igniting the clumped pieces of straw. Just like Faith, Monica was falling in her attempt to avoid the flames. "Hang on to the rope!" Laurel screamed. "Monica! The *rope!*"

Monica's gaze met hers and Laurel saw her reach with her left hand for the rope. Oh, God, she doesn't even have the strength of both hands, Laurel thought. She'd been shot in the right shoulder. Still, Monica clawed frantically with one hand, keeping herself from being choked by the noose.

"Damn you!" Crystal screeched at Laurel. "You *pushed* me. But you can't stop me!"

Monica shrieked. Laurel glanced at her. Monica's right pant leg was on fire. "Crystal, we've got to get her down!" Crystal looked at her coldly.

Laurel turned loose of Audra's hand and lunged forward, into the flames, just as she had thirteen years ago. She grabbed futilely at Monica's legs.

"Don't move!" A man's voice, Laurel thought. "I said don't—"

She looked back. Crystal whirled, pointing the Glock at a man in uniform. A shot. Then another. Crystal screamed and dropped the gun. Another shot.

Crystal weaved and fell backward into the flames.

Epilogue

Laurel's eyes snapped open. For a moment she thought she was in the freezing barn while Monica stood on a bale of straw with her head in a noose as flames licked at her legs. Her heart raced until the scene changed. She was lying in a warm, narrow bed. Across from her, mounted on the wall, sat a television. Light streamed through a window on her left. A hospital room.

Something pushed gently against her right thigh. She looked down. Neil sat on a chair beside the bed, bent at the waist, sleeping peacefully. She reached down and touched one of his sandy curls. So soft. She ran a finger down his cheek. Slowly his smoky blue eyes opened and he stared at her. Then he smiled. "I was afraid I'd never see those beautiful amber eyes again."

"I don't know about beautiful, but you never *would* have seen my eyes open again if you hadn't come to the farm. How's Audra?"

"Fine. Griping that she had to spend another night in here for exposure. By the way, she's one forceful little girl. She wouldn't rest until I roused a locksmith, went back to your house, got the dogs, and took them to Dr. Ricci. He says their eyes will be sore for a day or two, but otherwise they're fine."

"Thank goodness. What about Monica?"

"All right. Shot in the shoulder but no bone damage. Some first-degree burns on her legs. Suffering from exposure, of course, but she'll be all right."

"Crystal?"

"She's been taken off the critical list. She fired at the police but didn't hit anyone. One of them got her in the leg. She dropped the gun, it went off, and she was shot in the chest." He sighed. "I think it might have been better if she *had* died considering what's ahead of her."

Laurel closed her eyes. "My God. Life in prison without possibility of parole? Life in a mental institution?"

"That's for the courts to decide," Neil said.

Laurel shivered. "Well, I guess everyone is accounted for."

"Not quite. It seems Kurt went out to the farm earlier in the day to check out the noose you described to him. He went into the farmhouse. Crystal was there, too—"

"Oh, no!" Laurel cried. "Don't tell me he's dead!"

Neil patted her hand. "No, Laurel. She took her tire iron to him. Maybe she thought she'd killed him, but she didn't. He has a fractured skull, broken collarbone, broken arm. Also, he lay in that cold house unconscious for eight hours, but he had on a wool coat." He grinned. "*And* thermal underwear."

Laurel smiled weakly. "I used to tease him about wearing that underwear in the winter. I guess he'll have the last laugh."

Neil looked at her soberly. "You really love him, don't you?"

"Love him?" Laurel frowned. "We've been friends forever. I love him like a friend. I tried to love him romantically, but it didn't work for either of us." She sighed. "I'm glad he's all right, and I seem to be fine."

Neil hesitated. "Well, you did sustain a little damage. Frostbite."

Fear rushed through her. "I knew it! My feet! Oh, Neil, did they have to amputate my feet?" she cried, already trying to throw back the covers so she could see. Neil stopped her.

"Calm down, Laurel. You lost the little toes on both feet. That's *all*. The *little* ones. No one will even notice. It could have been so much worse."

She lay back against the pillows. "You're right. Considering what I went through, it's a miracle." She forced a smile. "I never liked sandals, anyway."

"That's my girl."

"Neil, how did you know where we were? How did you save us?"

"The police saved you. I just found you."

"Very modest. But how did you know something was wrong?"

"I've told you throughout this whole thing I wasn't the father of Faith's baby. I've always thought figuring out who *was* the father was the key. At the visitation I was talking to Crystal. She seemed a little strange, almost giddy but like she was trying to hide it. Then she started talking about how hard it was for Wayne to lose Denise, but it would have been even worse if he'd lost Audra. She said something about it being even worse for a father to lose a child than the mother. Then she went on about poor Chuck probably behaving so erratically lately because he'd lost *five* babies. I was only half listening, but after I went to bed, I remembered you telling me Crystal had three miscarriages and a stillbirth. That's four, not five."

"And that's it?" Laurel asked incredulously. "That one slip tipped you off?"

"No. I told you she wasn't acting right. She had this funny look in her eyes. I started thinking back to high school. Crystal was so pretty and dated Chuck. Then I thought of Faith and how she said she didn't think Crystal was quite as sweet as everyone thought she was. I also remembered how I was certain at one time that Faith had a crush on Chuck."

"Neil, Faith left a letter. She wrote it the week before Crystal killed her. It was hidden in my teddy bear. She entitled it 'In the Event of My Death.' She knew someone wanted her dead. I believe she thought it was Chuck."

"Speaking of Chuck, Kurt asked me to give you a message. He said, 'Tell Laurel the book of sonnets wasn't mine. I was keeping it for someone.' "

"Chuck. Why didn't Kurt just tell me at the time?"

"Still protecting a friend." Neil paused and his gaze drifted away.

"There's something else," Laurel pounced. "More bad news."

"It's not really *bad* news," he said slowly. "I talked with your parents."

"Good heavens, you've been busy this morning! The dogs, Audra, Kurt, my parents."

"Laurel, it's three in the afternoon, not morning. Anyway, I know your parents drive you crazy, but I had to call them. You're their child and you're hurt." She nodded. "Your mother was horrified." He drew a breath. "Your father was distressed, but he seemed equally distressed by the fact that last night your sister gave birth to twin boys."

Laurel grinned. "Twins!"

"That's right. Apparently Claudia knew for months she was expecting twins but didn't tell your parents."

"She was afraid that Dad would literally run for the hills. My God, two more little boys from *The Omen*." She reddened. "Oh, that sounded awful!"

Neil laughed. "No it didn't. Your father had the same note of horror in his voice. Your mother said Claudia and the babies are fine, although, and I quote, 'Claudia is a bit on the testy side today.' "

Giggles overcame Laurel. "That means Claudia is cussing her head off, sending nurses and doctors fleeing in desperation. Her poor husband. He's such a wimp. I sure wouldn't want to be in his shoes."

"There's more. Your father said he doesn't know if he can take all the commotion anymore. He told me to tell you he thinks he and your mother will come back to Wheeling in a couple of months."

Laurel's smile faded. "I see. That means Dad will want to take over the store again. He can't stand to be here and not be in charge even though I've increased business by thirty percent. And of course they'll want their house back.

They aren't dog lovers—I'll have to find a place to rent where they accept pets . . ."

"I know a place that accepts pets," Neil said. "My house."

"Oh. You're putting your father's house up for rent after he dies?"

"No, I meant my house in Carmel."

"*Your* house. *You* want to take my dogs?"

Neil closed his eyes and shook his head. "Laurel, I know you're a very bright woman, but I'm having trouble getting through today. I want the dogs *and* you, not necessarily in that order. I make enough money to support the three of us, but if you want to work, I believe the Carmel–Monterey area could support another floral shop. Lots of rich people and movie stars in that area, you know."

Laurel looked at him in astonishment. "Neil, are you asking me to move in with you?"

"If you want to try that first. Of course, I'm an old-fashioned guy. I'd prefer having you on a more respectable basis."

"*Marriage?*" Laurel squeaked.

"You sound like you just saw a mouse."

"I didn't mean to sound insulting, but Neil . . . I mean . . . we hardly know each other."

"We went to school together for twelve years. Besides, I feel like I've known you better than I've ever known anyone." He kissed her cheek, patted her hand, and smiled. "I won't be going home for at least a month until I get all the business around here wrapped up. In the meantime, we can see each other and you can think it over. In a few weeks, you can send me packing if you want, no hard feelings." He glanced at his watch. "Got to go, now. See you later, beautiful."

As he walked out the door, Laurel grinned. You certainly will be seeing me later, she thought impulsively. I hope you'll be seeing me for the rest of my life.